# Vampires

A Novel by Erik Burke

This book is dedicated to the memories of Nevaeh Buchanan
and Chelsea Bruck

*"I was. I still am."*

-Isaac Asimov

# PROLOGUE: MICHIGAN WINTER

It was a bright and empty day.

The detective peered out at the frozen landscape. She tied her dark hair into a neat ponytail. She double-checked the time on her phone. It was almost noon. The stone-faced rookie behind the wheel stared ahead wordlessly.

She felt bad for the kid. This had to be his first dead body. Popping someone's corpse cherry was usually a proud moment, but this case was different. This was no drug-overdose or suicide.

"Who found her?" She asked. "One of the volunteers?"

"A father and son. They were out in the woods for some rifle practice and stumbled on her." The rookie explained. "Their story's good. Everything checks out."

The kid took a deep breath, trying to ready himself. The detective simply stepped out into the deathly snow, her breath hitting the wintry air.

She walked with a purpose. Several officers scurried around her, taking photographs of the environment. A K-9 unit had been deployed. An ambulance pulled in alongside the police vehicles littering the clearing.

In the summer, this clearing would have been a nice little spot. It might even have been busy. Ash Township was a popular fair-weather hiking destination. The rest of the year demoted the area to a desolate backwater.

The detective was already covered in flaky precipitation. She impatiently tried to locate the crime scene. Eventually, her charge caught up with her. The rookie motioned ahead at a large, fallen log on a hill.

Its melancholy slopes were undisturbed. The ground was uneven. Any travel by foot would have been slow and treacherous. It was possible that a girl; lost, intoxicated, not dressed for the inclement weather, could have met her untimely end out here. It was the middle of nowhere. It would have been a lonely way to go.

Stepping carefully onto the hillside, the detective slowly made her way to the log. The timber was rotten. The way it had fallen suggested the ash tree had been struck by lightning a few years ago.

1

Yellow crime scene tape stuck out against the colorless snowdrifts. The blue uniforms gathered around the toppled tree parted instinctually, making way for the proud detective and her greenhorn assistant. It was freezing.

The heavy coat of the county coroner crouched over something beneath the broken boughs. His short grey beard and frazzled hair blended in with the surroundings. He reeked of coffee and sleep deprivation.

"What have we got, Finley? Hypothermia?" The detective asked, looking down at the body. She could hear the kid fighting back vomit.

"No. Not quite." Dr. Finley murmured.

The seasoned detective's confidence wavered at the sight of the remains. The red and blue hair dye seemed to be the only thing still intact on the girl's body. Her skin was paler than the surrounding snow. What was left of her face had been covered with dark purple bruises. One of her eye sockets had been completely shattered. Her mouth hung open in a silent scream of terror.

Her neck was worse.

Hardened as she was, the detective found it difficult to look at the large bite that had been taken out of the girl's jugular. Dried tendons hung frozen in the wind. There was no blood anywhere.

The detective ignored the rookie as he finally turned away. She ignored the analytical musings of the coroner as he reviewed his notes. She reached into her pocket and withdrew her cell phone.

She pulled up that weird email she had received. It was short. Only two sentences punctuated by little emoticon smiley faces. There was also a hyperlink. Clicking the link led to the Patreon account for someone named *DeathbringerBob:*

*For all your peril and snuff fantasies!* His webpage claimed.

Bob offered a sample story as proof of his writing ability. The detective had already read it a dozen times. Standing here, out in the woods, a mangled corpse at her feet, she read the story again.

A feeling of dread realization rose in her chest.

---

"It's not far now!" The hook-handed man exclaimed with a dashing smile.

The girl sighed. She had gone as Cinderella and ended up losing her shoes at the party. In some way, her predicament felt fitting.

The full moon shone overhead. The girl found herself captivated by her escort. He was young, with almond eyes and luxurious curly hair. His laugh was infectious. His smile could put anyone at ease.

He sported a vulgar tattoo on the back of his neck, but he was a far cry from the hook handed, hitchhiking serial killer your parents warned you about. He was a war vet. He had character.

She blushed. She wasn't one to run off with a stranger, but this man was her prince charming. He could do no wrong. Well, apart from the barefoot trek through Ash Township in the middle of the night.

Her long dress snagged on a fallen branch.

"Are you sure we're almost there?" She called out.

Her hero slid next to her. His hand gently took hers. He felt warm. He felt steady.

"Not far now." He crooned.

"We could have just hooked up at the party." She giggled.

"I have...performance anxiety." The man answered, danger in his voice.

The tip of his hook glided over her thigh. It was erotic. Her heart fluttered.

"Ok." She smiled. "I just don't want to step on a thorn or something. You'd have to carry me."

"Well, if you're so concerned...why don't we do it right here?"

She laughed. Then she looked into his eyes. He was dead serious. That only excited her more.

"Really?" She asked.

"Yeah." He winked. "Like Adam and Eve."

The hook tore through her costume. She moaned as the boy's fingers slid inside her. Her ecstasy swelled as hot kisses rained down on her neck. His prosthetic softly brushed her long, blonde hair. She thought she might climax right here.

That's when the hook pierced her back.

She was pulled horribly close to the young man's face. She tried to cry out, but the hook snared her lung, driving the air from her in a bloody spout. His teeth sunk into her neck. Her jugular hit the forest floor. The last thing she felt was her legs giving way.

3

*The man picked a stray tendon from his teeth with his hook. Another night, another kill. Another smile on his blood-drenched face.*

*He stared down at the lifeless corpse. Her pale skin delicately resting under that blue fabric. Her feet curled perfectly. Her eyes would never open again.*

*He thought she looked more beautiful now than ever in life.*

---

The detective looked away from her phone. She examined the lifeless heap before her. This girl was barefoot too.

The similarities were here. There were deviations from the story. There were no piercing wounds on this girl's back. This body was dressed as some comic book villain, not a princess.

But she was blonde. She was barefoot. She had a bite taken out of her neck. She went missing at a Halloween party, and she was found in the forested wastes of Ash Township.

There was no doubt in the detective's mind. Whoever had written this "fantasy" had done this. What exactly had the detective stumbled upon? What kind of person would write and act out such a vile perversion?

# I

Radiant daggers of frigid autumn sunlight cut across the unkempt room. Piles of half-read tomes littered the floor. The walls were akin to those of a derelict mausoleum. The air cloyed with an earthy aroma. Had he been in a better mood, the bedroom's sole occupant would have found the smell enticing.

Brian Stanhope lay on his back, his head covered by an overused pillow. He took a deep breath and held it in his chest. He lamented that sleep had not come in one luxurious eight-hour visit.

He released his breath. He blinked. He hated the sunlight. He hated his thin curtains for not containing the flickering blades of a dying star millions of miles away. The bright glare was almost worse than the roar of a semi careening into a head-on collision.

He shuddered at the thought. The voracious millipede of anxiety crawled down his back.

As much as Brian Stanhope desired redemption, he didn't think he would ever get it. He missed feeling like a human being. His bones sagged as he got to his feet. He cautiously opened his curtains.

Staring out the window of his one-story boyhood home, his eyes fell on the barren field across the street. He was disappointed that there were no deer out today. Maybe it was already too late in the day for deer.

He turned to the analog clock that had hung on his wall next to a crucifix for the past 28 years. It was not yet 7 AM. He shook his head. He wished the deer would come back.

It had been a wet spring. No one had been able to plant this season. The deer would not waste time in empty fields. They would find greener pastures elsewhere.

Brian's gaze drifted to the crucifix. Guilt impaled him. He averted his eyes.

He fled to the bathroom, sprinting past the abandoned rooms of his parents and his brother. He flicked on the lights, quickly hopping into the shower. As warm water washed over him, the anxiety faded into the corners of his mind. It would return, of course, but that was a problem for future Brian.

When he was finished, he dried himself lethargically. He observed dead roses in a vase on the toilet. The vase was an ugly off-

5

white thing. The roses had been dead for a while. Their brown, crinkled, twisted petals captivated him.

Brian contemplated his appearance in the bathroom mirror. The face that stared back at him was nearing 30. His once thick, black hair was gone. Women used to throw themselves at him, each one hoping they might run their hands through that hair, and stare into his deep, brown eyes. He still had his brown eyes, but they had developed an unsettling, piercing glint.

His beard was darker than a Ford Model T. Had he some natural social charm, the beard would have done many favors. Currently, it only hid his jowls.

His skin had paled from months of writing behind a computer. Permanent purple bags took up residence beneath his sunken eyes. His ears were starting to get hairy.

He smiled into the hated mirror and ran his tongue over his teeth. Sharp canines threatened to pierce his taste buds. His fangs had always been pronounced. In his youth, his mother had begged dentists to file them down. For some reason, every dentist refused, likening their defilement to taking a wrecking ball to the Sistine Chapel.

Damp towel around his waist; Brian made his way to the kitchen. His computer setup glowed from the living room. He wasn't in the mood to think about writing yet. He had to think about food first.

In lieu of *"Live Laugh Love"* or some other empty, white platitude, his mother had hung a photo of politician Bob Dole in the kitchen. Brian quickly dodged the statesman's prying eyes. It was best not to dwell on what mom had seen in the man. Thinking about his mother was worse than thinking about writing.

Brian searched through empty shelves, finding a lone sleeve of bagels. A brief scavenging of the refrigerator revealed a tub of hardened cream cheese. What remained of the spice rack peered down from a lofty cabinet.

He grimaced. Only garlic. Why did he even keep that around? The taste of garlic and the woman who loved it made Brian want to hurl.

He switched on a stained toaster and plopped in the bagels. When they were finished, he gingerly set them on a paper plate. He scooped out the cream cheese with a tablespoon. All the knives in the house had been discarded after an excruciating panic attack. The millipede had convinced him that he would stab himself, or worse, someone else. The knives had to go.

Mouth filled with bagel, he reached for his phone. He felt only his towel. He frowned. He needed a new cell *today*. He glanced at his computer, reminded of how carefully he had destroyed his last phone.

The anxiety stirred in his brain. He wolfed the last of breakfast down and retreated to his room.

Ransacking his meager closet, he hastily threw on boxers, a t-shirt, and a pair of jeans. His OCD forced him to slowly lace up a pair of high-top sneakers. He donned a ghastly hoodie that a polite fashion connoisseur might describe as "retro." Brian loved it. It was comfortable.

He applied a healthy dose of beard oil and grabbed some old sunglasses. After one last preening in the detested bathroom mirror, he stepped outside. The sun was still rising, and he felt the low heat of the October day.

Even for Monroe, Michigan, Brian lived in the boonies. His nearest neighbors were the chirping insects in the foliage. His property line drowned in barren cornfields. Weathered power lines choked by weeds were the only semblances of civilization. In his backyard, a towering dead white oak watched over the land. The lifeless tree made him sad for more than one reason.

He reached into the hoodie's front pocket, withdrawing a nugget of *Cannabis Indica*. He lifted it to his nose. He took a healthy sniff. This was skunk weed, alright.

Brian smiled at the overpowering aroma. Through the foul smell, he could detect light notes of pine and lavender. Fancy medical marijuana was sterile and bland. Cheap weed smelled like all the good and evil on Mother Nature's Earth. This weed made you work to get high. This weed rewarded you for getting high.

The anxiety roared like an injured beast. It threw itself against Brian's temples at the smell of marijuana. His pulse quickened. Sweat dripped from his bald brow. He needed to get his mental illness under control. Luckily, he had paraphernalia stashed in his ride.

Brian drove a Lincoln Town Car. Its fresh, bright red paint job didn't hide the rust, but if a car had four wheels and a seat, Brian could care less what it looked like. The leather seats were comfortable. That was a plus.

He sat down in the driver's seat. He popped open the glove box with a click. He snatched up a Bic lighter and fresh rolling papers from the overflowing compartment.

Brian smiled. The demon in his head recoiled. This was going to be a good smoke.

He rolled the leafy nugget into the paper gently, like a mother tucking a baby into a blanket. He placed the roll in his mouth. The lighter ignited with a spark. He touched the bare flame to the end of the joint. He inhaled.

Burning plant matter entered his lungs. All the blood, sweat, flowers, bird shit, decay, corpses, gentle rain, sparkling sunlight, and fresh soil that had gone into growing the weed entered his body. Acrid smoke caused his eyes to tear up. A novice smoker may have coughed uncontrollably. Not Brian Stanhope.

The veins in his eyes swelled, turning red. The anxiety floated away as gently as a leaf on a stream. This was a beautiful moment.

His body grew heavy. He put his stash back in the glove box. He turned the keys in the ignition.

The engine rattled comfortably. Enjoying his high a little too much, Brian threatened to drift to sleep. A loud cell phone commercial airing over the car radio snapped him back to reality.

That's right.

A new phone.

He needed to write.

Maybe some coffee first.

He backed out of his driveway, swerving gently onto the country road. He drove east wordlessly, joint dangling from his lips. The intrusive thoughts were gone. The sun reflected off the red hood before it vanished into the distant trees. The trees, who were the last remaining stalwarts against the light of day.

# II

Even cruelly scarred by time, Monroe was beautiful. Stunning churches adorned what was left of downtown. The River Raisin cut a brilliant path through the civilization. In this corner of southeast Michigan, Mother Nature slowly reclaimed her territory, hiding burned out buildings and needle covered streets in verdant veneer.

Mankind was slowly forgetting the small city, save as a port in the storm on a long road trip. Travelers spun tales of the food in the dying community, and how its restaurants stood a head above the other firmaments in the town. One eatery never left the hearts of those who ate there.

Zoe's diner had been born from the Detroit Race Riots and the collapse of the auto industry. It had survived the Recession of the Bush Administration and two wars in the Middle East. It was lauded as a regional institution like the Fermi Nuclear Power Plant or The La-Z-Boy Furniture Company. Monrovians looked forward to a meal at Zoe's almost as much as they anticipated re-enacting the River Raisin Massacre every year.

Zoe's used to be called Lou's Kitchen, but after a lengthy divorce, Zoe Jackson changed the name. She was one of eleven female identifying restaurant licensees in the city. She was also Monroe's only Black small business owner. Not an area known for diversity, even Monroe's more racist clientele had to admit Zoe made a damn fine cup of coffee.

However, no amount of renown, history, or happy customers seemed to satisfy the almighty dollar. The affairs of the little diner were starting to look grim. Zoe had already gone over her ledger twice this morning, and a third review showed no signs of improvement.

Zoe shook her head. October was never this slow. The kerfuffle over Custer Statue was driving away business. People were up in arms over that monument. Conservatives hailed the bronze likeness of General George Armstrong Custer as a national landmark. Liberals referred to the statue as "the butcher in the square."

Zoe couldn't decide if tearing down the horseback rider or leaving him up would be better for business. Zoe rarely thought of the statue, save for a chuckle every few months after reading *Monroe Evening News* articles detailing the recurring vandalism of the

9

monument. It seemed that some brave soul was spray-painting the balls on the horse blue; much to the chagrin of city council.

Zoe sighed as she glanced at her dining room. Three regulars and a stranger weren't going to pay the bills. She looked back down at her ledger. If things were this dead, she could at least help Reynaldo with the dishes, hang up Halloween decorations, and fix the toilet in the women's bathroom before lunch service. Her place still had standards, even if no one was there.

Zoe's brooding was interrupted by the newcomer slamming a fistful of bills onto the counter. She lifted her head with a start. She had to crane her neck back to get a good look at the unusually tall man.

He was pale. His long brown hair was pulled into a ponytail. He sported a goatee. His eyes were wide and bloodshot, as if he was on something. He was extremely muscled, and even with the barrier of the counter, he stood uncomfortably close.

"My apologies miss. It was not my intention to startle you." The man's voice was rough and animalistic, contrasting sharply with his eloquent speech.

"Oh! Don't worry. I was just lost in the music." Zoe smiled.

"The fare was delectable."

The way the man never broke eye contact was unnerving. There was a quiet hunger in his gaze. His eyes were like a shark's.

"I assume you must be Zoe?" he asked.

"You got it!"

"Nick Bowman." He introduced himself, unblinking.

"Where you from?" Zoe asked uneasily.

"North Carolina." Nick Bowman replied curtly.

"Is that so? I thought I heard a southern twang on you."

Zoe's hand drew close to the silent alarm under the counter. She had never used it in her decades of operation. Would today be the day?

Thankfully, fate intervened on Zoe's behalf. Nick finally blinked. He wordlessly walked out the front door. The chime rang, hailing his exit. Zoe drowned in a wave of relief.

She watched Mr. and Mrs. Vore observe the stranger as he got into a black Jeep Grand Cherokee. The Vores were regulars who always sat at the front bay windows. They were an elderly couple, known for their proclivity to gossip. As Nick drove off into the sunrise, the Vores tittered that he was "on the drugs." Zoe found herself agreeing with them. The growing heroin epidemic garnered daily headlines in the *Monroe Evening News*.

The only other patron in the restaurant, Alexis Knabusch, was typing away on a MacBook at the other end of the diner, oblivious to financial troubles and weird customers. Her coffee would need topping off soon. Zoe wondered if she'd have time to grab the Halloween decorations from the back before Alexis summoned her.

The chime at the front door rang again.

"Hey, Zoe." Sabrina Cunningham yawned sleepily.

Sabrina, despite having a reputation as a huge nerd, physically embodied the stereotypical All-American beauty. She was 23, blonde, blue-eyed, and athletic. She had a charming smile and a limitless supply of confidence. She was the girl-next-door mothers wanted their sons to marry.

"Sabrina! You look like you haven't slept all night." Zoe remarked.

It was true. Sabrina's hair was undone. Her eyes were tired, and her baggy *Silent Hill* sweatshirt was grass stained. Zoe heard the rattling of spray-paint canisters from within Sabrina's Harley Quinn backpack.

"Working on one of your art projects?" Zoe asked.

"You could say that." Sabrina gave a roguish smile.

"You're going to have to do another mural on the back wall of the place. I was furious when Lou painted over it."

"Yeah...that was a good one, wasn't it?" Sabrina pondered. "You seen Brian around?"

"He hasn't come in yet."

"Lame."

"You ought to get him to help you again."

"*Help?*...I guess he held the ladder." Sabrina snarked. "My partner-in-crime here?"

"She's over there." Zoe motioned at Alexis's table. "You want coffee or anything?"

"Nah, I can't stay long." Sabrina answered. "You should join us."

"We'll get a rush the second I do." Zoe answered sardonically.

"Suit yourself." Sabrina gave Zoe a wink. She adjusted her backpack and joined Alexis, launching into a spirited tirade as soon as she sat down.

Zoe filled a coffeepot. She couldn't help but overhear their conversation. In the food business, eavesdropping came with the territory.

"...with all the planning for the *heist*, I haven't slept in *days*."

"That doesn't sound healthy, Sabrina. Did you even read my blog about mental health and sleep?"

"Hey, you do you. Me? I'm more than happy to hide in the bushes at St. Mary's until 3 AM."

"So, you did it again?"

"Yeah! I gave him some nice blue balls as soon as the cops left! My dad and his big wig friends are going to be *pissed*."

"That's so funny."

"Right?"

"That thing is a racist eye sore."

"God, I wish I could tag some of those empty storefronts at the mall. Pat Catan's went out of business, that might-"

The two girls quieted as Zoe made her way over. She refilled Alexis's coffee. Alexis ran a hand through her hair, trying to make it look like she had been focusing on her MacBook. Sabrina simply smiled and drew Zoe into the conversation.

"I'll bet Zoe could kick General Custer's ass." She said.

Alexis's angry grey eyes warned Sabrina to change the subject. Sabrina either did not heed the warning or did not care. Zoe couldn't help but smile.

"Zoe, would you fight General Custer, if given the chance?" Sabrina asked.

"I'm not really a violent person. Besides, he fought for the Union." Zoe replied.

"I heard you whipped Lou with your belt when you caught him cheating on you." Sabrina laughed.

Zoe immediately went still. Her demeanor darkened. She glared at Sabrina.

"Don't believe everything you hear." She frowned.

"Well, I'll get out of your hair." Sabrina chuckled obliviously. "I gotta hit up Nikki and Talon. See you, Lexi! Let me know if you need more help with those pics! Zoe, say hi to Reynaldo for me. Oh, and tell Brian that we're going to smoke...I mean, smoke *up* some ideas at Munson Park. At the hill. There won't be kids around." Sabrina continued.

"Later, Sabrina. Don't talk yourself to death." Alexis rolled her eyes.

"She loves me." Sabrina teased.

She left in a whirlwind. Zoe gave a wry smirk. There weren't many girls like Sabrina Cunningham, that's for sure.

Shortly after Sabrina vanished from view, a familiar vehicle pulled into the parking lot. The blood red Lincoln Town Car parked as close to the building as possible. It's driver clearly considered nabbing a handicap spot for a moment.

Zoe brightened when she saw Brian Stanhope step out of the car. The morning sunlight reflected off his bald head. He wore sunglasses. He waved nervously through the glass front door.

*He's probably high.* Zoe thought with bemused sadness. She invited him in with the wave of an arm and wondered if she could trick him into doing the dishes again.

# III

Brian loved *Zoe's*: the exposed brick walls, the blue leather upholstery, the Edison bulbs, the Marcus Belgrave playing faintly in the background…it almost made him forget what a pathetic mess he was.

He sniffed his hoodie discreetly. Okay. Good. He didn't smell too much like reefer.

"Brian! How are you doing?" Zoe called out.

Zoe Jackson was thin and wiry. Her welcoming smile was enhanced by horn-rimmed spectacles. Her face was adorned with dark freckles, reminding Brian of Morgan Freeman. He swallowed nervously. He hoped that thinking about that similarity wasn't racist.

"Living the dream, Zoe, living the dream." Brian chuckled dryly. He hoped wearing sunglasses indoors wasn't suspicious.

"The usual?" Zoe asked.

"Extra sugar and extra cream. Is anywhere fine?" Brian motioned with a calculated arm.

"I'll be right back with that coffee." Zoe paused, "You know, it's good that you're friends with that girl."

"What?"

"I mean, you two are in here every day almost."

*Zoe playing matchmaker again.* Brian rolled his eyes behind his shades.

"She's my buddy." He answered. Despite everything, that was true.

Brian made his way over to the fashionably dressed 20-something sitting alone with a MacBook Air Pro. She was completely focused on the computer. In between furtive sips of coffee, her fingers gracefully glided along the laptop's track pad. Her blonde hair was streaked with oddly brilliant strands of blue.

Alexis Knabusch had dyed her hair every color of the rainbow over the past decade. One with an eye for hair care would have noticed the years of impulsive dyeing were beginning to take their toll. Alexis didn't seem to mind, and her scores of social media groupies certainly did not. They were more obsessed with her body.

She had a curvy build, or was "thicc" as the Instagram comments described her. Her grey eyes had a beauty belied by

14

emotional darkness swimming beneath the surface. Brian had been on the wrong side of those wrathful eyes many times.

Brian waved at Alexis, careful to avoid eye contact with Mr. and Mrs. Vore. They were Republicans. They were guaranteed to smell the weed on him.

Alexis didn't react as he slid in across the booth from her. He wondered why she tolerated him. He hadn't been the best friend as of late.

"Good morning, Brian." Alexis said coolly.

Brian lifted his sunglasses.

"I'm not too bloodshot, am I?" he asked quietly, trying to remain inconspicuous.

"*Well, good morning to you too, Alexis.*" She retorted sarcastically. "You realize Zoe knows you're high every time you come in here, right? That's how she guilts you into being an unpaid employee. Your eyes don't look red, by the way." Her expression turned playful.

"What? No she doesn't." Brian responded incredulously.

"So, you steamed the carpets last week out of goodwill?"

As if on cue, Zoe delivered Brian his cup of coffee.

"You two just holler if you need anything." She winked and made her way back behind the counter.

Brian smiled. Zoe was too kind. He doubted with every fiber of his being that she was using his altered consciousness for her own gain.

He took a long quaff of coffee. This is what the ambrosia of the gods must have tasted like. If anything, a little toke in the morning only enhanced the dark, sweet, milky bean water drowned in sugar and cream.

"How do you keep your teeth so clean? My dentist always complains about my coffee stains. With all that sugar, I'll bet you've dropped a small fortune on fillings. I certainly have." Alexis remarked jealously.

"Don't know. Never spent a penny on dentists. My mom wanted to, though." Brian took another swig of coffee. "Speaking of, I gotta drop off some money for her and Sam after I get my new phone...I'm thinking of getting the new iPhone? The one that came out two days ago?"

"My my. Mr. Moneybags. What is it you do again?" Alexis raised an eyebrow.

"I do what you do. I work online." Brian replied.

15

"You do not." Alexis laughed derisively.

"I do! Online fraud prevention consulting." Brian shifted his weight uneasily.

"That is *not* what *I* do. Besides, I still live in my absentee parent's house. I don't make enough to be self-sufficient like you."

"I live in *my* parent's house." Brian feigned wounded pride "People actually recognize you though! How many likes do your tweets get? 1K on average? When it's *not* socially relevant? Speaking of, I read your new blog post." Brian ran his tongue over his canines.

"You did?" Alexis asked excitedly.

"Yeah, gotta support my friends." Brian nodded.

"Speaking of friends, you want to hold Sabrina's ladder again?"

"What?" Brian blinked.

"Zoe might have her do another mural on the back wall." Alexis explained.

"Oh, cool! Yeah, I'd like to. I miss chilling with you guys. I've just been so busy with writing fraud stuff, you know…" Brian trailed off.

"Anyway, what'd you think?" Alexis smiled. "Of my article?"

"I think Buzzfeed is a good place for it."

The smile vanished from her face.

"I meant the subject matter." She said.

"Oh."

"You're my friend. Be honest with me." She stared at him expectantly.

"I had no idea slut-shaming was a thing." Brian began, "I mean, I guess I knew what it was, but I never knew it had a name. And I never knew that it was something people cared about outside of high school…*unless your last name happened to be Vore.*" he finished with a stage whisper.

Alexis smirked.

"Slut-shaming is something that stalks women throughout their lives." she articulated with growing passion. "It's a horrible double standard that plagues our society to the core. Men can sharpen their sexual experience on any poor innocent girl, but god forbid a woman try and find happiness if she isn't a virgin. Men perpetrate this toxic narrative in order for more helpless women to buy into the bullshit."

"It's fucked up." Brian agreed absentmindedly. He looked down at his mug. He needed another coffee.

"As a cisgendered man, can I ask your opinion on something?" Alexis queried.

Before Brian could react, she flipped her MacBook around so that he could see the screen. He blushed. Why was Alexis, in the middle of a family diner, without even so much as a hint of shame, editing a bathing suit pic? Of herself no less?

He supposed it was a nice pic. She was wearing a sensual black two piece. The image stirred something primal within him.

"Uh…" he scrambled to think of an appropriate reply. "It's September."

There was a pause.

"What?" Alexis asked; confused.

"Like, isn't summer over? It's like…wearing white after Labor Day. People don't do that. You don't post classy lewds after Labor Day either."

Brian was trying his best to sound woke. He hoped he wasn't coming off as sexist. Truthfully, he had no clue how to tell a younger female friend that she was smoking hot.

"Are you kidding? I can keep rolling these out all autumn thanks to global warming." Alexis beamed. "Huh, never thought I'd thank global warming for anything." She mused.

Something spurred Brian into giving up "being woke." Though he did not understand it, something about this situation felt hypocritical to him. He tried to put his reservations into words.

"Alexis, aren't you kind of…*contradicting* yourself? You're like, defeating your whole argument…of like yourself." he said.

Alexis stared. She looked astonished that he hadn't complimented her. The darkness in her grey eyes churned.

"What do you mean?" She asked through gritted teeth.

"I mean your article. Isn't this picture *encouraging* slut-shaming? Like, you posting that, people are going to call you a slut. Right?"

Anger flushed into Alexis's cheeks. She quickly turned her MacBook away from Brian and snapped it shut.

"Did you even read my article?" She accused.

"Yeah! You made such a compelling argument about not being called a slut. I totally get how that can hurt someone and affect their self-esteem and all that, but aren't you worried that you, and girls like you, are going to get called names online for posting things like that? It's kind of like, encouraging the toxicity." Brian rambled with half-baked conviction.

"Brian, it's important for women to feel empowered in their own bodies." Alexis glared.

"And you feel empowered by taking your clothes off?" It was now Brian's turn to be confused.

"Yes! Being comfortable with your body is so…I can't even begin to explain how important it is. Do you want this world to turn into *The Handmaid's Tale?*" Alexis was furious now.

"No, of course not, but like, you know dudes are just going to jerk off to you, right? How is that empowering? I don't want to kink shame or anything." Brian faltered. "Am I using that phrase right? *'Kink-shame?'*"

"You're hopeless!" Alexis exploded.

"Sorry. I don't really understand all this political nomenclature." Brian sighed. "I think that's something I admire about you. You actually try to think about world-view stuff. You really believe you matter."

Alexis gave a cruel laugh.

"You can't just spout your ignorance and then expect me to not say anything!" she countered.

"Well…uh…okay…what am I doing wrong?" Brian asked, desperate to pacify his friend.

"All right, so: a person's body is their own, right?" Alexis began, trying to bottle her anger.

"Yeah."

"And do you believe people should express their ownership of their body however they like?"

"I mean, sure."

"*However* they like. Whether that's tattoos, piercings, hair, or…?"

"Clothes?" Brian answered, taking the bait.

"Yes! If we insult or belittle someone who wants to express themself, then we are taking ownership of their body away from them." Alexis declared matter-of-factly.

"…but I wasn't trying to insult you. I think you look good. I was just saying the problem is a lot of weirdoes are gonna think you do too, and they are gonna do what weirdoes are gonna do." Brian protested. "I'm just trying to look out for you."

Alexis recoiled as if she had been struck.

"Where do you come off trying to baby me like that? I don't need you to be some sort of…*guard dog*."

"It's my fraud prevention instincts." Brian shrugged unconvincingly.

"I wish you had said I looked hideous. This is way more problematic." She sighed in frustration.

"I'm just telling the truth! Do you how many guys use Instagram and Snapchat just for masturbating?" Brian argued, "I just think you're better than that."

"I hope you never have a daughter." Alexis growled, "You'd probably tell her that it's okay for men to catcall her if she dresses a certain way. If she gets raped and murdered, you'd probably tell her ghost she was asking for it."

That last sentence touched a nerve.

"You're a bloodsucker." Brian snarled, "You're feeding off poor lonely boys who think giving you a like will get your attention. What happens when you don't give them attention? What happens when some guy comments and calls you '*sexy*' and you call him a '*Nazi*' just because he didn't comment with your consent? What happens when that jilted fuck comes after you in person?"

"It's a woman's right to do with her body as she sees fit. You don't get to tell me what to do just because you want to *'protect'* me. *You* don't get to do that."

Alexis blazed with rage and pain. Something about the fire in her eyes sucked the atmosphere out of the air. Brian suddenly found it hard to breathe.

"Look, do what you want." he sighed.

"You got a real problem with women, Brian." Alexis huffed victoriously.

"What? No I don't." Brian replied, worry in his voice.

"What about the Target meltdown? One girl didn't communicate with you the way you wanted her to, and now we're all just a bunch of bitches to you."

Mention of the incident was too much for Brian. His hands went clammy. A cold sweat broke out on his forehead. He stood quickly, throwing a few bucks on the table.

"Text you tonight?" Brian struggled to escape.

"Sabrina's the only one smoking. I'm taking a T-break." Alexis exasperated.

"You still got that 9297 number?"

19

"You memorized my phone number?" Alexis looked taken aback, and a little creeped out.

"I didn't mean to." Brian whispered.

Alexis paused.

"Look Brian, I'm sorry. Just be a little more aware of how your actions and words affect people." She said.

"Believe me: I'm well aware of their affects." He answered.

He hurried to the front door. Zoe tried to intercept him on the way out with a friendly good-bye. Brian lifted his hands in supplication.

"Sorry Zoe, I know you want people to pay at the register, I left my money on the table. Running late. Phone appointment. Catch you tomorrow!"

Alexis ignored his exit. She reopened her MacBook with disappointment. She looked at her swimsuit selfie on Photoshop. She saved her changes and closed the program. She didn't post the picture to any of her social media accounts.

Zoe glanced out the window, watching Brian as he drove away. She was sad that he was gone. Now she would need to clean the soiled dishes herself.

# IV

The dulcet, crooning vibrato of Post Malone enveloped Brian as he drove. He loved the dirty poetry of the music. Unfortunately, the local radio stations never seemed to air it. Brian had to purchase an actual, physical CD from Meijer just to listen to Post.

Brian admired downtown as it sped by. It seemed like fall was lasting forever. He hoped that it would. Winter was a jail sentence. He hated winter.

He fondly remembered the joint he had smoked before *Zoe's*. He'd have to pick up some more grass. Luckily, his phone dealer had no shortage of pot.

The gorged waters of the River Raisin vanished from view. The brown brick buildings of downtown were behind him. He had entered Monroe's East Side. The East Side had a reputation: only one gunshot after dark was a quiet night.

Abandoned cars rusted in the streets. Heroin addicts dozed off in overgrown yards. Decaying houses with broken windows blinked sinisterly at passerby.

Brian turned off the Post Malone. *Hollywood's Bleeding* was a little too on-the-nose for The East Side. Unfortunately, the radio only offered low quality, mainstream country music. The in-town station didn't play anything that came out after 2006.

He quickly turned the offensive sounds off. He didn't mind country music necessarily, but he was tired of hearing Toby Keith, Eric Church, and *Scarecrow*-era Garth Brooks for the hundred thousandth time. He honestly preferred the eerie similarities of the scorched neighborhood and the lyrics of *Hollywood's Bleeding*. He turned the CD player back on with a flick of a finger.

As the album began, he observed the few houses that were still occupied. The extreme beliefs of the East Siders were on full display without even a shred of self-awareness. One house harbored three beaten-down pickup trucks in its weed-covered driveway. A Confederate flag flew from a bay window. A small political sign in the patchy front yard urged residents to save Custer Statue.

"Custer fought for the Union; you dumb inbred fuck." Brian muttered angrily.

These assholes only liked Custer to piss off the liberals. It was common knowledge that most East Siders would vote to reinstate slavery in a heartbeat. What made this fact depressing is that almost all of Monroe's African American population lived in The East Side too.

He passed a tricked-out Cadillac worth more than the land it sat on. An aging African American man smoked a freshly rolled blunt and admired the vehicle from his front porch. The guy blasting mumble rap loud enough for the whole street to hear. He paid no attention to Brian's crimson Lincoln as it drove by; nor did he pay attention to his children. They were fighting on the gravel driveway, beating each other bloody, and shrieking in pain.

"Your kids are going to be in jail one day; you keep fucking raising them like that." Brian swore, "And make them listen to some 'pac and Biggie, they might learn something…wait, shouldn't these kids be in school? Fuck."

Brian was irritable. He hated when his viciously judgmental thoughts vocalized. He tried to calm himself with a deep breath. It didn't work.

Finally, he pulled up to his destination. It was a house that both blended in with the neighborhood and stood out like a sore thumb. The elm tree in the front yard was in good health. The hedges surrounding the two-story building were an acceptable level of unkempt. The yard was green. The driveway shone with fresh laid asphalt. Neither rot nor broken windows tarnished the exterior of the house, which was a relaxing dark gray.

Brian parked behind a new Honda in the driveway. Asian cars were a bit of an oddity in Southeast Michigan. Being so close to Detroit, *not* driving a Big Three car made right here in America was asking for trouble.

On the front porch, proudly displayed, visible from two blocks away, was a large white flag. The flag sported black lettering and the outline of an AR-15. It's text boldly declared:

*COME AND TAKE 'EM*

Brian left his sunglasses in the car. He tried not to mind the obnoxious slogan as he made his way between the wooden pillars of the porch. He was soon staring at his own reflection in the glass front door. He thought about knocking for a moment, but his eyes glanced down, espying a large welcome mat.

That was the only invitation he needed. The violent darkness of Talon Keener's home welcomed him. He stepped inside with nary a sound.

Brian jumped at the sight of the stair pumpkins.

The stairs to the second floor were obstructed by several large plastic jack-o-lanterns. The cutesy decorations were out all year round. While some may have taken this as laziness on the home-owner's part, Brian knew that this was an explicit warning to all guests to *never* enter the second floor. As such, he couldn't help but be intimidated by the leering plastic fangs of the jack-o-lanterns. Their eternally orange smiles broadcast malicious intent.

Brian truly did not know what happened upstairs. Quite frankly, he did not want to know. He could respect someone's privacy. Talon wasn't the only one with secrets.

He made his way to the kitchen, winding through several bare hallways. Pleasant warmth greeted him as he stepped onto the crumb littered floor. Nikki Keener leaned over the opened oven, munching away on some freshly baked cheesy garlic bread.

Brian's ears were repulsed by Nikki's sloppy chewing. The pungency of the garlic didn't help. He thought Nikki looked like a cow chewing cud.

Nikki Keener, formerly Nikole Dalton of Temperance, was a robust woman with brown hair. Her thirty-four-year-old face still clung to the last remnants of baby fat. Her ears were covered with piercings. Her green eyes seemed perpetually tired. She wore holey jeans and a pink tank top. She was barefoot. One ankle bore a tacky tattoo of a dove holding a banner reading "*Hope*" in its beak.

Nikki's shoulder blades had been inked with an actual tattoo artist's skill. The angel wings were cliché, but not ugly. Her left forearm, on the other hand, was tattooed with what looked like graffiti on a bathroom stall. The scrawling handwriting read: "*RIP SKYLAR 2-24-2004.*"

Brian knew better than to ask who Skylar was. The query always devolved into an hours-long diatribe from Nikki regarding her views on spirituality and the afterlife. No thank you.

"Hey Nikki." Brian tried not to step on the crumbs.

Nikki smiled, chewing with her mouth open. Noxious garlic fumes filled the air. More crumbs showered down on the floor.

"Talon's in the garage." She pointed to a narrow door on the opposite side of the kitchen, "I'll smoke you out when you guys are done."

"That sounds great. I can't stay too long though. I gotta hit up Sam." Brian replied.

He hopped over what looked like loose dog kibble. He fought back a gag. Nikki and Talon didn't own a dog.

"Tell your mom I said hi!"

Nikki took a gargantuan bite from her odorous meal. She leaned back over the oven and pulled out her phone. She scrolled through Facebook with an enthralled expression.

Brian went into the garage. The cold, sickly smell of oil greeted him. He took a meditative breath, clearing his sinuses of the garlic stench. He had never been happier to get away from Nikki.

No cars were housed in Talon's garage. Instead, several illegally modified assault rifles hung on peg board panels. Shelves and cupboards were efficiently placed at strategic locations around the space. A recently cleaned refrigerator was tucked neatly in one corner.

Sitting at a work bench, a cigarette lazily dangling from his mouth, Talon Keener tapped away on a brand-new iPhone. Talon had large gauges in his ears. A tattoo of the revolver-wielding Looney Tunes character Slowpoke Rodriguez decorated his right hand. Talon's mousey brown hair was tucked under a dark beanie, which itself hid under the hood of a black *Sublime* hoodie.

Talon had brown eyes, and a narrow, sunken face. A large, beautifully detailed tattoo of hawk's talons clutched his left eye. Unlike Nikki, he clearly invested in his tattoos.

Talon was in his forties, but looked much younger. His odd name was a gift from his drug-addled mother and deadbeat father. They hoped that a name deeply rooted in the animal world would give their son a special connection with the Earth. All the name really did was get Talon bullied. The bullying did not last long, as kids making fun of him soon owned broken noses and black eyes.

Talon had started seeing Nikki a few years ago. At that time, she had been dating a man named Damon Williams. Damon had been a portly, bearded fellow who only cared about snapbacks and vaping rigs. Talon met Nikki when he started dealing marijuana to Damon.

Nikki and Talon had different reasons to engage in their tryst. Nikki felt that Talon met her emotional needs. Talon just thought that Nikki was hot as fuck.

What started off as thoughtless hookups while Damon was at work at McDonalds turned into daily good morning and good night texts. Talon took Nikki out to dinner and movies in Toledo. The dinner and movies soon turned into walks in the park. Walks in the park turned into deep conversations about life. Romance blossomed.

One morning, after a busy third shift at the McDonalds on Telegraph Road, Damon stumbled upon Nikki lying in his bed sending nudes to Talon. Damon flew into a rage. He flushed Nikki's mother's earrings down the toilet.

Nikki, upon seeing her mother's keepsakes dishonorably destroyed, lost her shit. She took to Facebook as Damon ranted and raved. She set her profile to the "Public" setting and began writing a several paragraph long post. She claimed Damon had been beating her every day for years.

In truth, Damon had never raised a hand to Nikki. If anything, *he* had been emotionally abused by *her*. The libelous Facebook post being case-in-point.

Talon was in the middle of a meth high when he saw Nikki's post. Intoxicated out of his mind, and feeling intense anger, he decided to do a nice grav-bong hit. The drug cocktail brewing in his system only enraged him further.

THC now mingling with crystal meth, Talon promptly loaded a Sig Sauer P320 handgun and drove over to Damon's trailer. Nikki, upon seeing Talon pull up to the trailer park, rushed out to meet her Lancelot, leaving King Arthur cursing angrily at the front door.

Nikki threw herself into Talon's arms. Talon pushed her aside, drew his pistol, and fired three rounds at Damon. The bullets whizzed past Damon's head, barely missing him.

Damon turned to look at the bullet holes in his trailer. He then calmly pissed himself. He fled back into the double wide, pants soaked with urine.

Talon cursed loudly. Had he been sober, he would have killed that abusive son-of-a-bitch. He decided to shoot out the trailer's windows instead, which he accomplished with relative ease given his impaired dexterity.

As he was reloading the handgun, Damon burst out the front door. He ran down the street, wailing like a lost child. Talon took Nikki inside, where they smoked Damon's weed until the police arrived.

Talon was arrested without incident. He was charged with a menagerie of offenses, not the least of which was attempted murder. He used his drug-and-gun-dealer money to hire a skilled attorney, who managed to plead the charges down to misdemeanor breaking and entering. Talon only served one year in prison.

The year in the clink wasn't too bad. For one thing, it sobered him up. He kicked his meth addiction. He deepened his devotion to Nikki. On the day he was released, they were wed at the county courthouse.

Once the marriage was settled, Talon began modifying semiautomatics into full automatics. These weapons he sold to the more dubious members of society. The profits Talon divested into marijuana. Marijuana was legal to possess in Michigan, but as state lawmakers dragged their feet to establish dispensaries, Talon serviced a thriving black market. It was through the sale of black-market cannabis that Talon met and befriended Brian Stanhope.

"I got that phone ready." Talon glared at Brian. "I heard you trying to brush off my wife. Like you always do. She not good enough for you or something?"

Brian was all too aware of the large bulge near Talon's appendix that was certainly a firearm.

"No man, I'm just, you know, staying busy-" Brian began.

Before he could finish his sentence, Talon punched him hard in the arm.

"I'm joking, man! Lighten up!" Talon laughed.

He handed Brian the iPhone.

"All jailbroke and everything. VPN is as secure as the ones they got for the NSA." Talon coughed from laughing a little too hard for his smoker's lungs.

"What you need all these phones for anyway? You change 'em up every time there's a new release." He took another puff from his cigarette.

"It's for the…cyber security gig I'm doing."

After a quick inspection, Brian pocketed the phone. He drew forth his wallet. He counted out several hundred-dollar bills, giving the money to Talon.

"If you're some company's hired help, don't they provide you with the shit you need?" Talon asked suspiciously.

"Not necessarily." Brian answered quickly.

"Bullshit."

Talon deposited the money into a lockbox under his workbench. Brian noticed that the lockbox was full to bursting. Clearly, he had not been Talon's only customer today.

"You want a Faygo?" Talon asked. He crossed to the refrigerator and pulled out a colorful two liter.

"Got anything stronger?" Brian asked.

"If you mean liquor, no. I don't drink anymore." Talon drank the Faygo directly from the bottle. "Can't stand it. It makes me crave crystal, know what I'm saying? I been sticking to the program the judge put me on. Weed is all good, though. I also been doing that DMT shit Joe Rogan's always on about."

"That 15-minute trip shit?" Brian's eyes widened.

"Yeah bro. You gotta try it. It's like…a rig? For a dab? You smoke it, and you're gone. It's like…you see these spirits? Wikipedia says they're machine elves or some shit. They make you feel whole in the world. Like…you can really *see* the cosmos, you know?" Talon grew excited recalling his psychedelic pilgrimage.

"That's detailed, man."

"I've been going on it once a month for seven months now." Talon continued, "It was like; I knew I was doing the right thing. And you feel this presence every time. It be real chill. Except last time. I think I broke through." Talon grinned.

"What happened? I'm not too up on psychedelics. I just stick to Special K." Brian was curious now.

"Like, I smoked the DMT. I was laying on this floor right here. I saw the devil. He was like, on the wall, trying to trick me. Then I saw God. Like, there was this cross, and the devil wasn't there anymore. Then, I woke up." Talon's excitement blossomed in a fever pitch.

"Yo, I opened my eyes, and I was in the desert, bro. I was in a building, and I had a rifle in my hands. I looked out the window, and I saw this undead looking dude in a car. He had this beautiful woman next to him. He had this hunger in his face. Like, the hunger of a thing that hadn't eaten in thousands of years. A thing that hadn't tasted food in millennia. I knew he was gonna kill that woman. I couldn't let him do that. He was going to eat her, Brian. So I shot him. I did it, Brian. I killed JFK. And then I was back here, in Monroe. But the thing is: I know I killed Kennedy, and the Feds know I killed him too. That's why I carry a strap, 'cause they're looking for me. I've always known they were looking for me. It was subconscious, like, I always knew I had to carry a piece, but I never knew why."

Brian's mouth hung open. He was enraptured. He was so enthralled by his dealer's beatific vision that he had completely forgotten his creeping anxiety.

"Where do you get this shit? The DMT?" he asked.

"I got a contact. Name's Tommy Fenton. He'd hate your guts though." Talon ran a lazy finger across his Slowpoke Rodriguez tattoo. "You're a real fuck, Brian. He'd cap your ass. Some days *I* want to."

"…Thanks?" Brian tried to take the threat as a compliment.

"DMT. It's what's real. No laws of a fucking totalitarian late-stage capitalist bullshit country mean a fucking damn." Talon's voice grew resentful.

"You say all this shit after one year in jail, I'd hate to see you after ten to fifteen." Brian couldn't help but crack a smile.

"Fuck off, pussy. Wanna smoke? I gotta get motivated to jailbreak more phones."

"The iPhones came out a few days ago. Where do you get them all?" Brian asked.

Talon glared silently in response. Brian gulped. It was time to stop asking questions.

"I got some White Widow and Skywalker OG. I also got some Sour Monkey." Talon changed the subject but maintained his glare. He opened a cupboard, revealing shelves of neatly labeled strains of marijuana, all packaged discreetly in orange pill bottles.

"You know me, Talon. I like something a little more down to earth." Brian replied.

"Oh yeah, you're all about that skunk weed shit." Talon closed the cupboard with an annoyed sigh. He gestured at Brian to follow him into the house.

"I keep the well drinks away from the top shelf, know what I'm saying?" he winked.

The kitchen was now deserted. Cardi B echoed at a deafening volume. Dealer and client made their way to the living room, where Nikki was swaying side to side in time with the music. She perked up when she saw her husband.

"Need anything, baby girl?" Talon asked.

Nikki shook her head, smiling. Talon went upstairs, stepping over the menacing jack-o-lanterns. Brian, knowing better than to follow, plopped down on the couch.

Brian fiddled with an empty bong on the coffee table. He felt the anxious millipede pounding its feet angrily against his brain pan, deriding him for even being in the same room as a Cardi B song. He needed something to take the edge off, fast.

"He gettin' your special blend?" Nikki asked.

"Oh, yeah." Brian dropped the fragile glass bong. It spun around loudly on the table before coming to a stop.

"You know, people call what I smoke 'skunk weed' but I think it's a more pure, holistic experience." he explained, trying to cover his clumsiness.

"He keeps it in the back of the upstairs toilet, you know." Nikki said.

Brian sat stunned.

"What?" he asked in quiet disbelief.

"You know. The back part. Where the water drains in and out when you flush? That's where he keeps it. He dries it off so you won't notice. That's how it gets the flavor." Nikki explained.

"Bullshit." Brian chuckled nervously.

"It's true. You can ask him." Nikki shrugged.

"Does he like, submerge the whole bottle, or…" Brian began, doubt creeping into his voice.

Before he could finish, Talon came back downstairs.

"That'll be $20." He handed two bright orange pill bottles to Brian.

To Brian's horror, Talon's hands were slightly damp.

"Load the piece. I want to watch you smoke this trash." Talon pointed at the bong, taking a $20 bill from the trembling Brian.

A new Cardi B song started to play. The tune was boisterous and vulgar. Talon turned to Nikki with a frightening fury.

"You always gotta play that shit? It messes with my fucking vibes."

"You'd probably like it if you listened. You only listen to like, *two* artists. It's nice to change things up once in a while." Nikki replied, showing no alarm at Talon's growing anger.

"*Insane Clown Posse* is art, Nikki. You can never wear yourself out on high art. You absorb it again and again and you find new meaning. That's the whole appeal." Talon retorted.

29

"I think you just hate strong women." Nikki snarled.

"I just hate cunts who drug and rob innocent people."

"Like men don't do that?"

"You guys want any pot?" Brian offered, trying to defuse the situation.

He ground up a nug in a bedazzled, purple grinder discovered between the couch cushions. Talon and Nikki ceased quarrelling. Brian placed his salivating mouth over the opening of the bong and lit the reefer.

The noxious smoke hit his lungs like fresh mountain air in springtime. He could taste, smell, and feel freshly tilled earth, rotting carrion, stinking compost, and pine purity. It was a delight. He offered the bong to Talon, who politely refused it.

The anxiety may have been dispelled, but the weed quickly replaced it with paranoia. Brian coughed, violently expelling the fumes in his lungs. He paled as drained smoke passed over his tongue. He tasted filthy, oily, wet, sewage.

His dread intensified as he saw Talon look at the bong as if it were a bomb. That wasn't like Talon. Talon could clear hash pipes and one-gram dabs like it was nobody's business. Surely he could handle some shitty lowball reefer?

*Unless it's* actually *shitty. Like it was kept in a toilet.*

Brian's fear solidified as Talon offered the bong to Nikki, who also declined. Nikki's eyes met Brian's. She gave him a knowing smile.

"Are you sure you don't want to try it? The smokiness accentuates the flavor profile. It stimulates the palate." Brian pleaded.

"Bitch, its marijuana, not barbeque." Talon growled.

"Hey man, how do you store the kush?" Brian asked, "Like, before you sell it?"

"You know I keep it on lock. Don't tell me you're *that* high." Talon chuckled.

Brian wasn't convinced. He took a deep breath. He had no control over how Talon stored his weed, so he decided to live in the moment, man. He stared off into space, trying to enjoy the blissful sensation of low-quality THC coursing through his bloodstream.

As he silently battled anxiety, Nikki scrolled through Instagram, liking #livelaughlove posts. Talon finished his cigarette and lit another. For a moment, the Keener living room was filled with bliss.

"We ran into Christine the other night at Applebee's." Nikki stated, shattering the equilibrium.

Upon hearing her name, the four walls of the room shrank around Brian. The Cardi B turned to static. He looked at Nikki. Her innocent smile belied destructive intent. He looked at Talon, whose blank expression held only the neutrality of one who would support an oppressor. The plastic-jack-o-lanterns laughed with insidious glee, piercing Brian's heart.

He couldn't breathe. He couldn't think. He couldn't act. As his world collapsed into a singularity, he could only bring himself to say one thing:

"She hates Applebee's."

"I think she was there with that guy." Nikki gossiped.

Brian doubled over. He had been sucker-punched. The room started to spin.

"Mugsy's was her favorite. Why was she wasting her time at that microwave meal factory?" Brian stroked his beard, attempting to collect himself.

"I don't think she recognized us." Talon blew a ring of cigarette smoke.

"She totally did. I think she knew that we're friends and didn't want to talk to us." Nikki continued. "What happened between you guys, anyway? Didn't she move out of state?"

"I have to go. I'm late. Sam and my mom are expecting me." Brian made for the door.

"Don't try to dodge the question!" Nikki exclaimed gleefully.

"Let the man go, he's late." Talon said. "See you 'round."

Brian tried not to make eye contact with the plastic jack-o-lanterns as he slammed the front door shut. Rays of sunlight blasted his retinas, nearly blinding him. He was going to have a panic attack.

He pushed his way past the AR-15 flag. The keys to his car shook in his hands. Between the anxieties, heartbreak, and high, it took a solid thirty seconds for him to unlock his car door and sit down in the driver's seat. It took another twenty seconds for him to start the car.

The baleful melodies of Post Malone greeted his eardrums. He saw Talon and Nikki peering through the front window. His loud idling was drawing attention to their inconspicuously suspicious house.

*The gun banner probably draws more attention than me.* Brian thought.

He waved at his two hosts with fake cordiality. Turning the car westward, he cranked the speakers as loud as they were able to go. The music echoed down the road, announcing his panicked exit for miles to come.

# V

Geriatric facilities bothered Brian, but River Park Place Apartments had creeped him out even before he was a frequent guest. Its tiny parking lot on North Roessler Street was constantly overflowing. Were there that many old people in Monroe? He barely had enough room to get out of his car. He squeezed between vehicles, careful not to hit any stray side mirrors.

River Park Place was owned and operated by the Monroe Housing Commission. While run as a for-profit institution, they provided a variety of amenities for the infirm, elderly residents who called the brick building home. Brian's favorite amenity was the free Wi-Fi. Without that, the whole property would have been overwhelmingly depressing.

Brian pulled out Talon's hacked iPhone. He accessed the River Park Place network by entering: *Password1*. He sighed.

The lax security was for the benefit of the residents. Most didn't know what texting was. Some struggled to operate even laundry machines.

He entered Alexis's number and sent her a one-word message:

---

Hey

---

Almost immediately, the phone vibrated with a response.

---

What sort of juggalo magic does Talon cast on your devices?

---

Brian chuckled.

---

What? lol

Whenever you text me, your number comes up as a random string of letters.

---

Talon had come through yet again.

---

I'll talk to you later.

Ok loser :P

---

Brian pocketed his phone and checked in with the front desk. The security guard was a scowling Mexican man who wore a blue uniform and matching cap. A tin badge proclaimed his status as "*security personnel.*" Brian avoided small talk with the guard. Embarrassingly, he had never learned the man's name.

Brian gave a meek smile as he signed his name on the check-in list. The guard merely nodded without changing his expression. The man leaned under the table, flipping a switch. A loud bell signaled that the entry doors were unlocked. Brian slipped through them wordlessly.

In the carpeted hallway, the smell of mothballs and cinnamon greeted him. Brian recognized the door with a spooky plastic skeleton on it as his destination. The skeleton was dressed like the Dracula from silent films.

Brian raised one hand to knock, but hesitated. His head was throbbing. He wished he could smoke weed in here. He tapped on the door nervously.

He scratched his nose, ran a hand through his beard, and shifted his weight from foot to foot. The nervous ticks only amplified his fear. He smiled through his sunglasses as his little brother Samuel opened the door.

Even with his contemptuous expression, Sam was an attractive young man. He was clean shaven. He wore a stylishly grungy brown coat with elbow pads. His green trousers and black high-top converse proclaimed his hipster status. With long, perfectly unkempt blonde hair, deep blue eyes, and a healthy complexion, there was no doubt that the mid-20s were being exceedingly kind to Samuel Stanhope. That was good. He needed all the kindness he could get.

"It's a bad day." Was all Sam said.

"Shit. I'm sorry I'm so late." Brian squeezed past his brother. Low, pulsating guilt took anxiety's place in his brain.

Despite the sunglasses, his eyes took a moment to adjust to the yellowed artificial lighting in the room. The small apartment

34

opened to a modest kitchen, a sparsely furnished living room, and a bedroom at the end of a narrow hall. There was a glass sliding door that led out to a patio, which was perpetually being repainted or remodeled by the building's staff.

"Were you picking up from that loser Talon again?" Sam arched an eyebrow with annoyance.

"Only until the dispensaries get the all-clear from the Monroe Inquisition." Brian joked.

Sam didn't laugh.

"How bad is it?" Brian cleared his throat.

"She thinks we're presenting at the Raisinville Science Fair tonight." Sam answered.

"Ah, the prime of my child prodigy days. Remember when all it took to be a child prodigy was to show up and get A's?" Brian ribbed Samuel playfully.

"Don't bring up that bullshit today."

"Sorry…talked to Raoul lately?"

"What do you think?"

"Did you tell him I'm sorry about the…you know…incident?" Brian's mouth suddenly felt very dry.

"You can tell him yourself." Sam folded his arms.

"By the way, I got last month *and* this month taken care of." Brian, who was eager to change the subject, pulled out his wallet. He counted out a fistful of hundred-dollar bills.

"You can pay at the front desk, you know." Sam glared at the money in his hands.

"I can't. Legal stuff." Brian rapped his fingers on the kitchen counter with nervous frivolity. "I'll have the medical covered on Friday. Want me to drop the check off with you and Raoul at your place?"

"*Legal stuff?*" Sam shouted.

"Yeah." Brian shrugged.

"I don't care what the judge says. Fainting in court was *not* proof that you're an incapable caregiver. Where do you get all this money from anyway?" Sam no longer attempted to hide his contempt.

"I'm *not* a capable caregiver. That month…screwed me up forever." Brian's own tone grew sharp. "And I told you, I do fraud consulting. Big business now that there are all those leaks. Do you even watch the news?"

35

"That month was hard for all of us. I had a label interested in *Parts Unknown*. I had to put my life on hold while you were doing…*what*, exactly?" Sam's accusations cut Brian to the quick.

Brian took off his sunglasses. He turned away from his brother. He eyed some dying flowers on the kitchen table and was reminded of the roses in his bathroom.

"Can't we get her some new flowers? Or some fake ones? Jesus." Brian sighed.

He started opening cupboards in the kitchen, trying to do a spur of the moment inventory. Maybe some fake flowers were hidden away somewhere. What he found made him jump with fright.

"What the…who put this here?" Brian angrily pointed out a small jar of minced garlic.

"Are you kidding me right now? You hate her so much that now no one can enjoy her favorite *seasoning*?" Sam rolled his eyes.

"Well, when Raoul fucks you over and ruins *your* fucking life, don't come crying to me!" Brian exploded.

"Raoul didn't do anything. We all have bad days. *I* have regrets. You don't see *me* letting *my* life fall into complete shit!" Sam took a step towards his brother, hands clenched into fists.

Brian considered escalating the situation. Then, a quavering, melodious voice like a dying bird cut through the room. The hostilities ceased.

Brian's head momentarily cleared. Sam released his fists. The voice echoed within the bodies of the brothers before finally reaching their ears.

"Dinner's almost ready."

The boys looked down the interior hallway. The bedroom door leaked natural light onto the sterile floor. Before they could react, the voice called out again.

"Brian, leave your brother alone and go set the table."

Silence.

"Oh, Jesus." Brian groaned.

"Sorry." Weariness too deep for someone so young pervaded Sam's voice.

Brian turned back to his brother.

"Do you remember what my project was?" he asked.

"Fifth grade? I think you did that thing with the weed killers. Which brand was more effective or something?" Sam squinted in deep thought.

36

"Thanks. I'll take care of this." Brian clasped his brother's shoulder comfortingly.

He cautiously made his way to the bedroom. A pit formed in his stomach. He tentatively opened the pinewood door. Fierce sunlight swept over him. He quickly replaced his grim, firmly held jaw with a youthful smile.

A hospital bed wired to respiration devices and heart rate monitors was the centerpiece of the room. Two sets of windows illuminated the space with a radiant glow. A shoddily constructed IKEA chair was the only other piece of furniture in the bedroom. Lying on the bed, attached to all the mechanical instruments keeping her alive, was Brian and Samuel's mother.

Her hair had grayed considerably. Her legs withered from misuse. Childlike fear haunted her eyes.

"Hey, Mom?" Brian asked. He cautiously sat down on the IKEA chair and scooted closer to the bed.

"What is it, Brian?" his mother asked.

"Do you know where I left the dandelions? I don't know if the Roundup killed them or not." He played his part well, taking his mother's trembling hand in his.

"They should be in the garage. Ask Mr. Salisbury if *I* can get some credit for doing all the work for you." she replied.

A smile spread across Mary's wrinkled face. Her dull brown eyes stared off through the windows. Brian couldn't help but follow her gaze for a moment.

"Mom, can I use the printer? I have to print the last page of my report. Mr. Salisbury said we could turn the paper in tonight as long as we...we..." Brian pretended to search for the phrase. His mother picked up on the answer.

"As long as you cited your sources?"

"Yeah! I used Wikipedia and everything."

"Ask your father." Mary's voice wavered painfully.

"Okay. Dad said to take it easy. He said take your pills for your migraine."

Brian reached for a pill bottle on top of the heart rate monitor. He shook out two tiny rose-colored tablets. He offered them to his mother, who dry swallowed them before he could stop her.

"Tell Sam...tell him...to listen...to...his mother..." Mary's voice faded off into a faint whisper.

Putting the pill bottle aside, Brian kissed his mother on the forehead. He held her hand as she drifted off into a mercifully dreamless sleep. Had he not been so invested in playing his part, he might have noticed he was fighting back tears.

He closed the door and swept into the living room like a thief in the night. Sam leaned over the counter, staring at his elder brother with a mixture of awe and suspicion.

"*Bad day.* What are you talking about?" Brian spoke with bravado. He subconsciously brushed a tear away.

"What did you do in there?" Sam asked.

"Just played along. I asked if I could use Dad's printer." Brian plopped down on the couch. Man, he could use something to take the edge off.

"Brian! Dr. Powers said we can't keep feeding her delusions." Sam bristled.

"Sam, the woman is brain damaged. The car flipped what, a dozen times?"

"We have to challenge those thoughts. If we do, her cognitive function might—" Sam began.

"She's not reliving the wreck today. That's all I can ask for." Brian's haunted eyes bore holes into his brother.

Sam went silent, drowning the room in eerie disquiet.

"Have you been seeing anyone?" Sam's question was a peal of thunder.

"Are you kidding me? Not since Christine left." Brian laughed a hollow, cold laugh that worried Sam.

"No, I mean...like a therapist. A doctor." Sam elaborated, "It's done wonders for me."

"I don't have insurance." Brian sighed.

"Well, it seems like you're making *a lot* now." Sam prodded.

"Hey, everything I'm doing is legal. Don't worry about it."

Brian met his brother's inquisitive eyes. Sam was always eager to get to the truth. He was a lot like their father in that way.

"You know, if you have to explicitly tell me that what you're doing is legal, it probably isn't." Sam countered.

"Look, Sam, I want you and Mom to be as comfortable as possible. I'm sorry. You deserve to spend time with your boyfriend and live your life. This fraud prevention work is good for me." Brian started sweating.

"I just think you should talk to someone about how you feel. You *have* been through a lot...loathe as I am to admit it." Sam leered.

"That's what you're here for, right?"

"I'm not equipped to deal with everything."

"Well, I'm here for you too!" Brian ignored his brother's valid point. "*Parts Unknown* playing anywhere yet?"

"We have some gigs in the pipeline. Nothing too earth shattering." Sam gave a begrudging smile. "We've improved since our set at *Trapper's*."

"Oh, that was a great show! Was that the last time I saw you play?"

"Yeah." Sam glowered.

"I'll see your next few shows. You know, I could get you guys some exposure. My friend Alexis has a big social media following. Maybe she can give you guys a shout out?"

"That basket case? No thanks." Sam said dismissively.

"She could be a big help." Brian argued.

"You certainly know how to pick them." Sam laughed.

"What? No. We're not like that." Brian frowned. "She's like, half my age dude."

"She's 21." Sam stifled a chuckle. "Hey, come to dinner with Raoul and I sometime. You two should clear the slate."

"I'm busy. Doing fraud overtime. Gotta get those big bucks."

Brian stretched and looked at the clock on his phone. Was it that late already? He could still grab some dinner from McDonalds and get some writing going before dark.

"See you Sam."

"Don't be a stranger." Sam said.

"I've been a stranger my whole life." Brian half teased as he left. "Let me know if you need more money."

Sam was alone in the apartment now. He reached into his pockets and pulled out the cash Brian had given him. There was more than enough for the next two months of Mom's upkeep. That only made Sam worry more. He could see through the cracks of his brother's façade better than anyone.

Sam hated that Brian had left him to care for their ailing mother alone. Brain damage mixed with dementia was a daunting foe few could conquer, and that didn't even account for the bodily injuries Mary sustained. Sam could barely wrap his head around what Mary's reality was.

He locked the apartment door behind him as he left. The air was still and heavy. A musty odor of decay inched its way into his nostrils. He was more than happy to leave this living mausoleum. He had band practice tonight. His guitar was waiting. It was the only thing he had ever excelled at, and the only thing that hadn't abandoned him.

He shook his head. He was starting to sound like Brian. Raoul hadn't abandoned him. Raoul had been a lighthouse in a stormy sea. He had been there when his older brother had fled.

He missed being friends with Brian.

Even though the sun was setting, Sam's day was just beginning. He ruefully pondered the prospect of pouring his heart into his music, going in for a late shift at the hospital, followed by more care for his mother, followed by more attempted artistic catharsis, followed by another late shift, rinse and repeat *ad nauseum*. He watched the sunset, seeking a reprieve from his despair.

# VI

The dead white oak reached vainly into the night sky, lifeless branches amongst distant stars. Stars: once believed to be lights of heaven peeking through the firmament. Stars: nothing but empty balls of burning gas. Void. Empty. Not very comforting.

It's comforting to believe that someone is out there looking after you. Holding you close. Keeping you safe. Telling you comforting stories. The kind of stories Brian wished to write more than anything.

But those were not the stories he wrote.

He took another hit of Talon's sketchy marijuana. Eying his digital handiwork, he set his glass pipe (or "bowl" as the youngins called it) aside. He ran his hands over the keyboard.

He built the computer after his father's funeral. Its purchase had been justified self-care. He could use the device to take some freelance film editing gigs.

It was disappointing that the computer was now a glorified word processor. He would have loved to enthrall audiences with stunning visuals. He had the skill to animate such stories.

But those were not the stories he wrote.

Brian loved the power writing gave him. He had the power to make the heart ponder. He had the power to hold a mirror up to the human condition.

But those were not the stories he wrote.

His lucrative Patreon page was displayed on one monitor. The other contained a half-written rough draft. His calculating eye corrected errant words.

His eye would have been good for fraud analysis. Maybe one day he could go back and write a screenplay about fraud prevention. It might make a good slice of life story.

But that was not the story he was writing.

*DeathbringerBob*'s cell phone buzzed. He opened the unread text message. The cryptic sender told him everything:

---

The death of a beautiful woman is the most romantic thing there is :)

---

Brian couldn't believe what he was reading. For the millionth time, he wondered if he was demented. His eager readers didn't mind crazy.

There were many names for the genre Brian wrote: Neo-gothic-erotica, peril fetishism, hardcore humiliation/defeat fantasy, snuff, limp fetishism...the name didn't matter. It was all the same truth:

Brian Stanhope wrote murder porn.

He discovered the subject after his life collapsed last year. He had gotten high alone in the very chair he sat in now. He wanted to play some video games, but they reminded him too much of Christine. She loved gaming.

He turned on Netflix instead. He needed to consume media before his anxious depression consumed him. He browsed through the app like a madman. Comedies proved repulsive. Academy award winning dramas angered him. Tragedies hit too close to home. Documentary on the other hand, he could process.

He unearthed something about Dark Tourism. Brian had never heard of Dark Tourism before. The grim phenomena connected with his unhallowed brain. Brian couldn't look away.

The documentary explained Dark Tourism as an unofficial moniker for visiting places deeply tied to death and suffering. It was different from paying respects at a Holocaust museum or bloody battlefield. Dark Tourists voraciously enjoyed places where people lost their lives. Some enjoyed it a little too much.

A woman was interviewed by the film crew. She was a short, plump, aging lady on a guided tour of Jeffrey Dahmer's murder sites. A huge smile inhabited her face. She told the documentarians that this was her 12th time taking the tour this year.

*"It helps my research, you see. It's very inspiring."*

Her smile contrasted sharply with the film's morbid atmosphere. It enhanced what the filmmakers were trying to convey. It was brilliant.

*"Inspiration for what?"* The crew asked.

The woman's smile turned coy.

*"Oh, Jeffy is a frequent guest star in my fan fiction."*

Her eyes were flirtatious.

The film quickly cut to gruesome photographs of "Jeffy" and his handiwork.

"No fucking way." Brian laughed in disbelief.

Eager to prove the documentary wrong, he closed Netflix and opened a new tab. That old bat had to be full of shit. No one wasted their time writing erotic fan fiction about serial killers.

Brian set his chrome browser to *incognito* just in case. No need to summon the FBI to his door. He took a deep breath and dove in.

Google revealed pages upon pages of links to websites with names like DeviantArt, fanfiction.net, archiveofourown, and deadskirts.com. Brian blinked in shock. Whatever this was, it was alive and well beneath the surface of the internet.

Morbid curiosity seduced him. He selected the first link. Soon he was reading smut about The Black Dahlia Killer:

---

*...her delicate fingers dug into The Dahlia's back. They made passionate love. Each thrust was ecstasy. Each kiss elevated intensity. Every caress, their hearts beat faster. The woman moaned...*

---

Brian was getting hard.

---

*...the heroine sighed. Glistening with sweat, panting with exhaustion and desire, her eyes met his.*
*The Dahlia stabbed a large knife into the girl's throat.*
*Shock and dismay engulfed her. Blood spilled over her marbled skin. Heavy coldness swallowed her fingers and toes. Death worked its way into her heart. She stared in horror at The Dahlia. Her eyes closed one last time. With her last breath, the poor, delicate thing had found her way to an early grave.*

---

It was the taboo of the whole thing. It was outside the realm of reality. It was the perfect fantasy in that way.

The detail of the girl's every breath, every kiss, every flex of the foot...how her breasts felt in The Black Dahlia's strong hands, how her pulse raced as he kissed her, how wet she was with literal death...It was the most titillating thing Brian had ever read. The fact that this *existed* was pure lunacy.

He spent hours digging through every link.

To his surprise, real serial killers were a rare occurrence. Most compositions featured heroines sleeping with actual monsters, which then killed the foolish women. Some stories featured no sex at all, only pages of brutally specific deaths. The further Brian dug, the

43

further the erotica declined in quality. They began to read like fantasies of high school Goths.

One stinker starred a woman with a fetish for Deep Ones, the fish creatures of Lovecraftian Lore. She believed they would leave her alone if she slept with enough of them. What started as some sort of on-the-nose literary joke eventually ended with the poor protagonist being killed by a rusty trident through the vagina. The weapon made her lubricate as it killed her. The last line of the story read:

---

*"...and her luscious cum spattered from her lifeless flaps."*

---

"Jesus Christ! I could write something better than that!"

Brian laughed uproariously. He prayed that the goofy woman from the documentary had written that. He wouldn't be able to stand it if she had written The Black Dahlia tale.

His guffaws subsided, and he stared at the computer screen. His anxiety was silent. He clicked back on the first story.

Ancient, dark, primal hunger rose in his throat. He thought he might puke. He opened his mouth to retch, but only one sentence came out:

"I *can* write something better than that."

He fired up Microsoft Word. He cracked his knuckles. He was ready to write.

Something tried to stop him. Maybe it was one last shred of reason, crying out that this was wrong. This was exploitative. This was necrophilia. Couldn't he see that?

Perhaps the Doubting Thomas in his head was right. He shouldn't do this. Maybe he should call someone.

He opened his phone. The sad, tired old android had lived far too long. He thought of his family.

He couldn't tell Sam about the snuff. Maybe he could just tell his little bro that he was feeling lonely. He could tell Sam that he wanted to apologize, and that he really *was* helpless at the courthouse, and that when he saw Christine at Target-

*Christine.*

Her name popped up on the phone screen. He had been texting her every day. He cringed as he re-read his lengthy outbound apologies. None garnered a reply.

He *was* sorry. He had jeopardized her job. He was sorry about that. But didn't she realize she never communicated? She may as well have been cheating. She fled from conflict and he had no choice *but* to trash the store and get thrown out. He was *sorry*! She had *hurt* him. She lied.

He bent over backwards, and she lied and she slept around and he was *sorry* and now *he* was the clown for texting her endlessly and she didn't even have the guts to block his number *even after* she moved away out of *shame*!

He angrily started writing.

All he could think about was Christine: Her curly red hair. Her light blue eyes. Her dimples when she smiled. Her gleaming white teeth. Her soft, perfectly sculpted hands. Her muscular legs, her breasts, her ass, her feet; everything about her surged into his mind, fueling the dark vortex now swirling within.

When his fervor passed, he discovered he had written a story.

---

*Two friends drove through the cornfields of Nebraska. They were enjoying themselves. Going on a road trip with your bestie: That's what the early twenties are for.*

*The driver was a grey-eyed redhead with heartbreaking dimples. Her back-seat passenger was a brunette with great legs. The limbs had done her many favors on the college track.*

*The girls encountered a hitchhiker. He had a hook for a hand. The friends were reminded of urban legends. They recalled tales of a hook handed serial killer hitchhiker haunting the roads.*

*The killer could not be this man. This man was handsome. He was tan. He had dark, curly hair and a perfect complexion. His smile was charming and disarming.*

*The girls' hearts melted. They eagerly invited him along. They asked where he was going.*

*"Not far." The hook handed young man replied.*

*His car had broken down a few miles back. He just needed to get to the next town. His family lived there. They could get him a tow truck.*

*The redhead eyed his prosthetic hook.*

*The man explained he had lost the hand in Iraq while disabling a roadside IED. His valor saved an innocent mosque but left him disfigured. Now, he was simply happy to be out of the Middle East.*

*"That's so brave." The redhead replied warmly.*

*She loved heroism. She was getting wet. The car gently swerved in and out of the lane.*

*"Do you want to touch it?" The hitchhiker flirtatiously offered his hook. A boyish grin lit up his face.*

*The driver bit her lip. She flashed a sensual smile. Her finger brushed against the hook.*

*In the backseat, alarm bells rang in the runner's head. They hadn't passed any broken-down cars. The man didn't seem to have a cell phone on him, nor had he asked to call his family on their phones. If he had served in the United States Armed Forces, why was a tasteless tattoo on the back of his neck? She could clearly see Calvin from* Calvin *and* Hobbes *peeing on the American flag.*

*"Do you want to call your folks?" The runner asked. She instinctively pulled her legs close to her chest.*

*"They know I'm coming. Besides, I don't want to intrude on your hospitality." The man leaned between the two front seats, smiling.*

*Her legs relaxed. Such a beautiful smile. She could trust him.*

*In the driver's seat, the redhead took hold of the man's hook. She loved the feel of it. It was cold. It was sharp. It was sensual.*

*The car swerved ever more precariously.*

*She dragged his prosthetic across the skin on her leg. She shot the man a loaded gaze. He smiled lustily.*

*"You ever given road head?" He asked.*

*The redhead nodded, biting her tongue between her teeth.*

*"You ever received road head?"*

*"No."*

*The man reached over, gently unzipping her shorts.*

*Her heart raced. He gently kissed her where she was most vulnerable. Her gasp turned into a low moan when she felt his tongue. The hook traced along her thigh. Its tip only amplified the pleasure.*

*The runner watched the action unfold from the backseat. She was oblivious to motion of the car. Her repressed voyeurism blossomed. In a way, this was her fantasy come true.*

*As the moaning grew louder, primal pleasure intensified. The redhead was unaware of the hook inching its way up her body. It slowly scraped past her stomach. Soon it reached her ribcage. The brunette realized what was about to happen, but it was too late.*

*With a single, powerful stroke, the hook tore flesh, ripped skin, and punctured organs.*

The redhead's chest opened scarlet down to her bellybutton. She did not have enough breath to scream. She painfully sighed, losing control of the car.

The vehicle swerved into a ditch. It then flipped into the air. It turned end over end, landing upside down in the cornfield. The wreck left a path of devastated earth and flattened cornstalks in its wake.

The redhead lay twisted and broken. She slumped over the crumpled steering wheel, suspended only by her seatbelt. Life drained out of her wound. Her vision grew dark and blurry. Her extremities twitched uselessly in a feeble attempt to save her life. Her consciousness began to fade. Her final thoughts scattered themselves across her dying mind. She hoped that her family would forgive her for being so foolish. She was sorry that she had failed her best friend...

...with that, her now dull, grey eyes rolled up into her skull, closing forever. A faint breath escaped from her blood-spattered lips. Her road trip reached an untimely end.

The brunette had been knocked unconscious. She awoke with a groan. Bruises crudely blossomed over her skin. She blinked, getting a clearer view of the car's pulverized interior. Had everything been some horrible dream?

She did not see the hitchhiker. When she went to brush the hair out of her face, nothing happened. She looked down.

Both of her arms were horribly broken. Yellow bone stuck out of her right arm at the elbow. She cried out in shock. Pain arced into her shoulders.

Her runner's legs remained mercifully unbroken. She screamed her friend's name. She heard no reply. Fear clutched her heart.

The windows had been shattered in the crash. If she could just wriggle her way out, she could run. She could get help. She could –

Her train of thought was derailed by a bloodied hook piercing her left shoulder. She screamed. Her broken arms flailed wildly, but to no avail.

The charming, sensual smile of the hitchhiker loomed inches from her face. Her blood ran cold at his calm expression. He winked.

"Stranger danger."

He covered her mouth and nose. The runner was taken aback. His hand was warm and calloused.

She choked, coughed, struggled, and kicked, but it was no use. She just had to keep her eyes open. If she could see, she could breathe.

Her lungs disagreed with her.

*Her deep brown eyes turned glassy and lifeless. Her legs gave one final twitch in a desperate, last-ditch effort to escape. She wondered if she would be reunited with her friend in heaven.*

*The hook handed serial killer of legend sat over his victims. The media would glorify him for weeks when they found the bodies. He couldn't have done it without miss horny redhaired driver and miss leggy passenger. He needed to thank them.*

*He leaned over the open eyes of the runner. He planted a tender kiss on her limp lips. He brushed her hair aside. He closed her eyes with his good hand before crawling out the back window.*

*Reaching through the shattered glass of the driver's side, he cradled the upside-down corpse of the redhead. He kissed her bloody lips passionately. He gave her hair a playful tussle.*

*He stood. He brushed himself off. He strode into the cornfield with nary a look behind him.*

---

Brian beheld his creation. It was dark. It was perverse. It was profane. It was deeply erotic. His anxiety and depression had been replaced by satisfied stillness.

He needed to share this.

He created a DeviantArt account. He chose the username *DeathbringerBob* for a few reasons. The first, most important, and most obvious reason; was that no one could ever find out that he had written this under any circumstances. Not ever.

He had brought death to those two girls. "Death bringer" had a nice ring to it. That was reason number two.

The third and final inspiration for the name was that damned picture of Bob Dole on the wall. Why his mother had been so smitten with Mr. Dole? He wasn't from Michigan.

Brian posted his story and went to bed. His dreams were not easy that night. Something deep in his mind tried to tell him that what he had done was wrong.

*No one will find out.* He tried to calm himself.

*Character is what you are in the dark.* His subconscious answered.

After a fitful sleep, the first thing Brian did was check his computer. He rubbed his bald head anxiously. He ran his tongue over his fangs. He logged in to the *DeathbringerBob* account.

What he found shocked him. In less than 8 hours, his story had racked up two hundred likes and five favorites. He had ten new private messages.

Astounding.

He opened the messages with pride. Seven simply said "nice job" or "good work." Banal. Still, Brian replied, thanking their composers for the compliments. One message was revealed by Google translate to be Russian. It offered to sell him "male vitality enhancement" supplements. It was quickly deleted. Another message called him a freak. Furthermore, it told him he should commit suicide for writing something so grotesque.

*Whatever. It's not like I don't consider it every day.* Brian deleted the rude message with a smirk.

The final message was something completely different.

---

I haven't read something so fresh, so enticing, or so romantic in quite a long time. :)

You have piqued my interests, newbie :)

---

Something about the enigmatic smiley faces caused Brian to investigate the sender's account. Their profile was bare. There was no evidence that the account was active. The username was as mysterious as the message.

It was just "Paul." It was simple. It was innocuous.

The "About Me" section simply contained the colon-parenthesis smiley face. The pixels of that little black smile were all at once inviting and disconcerting. Behind that little text-based smile was something dark. Something secret. Something vindictive. Something horrible. Something erotic. Most of all, it was something that offered Brian comfort in the virulent turn his life had taken.

The millipede of anxiety tightened around his throat. He swallowed hard. If he replied to Paul, there would be no going back.

# VII

---

Yo!

I appreciate the kind words

---

Paul's response was instantaneous.

---

Of course! :)

Always happy to give credit where credit is due :)

So what's with the happy faces? lol

Oh, they're just happy :)

Like your fic <3 :)

I've never written anything like this before

Wasn't sure how it would be received

I thought it was hot :)

You should be proud. :)

You should post your work to archiveofourown and fanfiction.net :)

It's better than the tripe on either of those websites :)

Can't wait to see what you do next :)

Do you know if a lot of people like stories like mine?

Not nearly enough of them do :)

I mean, we're a niche community :)

But we're out here :)

So who are you?

Oh, I'm just a fan :)

Is Paul your real name?

Ok boomer XD

Are you for real? :)

I don't use my real name. :)

People tend to look on us with disgust, as you can imagine :)

Personally, I think there's nothing wrong with romance in its purest form :)

Sorry.

Not a boomer lol

I should know better than to ask that lmao

I'm just worried you're an FBI agent or something

The FBI have bigger fish to fry than little old you :)

That's exactly what an FBI agent would say

XD

What's the name of this?

What do you mean? :)

Like, you know

Furries, BDSM, etc.

You said this was a niche community

Are you sure YOU'RE not the FBI? ;)

Sorry

I had no idea people appreciated death

That might be putting it lightly 3==D ;)

Some people refer to it as peril fetishism :)

But even that is a big umbrella! :)

Ok...I think I gotcha

Try not to think too hard about it :)

I really hope you write more, Bob <3 :)

---

Brian took Paul's advice and wrote more. He had not been this inspired since his last directing gig in Chicago. Peril fetishism was a great way to get back at Christine. Peril fetishism was a newfound passion. It needed to be explored.

He published another story the following day, and another one the day after that. Before long, he had crafted an impressively bloody body of work. Each story was more popular than the last. He wasn't sure whether this was because his writing was getting better, or because he was building an audience. His new friend Paul assured him that his success was a combination of both.

As *DeathbringerBob*'s notoriety grew, Brian left the house less and less. That suited him fine. He wasn't ready to go out into the world. His trauma was still too fresh.

Brian killed Christine more than a dozen times in his tales. She took the form of a lady knight slain by a dragon, a housewife savaged by a werewolf, an unlucky diver devoured by a shark. Each new death grew more fantastical.

His readership never knew he was murdering his ex. They had no idea who Brian was, where he was from, or what he had done. All they knew was that he produced high quality content they could not get enough of.

Brian was happy. Writing calmed his anxiety. The intrusive thoughts quieted. The creativity, positive reinforcement, and marijuana were doing wonders.

Something else started nagging at him, though. He ignored the new feeling. He knew it was a deeper guilt, a deeper shame. He was still too happy to give up his new hobby, however.

*If it ain't broke, don't fix it.* He thought unconvincingly.

He published new short stories every day for a month. The readers loved his rate of production. None more so than Paul.

---

30 stories in 30 days? :O

You're a regular Stephen King! :)

More erotic than him though ;)

The way you describe the final moments...particularly that one about the

dragon...the way she struggled until the bitter end...it's sad...its exciting

3===D :)

You should be compensated for your talents :)

---

Not leaving the house for a month hadn't slowed Brian's financial crisis, however. He was still on the hook for his father's funeral costs, his own court fees, and keeping his marijuana stocked. Paul's words were intriguing.

---

People get PAID to do this?

Damn

Do what you love, and never work another day, right?

Haha :)

Something like that :)

How do I get paid?

Well, you could do commissions on Patreon :)

I'd back you ;)

I know some people. People like me :)

People who would pay you to write any number of deadly encounters :)

---

The anxiety stirred. Brian wondered if being paid for his work would be considered exploitative. He thought about his dry bank account. He could be homeless soon. Being homeless in Monroe, Michigan was not a scenario he liked to imagine.

His temples pounded as he typed out a reply:

---

I will open a Patreon. Thank you for the advice.

I can't wait to support you. :)

I'll text you some ideas I have for a commission :)

My friends will want to text you too :)

---

Brian froze.

---

Text?

Just send me your number. I promise I'm not a honey pot. :)

Honey pot?

Those things the FBI use to find criminals :)

I thought you knew ;)

Since you're so worried about the feds and all ;)

They wouldn't use that for deadly

smut, would they?

Lol

Oh Bob XD

There's a reason no one in our community worries about the FBI :)

Nothing we do is illegal. :)

No one's getting hurt. :)

It's like pro wrestling! :)

People sometimes get hurt in pro wrestling

Just send the number, cutie :)

---

*Oh, shit.* Brian thought.

This was supposed to be just for him. Money would be nice, but giving his number out to some internet stranger? No way. Things could bleed over into real life. He couldn't have that.

On the other hand, Paul *was* right. What he was doing wasn't illegal. Was it *morally* wrong?

He wasn't *actually* hurting anybody. He wasn't putting Christine to death *literally*. He never used her name. He only used bits and pieces of her here and there. Isn't that what writers did? They write what they know. He knew he would never *actually* take revenge on Christine. This whole thing was just do-it-yourself-therapy.

He deserved to be financially compensated for his artistic catharsis. He was just writing words that people jacked off to. Don't

54

pornographers get paid? That's all he was: a highly specialized pornographer.

He created a *DeathbringerBob* Patreon account. He spent some time brainstorming what his reward tiers would be. Eventually, he composed a list that he believed would satisfy everyone:

For five dollars a month, he offered a personal thank you for anyone willing to donate. For twenty-five, one could access his original stories on Patreon before he posted them anywhere else. Finally, he offered to write one custom monthly story for whoever was willing to part with seventy-five dollars a month.

Immediately, two people signed up for the $5.00 tier. Five people signed up for the $25.00 tier. One person signed up for the $75.00 tier. Brian was unsurprised to see that the largest backer was Paul.

With this, he would be getting $210.00 a month. That wasn't too shabby. He hopped over to his bank's website. He only had one credit card that was not maxed out. Brian took the money left on that card and purchased a burner phone from a nondescript local drugstore. It was a rudimentary flip phone that still needed to have minutes added to it.

He anxiously messaged the phone number to Paul. After a half hour, he received a text from a restricted number. Brian's blood ran cold when he read it:

---

A burner phone? Really? :)

Don't you trust me? :)

Okay that is fucking creepy that you know that

Sorry ;)

I'm glad you didn't just give me your actual number. You have some brains :)

Well Paul, thanks for backing me on Patreon!

What do you want your story to be about?

Female wrestling :)

Really?

Yes. Just two female wrestlers going at it. ;)

One takes it too far and kills the other. :)

That's all?

Yeah? :\

PHEW

I thought this was going to be some pedo shit lol

Oh no. I'm not an animal :)

It's just that I, and others like me, prefer to be a little discreet. :)

I understand completely.

I knew you would :)

Thank you, Bob <3 :)

---

In the coming weeks, more backers pledged their hard-earned money to Brian's Patreon account. After a month, he was making enough to pay all his bills. After two months, he repaid all his credit card debt. After three, he started helping Sam take care of their mother. After four, he was able to hit up Talon for VPN wired, jail broken phones. The VPN access was nice. The less Paul knew about his location, the better.

The black-market phones were crucial in other ways. True to Paul's word, all the high tier patrons preferred anonymity. They weren't animals. They didn't want bestiality, necrophilia, or pedophilia. Some wanted graphic blood and gore. Most wanted more hook-handed serial killer stories. All wanted their desires fulfilled.

Any reservations Brian had were soon cast away. If the money was good, and killing was involved, he would write it. It was nice to feel needed again.

# VIII

Sitting in front of his computer on that lonely autumn evening, Brian felt strange. Something was wrong. He was smoking more heavily. He was constantly irritable and paranoid these days. The hatred against Christine had burned out, but something else had taken its place. Something that frightened him. Something that had been there all along.

He rubbed his eyes and recalled his day: He went to *Zoe's*. He got in that argument with Alexis. He bought the new phone from Talon. He fled in shame upon the mention of Christine. He helped his angry brother care for his mom. It was a typical day. Why was he so on edge?

Proofreading Paul's monthly commission revealed the truth.

Paul loved fantastical, gothically romantic deaths. This month, Paul wanted a piece about a mermaid. A mermaid who desperately wanted to be human. Her name was to be Echo. It was a little cliché, perhaps, but Paul was very particular.

Brian had given Echo dark brown hair, freckles, olive skin, and grey eyes. Echo discovered a magical seashell that would grant any wish her fishy heart desired. Of course, Echo wanted lungs, and legs, and feet, and toes. She wanted to breathe the air and feel the sand beneath her.

The ornate shell granted her wish. She was now unable to breathe underwater. She had no choice but to make a mad swim for the surface. Brian toyed with the idea of having Echo drown, but that wouldn't have been satisfying enough for Paul.

Paul liked the hardcore.

---

*Echo washed up on the shore; alive, unharmed, and breathing air for the first time. It tasted light and fresh. She could smell the salt. She could feel the sand beneath her toes.*

*She stared at her feet with excitement. She fawned over her legs like a land-walker might dote on a puppy. She loved her high arches, her shapely ankles, her leggy muscles...oh, how good it felt to be human!*

*It was time to try walking.*

*She was a little unsteady at first. It took a few minutes to find her balance. Clinging to rocks for support, she took one baby step, and then* another. After an hour of trial and error, Echo was sprinting across the shoreline.

She laughed as the sky changed colors. It would be evening soon. She turned to the sea. Sadness drowned her heart. The ocean had raised her. It was all she had ever known.

Maybe the earthy world of mankind would surpass her wildest dreams. Maybe a day would come when she would not think of the ocean. Echo hoped not.

A heavy sea breeze enveloped her. Her vulnerable flesh burst into goose pimples. A slow realization hit her: she was stark naked.

Echo had seen sailors covered in heavy cloth, and sunken ships filled with silken ornaments. She had always wondered why humans bothered with the silly things. Standing on the shore, laid bare to the elements, she hypothesized that the clothes had a utilitarian purpose. That purpose: warmth. Survival.

The sun was setting. Night would bring only more cold. Echo needed to find some clothes, fast. She would have to look for some fishermen and see if they had a spare set lying around.

She made her way up the shoreline. There were no humans in sight. Echo did not worry. She would find someone soon. Humans loved playing in the water.

As the sun fell low over the waves, Echo caught sight of a large fishing skiff on the shore. She picked up her pace, eager to have her first human interaction. It never crossed her mind that it was unusual for her to be naked. Surely this sort of thing happened to humans all the time.

Her heart soared when she saw a fisherman on the boat. His back was turned to her, but she could see his dark, coarse, curly hair, and strong, well-built body. The top of a tattoo peeked over the hem of his coat. He hunched over the deck of the watercraft, running some loose fishing net through a curved hook. He hummed as he worked.

"Uh...excuse me? Hello?" Echo called out.

Speaking for the first time was not as precarious as she had imagined. The air flowing over her tongue made it easy. The magic shell truly had power.

The man merely turned his head over one shoulder. He had some light stubble covering his face. His eyes were a rich almond. He threw a smile at Echo. His smile was not threatening in the slightest. It was welcoming and warm.

"I'm sorry to bother you, but do you have a spare set of...uh...clothes...lying around? I seem to have misplaced mine." She said.

Echo was standing a hairsbreadth away from the fisherman now. There was something magnetic about him. Something alluring. Maybe the tall tales about attractive human men held some water after all. She smiled.

"Clothes? Sorry, I don't have any lying around...but I do have something *for you.*" The man winked. It was the wink of a shark on the hunt.

Before Echo could react, the hook lunged towards her. As it tore into her belly, she realized it was not attached to the skiff at all. It was attached to where the fisherman's left hand should be.

The hook gutted her as easily as it would a fish.

Echo locked eyes with her murderer. He was still sporting that carefree, charismatic smile. Her grey eyes fluttered.

Echo found it hard to breathe. She gasped for air as the hook tore through her. It caught under her ribcage. Pain like nothing she had ever felt blinded her. Her newfound legs, now weak as jelly, helplessly gave way as the man pulled her close.

He arched his head backwards, still smiling. He bit into her jugular. Echo saw her crimson blood splatter onto the sand. She knew that the pain didn't matter anymore. Her grey eyes closed one last time. The final sensation Echo felt was disappointment. She would never know what it was like to walk all over dry land.

The hook handed serial killer took a moment to wipe the blood from his face. He then tossed Echo's corpse into the skiff. He gazed at his victim, a hunter beholding a prized catch.

Another mermaid. He chuckled derisively. Too trusting.

He would pilot the skiff out as far as it could go. Then he would dispose of the body. The corpse was bloody. The sharks would scavenge it, removing all traces of Echo's existence.

He hopped aboard. He started the engine. He sailed the little boat off into the horizon. The sun was beneath the waves now. All that was left was endless night.

---

The veins in Brian's temples throbbed. This was good work. He had even pleasured himself while writing it.

Paul would love it. Maybe he would tip a few extra dollars in addition to the monthly Patreon pledge. He was generous with his money.

Brian gasped. His pulse quickened. He was sweating. He was sick to his stomach. Why, oh why was he so anxious?

It was Echo's grey eyes that gave it away. They were the same eyes he had given the redhead in his very first story. Bits and pieces.

Christine didn't have grey eyes.

It wasn't just her eyes that Brian killed. It was her legs. Her arms, her hands, her breasts. Her whole body had been killed in more ways than he could count.

*She's my buddy.*

Shame rushed in. The anxiety was painful. He was scared that if he turned off his computer, the darkness of the room would swallow him up. His breathing grew panicked. The room spun.

Brian sent the story to Paul. This only made him more ashamed. He placed his head in his hands. He feared his brain might pop out of his skull.

He didn't want to hurt her. He didn't want to see her grey eyes close forever. Why, oh why had he been using her likeness?

Brian cried out her name in frustration. He was alone in an empty, soulless house. No one heard him.

Her name echoed into silence. It was a silence that threatened to shake the building to splinters. It was a silence that threatened to fell the dead white oak and smash Brian to pieces.

His phone vibrated.

Mental illness still feasting upon him, he reached for the phone. He shook his head. There was no way Paul had read the story that fast.

Brian's heart fell when he saw the name on the caller ID.

"Speak of the devil, and she shall come." He whispered tearfully.

He opened the text message.

# IX

Alexis sat on her bed; legs crossed beneath her. She glared at her MacBook, careful not to spill her diet coke. Her bikini selfie dominated the laptop's screen.

"Fuck him."

Brian's ignorance still angered her. Alexis posted the selfie to her Instagram. Her description of the photo was an out-of-context Nora Roberts platitude plagiarized from goodreads:

---

*"If you don't go after what you want, you'll never have it. If you don't ask, the answer is always no. If you don't step forward, you're always in the same place."*

---

The likes poured in. Alexis grinned. Numerical validation was more gratifying than any sexual encounter or mind-altering substance.

"Hey! Are you listening to me at all?"

Alexis blinked and looked away from her screen. Sabrina sat on the floor, giving a belly rub to Lily, Alexis's hyperactive German Shepherd. Sabrina was pouting.

"Oh, sorry, I got distracted." Alexis took a sip of diet coke.

"Ugh! You're worse than my dad." Sabrina vented. "He was too busy talking up his friends at the Housing Commission to even listen to me. I practically screamed: '*DAD, I PAINTED THE BALLS ON THE HORSE BLUE*' and he just said he would: 'ground me later.' *Later!* What does that even mean? *Ground me later.*" Sabrina sighed and changed course; anger completely gone. "Do you want to see how my portrait of Lily turned out? I might have gotten some spray paint on the fence."

Alexis bolted upright, knocking her MacBook aside.

"You're joking!" she gasped.

"Relax; I have some white. We can cover it up." Sabrina chuckled.

"If my parents see that-"

"Your parents are never here. Besides, you hate your parents."

"That doesn't mean you can deface their property!"

Sabrina shrugged. She went downstairs. Lily followed close behind. Alexis clenched her fists. Her absentee parents *intensely disliked*

Sabrina's artistic endeavors. If any traces of her "artwork" stained the residence...what was she thinking? Fuck her absentee parents. Fuck their upbringing for giving her the compulsion to constantly clean house. They should come home and clean it. Assholes.

Alexis lethargically followed Sabrina downstairs. Opening the sliding glass door to the backyard, she found Lily enduring the zoomies. The dog ran around the perfectly manicured grass full tilt. Sabrina stood on the porch, gazing up at the clouds.

"I wish I lived here." Sabrina daydreamed.

"No, you really don't." Alexis scowled.

"Carrington Farms! Just look at it. All these perfect white fences...it's like *Tom Sawyer* if corporate housing existed in the 1800s." Sabrina proselytized.

She proudly gestured towards a large canvas propped up against the wooden fence posts. A beautiful abstract of Lily mid-run was perfectly sprayed onto it. Blue, brown, and black splotches tarnished the white property markers behind the painting. Mr. and Mrs. Knabusch would go into conniptions if they saw it.

Alexis sighed. She reached into Sabrina's discarded Harley Quinn backpack and pulled out a can of white spray paint. She began painting over the fence. Sabrina grabbed her artwork, admiring her creation while Alexis swore under her breath.

"Wow, she's just running along!" Sabrina beamed at the real Lily, who was still happily frolicking. "Dogs just need nature! Who'd a thunk?"

"Don't be such a wook, Sabrina. Dogs need us more than they need the great outdoors." Alexis sulked.

"What did you call me?" Sabrina's smile vanished.

"A wook." Alexis covered the last of the accidental graffiti and put the spray paint aside.

"A wook? Like Chewbacca from *Star Wars?*"

Alexis was dismayed to see tears in her friend's eyes.

"No! Don't be vapid. Those are *Wookies*. You are not a Wookie. Wooks are just...you know those girls who read tarot cards all day? They go to hippie festivals and beg for money? That's what a Wook is. I was making a joke. Your comment about nature and all." Alexis explained.

"But I like tarot readings." Sabrina was not convinced.

"Sabrina! If I wanted to call you an ugly cunt, I would just say you're a hairy, ugly, uncoordinated cunt! You're not." Alexis exasperated.

Sabrina blinked in confusion.

"Sorry about the microaggression." Alexis groaned. "Let's go inside."

She gently placed a hand on Sabrina's arm and guided her friend back into the empty house.

"I just...never heard that before. You must be really up to date on all the dank memes." Sabrina tucked her painting of Lily under one arm.

"I have to be! Memes are important in educating the masses about the crimes of the patriarchy."

"I get you." Sabrina turned back to the fenced-in yard. "Do you think we should bring Lily inside? I mean, if dogs need us more than they need nature, it might not be good for her to be out there alone."

"Sabrina, I didn't mean it literally, she'll be fine." Alexis headed back upstairs.

"Ok...you want to smoke? I picked up from Talon." Sabrina offered.

"I'm okay right now." Alexis declined.

Sabrina set the painting at the base of the stairs. She followed Alexis back to her room, pulling a one-hitter out of her pocket. She sparked up and winked at her host.

"Smoking while I'm grounded is *really* going to piss my dad off. Who grounds a 22-year-old, anyway?" Sabrina smiled through a mouthful of smoke.

"Why do you even want your dad to be pissed at you?"

"So he can finally care about something other than the assholes whom'st run this shitty town." Sabrina exhaled a dank cloud. "Hey, do you want to do a podcast now that I'm grounded?"

"How are we gonna do that if you're grounded?" Alexis countered.

"We can do it over Skype or something. It can be about whatever." Sabrina hopped onto Alexis's bed before Alexis could stop her.

Alexis glared. Once upon a time, she had been jealous of her best friend. She could never be as conventionally beautiful as Sabrina or cultivate perpetual calm like she did. The friendship started off as a one-sided attempt to dispel Alexis's haunting specter of envy. Despite this, the friendship blossomed. This was helped by the fact that Alexis learned Sabrina was just a fucking spastic.

"You know, as much as you activate my OCD by ruining my bed, the world's gonna be real lonely when you're grounded."

"I'll fix it." Sabrina made no attempt to do so. "Maybe we podcast about whatever you wrote. How'd the writing go by the way?"

Alexis picked her MacBook up off the floor.

"Look! They loved my article! They want me to write another one." She smiled, showing Sabrina her email.

"Wow! Now I can tell people my bestie writes for Buzzfeed." Sabrina glowed.

"It's not all that impressive. All I did was explain how slut-shaming degrades women. You'd be surprised how few people understand that." Alexis said smugly.

"Wow, it must be hard being woke all the time…Do you know what your next article will be about?"

"I want to write about Brian Stanhope." Alexis revealed.

"Shame about his hair. He used to have such nice hair. You remember how I had such a thing for him? He's *terrible* at conversation, but he was so handsome. He's a better *friend* than anything though. I miss just smoking and listening to music with him. You think his looks went away because of his mental trauma? I read that can happen. I saw it online. At least his brother is still hot. Too bad he's gay. We all should have known he was gay though; don't you think? Sam is *so* talented at music. *Parts Unknown* is playing at Big John's this year. Are you gonna go? What are you going to dress up as?" Even high, Sabrina was a one-person conversation.

"Sabrina! Pay attention!" Alexis clapped her hands.

Sabrina went still.

"Anyway, yes, I do want to write about Brian. I want to show him how ignorant he's being-" Alexis began.

"You shouldn't write about Brian. You're doing that thing you do." Sabrina interjected.

"What thing?" Alexis asked, confused.

"You know…you like…okay…it's like someone is mean to you, or does something that upsets you, so you go through a roundabout way to get back at them, but you don't actually confront them. You'll probably write some big article about how a bald stoner raped you with his eyes or something, and you won't explicitly *say* it's Brian, but everyone who knows you will know that it's him." Sabrina took another hit. Her blue eyes were now quite bloodshot.

"When have I *ever* done something like that?" Anger began to boil within Alexis.

"I mean, I'm your friend, I'm just trying to help you." Sabrina replied defensively. "It's just like why you're trying to be a social media personality: your parents focused on their careers, didn't really want a kid, but they felt obligated to pop one out, so you came along. You were a cute little kid, but they had lives and parties and *whatever,* so they left you alone to grow up in this big empty house, and you felt you were neglected. I mean, you *were* neglected, so now you make fun of their boomer values by writing famous online articles about slut-shaming. It's the perfect passive-aggressive revenge."

Alexis was flabbergasted. She flushed red with rage. She had never experienced such an accurate takedown.

"Fuck you!" she swore.

"Aw, yay! I've been trying to get you to say that to me for years. Now help me make a podcast." Sabrina went to hug Alexis.

"Don't touch me!" Alexis snarled.

"Oh sorry, safe space and all that. Slipped my mind! Anyway, I was thinking we should do a podcast about sex from the girl's point of view. But not like vanilla stuff. We should look at weird fetishes and porn and stuff. Wouldn't that be cool?"

"Sabrina!" Alexis shouted.

"What?" Sabrina asked innocently.

"You are insufferable. I'm not going to help you make that."

"Fine. You're missing out." Sabrina went over to the mirror that hung on the back of Alexis's door.

"Do you think I should dress up for Big John's? He's doing it on Halloween after all." Sabrina played with her hair, examining the canvas that was her body.

Alexis stared daggers into Sabrina. She could not fathom that her friend's mind was already one million miles away, completely indulged in a new subject. Alexis assumed that undiagnosed ADHD mixed with being a Sagittarius was the likely explanation for Sabrina's behavior.

"I was thinking of doing like, Belle, from Disney, but what if the Beast had like, beaten her to death? Something real macabre. Or like, remember *Jaws*? What if I was like, a shark attack victim and had a bunch of bites taken out of me? My little sister's friend Ally does special effects make-up. I think she could hook me up." Sabrina's excitement swelled at the prospect of a gory costume.

"Sabrina, that's cool and all, but you shouldn't have too many moving parts. What if one of the fake wounds falls off, or gets stuck on a tree or something?" Alexis resigned to wherever Sabrina would take the conversation.

"Oh, good point. I should probably just go as a superhero or something." Sabrina spun around, facing her best friend. "What about you?"

"You know Big John. He loves puns and ironic humor. I figure I'll go as something clever."

"See, this is why we're friends! I go with the scary costume; you go with the funny costume. We're like yin and yang!" Sabrina smiled.

"You said *Parts Unknown* was playing this year?" Alexis asked.

"Yup! They're the *headliner*, can you believe that? I'm so happy for Sam."

"That's cool. It's about time something good happened to the Stanhope family."

"Maybe he'll get another record offer? He and Raoul are so marketable right now. How many gay punk bands do you know?" Sabrina giggled, "Big John's is perfect for them. His raves are totally like the CBGBs of Michigan."

"Hey, that's not a bad analogy." Alexis agreed, "It's the one good cultural thing in this whole town, and it's not even advertised."

"We're so exclusive." Sabrina laughed. "You should totally invite Brian."

"What." Alexis froze.

"Yeah! You could work out whatever it is you're feeling about him." Sabrina suggested.

"I don't feel anything about him." Alexis replied with dismay.

"Yeah, sure." Sabrina rolled her eyes.

"What is that supposed to mean?" The anger rose again.

"Whatever. I'll go let Lily back in. Oh, and I'm gonna go look for weird fetish stuff for the podcast." Sabrina stuck out her tongue.

She was back downstairs in the blink of an eye. Alone, Alexis shook with fury. She punched the wall.

How dare Sabrina insinuate that she had feelings for Brian? He was pathetic. He kept letting one traumatic experience detach him from the world.

Being cheated on was one thing. It sucked. She had been cheated on in the past. But based on what little Brian had told her about the Christine situation, it didn't sound like cheating at all. It sounded like miscommunication.

Alexis didn't like that Brian was skewing the truth to compensate for his hurt feelings. She also didn't like how he treated Christine as an object that existed solely for his pleasure. Even a cheating ex didn't deserve to be dehumanized like that.

Alexis *hated* that Brian was clearly lying about how he got his money. He didn't do "fraud analysis" or whatever he always prattled on about. He probably dealt drugs for Talon. It was the only explanation that made sense.

She hated that Brian spent every night locked up in his house like a hermit. He lived in the middle of nowhere with a big dead tree as his only company. That wasn't healthy. Alexis knew firsthand how destructive loneliness could be.

Brian reminded Alexis of herself. This angered her to no end. Brian had a way better childhood than she had. He wasn't an only child. He hadn't been abandoned in a lifeless house while his parents played at being corporate executives.

Even so, Brian *was* hurting. So what if he wasn't the best ally? So what if he had open disdain for the world? He was her friend. If she could just rehabilitate him…maybe…

Maybe if she could turn Brian around, and get him to care about something, she could document it. She could write that article! She could get likes. If she could just convince this one, narrow-minded, cisgendered, heterosexual man that he wasn't the only thing in the world that mattered, she would have her ticket to internet stardom.

She brushed blue hair out of her face. She shook her head. She was disgusted that she actually cared about Brian. She wanted to throw up. Wanting to throw up didn't make the inkling of affection any less true.

*Damn you, Sabrina.*

Alexis pulled her phone out of her pocket.

*No, texting him is stupid.*

She put the phone away.

*No, I should tell him I'm going to the rave.*
She pulled the phone out.
*No, he's a loser.*
She put the phone away.
*No, he can help me.*
She stared at her phone.
*No…we can help each other.*

Brian might be almost ten years older than her. He might be bald. He might be gross. He might have bad coping skills. None of that mattered. She was going to clean up his act and turn him loose on the world.

She shuddered. She was a little frightened by the idea of a self-actualized Brian Stanhope wandering the earth. She laughed.

She shot him a text message.

# X

When Brian was a film student, he had been given the opportunity to interview a famous horror director. It was one of his fondest memories from college. He had asked the man if the process of making horror was scary.

*Oh no*, the director chortled. *There is nothing frightening about making a scary movie. Something about the day-to-day menial work…setting up the camera…reviewing blocking…making sure the actors and stuntmen are safe…checking and double checking that you have the exact right shot…it takes all the fright right out of you.*

Brian wondered if pornographers felt the same way. Days on end of recording cum shots, o-faces, and intimate close ups probably took all the joy out of sex. Hell, *thinking* about porn production made factory assembly lines look sexy.

He wondered if writers ever grew bored of writing. Whether actors phoned in performances just to get that next paycheck. Whether artists mindlessly labored over commissions they cared nothing about. Yes, artistic inspiration replaced by routine equilibrium seemed likely, if depressing.

Brian concluded that he must *especially* be abnormal. He lived for writing peril. Every sigh, every death, every last word was pure bliss. If filmmakers could capture such passion, pornographers feel every orgasm, writers know the soul of every word, every actor live as their characters, every painter see each color as if for the first time…if only all creatives could feel what he felt when he took a life on a page, the world might be a better place.

When Brian wrote the death of a woman, he was sharing a human experience so intimate and delicate, that in reality, no one can ever know it. When humans die, they die alone. The embrace of death is solitary.

Just as he killed his heroines, he died with them too. To reach the journey's end with another person, with a beautiful woman…what was that if not tender? If not sorrowful? If not joyful? If not orgasmic? If not spiritual?

He got to live death every day. He got to know it. Fall in love with it. Be aroused by it.

It scared him more than anything. He thought of the crucifix on the wall. Shame filled him. Why was he turned on by this?

*Why peril fetishism?* He thought.

Sometimes he would get stoned and browse psychology articles online. Every single one explained that childhood experiences and traumas informed adult behavior. He would then think back to his youth. He and his friends used to play cops and robbers on the playground. Epic pretend bank heists had their fair share of casualties. One of his friends, a tomboy eager to roughhouse with the fellas, had put dramatic bravura into her play-deaths. He had been fascinated by her performances. He always tried to be the cop that brought her down.

Was that it? Was that why he was fucked up? If experience informed behaviors, did that mean that he was going to kill someone in real life? Brian wasn't sure Paul was telling the truth about peril fetishism being inconsequential. He was seeing the consequences.

Alexis…he didn't want to see her get hurt. She had been there when his father died. She had been there when Christine left. She was here now. Her words filled the screen of his phone. Her presence in the room was just as real as his.

---

Hey are you going to Big John's?

Idk

Your bro is playing.

---

Of course Sam was playing at Big John's. Everyone who showed up to those raves knew a guy. That guy knew a guy. Pretty soon, a small label would want to hear your sound.

---

Sam told me

Don't know if I'll go tho

Why not? He's your brother! You gotta support him

I don't know if I'll know anyone there

I'll be there

---

70

Brian got a sudden mental image of Alexis holding his hand. Why did he think that? He didn't like her, did he?

As suddenly as it appeared, the image was replaced by one of her lifeless corpse on the forest floor. Her grey eyes, now glassy, stared emptily up at him. Blood dripped from her broken jaw.

---

I don't think I'm gonna go :(

Brian, you can't stay in that house forever.

I've got a big work project

Fraud isn't constantly happening!

Fraud literally happens every second of every day lol

It'll be fun

It's a great opportunity for you to see communities interacting together in

a safe space

Meh

Come on, I'll buy weed.

---

The mental image of her dead body vanished. Brian was hyperventilating. His hands shook feebly.

---

I only buy from Talon

He might get mad

What kind of pothead has brand loyalty?

I'm not a pothead

LOL

I just use it for my nerves

Yeah and I use oxygen for my life

What if Raoul's still mad at me?

What if she's there

She moved away dumb dumb

71

I'll be there

---

Alexis wanted to be his date? Was his anxiety was playing tricks on him again? When would his hands stop shaking? When would he catch his breath?

---

I'll help you patch things up with Raoul.

He's probably not that mad anymore.

Cool

So are you going?

---

The intrusive thought had retreated, but Brian could still see Alexis's battered, broken body. He was aroused. He was disgusted. Cold sweat dripped slowly down his neck.

---

"Sure, -if you want to be fucking miserable."

---

Brian wanted to type that. Swearing at Alexis would end the conversation. She'd blow up. She might even end their friendship. But she'd live.

At the exact moment Brian typed out "*Sure*," his phone vibrated. Another message from Paul. A vibration from the phone you're texting on is completely, utterly normal. However, in Brian's sweaty, slippery, shaking hands, this simple vibration was enough to launch everything out of control. The electronic motion of the device caused an erratic finger to hit "send."

---

Sure,

---

Brian's heart stopped. He was going to black out. He was going to drop dead right there. He was scared of dying.

Fuck! Was that why he was so obsessed with death? Why didn't he think of that before!

Fuck! Alexis was going to wind up dead because of him. Fuck! He was going to kill her.

Fuck! Fuck! Fuck!

Just when things couldn't get any worse, Alexis replied:

---

Great! Can't wait! :)

You're making progress. :)


---

Brian dropped the phone on the floor. He darted to the bathroom. He threw open the lid of his toilet, collapsed to his knees, and vomited. The horrible stench only made him throw up more. Of course his vomit smelled vile. *He* was vile, and every cell living in him was wretched and cursed beyond redemption.

He couldn't go to the rave. If he did, Alexis was dead. He puked a little more.

In the middle of the night, in the boonies, with drugs and music and people, anything could happen. Brian didn't *want* anything to happen. Would that be enough?

He desperately tried to catch his breath. He clutched the toilet as if it were a floundering life preserver. The tiled floor of the bathroom suddenly seemed quite cold beneath his feet.

He wanted to retch again, but there was nothing left inside his churning stomach. He wiped the vomit from his beard. He collapsed on his ass, legs outstretched, back against the wall. He stared up at the damningly bright yellow light.

As he sat there, gasping for air, he felt his hand crush a dried rose petal. He looked at the dead flowers on top of the toilet. They were taunting him. Would Alexis get flowers on her grave one day? Would he get flowers on his?

He thought of his father. He hadn't visited his grave in months. Maybe he could do that instead of going to the rave and killing Alexis. She might accept that excuse.

Fetid, putrid, voraciously hungry anxiety threw itself against his skull. His consciousness wavered. He wished he had a blunt.

He took a deep breath. He clenched his jaw and closed his eyes. It didn't help. He couldn't hide from the fact that his fetish was fundamentally wrong.

*You're jerking off to death! You're sick! You want to kill people! You might as well! Why dance around it? The world has fucked you, and you want to fuck it back! You are worthless. No living woman would ever want you. Corpses can't say no, is that it? Foot fetishists, furries, scat enthusiasts; all have a higher rung on the ladder than you. You exploit tragedy to get your rocks off. You get paid for it too. Fucking perverted sellout. You are <u>disgusting</u>.*

Scared as he was, his tongue formed words. Breathlessly, he began to speak. He threatened to choke on his own counterargument.

"I need...I need..."

His ears shut. He closed his eyes. He was so scared of his internal monologue he nearly fainted when he heard its mocking reply:

*What do you need? Pervert.*

Brian opened his eyes. He didn't need weed. He didn't need reassurances from Paul or Alexis or his brother or his brain-dead mother or cold dead father.

He needed coffee.

# XI

Zoe placed a freshly carved jack-o-lantern on the edge of the counter. She clicked her tongue. She always was a late decorator. Halloween would soon be gone. She placed a second jack-o-lantern next to the first one. If she was going to be late, then she was going to turn her diner into a haunted house; damn it!

Reynaldo prepped for breakfast in the kitchen. The sizzling of stovetops, the cracking of eggs, and the sharpening of knives reverberated through the restaurant. Zoe found the echoes comforting. It was 5 AM. There was no better way to start the day.

She hung a smiling plastic bat in the front window. When the sun rose, she could admire the changing of the leaves. Maybe the sun was rising early? Reds, yellows, and oranges were amplified by a brilliant blaze racing towards the building.

A scarlet Lincoln pulled into the closest non-handicapped spot. Its headlights went dark. The engine rattled to a halt. A muffled Eminem song went silent as the driver's door opened. The dull neon glow of the diner's sign illuminated an all too familiar customer as he stumbled out onto the blacktop.

Zoe was puzzled. Why was Brian Stanhope here so early? The doors didn't open until 6. He knew that. Why was he tugging on the locked front door?

He looked bad. His bald head was grimy with sweat. His expression was despondent. He reminded Zoe of what her own reflection had looked like when she was with Lou.

"Brian? What are you doing here so early?" Zoe asked incredulously. She did not move for the glass door.

"I just need some coffee, Zoe." His voice was a forced echo.

"It's too early. We're not ready."

"Zoe. Please let me in." Brian angrily replied.

"Brian, you know when we open. Nothing's prepped." Zoe held her ground.

"Zoe, I am your most loyal regular. I buy your coffee every day. You trick me into doing chores around here. For the love of God, let me in and let me have some coffee." Brian's voice cracked as his pleading; bloodshot eyes met hers.

The look in those eyes scared Zoe.

She unlocked the door and let him in. He made a beeline for a stool. He collapsed onto the counter.

Zoe quickly locked the door behind him. She double-checked the empty parking lot. She didn't need other early birds.

Clearly illuminated by the golden electric lights, Brian's slumped form looked no better. One arm simultaneously held him up and covered his face. The other sat unmoving. He breathed quietly. What little of his expression Zoe could see was morose. He needed coffee, all right.

Soon, the black, caffeinated elixir filled an earthenware mug Zoe clasped in her hand. Even through the stone chassis, the coffee threatened to burn her fingers. She swiftly applied generous helpings of cream and sugar to the liquid. Its harsh black tone transformed into a gentle mahogany. She expertly placed the mug on a discounted doily and set it in front of Brian.

He did not react to the presence of the steaming beverage. He sat motionless; his face hidden. His lips made a thin, flat line.

Zoe shook her head. This wasn't like him. He could down coffees in one go.

"You know, I'm gonna need your help taking out the trash later. Reynaldo's athlete's foot is bothering him again." Zoe reprimanded.

"Whatever." Brian's voice was barely a whisper.

"What is it? A girl?" Zoe placed her hands on her hips.

Brian reacted as if he had been electrocuted. His hand flew from his face. He nearly fell out of his stool.

His inflamed, exhausted eyes were panicked. These were not the eyes of someone who had hit the reefer. These were the eyes of someone in great turmoil.

"What happened?" Zoe softened her voice.

"I haven't slept all night." He finally took a long sip of coffee. "How did you know I was thinking about a girl?"

"You had that look in your eye." Men and their romances!

"Yeah...I mean...kind of?" Brian hesitated, "Do you ever...think about someone? Like, *really* think about them?"

"I've been in love before, Brian." Zoe didn't like the deceptive tone he had taken.

"Okay, but have you ever had feelings for someone, but like, you knew it wouldn't be good for you guys to be together? Like, if you dated someone, it might actually end up hurting them?" His questions were desperate.

"What on earth are you on about?" Zoe poured herself a coffee.

"It's kind of...hard to explain. What if, you got yourself into a weird situation, and you aren't even able to figure it all out yet, but you hate being alone, and maybe you do like this person, but maybe you're just not sexually compatible...like...what if they get...*hurt?*"

"Drink your coffee, Brian." Zoe sighed, "Your brain is doing laps around Lake Erie."

"You ever feel like you're decaying? Like you're just a reflection of where you are? Like maybe this Earth is Detroit, and I'm Brightmoor?" Brian didn't drink.

"I grew up in Brightmoor. It's a shame." Zoe wondered where Brian was going with this.

"Do you ever think about death?" he asked.

"What are you talking about?" she frowned.

"Do you think death and control are maybe related?"

"I don't understand a word of what's going on here."

"Sorry. I just...what if you were with someone, and they died, but like... you were *happy* they died?" His voice was quiet and serious.

"They got an inheritance or something?" Zoe laughed. "Whatever is eating at you, you're giving it too much attention. Do you really want my opinion?"

"Sure, yes, anything." He was gripping the counter now. His knuckles were turning white.

"You need to take a deep breath and focus on what's right in front of you. Nothing good comes from ruminating." Zoe smiled, "Reynaldo's got a new special I want you to try. He's got some nice huevos rancheros with minced garlic that are gonna bust you right outta your head."

"God, if I have garlic, I'm gonna throw up again." Brian put his head in his hands.

Zoe glared at him.

"Brian Stanhope, when your mom and dad brought you here as a little boy, you ate anything and everything I put in front of you. Where did this garlic allergy come from?"

He sighed.

"It's not an allergy. It just...it reminds me of her."

Zoe slammed a hand on the counter. Brian jumped. He almost fell over again.

"You gotta put that girl behind you. You made a mistake. So what? People forget about that stuff. People move on. You need to move on too. The only person you're hurting by holding on is yourself." Zoe said, "You and that Knabusch girl are here every morning. Why not get together with her?"

"Alexis…she…no, she knows all about my bullshit, Zoe. She doesn't forget anything. No one forgets…She…I…" Brian grew paler than before. His hands trembled.

"So what? *She's on the internet all the time so she doesn't forget anything?* Ha!" Zoe laughed, "She doesn't care about your whoopsies."

"I didn't make a '*whoopsie*,' Zoe." Brian gritted his teeth, "Alexis is a paragon of women's rights and survival. I'm like the opposite of women's survival."

"Brian, that little fit you threw at Target-"

"*Little fit?* I screamed at the top of my lungs that I was going to kill Christine. I called my brother's boyfriend the *f-word*. I was out of control when I needed to be in control, and now all I care about is having *ultimate* control!" Brian shouted indignantly. His bloodshot eyes filled with despair. "People don't forget *anything* in this town. I don't think anyone in the state of Michigan can forget *any* transgression! Zoe…when I told Christine I wanted to kill her…I meant it. Raoul knows I meant it. There are people out there that know I meant it."

He deflated into the stool. Stillness swept over the restaurant. The proprietor stared at her customer, unsure of what to say. His words were frightening. Death? Control? *What?*

For a moment, Zoe thought Brian might cry. She adjusted her glasses. Then, she answered him carefully.

"Listen: whatever happened in the past…is in the past. I'm sorry we live in a corner of the world where that past haunts us every day. The thing is Brian: I see you every day. You're working hard. You're taking care of your mom. You're trying to patch things up with your brother. You're trying to connect with this girl. That's all that counts, Brian. You're trying."

Brian raised his weary head. He stared directly into Zoe. She felt a chill run down her spine, but she wasn't sure why.

"If you knew what I did every day, you'd know I'm not trying." He said.

Zoe fought through her fear. She took his hand. He wasn't shaking anymore.

"You can always start." She replied.

A splash of color returned to his face. Without a word, he withdrew his hand from hers and finished his coffee. He stood, pulling out his wallet. He placed a couple of bills on the counter. He smiled.

Zoe couldn't help but stare at his large canine teeth. Those fangs made his smile wicked. His mother had always fussed over his teeth. For the first time in her life, Zoe understood why.

"I'm going to start. I'm going to show them. Thank you, Zoe."

"You can start by trying the huevos rancheros." Zoe suggested.

She motioned for Brian to return to his seat. He shook his head. He lifted his hands and cracked his knuckles menacingly, like a prize fighter before a big match.

"Baby steps, Zoe."

He flashed another toothy grin. He brushed past her, going out the rear doors in the kitchen. Reynaldo hurled insults in Spanish, but Brian ignored him and went outside.

Zoe sat quietly, trying to make sense of this encounter. Something about his demeanor, his talk of women, and control, and death, and what he did…it didn't sound good. She was worried about him, but she had bigger problems. She hadn't finished decorating.

The sun rose over the tree line. She finished her coffee. She grabbed the two dirty mugs. She darted into the kitchen and dropped them in the sink. Seeing the soiled earthenware, Reynaldo began a profanity laden protest. Zoe threw him a violent look. Reynaldo went silent.

The large engine of a semi-truck moaned as it pulled into the parking lot. Zoe turned the "Open" sign on with a pout. She'd have to finish decorating later.

†

Watching the behemoth truck find a spot, Brian turned the keys in the ignition. His rusting Lincoln Town Car lurched to life. The Eminem album played.

He reached into to his glove box. He pulled out a CD and a pre-rolled joint. He ejected the Eminem album with one hand. He placed the marijuana cigarette in his lips with the other. Kanye West's *My Beautiful Dark Twisted Fantasy* soon played.

He lit the joint. Skunky aroma filled the car. He grabbed his phone. He sent a message to Paul:

---

I need to talk to you.

---

# XII

Munson Park was nearly deserted. It was noon. The children of Monroe were all still in school. Joggers made their laps along the park's winding footpaths. Neighboring Custer Airport was serenely quiet. Lethargic autumn clouds drifted above the hill at the center of the park. The man-made knoll was one of the highest points in Monroe County. From up here, fall was on full display.

Sabrina had packed her vape with a stout *cannabis indica*. Alexis watched Sabrina blow her own heavy clouds into the sky. The two girls lay at the top of the hill, sky-gazing and reminiscing.

"Do you remember when we used to play lava tag?" Sabrina asked.

"Yeah...should've been called splinter tag." Alexis shuddered. "Everyone called me a fat porcupine."

"That's because you'd always land ass-first on the woodchips. Do you remember Jordan Donahue? He used to only chase me when he was it."

"That's 'cause he liked you." Alexis folded her arms.

"Really?"

"Totally."

"Damn it! I should've smooched him. I heard he's a lawyer now. He could easily take care of an old spinster like me." Sabrina sighed.

Alexis prickled in offense. She glared at Sabrina. A righteous fury churned in her stomach.

"Sabrina! That is so triggering!" she snapped.

"What is? Kissing a boy?" Sabrina exhaled another cloud.

"No! Calling yourself a *spinster*! Needing a man to take care of you. Statements like that reinforce harmful stereotypes about a woman's role in society." Alexis explained angrily.

"Oh, shut the fuck up, Alexis. Not everything has to be political all the time." Sabrina went to take another hit from the vape.

Alexis reached over and slapped the device out of her friend's hand. Sabrina recoiled in shock. The cartridge landed on the grass without a sound.

"What the hell?" Sabrina protested.

"You're starting to sound like Brian." Alexis snatched the discarded vape and took a hit.

"Whatever...do you think he'd do a podcast with me?" Sabrina pulled out her phone.

"Aren't you supposed to be grounded?" Alexis asked.

"Yeah, but my dad's a little bitch." Sabrina exasperated. "Check this out: there's a community of people on the internet who jack off to death. Isn't that weird?"

"What are you talking about?" Alexis coughed. This was a tough strain.

"Yeah. It's like peril...*something*. Look at this!" Sabrina shoved her phone into Alexis's face.

In between marijuana-fueled wheezing, Alexis made out the Patreon account of someone named *DeathbringerBob*.

"These writers on Patreon do serial-killer commissions. *This* guy writes about the hook-handed-hitchhiker. Wild. We should totally cover this." Sabrina elaborated.

"No one would listen to that shit." Alexis retorted in confusion. "Where did you even find this crap?"

"Oh, so talking about underrepresented fetish communities is *weird*, but when you fantasize about Brian Stanhope becoming a soy-boy simp, its *progressive*?" Sabrina countered.

"It's not like that!" Alexis clutched the vape defensively.

"What are you going to do, parade him around like a pet on social media after you indoctrinate him?"

"He's not a pet. He's a person. He can be an example." Alexis argued.

"That's the most sensible thing I've heard you say all day. *He's not a pet, he's a person*" She echoed mockingly.

"...hey, Brian." she continued with a seductive tease.

Alexis whipped around, dropping the vape. Sure enough, Brian Stanhope trudged up the hill. He was out of breath. He looked exhausted. He was wearing the same grungy hoodie as the day before. His bald head was a little paler than usual.

"Hey guys." He waved, gasping for air.

"God, you're so out of shape!" Sabrina giggled.

Alexis thought that Brian would sit down, pull out a joint, and spark up. He didn't do that. He simply stood on the precipice of the hill, staring at her. She was disquieted by the look in his eyes. Normally, it was a battle to maintain eye contact with him. Today, he bored holes into her. She was used to this gaze from other men, but not from Brian.

"Uh...everything all right, Brian?" Alexis asked.

"Gonna sit with us, handsome?" Sabrina winked. Alexis elbowed her, hard.

"Oh, yeah, uh, sorry." Brian blinked. He did not move.

"Are you feeling all right?" Alexis raised a concerned eyebrow.

"Yeah. I just didn't sleep at all last night. I'm a little out of it." Brian yawned.

"Did you get high and stay up 'til 3AM watching YouTube videos without me?" Sabrina whined.

"I wish." Brian responded.

His baleful eyes turned back to Alexis.

"I'm really looking forward to going to Big John's with you." He said.

"You could have just texted me that." Alexis answered with cautious happiness.

"Sure. I know. It just means a lot." He replied.

"*Alexis and Brian, sitting in a tree, K-I-S-S-*" Sabrina began.

Alexis punched her friend in the arm.

"Ow! Violence against women! Violence against women!" Sabrina laughed.

Brian's eyes widened in alarm. His arms shook. He turned away.

Alexis and Sabrina tussled. Alexis eventually shoved the hysterical Sabrina aside. She looked at Brian. It sounded like he was trying to catch his breath again. He stared at the small airfield below the hill.

Brian watched a small Cessna 172 Skyhawk take flight. The petite aircraft was white, with large red stripes running along its sides. The little sky hopper looked like a tiny crucifix soaring into the overcast sky.

"What?" Alexis asked him. She was starting to get concerned.

Brian shook his head. He turned back around. He looked at Alexis with that same unsettling gaze. He resembled a deathly skull.

"I think I gotta go see my mom."

"Brian! Come on! Smoke with us! Your mom will still be infirm later." Sabrina taunted, taking a surreptitious hit from the misplaced vape.

"I don't know if that's a good idea." Brian finally broke eye contact with Alexis. He stared down at his shoes.

"If you don't want to smoke, you can just hang for a little bit." Alexis offered. "We were talking about lava tag."

"Yeah." Sabrina nodded.

"You never bullied me when I fell." Alexis smiled.

"I guess." Brian still made no move to sit down.

"Are you sure everything's okay?" Alexis felt a weird sensation in her heart.

"Yeah..." Brian didn't sound very confident.

"Hey, Brian. You're an artistic type." Sabrina interrupted with a wink.

"I was. I still am." He answered quietly.

"I mean, you went to school to make movies in Chicago or whatever." Sabrina elaborated.

"I guess I did." He smiled nervously. Alexis stared at his fangs for a little longer than she should have.

"Have you ever done a podcast?" Sabrina asked.

"What kind of podcast?" Brian fidgeted with his hoodie.

"Brian, ignore her, she's being weird." Alexis rolled her eyes.

Sabrina kept talking:

"Check this out: I found a group of people that write murder porn. I want to talk about how women react to shit like that. Check this out: there's a story I read about this girl getting murdered in fucking *Ash Township* of all places! The closest middle of nowhere to here that there is! There could be someone living nearby that is into this stuff, and we'd never know about it! Wouldn't that make a great concept for a show? Covering all the weird fetishes of the world? Check this out: we should talk about this over *Vince's*. I could *kill* for some chili dogs."

Brian looked like he was going to be sick.

"I think I should go now." Brian began the precarious trek downhill.

"Your loss." Sabrina shrugged. She went back to the vape.

Alexis got to her feet. She followed Brian despite her better judgment. Weed did that sometimes.

"Hey!" She called out.

Brian turned around. Alexis stopped in her tracks. He looked like he was going to cry.

"Sorry about Sabrina. She's being weird." Alexis shrugged.

Brian stared at her again. She felt an icy lump form in her throat. She shifted uncomfortably.

"So, we're going to the rave?" she finally asked.

Brian looked up at that little plane. The cross it made against the sky seemed to frighten him. Alexis reached out to grab his arm. He pulled away. There was pain in his brown eyes.

"You're my buddy...I don't know. I guess. See you." He croaked.

He nearly tripped over every step back to his car.

Alexis slowly returned to the summit. She felt spent, though she hadn't cried. She touched her stomach.

"He likes you." Sabrina smiled.

Alexis did not respond. She watched the plane. The red and white rood made her feel self-conscious. What had Brian seen in it?

"God, I'm hungry." Sabrina moaned. "I'll buy if we go to *Vince's.*"

"Sure."

Despite how unsettled she had been by Brian's starved eyes, the feelings in Alexis's stomach were not the frustrated pangs of hunger, but the light flutter of butterflies.

*Fuck.* She frowned.

# XIII

*They know. They fucking know. God damn it! Why did I have to use Ash-fuck-all-Township? "Write what you know." What a load of horseshit. I swear to God, I am going to chuck my computer into the River Raisin. Then, I'm going to throw my phone in after it. Then, I'm going to pick a bunch of hypodermic needles up off the street and stab myself to death with them. Fuck me. This is some fucking-*

"I wish you would do something about those teeth."

The machines behind his mother's bed whirred quietly. Had Brian been more focused on the conversation, he would have rejoiced. She mentioned his fangs. It was a good day. It was not a bad day. Sam didn't know what bad days were.

Brian remembered his mother regaining consciousness. He remembered her opening her eyes and screaming. She screamed for hours on end. She screamed until tears ran down her face. She screamed until her voice was hoarse.

The doctors told Brian that she was constantly reliving the accident. She was seeing the car flip time and time again. She was seeing Andrew Stanhope's neck snap as he tried to shield his wife from the impact. She was seeing the semi-truck collide with her car. She was seeing the wreck come to a horribly still rest. She was seeing the drunken truck driver feebly trying to pull himself out from behind the wheel. She was seeing him bleed to death before the paramedics could arrive. She was seeing her beloved husband carted away in a body bag. She was seeing an EMT hold her head together.

Brian stayed awake with her that first night. He stayed up with her for a week straight. Her voice failed, but still she tried to scream. He begged her to take the medicine that would sedate her, but she only wailed silently. Eventually, the screams turned to moans. That was worse.

"She's got severe brain damage." The doctors explained, "It seems that the blunt force trauma accelerated her early onset dementia. She won't ever return to the way she was."

"Can you at least make her forget?" Brian begged.

They put Mary Stanhope on an experimental drug. It helped the brain recover from extreme trauma, but its effects on the memory were disastrous. Brian wondered how many others chose medications based on side effects.

His scheme worked too well. The day of the accident became a complete blur to Mary Stanhope. Soon, everything was a blur to her. At least she stopped screaming.

Putting someone on a non-FDA approved treatment was expensive. Brian spent all his filmmaking money. It wasn't enough. The state tried to go after Sam when Brian went bankrupt.

Brian remembered stumbling up the stairs of the courthouse. He had been hungry, sleep deprived, and higher than the moon. The last of his hair was gone, claimed by his mother's screams. It was the first time he had been bald in public. He remembered the stares.

He had not dressed for court. He showed up wearing an outfit not too dissimilar from the one he wore now. His beard had been a scraggly mess. He remembered Sam and Raoul standing before the judge. He remembered Sam's gasp upon seeing him.

*Why are they going after Sam? He has a life. Without Christine, I have none.*

He remembered the judge asking him about his income.

"None." he had slurred.

Surely, he must have assets?

"Funeral took 'em all." the room was starting to spin.

Well, young man, how can we expect you to care for your mother?

He couldn't think about financial liability. He could only think about the last text Christine had sent. The text that pushed out his suffering mother, his dead father, his younger brother, everything.

"Christine never loved me."

The next thing he remembered was waking up on the floor. He saw the bailiff and Raoul looming over him. He heard his brother pleading with the judge.

"-your honor, continued joint custody of my mother's affairs is the only way an undue financial burden can be alleviated-"

The judge decisively silenced Samuel:

"-he shows up intoxicated, and he has provided no evidence of income. Clearly Mr. Stanhope has a mental handicap himself to behave in such an abhorrent, unruly-"

Then everything went black.

"Have you talked to Dr. Gonzalez about those fangs of yours?"

Brian looked at his mother. Her eyes were full of worry. He forced himself to smile. He squeezed his mother's hand and brushed her hair behind her ear.

"He says it's more trouble than it's worth."

"Ugh...*dentists*. Useless, the lot of them! We'll just take you to someone who *does* see the problems your teeth cause you." Mary blinked.

"They don't hurt me, Mom. They don't hurt anyone." Brian stood and kissed his mother on the forehead. "Would you like a glass of water?"

"No, I need a nap. I'm working the midnight shift tonight." Mary yawned. "There are some hot pockets in the freezer for you. Love you, sweetie."

He quietly closed his mother's bedroom door. He flopped onto the off-white couch in the meager living room. It smelled like mothballs and sterile cleaner.

He stared out the patio doors. All he saw was the dying community of Monroe. He saw the faces of Alexis and Sabrina. He saw Sabrina reading his work with disgust. He saw himself killing Alexis at Munson Park.

He pulled out his phone. He reread the thread of texts from Paul. He swallowed hard. He was jittery and full of nervous energy. He saw Alexis's grey eyes. He kicked himself for staring at her so stupidly. She must have been able to see his dark, twisted subconscious.

*Shit!*

His trepid finger scrolled through the messages for the umpteenth time:

---

Thank you for all you do, Bob <3 :)

This month's offering was some of your best work yet :)

The way poor barefoot Echo met her end was simply delectable :)

Love your recurring hooked man character :)

Glad you liked it Paul

I'd love to talk about next month's commission :)

When you get the chance :)

About that

What is it? :)

Eager to begin work for your most gracious patron? ;)

I canceled next month

For everyone

Sorry

What? :O

Why on Earth would you do such a thing? :O

Are you unwell? :(

I can start a GoFundMe if you'd like :)

No I'm just done

Why? :O

I think this shit is starting to get to me

I need to stop

For my own mental health

Bob, just take a month off. Recharge your batteries :)

I'm DONE done

Why? :)

I'm in a dark place

This is all I think about

I look at people in real life

I think about what if I killed them

Do you ever feel that way? Does this fuck you up at all?

No, because I'm not a psycho like you :)

I just like to get my rocks off :)

People think about sex all the time :)

That's all this is :)

It's just pretend, a fantasy :)

A sexy fantasy ;)

Wow, I'M the psycho???

Sure :)

It's why your work is so good :)

Makes me feel some kind of way ;)

I'd be very sad if you stopped :(

Sorry Paul. I can't do this anymore

I appreciate your encouragement but I really am done

Please don't quit Bob :(

It's over. Sorry

You're making me feel like I'm dumping you or something

:(

If your card got charged for next month it'll be refunded when I

close my Patreon

You can't quit! You're the only one that makes me feel anything anymore

:(

Paul, if I can, I'm going to see a therapist

You should too

Why? :O

This isn't normal

It is to me :(

It's not to me!

It's hurting me, and I have to stop!

Is it the money? I'll pay double :)

No! I'm sick of this

I want to sleep with a girl and NOT want to kill her you know?

I don't :)

Then you're a fucking freak!!!!!

:O

I've had to change my whole fucking life because of people like

you!

Money and paltry e-fame isn't worth this

Don't you worry about how disgusting this is?

So you're kinkshaming me >:(

Oh FUCK OFF PAUL

So I'm not going to hear from you again? >:(

You're just going leave me alone? >:(

You are a sick fucker >:(

Right back at you

What you're doing is worse than rape >:(

Like you'd even know what that is

You don't have any fucking guts asshole

No wonder you can only score dead girls

You're going to fucking regret this Brian :)

What the fuck did you call me?

That's not my name

Are you retarded now too?

Sure it's not :)

I'll be seeing you real soon Brian :)

When I find you, I'm going to make what you did to Echo look like a tease

;)

---

Brian's hands were shaking again. He set his phone down on the couch and reached into his hoodie pocket. He withdrew a lighter, a small glass piece, and the prescription pill bottle filled with Talon's hopefully-not-toilet-washed strain. He quickly packed the bowl and sparked up, eager to stop the anxiety millipede before it tore chunks out of him.

*Damn it. How did he know? He always knew. He even knew about the trac phones.*

The odorous marijuana moved quickly through his bloodstream, but the threatening final message from Paul imprinted itself into Brian's brain. Paranoia consumed him. He considered sleeping on this couch tonight.

*I wish this were a La-Z-Boy. Not that people in Monroe can even afford La-Z-Boys. The one thing this city is known for. Fuck Monroe.*

Should he go home? Did Paul know where he lived? Would Paul attempt to break into his house? Maybe he should change the locks and install some security cameras. He shook his head and took another hit from the bowl.

What if breaking into Brian's house and driving a stake into his heart wasn't Paul's taste? What if Paul just showed up on the streets of Monroe, walked up to Brian, and shot him dead? Brian had no idea what Paul looked like.

He exhaled noxious smoke. The VPNs from Talon had all been useless. Paul knew who he was. Sabrina was close to figuring out who he was too. Maybe he should move.

*Damn it!* Talon's juggalo skunk weed wasn't working.

His pulse throbbed painfully. He feared his veins would burst out from under his skin. Brian took another foul-smelling hit and held it in his lungs.

*Okay...let's think here.*

Should he go to the police?

*Oh, hi officer. I write murder fetish erotica. I think one of my psychotic subscribers might hunt me down and kill me. Can you help?*

Maybe he could stay with Sam for a while?

*Hey bro. A guy paid me some money so I could help him jack off to a mermaid being killed. I think he's gone off his rocker and he might attack me. Can I lay low with you for a few days? Sorry I called your boyfriend the f-word by the way.*

He had to think harder.

*Patreon...hey, Patreon!*

Of course! Patreon would have to keep some of Paul's personal information on file. Brian wasn't sure Paul used real card info, but it was better than nothing.

Brian would go home. He would put in a request for Paul's personal details. He would cite harassment as why he needed the information, and he would show Patreon the texts as proof. Then, he would scrub all traces of *DeathbringerBob* from the internet. That way, Sabrina couldn't find out who he was in the dark.

Brian smiled. This plan was brilliant. He let out a sigh of relief, and the fumes contained within his lungs shrouded the entire room in smoky haze so thick it impaired his vision.

A key turned in the front door.

Brian leapt to his feet too quickly. He began to cough, hard. The fear of being discovered mixed with the mental turmoil Paul had inflicted was enough to cause Brian to hack up a lung.

He ineptly tried to hide the bowl in his hoodie pocket while fumbling with his sunglasses. He tried to fan away the smoke plumes. The cloud of secondhand marijuana only grew more dense. What was worse, he was still coughing.

He turned around. Sam and Raoul stood in the doorway. The two lovers stared at him as he flailed and wheezed. Sam's radiant face darkened. Raoul gave a bemused half smile.

"I didn't realize we were hotboxing today." Raoul smirked.

"What the fuck, Brian?" Sam growled. He slammed the front door behind him.

Brian threw open the sliding glass patio doors between coughs. He fanned his arms, driving the smoke outside. It was too late. The damage had been done.

"What the fuck are you thinking?" Sam furiously turned on the overhead fan. "How do you think Mom is going to react if she smells that?"

"Well, currently she thinks I'm ten, so I think she'd think Dad did it." Brian coughed. Out of the corner of his tear-filled eyes, he swore he saw Raoul suppress a laugh.

"Keep your damn coughing down!" Sam shouted.

"Come on, bro. You never took a fat rip? You used to smoke more than me. You know, if you don't cough, you don't get off." Brian chuckled nervously.

"If that security guard smells this shit, she's gonna get evicted!" Sam snarled.

"My cousin can hook you up with some good strains. Real south of the border shit." Raoul teased.

Raoul was a tall, muscular man of Hispanic descent. His eyes were rich and full of life. His dark hair was neatly trimmed and faded. Brian believed that if Marlon Brando had been a gay Latino, he'd look remarkably like Raoul.

"It would smell a lot better than this reefer you're poisoning yourself with." Raoul laughed.

He had a charming laugh. Damn! He was so charismatic. Brian thought Raoul needed to quit his job as a Target manager and perform with *Parts Unknown* full time. Brian kind of fucked that prospect up at court, but still.

"I appreciate the offer. I just prefer the natural earthiness of real, unpurified cannabis. It's a better smoking experience." Brian argued.

"Could have fooled me." Raoul threw an arm around Sam. Sam was a lucky man.

"Sorry I didn't let you know I'd be here. I just had the day off and wanted to spend some quality time with Mom." Brian continued.

"How is she today? Apart from nearly being kicked out on the street over your foolishness." Sam haughtily flipped his golden hair out of his face.

"She's great, man. She's gotta go to work later."

"Please don't joke about her delusions."

"I'm not joking. She's working midnight shift tonight."

"Brian…" Sam was genuinely hurt.

"She's like, okay now, Sam." Brian tried to comfort his brother, but he was too high.

"Whatever. Just don't antagonize her more."

"I would *never* do that." Brian harshly protested.

"I'm going to see what I can throw together, babe." Raoul pecked Sam on the cheek and began rummaging through the kitchen.

"I, uh, hear you guys are playing at Big John's." Brian stammered.

"Yeah. Are you going to come?" Sam asked.

"Hell yeah. It's been too long since I've rocked out to *Parts Unknown*." Brian smiled.

"You sure you don't have work or something? You go out of your way to not support us." Sam retorted.

"No! No. My uh, contract ended. Yeah. I got loads of free time. I want to chill with my little bro. He's the best musician I know! Hey, I rhymed." Brian laughed. He was a little too spacey for his own good.

"Wow...well, hey, it'll be good to see you there." Sam warmed slightly.

"Awesome. I need to clean my act up. Too much work makes Brian a dull boy." Brian tried to laugh, but nothing came out. "I've been in a dark place, man. I just think about death and killing all the time, you know? It's all I care about these days."

"Wait, what?" Sam went pale with shock.

"You going to stick around for dinner, Brian? I've got just enough ingredients here for some mean jibaritos." Raoul offered obliviously.

"No thanks. Speaking of death, I gotta take some measurements of that white oak in the backyard. I think it's time I finally hired someone to cut it down." Brian lied.

The thought of the garlic-laden sandwiches made Brian's stomach turn. He turned to Raoul. He cleared his throat.

"Hey, Raoul." he began.

Upon meeting Raoul's curious gaze, his intoxicated courage fled.

"I've been meaning to tell you, Raoul, I mean, I wanted to say, that I just wanted to let you know, that I've been meaning to tell you, that I wanted to let you know, that I wanted to say, that I *wanted* to say, that I am, you know, wanting to let you know, that I want to say, that I'm wanting you to know that I've been meaning to say...you know. I've been thinking. I wanted to tell you that I wanted you to know that I wanted to say, that, *you know*, I wanted to say I'm letting you know that I wanted to say I was thinking about wanting to tell you...that I wanted to let you know."

Without waiting for a reply, Brian stepped out of the unit. His hands trembled something fierce. He was barely halfway down the hall when he heard Sam's voice call out:

"Hey! Brian!"

Sam caught up to him quickly.

"Are you...doing okay?" Sam asked with brotherly affection Brian didn't deserve.

"You know, not really. But I'm taking steps." Brian answered quietly. "I cannot wait to see you play. You're really talented, you know?"

"You're really going to come?"

"Nothing in the world could stop me. Catch you later." Brian would uphold this promise. He would be better.

He made his way outside. He took a deep breath and coughed one more time. He felt the weight of the phone in his pocket as surely as if it were a bomb on the brink of detonation.

Mercifully, Paul stayed silent.

# XIV

It was the dead of night. The red Lincoln painfully limped down the gravel road. Brian's anxiety tore through his body. The ambiguity of anxiety was the worst thing about it. It could be the millipede with hundreds of needly sharp feet piercing his skin. It could be the angry monster stomping on his brain. It could be the ocean of thoughts drowning his psyche in death. It could be all three at once.

He had not smoked for days. He had not masturbated, slept a full night's sleep, or written as much as a shopping list in over a week. Had it been a week? It was getting difficult to keep track of time.

Why had he sobered up? The thoughts were worse sober. He would surely kill Alexis tonight.

He tried blasting some *My Chemical Romance*. The strumming guitar, pained vocals, and haunting lyrics of *Early Sunsets Over Monroeville* did nothing to pacify him. Could he not even enjoy music now?

Was he depressed? He didn't think so. Perhaps he didn't *want* to die, but he would be *willing* to die, if it meant not enacting his murderous fantasies on the living.

He sighed. These thoughts had been simpler when he was high.

Past endless, barren cornfields, a lone farmhouse guarded the mouth of a forest. A sea of parked vehicles surrounded the building. Pulling into a long driveway, Brian snaked his way through the labyrinth of cars and costumed party goers. It was hard to believe that this event was once a tiny jam session around a bonfire.

He parked behind a black Jeep Grand Cherokee. Its North Carolina license plate caught his eye. One of Big John's acts had that kind of draw?

The CD player died with his engine. He feared he would be struck by lightning the second he stepped outside. He squeezed his eyes shut, took a panicked breath, and stepped into Halloween night.

Brian dizzily stumbled through the improvised parking lot. Faint electronic music echoed from the woods ahead. Port-a-potties were arranged along a dirt path into the wilderness. String LED lights hung next to security cameras on trees.

The sky vanished under the canopy. Lights danced through the undergrowth. Songs pulsed between tree trunks. The cold wind smelled of fallen leaves, fresh dirt, tobacco, marijuana, and liquor. Brian saw zombies, ghouls, superheroes, movie characters, robots, and clowns all following the forested path. He looked down at his dark jeans and black hoodie. He had forgotten to wear a costume.

His heart raced. His ears rang in time with his palpitations. The music grew louder. The lights grew brighter. The trees grew thicker. The crowd compacted as the path narrowed.

Finally, the synthetically lit trail opened into a massive clearing. A bonfire sweltered at its center. A mob of costumed peopled danced around the flames. Smokers and drinkers converged under a grey tent. A large, makeshift stage was surrounded by an army of bodies. The music was deafening.

He did not he hear the bright tenor of Raoul. He was still early. He headed for the grey tent.

It was slow going through the undulating masses. Beer and liquor were knocked back around him. Cigarettes, vapes, and joints exhaled a healthy haze around the fire. The glow of the flames and the colorful lights from the stage cut through the smog, forming vibrant, laser-like effects in the air.

Peering through the crowd, Brian failed to recognize anyone. He saw a girl sporting a home-made mermaid costume. She laughed with a man dressed in pirate attire purchased from Family Dollar.

Brian felt the color fade from his face. The girl had brown hair, freckles, and went barefoot despite the obvious safety hazard. Her feet rocked back and forth on the leaves playfully. The cheap pirate poked her with a cartoonishly fake plastic hook. The barefoot mermaid laughed and threw her arms around him.

Brian tried not to vomit. All sound became white noise. He felt the beast dive bomb onto his brain. He felt the millipede wrap itself around his mouth. He felt the ocean of disembodied intrusive thoughts swallow his heart.

"Hey! Watch where you're going!"

Brian looked up from his invisible, internal strife. He had nearly run over a pair of female zombies. One was a brunette with a fake bone jutting out of her arm. The other a redhead with a steering wheel expertly wrapped around her neck. Another echo of his work taunting him. He apologized under his breath, fought back tears, and pushed his way past the indignant women.

Desperately scanning for anything else, he saw men scattered throughout the throng. They were clad in camouflage fatigues. Camouflage gear was not uncommon in Monroe, especially in colder weather, but there were way too many of these guys for this to be coincidence. The military-like gear must have been a cheap group costume. Brian looked down at his normal clothes. He felt even more like an outsider.

Eventually, he reached the grey tent. It was crowded. Large coolers filled with PBR and Coors Lite had been placed at each corner of the enclosure. Several recycling bins helped mitigate litter. Three hookahs were surrounded by guests clamoring for a hit.

"Hey, you real fuck!" A tattooed hand clamped down on his shoulder.

He spun around, meeting the face of Clyde Barrow. Wait, Clyde Barrow didn't have tattoos, especially not a Slowpoke Rodriguez tattoo. It was just Talon. Behind him, Nikki postured as a scantily clad version of Bonnie Parker. She chuffed on a large cigar with gusto, her own ink peering through the little clothing she wore.

"Whoa. Didn't recognize you with the fedora." Brian mumbled.

"Yeah man. It's sick!" Talon stared at Brian. "You don't look so good, my guy."

"I think I just need to have a drink or something." If he were numb, he couldn't hurt anybody.

"Why aren't you in costume, Brian?" Nikki asked, exhaling wispy cigar smoke.

"I forgot." Brian spoke over the crowd.

"You forgot to dress up? On Halloween night? No wonder Christine fucking left you." Nikki remarked.

Her words accelerated his growing panic. Brian's chest rose and fell. His hands went clammy. He worried he might explode.

"I'm not the only one! There's all these guys in camo or something." he deflected.

Talon shifted threateningly. Nikki smirked.

"What? *Are* they in costume? Did a new *Call of Duty* game get released?" Brian asked between gasping breaths.

"Those fuckers are those fucking American Guard assholes from Toledo. I don't know why Big John let them in here. They're probably trying to push meth on our turf. Fucking Ohio." Talon explained angrily. "Makes me want to start drinking again."

99

"Never heard of 'em. Are they a hate group?" Brian worriedly thought of his brother.

"They wish they were a fucking hate group. Pussies don't know the meaning of the word 'hate'." Talon adjusted his fedora. "I swear to God, if they push meth here, I'm going to get my shooters."

"They don't seem that bad." Nikki observed casually.

"Meth! Here! What the *fuck*? This town has had it bad enough with heroin and other shit drugs. Fucking drug shit man." Talon sighed. "Want to drop some bombs?"

Talon reached into his jacket pocket. He withdrew a handful of Ketamine bombs carefully wrapped in cigarette paper.

Brian's mouth watered. He ran his tongue over his large teeth. The cold sweat on his bald head evaporated. The music sounded less fuzzy to his ears. The last time he had taken the light horse tranquilizers was as a film student in Chicago, long before Christine entered his life. His college sweetheart at the time had been very into the club scene. She had turned him on to "Special K."

Brian loved Ketamine. Ketamine gave him energy. It made him feel euphoric in a way that marijuana never could. The sense of calm and serenity the drug imparted was heavenly. If one took enough Ketamine, one experienced spiritual visions, but the best part of Special K was the connectivity. While tripping, it was easy to feel one with the world and the people around you. K-holes weren't always fun, but Brian needed connectivity.

He knew the drug was less potent as a bomb. Bombs provided low intensity trips, but lasted longer than a snort. Bombs took longer to kick in as well. Brian needed this trip to kick in fast and last as long as possible, so he quickly grabbed four bombs out of Talon's hand. He downed them all before the dealer realized how many had been taken.

Talon did a double take. He gave one bomb to Nikki. He glared at Brian.

"Hey man, I still gotta sell this shit. Don't be a pig." he grumbled. He then took one bomb himself, pocketing the rest.

Brian took four deep breaths. He tried to focus on the main tent pole. Maybe the Ketamine took effect immediately. Maybe he stared at the pole for ten minutes. Time distortion was a substantial K bomb side effect.

Brian soon felt refreshed. Ketamine was better than a comforting cup of coffee. The anxiety in his brain and body fell silent.

It was as if anxiety never plagued him in the first place. He felt like a child again.

He saw Nikki and Talon nodding along in rhythm with the music. Hey, those were some pretty good tunes floating in the air. He gave a high five to Talon and winked at Nikki. He felt great.

Sam would be going on soon.

Absolute serenity enveloped him. He danced his way out of the tent. He grooved through the crowd. A man in a blowup T-Rex costume did a little shimmy with him as the music crescendoed.

He saw one of the American Guard guys chatting up a Dora the Explorer. This man was also bald, so Brian went up and rubbed the stranger's head. The stranger turned angrily but stopped at the sight of Brian rubbing his own bald head.

Camouflage man and adult Dora laughed as their anger fled from them. They each gave Brian a good-natured knuckle rub on the dome. Brian smiled.

*This is what being alive is all about.* He drifted away.

The stage drowned in speakers, amps, and subwoofers. Synth melodies rose and fell in harmonious cacophony. It was orgasmic.

*I love you, Ketamine.* Brian glowed.

Leaves crunched beneath his feet. The chill autumn evening no longer felt so cold. He brushed past a Jedi Knight and a Joker as he searched for his brother's band. There had to be a backstage greenroom area somewhere. After what Brian thought was a few minutes of aimless wandering, he came across a camping tent behind the stage.

*Bingo.*

A large, red-bearded man stepped out of the tent. He was a good foot-and-a-half taller than Brian. He was dressed as the character Tormund Giantsbane from HBO's *Game of Thrones* adaptation. He held up his hands in a gesture that was both apologetic and firm.

"Sorry, bands only."

"Big John! I'm with the band!"

"Holy shit, Brian? Hey brother!" Big John lifted Brian up in a powerful bear hug. Big John's hugs normally knocked the wind out of Brian, but with all the Ketamine flowing through his veins, Brian couldn't feel a thing.

"Is Sam back there?"

"Oh yeah. He said you'd show up. Go right on in, buddy."

Big John set Brian down and gave him a hearty slap on the back. Brian returned the favor with a goofy thumbs-up. He went inside.

"Yo! Brian!" Sam cried.

The makeshift greenroom had a dirt floor. Portable lights hung from the tent poles. Instruments and sound equipment were haphazardly scattered around the small space. *Parts Unknown* sat on plastic lawn chairs in the center of it all.

Raoul nursed a half-finished bottle of Corona and sat next to Emily Felder; a drummer covered in piercings. She had gotten them solely for the band. She sat with her legs crossed, a cigarette in one hand. Sam sat behind them, putting a new string on his electric guitar. All three members of *Parts Unknown* wore khaki uniforms with white pith helmets.

In his haste to join them under the dim yellow lights, Brian tripped over the entrance of the tent. Deep in a K-hole, he hardly felt the ground. He looked up at Sam. His brother looked like a disappointed angel.

"Whoa! You all right, Brian?" Sam asked with a laugh.

Brian began to cry.

"Yo, everything all right, man?" Sam knelt beside him.

Brian's tears landed in the soil.

"Yeah man. Sorry. I'm just so happy to see you. You're going to kill it up there." he sobbed.

"No need to get all weepy, Brian. I'm just glad you showed up." Sam replied.

"I just...it's the first time I've seen you play in such a long time, and what if it's the last time I ever see you play?" Brian asked, laughing and crying all at once.

"Brian-" Sam began worriedly. His elder brother cut him off.

"Hey, what are you all supposed to be, anyway?" Brian wiped his tears away with an uneven hand.

"Oh, we're supposed to be explorers! You know, *Parts Unknown*? We're like on a safari." Sam explained, concern fleeing from his voice.

"I thought you guys just liked Anthony Bourdain." Brian struggled to his feet.

"Will those Ohio *gringos* think we're fellow white nationalists?" Raoul interjected. "Just look at our helmets."

"Do you know why they're here?" Brian asked fearfully.

"Big John thinks they're here to buy drugs or something. He said he's keeping an eye on 'em." Sam explained.

"Well whoever they are, I'm going to give 'em a show." Raoul gave a sexy wink. "You guys ready to kick some ass?"

Emily nodded and finished her cigarette. Raoul adjusted his pith helmet. He stepped past Brian to get outside. Sam finished fitting his guitar string.

"It really means a lot that you're here." Sam smiled angelically.

Sam's teeth were perfect. Brian couldn't find the words to reply to his younger brother. He closed his eyes.

When he opened them, he was standing in the audience. Sam walked up and down the stage, guitar in hand. Emily twirled drumsticks. The crowd threatened to overflow onto the boards. Brian couldn't breathe with all these people around. He poked his head above the crowd. He saw Raoul stride up to the mic and take it in his hands.

"You motherfuckers ready to get fucking sexy?"

The crowd roared in approval. The band played. Brian lost himself again.

He awoke in the center of a mosh pit. Bodies ran into each other with kinetic forces rivaling those of the Large Hadron Collider. Brian couldn't feel anything.

He discovered that he could see with his eyes closed. He was happy. His newfound superpower would allow him to catch every second of his brother's show.

Emily's heavy drumbeats made Brian believe his hair would grow back. Raoul's gorgeous tenor shook him. Sam's sick shredding made Brian ecstatic and remorseful.

Brian felt his eyes close. Now he was standing on the stage, staring out at a sea of faces. They were all his own face staring back at him. He let out a howl. The crowd of mimics echoed him.

He closed his eyes, still seeing. He smiled. He saw Paul's threats play out before him. He saw the hook-handed man in a Target, puncturing Christine. He felt a pair of arms wrap around him. He was pulled from the heart of the mosh.

It was Alexis who had rescued him. She was dressed in a black beanie with cute, animal-like eyes and ears sewed on to it. Her heavy camo had been artfully altered to support wings under the arms. She sported black boots. She looked fantastic.

"What are you supposed to be?" Brian laughed.

"I'm a Com-*Bat*, get it?" Alexis chortled. In the surreal glow of the rave, her grey eyes were enchanting.

"Oh! You blend right in! Didn't see you there." Brian winked, but still saw.

"Ugh, don't remind me!" Alexis shouted over the dull roar. "Everyone thinks I'm part of those American Guard losers. I read about them on the Southern Poverty Law Center."

"Hey bitches! Woo!!!"

Sabrina approached. She was dressed as an impeccably lewd Harley Quinn. Her freshly dyed hair glowed in the dim light. She held a small wiffle ball bat in one hand, and a joint in the other. She snuggled herself between Alexis and Brian.

"Aren't we such a cute group of friends?" She asked, kissing Alexis on the cheek.

"We sure are." Brian snatched the joint from Sabrina. He took a hit.

"You're the only Harley Quinn I've seen tonight, surprisingly." Alexis said to Sabrina.

"I know, right? Thought there'd be more of me with *Joker* out." Sabrina smiled.

"I think you really underestimate how much people hated *Suicide Squad*." said Brian.

"Joker and Harley's toxic relationship is going on the podcast!" Sabrina cheered.

She playfully whacked Brian with the wiffle bat. This surprised him just enough for her to snatch the joint back. She took a huge toke.

"It sucks that my costume was culturally appropriated by those skinhead assholes." Alexis growled. "They're giving this whole party a bad vibe."

"Oh, come on! I don't think they're that bad. One of them is really cute! He hasn't been able to keep his hands off me all night! You guys want to meet him?" Sabrina offered excitedly.

"Sure." Alexis rolled her eyes.

"Come on!" Sabrina grabbed Alexis's hand.

Alexis sighed. She held Brian tighter than before. Brian grew cold and lifeless. He gulped. His perception of reality was starting to decay.

Sabrina guided them through the writhing herd of people. Claustrophobia set in. There was no way out. Brian started sweating again. He looked worriedly at Alexis. She had probably worked really hard on her punny costume. He didn't want to soak it with his perspiration.

They wound their way through a group of zombified ravers. The zombies were passing around a bottle of apple flavored Crown Royal. As the slugs of liquor went down, the alcohol leaked out of the zombies' stomach wounds. One zombie girl took a huge swig. Then her arm fell off, hand still clutching the bottle. The other zombies laughed.

Brian turned his head away from the ghoulish spectacle, only to see that he had taken a bite out of Sabrina's neck. He felt her blood drip down his face. Sabrina gave him a wink.

He was scared of what he would see if he looked at Alexis.

Sabrina's neck sewed itself back together. Her blood evaporated from his jaws. The vision faded.

*I hate you, Ketamine.* Brian lamented.

They were back at the grey hookah tent. Brian felt Alexis let go of his arm. A wave of relief washed over him.

Sabrina rushed towards Talon. Alexis followed close behind. Brian could barely keep up with these spry young twenty-somethings. Had the ground been this uneven a few hours ago?

In the firelight, Brian saw that Sabrina wasn't actually rushing towards Talon. Rather, she was heading towards the man he was talking to. Talon shook hands the camo jacketed male. He discreetly passed the stranger a few Ketamine Bombs.

Maybe Sabrina and Nikki were right. The bad vibes were gone. This guy didn't look like an Ohio skinhead. He had a full head of black hair. Also, he was clearly Asian. The guy wore a pair of thin designer glasses that gave him a nerdy aura despite his Bass Pro Shops jacket and pants.

Sabrina giggled as she hugged the skinny Asian man. She nuzzled his neck. The man smiled and popped a Ketamine bomb. He offered one to Sabrina, who took it from his fingers with her mouth. She sucked on his digits longer than she should have.

"Ithoughtyoudidntlikethoseguys." Brian slurred.

"Nah, man. *I* was fucked up. They're cool." Talon yelled over the crowd.

"Whoisthat?" Brian asked.

"My hookup." Talon answered.

Sabrina laughed and tugged at the Asian man's camouflaged jacket.

"Come with me! Big John said he stashed some jello shots somewhere." Sabrina dragged her new boo into the ever-growing crowd in the clearing. They disappeared.

"I wish you would have punched that guy, Brian." Alexis pouted.

"WhatAlexisthatsnotlikeyoutobeviolent."

"You should always punch Nazis. Always." Alexis glared.

"Thatguywaslikejapaneseorsomethingitsfine." He thought his eyes had closed again. Alexis *was* staring at him intently, so maybe they were open.

"Brian! I could have filmed you punching him! You could have learned something. You could've been an online inspiration!" Alexis exclaimed.

Brian's brain unraveled. He saw everyone at the rave drop dead at once. He heard *Parts Unknown* fade into nothingness. He turned to Alexis.

"Lexi...are you...trying to like...use me...or something?" He said as slowly as he could.

Alexis's eyes widened in surprise. She went as white as a sheet. Blood dribbled from her mouth.

"No! What? No." Her protest was not convincing in the slightest.

"Buddy. You are. You're using me." Brian drew close to Alexis.

He was too close to be a friend. He felt her hot breath waver against his skin. He wiped her bloody chin with his thumb. He wasn't sure the blood was real.

"It's okay. I've used you too." He said.

Brian Stanhope grabbed Alexis Knabusch by the neck and kissed her.

Deep in the K-Hole, what was meant to be a playful tug at the back of her neck turned into a full-on grab of the jugular. Alexis's blue-blonde hair flew in her face. She gasped for breath. Her hands clawed at Brian's.

The terror in her hands and lips made Brian stop. He relaxed his grip. Alexis shoved him away. Her sweet taste vanished. He realized he had accidentally choked her.

"What is the matter with you?!" she sputtered.

Every single cell in Brian's body went cold. He had done it. Not even Ketamine had been able to stop him. He was finished.

"Alexis..." Brian began. "I didn't...I mean...I..."

"*Asshole.*" Alexis spat. She stormed off into the crowd after Sabrina and the mysterious Asian.

Brian's brown eyes were wild with fear. His heart threatened to rupture. The air now seemed as thick and cold as a block of ice. He stared off after her, wondering what he had become.

"I think you're supposed to sleep with them first. You know, before you choke them out a little. You certainly have a way with women, Brian." Nikki laughed. She wrapped an arm around Talon.

"Did you do this at Target too? No wonder Christine skipped town." She continued.

Brian felt fury rise in his battered heart. He glared at Nikki and took a step toward her. He lifted a finger right into her face.

"You shut the fuck up, you stupid cunt." Brian roared. "You always gotta bring my ex up? How would you feel if I brought up Damon every two seconds? Hypocritical bitch."

"Hey!" Nikki snarled. "You can't talk to me like that!"

"Brian, chill the fuck out." Talon would have scared Brian out of his wits had he been sober. In his current altered state, Talon was only another provocation.

"Who the fuck is *Skylar*, anyway? Fucking cow. Was he before or after you left Christ or whatever?"

Brian shoved his angry finger into Talon's chest.

"Tell your woman to take care of herself. I can smell her from here."

Stars exploded into Brian's vision. He hit the ground. Talon had punched him in the face. His whole jaw smarted something fierce. He wondered if this was the sort of pain his heroines experienced in his stories.

"Talk to my wife that way again and I'll put a hole in your head! Fucking burn-out!" Talon spat on Brian's dark hoodie.

The thick white loogie soaked Brian to the skin. Talon made a move as if to kick Brian while he was down. The nearby partygoers wondered if there would be a good old-fashioned beat-down. Any further physical violence was prevented by the appearance of Big John, who pushed his way through the now enraptured crowd.

"Hey! No more of that!" Big John yelled. He placed himself between Talon and the prostrate Brian.

"Get your fix from someone else, faggot." Talon yelled at Brian.

"Hey! Get out of here! Go home, Talon!" Big John shouted.

Talon adjusted his fedora and walked away. Nikki followed him. She threw a middle finger at Brian as she went.

Brian was cripplingly discombobulated. Mind altering drugs and physical assault were not a good combination. He struggled to stand. Dead leaves crunched beneath his hands. His vision blurred. The leaves, dirt, and feet of onlookers swirled like a kaleidoscope before him.

A large set of hands picked him up. His feet were beneath him again. He swayed from side to side like a spinning top. He felt Big John steady his unbalanced frame. His head lolled from side to side.

"You gotta go too, Brian." Big John said.

"Imwiththebandman." Brian murmured.

"I heard what came out of your mouth. That kind of talk is unacceptable. You gotta go home. *Now.*" Big John ordered with hard authority.

Brian shoved himself away from Big John. He staggered, feeling Talon's spit between his fingers. He faced the bewildered onlookers.

"Imgoing." Brian walked off into the tree line. He didn't bother to take the path.

In the woods, the lights and music faded away. Soon, Brian was stumbling blindly in the dark. He tripped over roots and fallen branches, barely able to keep his footing. He could not see inches in front of his face. He wasn't sure whether he was heading towards the parking lot, or back to the rave, or deeper into the middle of nowhere.

He grabbed the trunk of a nearby tree. He felt his head do a flip. He felt hot vomit leave his mouth. He held the side of the tree, retching.

The black silence of the empty woods absorbed him into its hallowed ecosystem. He didn't feel the vomit anymore. He felt all his senses dissipate into the shadows. He was nothing but a disembodied consciousness floating in the night.

*This must be what death feels like.* Brian thought. He didn't know if he was thinking or speaking anymore. What was death but total disassociation from reality?

He caught a whiff of the earth beneath him. It smelled like skunk weed. He felt the wind howl. He heard a pair of footsteps ahead of him. He wasn't alone. He needed someone, anyone, to be with him now.

He rushed into the void. Not seeing, not hearing. Only feeling hunger. He quickened his pace. His hands touched something solid and hard.

"Let go of me! Please! Don't! You're hurting me!"

He fell onto something warm.

"Stop! Stop! Let me go!"

He heard a scream. He heard a grunt. He felt something warm and wet explode from his mouth. He fell onto his back. He stared up at the night sky. He could see no stars. Something cold and wet fell onto Brian's face.

He wasn't sure if his eyes were opened or closed.

# XV

Detective Cassandra Johnson frowned as she watched the heavy snowfall from her office window. She set down her mug of rapidly cooling coffee. She pulled out a hair tie and adjusted her tight bun. Another all-nighter was no excuse to be out of regs.

Cassandra, or "Sandra," as she preferred, was not a Monroe native. She had grown up in Ludington, on the western side of the state. Monroe was supposed to be a temporary assignment. She planned to earn her stripes and transfer to Detroit. 20 years later, she was still in Monroe. She had fallen in love with the post. The slow pace of life in Monroe County, combined with an abundance of crime, allowed Sandra to make lieutenant quicker than she would have in Detroit. Plus, being the only female detective in the county provided job security.

At first, the Monroe cops joked about having a woman on the force. Sandra showed them she was no damsel in distress; nor was she some air-headed trophy detective that the precinct could use to showcase diversity. She was a tomboy. She kept a clean record. She put up with no nonsense. She had an indomitable pride that governed every action. Most importantly, she enjoyed working convoluted cases.

She appraised the meticulously organized chaos of affidavits, maps, and paperwork that flooded her desk. She reviewed three statements with a glance. One was made by Alexis Knabusch. One was made by Zoe Jackson. The last was Samuel Stanhope's.

She applied some lotion to her weathered hands. Her Glock 17 hung on her belt. She checked her watch. It was nearly 7:30 AM. The special segment on FOX News Detroit would air shortly. Her pride swelled.

She flicked on the television opposite her desk. The FOX News logo appeared on the screen. A sharply dressed anchorwoman turned to the camera and began her story:

*"The search for a missing Monroe girl continues one week after her disappearance. 22-year-old Sabrina Cunningham was last seen Halloween night on the property of Jonathon Baumann, a local Monroe man with a fondness for live music."*

Sabrina's photo flashed across the TV. The broadcast cut to footage of K-9 units searching the snowy woods behind Big John's. The anchorwoman continued:

*"Located in northern Frenchtown Township, Mr. Baumann regularly hosts large parties that celebrate up-and-coming local bands. Sabrina Cunningham vanished at one such event. She was last seen dressed as the comic book character Harley Quinn. Authorities were alerted to Sabrina's disappearance when she failed to return home to her parents the following morning."*

The segment cut to a close-up of Big John. He looked terrible. His red beard and hair were in disarray. He had been crying.

*"I should have called the whole thing off."*

Big John's voice trembled.

Sandra felt bad for Big John. The Housing Commission had publicly called for his arrest. Small wonder. Sabrina's father held a seat with that glorified subcommittee.

Luckily, the Chief had cowed the bloodthirsty bureaucrats. This was a missing person's case. Big John had been completely cooperative with the investigation. He even handed over his security camera footage without a warrant.

The TV cut back to the news studio:

*"The presence of drugs and alcohol at the party have left many worrying for Sabrina's safety. The low temperatures and heavy snowfall across Southeast Michigan have only worsened fears."*

The news transitioned to the old northside Monroe Bank and Trust Office. The building, once abandoned, now teemed with dozens of civilians wearing bright yellow vests over winter gear. It's decrepit parking lot overflowed with vehicles.

Organizing the search parties was the only useful thing Mr. Cunningham had done. He spent the rest of his time bemoaning the early November blizzard, or disparaging hard working police officers. Sandra had enjoyed watching the Chief put Cunningham in his place.

*"Still, this has not deterred spirited volunteers from searching the woods for any signs of Sabrina."*

A clip from the Cunningham press conference played. Sabrina's parents stood on the front steps of the old bank. They were surrounded by reporters. The falling snow gave the segment a renaissance-painting feel.

*"If anyone has any information on where Sabrina is, please, call us. Call the police. Let us know. We just want our daughter back."*

Mrs. Cunningham choked back tears as her husband spoke.

*"We've been taken aback by all the kindness. Thank you. Every little bit helps."*

Mr. Cunningham held his wife while she wept.

The anchorwoman took over:

*"Dozens of witnesses have provided insight into the events on Halloween night."*

The newscast cut to a man and woman standing in the snow. Sandra grimaced at the sight of them. She took another sip of coffee.

Nikki Keener sobbed into the camera:

*"There were just so many bad vibes at that party. I pray that Jesus will find that girl and bring her back to us."*

Talon Keener shook his head:

*"We're going to find her. We're out here looking with everybody else. This is messed up, man."*

He wiped away Nikki's crocodile tears.

Sandra clenched her jaw. She had arrested Talon after the two-bit dealer tried to shoot Damon Williams. She knew the Keeners were out on Halloween to do a little more than have a good time.

*"21-year-old Monroe native Alexis Knabusch was the last person to see Sabrina on the night of her disappearance."*

The TV played a Snapchat video featuring Alexis dressed as a camouflaged bat with Sabrina as Harley Quinn. It was the night of the rave. The two girls made duck-faces into the camera. They laughed.

The lighting in the video was extremely poor. Sandra's head throbbed with frustration. The headache was interrupted by Alexis Knabusch speaking at the bank.

*"I've been calling and texting Sabrina every hour. If anyone, anyone can find Sabrina, please, hit me up on twitter or Instagram. I made the hashtag #savesabrina. If you put that in your posts, I will read it. Please help me find my best friend."*

Alexis looked paler than when Sandra had interviewed her.

"He choked you?" Sandra had asked.

"Yes...but...I think it was on accident? He's been weird for a while, but I don't think he kidnapped Sabrina. It was probably those skinhead fuck-boys." Alexis had stammered.

"He was weird for a while? Like that day he met you and Sabrina at Munson Park?"

"Yeah."

"Can you remind me what happened at the park?"

"Sabrina was going on about some weird death fetish thing she wanted to do for a podcast. She was even weirder than Brian, you know what I mean? But Brian...he looked and acted like...hell."

*Sabrina knew.* Sandra thought.

"I find it interesting that Brian Stanhope followed you guys for most of the night, assaulted you, and now no one can get a hold of him." Sandra had mused.

"Well, he was high; and he has a shitload of issues with women." Alexis had growled.

*"Anyone with information on Sabrina is advised to either use the #savesabrina hashtag or file a tip with the Monroe County Police Department."*

The television showed Sandra herself. Last night's press conference at City Hall had been some of her finest work. Sandra beamed with pride as her recording spoke.

*"We are using all of our manpower to find Ms. Cunningham. I want to thank all the volunteers who have come forward and aided us in our search. We are going to find Sabrina and bring her home."*

The anchorwoman smiled from her studio:

*"Now, over to Joe for the weather..."*

Sandra swallowed her proud fantasies with her coffee. She turned off the TV. She returned to her desk, and the anonymous tips about Sabrina. They all contradicted each other:

There had been members of the American Guard at the party. There were no American Guard at the party. There were no fights. There *was* a fight. No one agreed on who had been fighting. There had been drugs at the party. There had been alcohol. It was a sober event. Sandra's team had spent sleepless nights trying to validate *anything.*

The mentions of the American Guard concerned her. Those Ohio radicals had been a thorn in her side ever since the presidential election. The group splintering didn't help. All Guardsmen still claimed to be civil servants fighting the evils of immigration. Some became right wing bloggers. Others used their notoriety to engage in criminal activity. It was a pain in the ass trying to catch these fools before they jumped the Ohio border.

If there had been American Guard at Big John's, Sandra hadn't been able to identify any on the security camera footage. The clash of firelight and electronic displays created dozens of hours of blurry footage. She didn't have the heart to tell Big John that his cameras were worthless.

American Guard aside, Sandra had other problems: the blizzard for one. The untimely precipitation had buried any traces of footprints, personal items, and smells. Not even the K-9s could pick up a scent. Most likely Sabrina had blacked out and frozen to death beneath the snow somewhere. But maybe not.

The truth had been revealed to her a few nights ago.

It was late. The first few all-nighters were rough. Sandra had been going over tips when an email appeared in her personal inbox. Not the tip inbox, her *personal* email account.

It was from an encrypted sender. Normally Sandra would have deleted it. Unknown senders were usually trouble. Just as she was about to click the trash button, she read the subject of the email:

---

## ANONYMOUS TIP REGARDING SABRINA

## CUNNINGHAM'S FATE

---

She didn't like the use of the word "fate." She didn't like that someone had found her private email. She liked the contents of the message least of all:

---

Brian Stanhope killed Sabrina Cunningham. :)

If you need proof, just look into what he does for a living :)

---

The link to the *DeathbringerBob* Patreon account...if this was Brian Stanhope, he was into some fucked up shit. The serial killer fan fiction certainly fit the psychopath profile. His only public records were dockets from a court case a little over a year ago. His power of attorney over his crippled mother had been revoked. Apparently, this was due to "mental instability."

Eager to investigate this *"mental instability,"* Sandra asked around about Brian. She discovered he was a regular at *Zoe's*. She swung by to grab a cup of coffee and ask a few questions.

"Detective Johnson! I thought you left this Republican Mecca." Zoe had chortled.

"Oh, it's not that bad." Sandra had replied. "You know Brian Stanhope?"

"I sure do."

"Do you know where he works?"

"He does some computer thing for a living. He rarely comes out of that house, save to come here or check on his mother." Zoe had adjusted her glasses while she spoke.

"What do you know about his *computer thing?*"

"He investigates fraud, I think. It gives him a lot of stress."

"Stress?" Sandra raised an eyebrow.

"That boy has been through a lot. His Dad died in that car accident. Not to mention what it did to his mother." Zoe had explained, "The last time he was in here, he was talking about dark thoughts or something. It was odd. Unlike him. Usually, he flirts with that Alexis Knabusch."

"What kind of dark thoughts?" Sandra's interest intensified.

"He said something about being with someone, and not wanting to be with them. He said he'd be happy if they died. He was going on and on about control and death. I don't know. He mentioned his ex and some girl. He was scared he'd hurt this girl he liked. He said he hurt his ex in the past. He was in a real state. Do you want to take a look at our breakfast menu? Reynaldo has some delightful eggs benedict today..."

Sandra tracked down Brian's mother at the old folk's home next. River Park Place Apartments... was it mere coincidence that Sabrina's father managed the building? It was a crown jewel for the Housing Commission. Had Brian fixated on the Cunninghams?

River Park Place had almost been fruitless. The mother was not much help. His brother on the other hand, was extremely helpful.

"I haven't heard from Brian all week! They should be looking for him too!" Poor Sam had been really upset.

"When was the last time you saw your brother?" Sandra had inquired.

"The night of the party! He was all crazy.... falling over himself...he said that night might be the last time I'd see him *ever.* He got kicked out of the party for threatening a girl or something." Sam had elaborated.

"Really?"

"Something got into him, some bad weed, some drug, or...*something.* He loves drugs. He smokes here a lot. He practically hotboxed my mom a few weeks ago."

"When he was...*hotboxing*...your mom, did he say anything out of the ordinary?" Sandra had pulled out a notebook.

"He said he was thinking about death, killing, and dying. He said they were the only things he thought about anymore." Sam's eyes widened. "Now hold on, you don't think-"

"Thank you for your time, Mr. Stanhope." Sandra scribbled down her notes and left.

Returning to the station, she re-read all the tips. They weren't a quagmire like she previously had thought. All the stories had a through-line: Brian had been with Sabrina most of the night.

Sandra read all the "stories" on Brian's Patreon page. He fetishized the deaths of nubile young women. She thought about Alexis, Sabrina, the ex, and Brian's mother.

*"...he does have a shitload of issues with women."*

Sabrina had figured it out. It was impossible that she had discovered his work by accident. The case against Brian Stanhope looked solid. If they found a body-

The door to Sandra's office burst open. A young officer she had taken a liking to panted in the doorway. Cal Stewart was his name. He had potential, even if he had disrupted her thoughts.

"Lieutenant! We found her. You got to come with me." Officer Stewart gasped.

"Where is she?"

"Ash Township. She...She didn't...she's..." Tears formed in Cal Stewart's eyes.

Sandra knew what those tears meant. She chambered a round into her Glock 17. She put on her winter coat. She threw her badge around her neck. She followed Officer Stewart into the cold light of day.

# XVI

Sandra peered out at the frozen landscape. She tied her dark hair into a neat ponytail. She double checked the time on her phone. It was almost noon.

Cal stared ahead wordlessly.

She felt bad for him. This had to be his first dead body. Popping someone's corpse cherry was usually a proud moment, but this case was different. This was no drug-overdose or suicide.

"Who found her?" She asked. "One of the volunteers?"

"A father and son. They were out in the woods for some rifle practice and stumbled on her." Cal explained. "Their story's good. Everything checks out."

He took a deep breath, trying to ready himself.

Sandra simply stepped out into the deathly snow, breath hitting the wintry air.

She walked with a purpose. Several other officers scurried around, taking photographs of the environment. A K-9 unit had been deployed. An ambulance pulled in alongside the police vehicles littering the clearing.

In the summer, the clearing would have been a nice little spot. It might even have been busy. Ash Township was a popular fair-weather hiking destination. The rest of the year demoted the area to a desolate backwater.

Sandra was already covered in flaky precipitation. She impatiently tried to locate the crime scene. Eventually, Officer Stewart caught up with her. He motioned ahead at a large, fallen log on a hill.

Its melancholy slopes were undisturbed. The ground was uneven. Any travel by foot would have been slow and treacherous. It was possible that a girl; lost, intoxicated, not dressed for the inclement weather, could have met her untimely end out here. It was the middle of nowhere. It would have been a lonely way to go.

Stepping carefully onto the hillside, Lieutenant Johnson slowly made her way to the log. The timber was rotten. The way it had fallen suggested the ash tree had been struck by lightning a few years ago.

Yellow crime scene tape stuck out against the colorless snowdrifts. The blue uniforms gathered around the toppled tree parted instinctually, making way for Johnson and Stewart. It was freezing.

The heavy coat of the county coroner crouched over something beneath the broken boughs. His short grey beard and frazzled hair blended in with the surroundings. He reeked of coffee and sleep deprivation.

"What have we got, Finley? Hypothermia?" Sandra asked. She looked down at the body. She could hear Cal fighting back vomit.

"No. Not quite." Dr. Finley murmured.

Sandra's confidence wavered at the sight of the remains.

The red and blue hair dye seemed to be the only thing still intact on Sabrina Cunningham's body. Her skin was paler than the surrounding snow. What was left of her face had been covered with dark purple bruises. One of her eye sockets had been completely shattered. Her mouth hung open in a silent scream of terror.

Her neck was worse.

Hardened as she was, Sandra found it difficult to look at the large bite that had been taken out of Cunningham's jugular. Dried tendons hung frozen in the wind. There was no blood anywhere. The girl's feet were bare.

*Brian Stanhope.* Sandra pulled out her phone. She re-read Brian's Patreon.

"Maybe some wild animals found her...you know...and..." Officer Stewart threatened to faint.

"No." Dr. Finley shook his head. "Had she frozen to death and then been a meal for the carrion eaters, they would have gotten more of her."

"What are you saying?" Officer Stewart was not comforted by clinical observations.

"That party was miles south of here. With the weather, there's no way she could have made it on her own." Finley continued.

"So...that means..." Cal retched.

"Sabrina Cunningham sustained these wounds while she was alive. Someone left her here." Sandra pocketed her phone.

*Brian fucking Stanhope.*

"The tips said she had a wiffle ball bat or something. That's not here." Officer Stewart stammered.

Sandra looked at Cal with concern. He was starting to break down. She needed to give him purpose, otherwise he was liable to puke on the body and contaminate the crime scene.

118

"Has the Chief been contacted?" She asked.

Officer Stewart shook his head.

"Contact him." Lieutenant Johnson ordered. "This is officially a homicide. Get Hoppert on the line too. I got a lead on the bastard who did this."

Officer Stewart nodded. He marched back to the car, speaking into his walkie-talkie as he went. Sandra knelt next to Dr. Finley.

"I'm sorry, Liam. I know your families were close."

"The last time I saw her was Thanksgiving. Nearly a year ago…" the doctor sounded like a tattered scarecrow.

Sandra examined Sabrina's ruined face. Even now she cried for help. It was a silent cry echoing through the trees. Sandra couldn't save Sabrina, but she could give her justice.

"The bruises on her face look like they came from a fist." Sandra began. "But the neck…are we sure that's human?"

"Positive." Dr. Finley nodded grimly. "What's remarkable is that it was a clean bite. Her jugular was completely severed in one go. What's worse…"

"What?"

"Whoever did this drank her blood."

"You're positive?" Sandra retrieved her notepad from her coat pocket.

"Look how pale she is. Look around. There should be a nice little trail for us. There's not. There's no blood anywhere."

Sandra added to her notes in earnest.

"Dr. Gonzalez is on his way over to my lab right now." Dr. Finley rose and adjusted his coat.

"The dentist?" Sandra asked.

"The very same. I'm making a mold of the neck wound. Perhaps we can match it up with the bite profile of the perpetrator." Dr. Finley took off his glasses and cleaned them with a small cloth. "Do you still need her out here? I'd like to get her inside."

Lieutenant Johnson was lost in thought. She had the Patreon. She had the statements. The lack of physical evidence didn't matter. In fact, its absence strengthened the case. The motherfucker had known what he was doing.

Sabrina had discovered Brian Stanhope's dirty little secret. Brian killed her to keep her quiet. He even did a little bloodsucking too. Just like his stories.

"Sandra? Can my boys start preparing Sabrina for transport?" Dr. Finley repeated, impatience fraying his voice further.

"Of course."

Sandra snapped her notepad shut. She made her way down the hill. Dr. Finley followed her. The crunching snow beneath their feet was the only sound other than the rising wind.

"I'll have a preliminary report ready before the end of the day." Dr. Finley shattered the silence.

"I appreciate that." Sandra said.

"This is worse than Nevaeh Buchanan in '09." Dr. Finley had tears in his eyes.

"This one won't go unsolved. I promise you that." Sandra vowed.

"That kid is calling Hoppert? You have a lead?"

"More than that. I think we have enough for a warrant." Sandra smirked.

"Who?"

"You ever heard of someone named Brian Stanhope?"

Dr. Finley paused.

"I have not heard that name in a long time." He chuckled, "His mother used to bother me about getting his teeth fixed. I had to tell her I'm not a dentist at least four or five times. She always was a bit batty, even before that tragedy."

"What was wrong with his teeth?"

"He had some impressive canines. I don't know a dentist who would have touched them. They were incredibly healthy by my recollection. Of course, that was nearly twenty years ago."

"Canine teeth?" Sandra's smirk widened into a smile.

Dr. Finley's eyes went wide. He opened his mouth to speak. Sandra politely stopped him with a raised hand.

"I *know* we have enough for a warrant." She pocketed her hands proudly. "Text me when you and Dr. Gonzalez finish the report."

More police cars arrived on the scene. A group of young gentlemen working for Dr. Finley made their way to the log, stretcher in hand. *The Monroe News*, *Detroit Free Press*, and *Toledo Blade* would soon be here. It was a small blessing that Dr. Finley had arrived *before* the press. The last thing anyone wanted was some frontpage spread of Sabrina's corpse.

Officer Cal Stewart waited in the car. He sat in the driver's seat, morosely staring off into the snowbound woods. Sandra quietly sat next to him. She knew he had been crying.

"You did good out there today. It's not easy seeing something like that." She comforted.

"I knew Sabrina back in high school. She took me to a Sadie Hawkins dance sophomore year." Cal uttered softly. "We weren't close after graduation or anything. I...didn't think I'd ever see someone I knew...like...*that*."

"I'm sorry Cal." Sandra thought of the Finleys friendship with the Cunninghams. "I had no idea."

*Fucking small towns. Should have went to Detroit.*

"Thanks." He responded.

Officer Stewart ran a hand through his dark hair. He put the keys in the ignition. The interceptor purred to life.

"Where to, Lieutenant?"

"The station. We need to debrief the Chief. After that...we make an arrest."

"Good." Cal growled. "Let's get the son-of-a-bitch."

Sandra looked out the windshield. A large crow sat in one of the bare trees. It cawed. Its cry echoed through the frigid forest, a tardy omen of death. Sabrina's frozen; terrified, broken, bloodless body greeted Sandra whenever she blinked. The crow cawed again. Maybe it was an omen of retribution.

Sandra couldn't help but smile. She knew the secret of homicide: murder was rarely complicated.

The interceptor turned onto the black highway. Heavy clouds gathered overhead. The car hit eighty miles an hour. Even at this speed, it could not outrun the gloom of winter, which closed in more quickly with every breath.

# XVII

"Christine!"

"Brian?"

"Christine!"

"What are you doing here?"

"We need to talk-"

"I'm at *work*-"

"I need to talk to you, Christine."

"Go home. I'm on the clock-"

"Is it true?"

"Is what true?"

"Colin."

"...I'm not having this conversation."

"Did you hook up with Colin?"

"What did I just say?"

"Please, Christine...don't do this to me, not after everything-"

"Brian, if you don't leave me alone, I am going to-"

"CHRISTINE! MY PARENTS JUST GOT INTO A FUCKING CAR ACCIDENT!"

"Brian..."

"MY DAD IS FUCKING DEAD! MY MOM IS FUCKED! MY LIFE IS FUCKING OVER! ALL I WANT TO FUCKING KNOW IS DID YOU FUCK COLIN OR NOT?!"

"Don't you dare use that...don't you *dare*..."

"My life is fucked. Christine...please..."

"I don't care...your parents have nothing to do with me."

"Did you fuck him?!"

"Let go of me!"

"Is he here? I'm going to fucking kill him."

"Get off! You're making me uncomfortable-"

"*UNCOMFORTABLE*? HOW DO YOU THINK I FEEL AFTER THE FUCKING WEEK I'VE HAD?! NOW I HAVE TO DEAL WITH THIS BULLSHIT?!"

"You're a fucking asshole, Brian!"

"HEY! What the hell is going on here?"

"Pick that shit up, Brian! It took me an hour to set up that display-"

"An *hour?* Well how long do you think it took me to find out about Colin? LONGER THAN THAT!"

"Brian. You're making a scene. You need to go right now."

"This doesn't concern you, Raoul. Go back to doing whatever the fuck it is you do here."

"Get the fuck out, Brian! Raoul, I'm sorry-"

"You owe me, Christine. After everything we-"

"I don't owe you shit. We. Never. Dated. Get that through your head! You were fun, okay?! Colin...I never had feelings for anyone before. Fuck! You knew this! You want me to spell it out for you?"

"What...?"

"Brian, get out of my store. Now. It's time to leave."

"Shut up, Raoul! Christine, come on, you don't mean that..."

"Colin actually fucking listens to me! He cares about me! I'm in love with him! I know it's not what you want to hear, but I am *sorry*, ok?!"

"Brian, come on."

"...did he really serve in Iraq?"

"What?"

"Brian, you're going to be charged with trespassing if you don't get the-"

"I. Am. Not. Talking. To. You. Raoul. Christine, did that fucking prick actually serve in Iraq?"

"I don't-"

"He's a tough guy, is that it? You want to date some big ass war hero who still has hair and a prosthetic hand? I didn't know you were into Captain Hook. Another white girl fucked by Disney. Tell me Christine, does he fuck you with the prosthetic on or off?"

"Fuck you, Brian!"

"You cheating...why didn't you just tell me!? You led me on!"

"Brian, you're way out of line."

"This doesn't concern you, you fucking faggot!"

"Brian!"

"Brian...do you know who your brother is?"

"OF COURSE I FUCKING KNOW WHO MY BROTHER IS! I'VE KNOWN HIM A LOT LONGER THAN YOU!"

"Go to hell, Brian."

"I'm calling the cops."

"CALL THEM! THERE IS GOING TO BE A FUCKING MURDER IF YOU CALL THEM, SO YOU DAMN WELL BETTER CALL THEM."

"Just try it, *cabrón*."

"Brian, stop!"

"I'm going to kill you, Christine! You fucking whore!"

"You just try, you mother-"

"FUCK!!! GAH!!!"

"Yeah, keep trashing the store. That's trespassing *and* vandalism, *pendejo*. Christine, come with me-"

"DON'T TOUCH HER! YOU LED ME ON! YOU LED ME ON! HOW MANY PEOPLE KNOW ABOUT YOU AND COLIN? WHY WAS I THE LAST TO KNOW?!"

"Brian, I tried...I tried to tell you...you never listen..."

"Last chance, Brian. Get the fuck out of here."

"Brian, *let go of me-*"

"You want assault added to your charges, Brian?"

"IF YOU DON'T LET ME SPEAK TO MY GIRLFRIEND, I WILL KILL YOU! THIS IS A PRIVATE CONVERSATION!"

"That you're making public."

"BECAUSE SHE *LIED!*"

"Get the hell out of here, Brian!"

"You're coming with me! We are going to talk this out!"

"You can't reason someone into loving you, Brian. Especially not the way you're acting."

"Like you'd know! How's the hookup culture, Raoul?"

"BRIAN! GET THE HELL OUT!"

"Christine! No! I am not leaving!"

"GET OUT!"

"Ow! What the..."

"The cops are on their way. They're coming. Christine, let him go."

"GOOD! I'M GOING! FUCK YOU, RAOUL. AND FUCK YOU, CHRISTINE! FUCK MONROE! FUCK MICHIGAN! AND FUCK ME! FUCK!!! YOU!!!"

"Christine, it's okay. Don't cry, he's leaving. The cops will be here soon."

"I...I...I..."

"Come on, just get in the back room, he's gone..."

Sufferers of Ketamine hangovers replay the most low-down, fucked up moments of their lives whenever they close their eyes. Some claim that this process is necessary to trigger an awakening. Brian didn't need an awakening. He already knew the dark truth about himself:

He wrote what he did because it always existed inside him. He had always been a piece of shit. There was no redemption in this world. Owning up to your mistakes just got you killed, or worse, canceled.

*Fuck Ketamine.*

Ketamine hangovers weren't supposed to last ten days. The hangover would cause some puking, some disorganized thinking, and some minor memory loss, but only for a few hours. Brian believed he must have contracted the flu from the snowstorm.

He remembered opening his bloodshot eyes and seeing only white. The air was unbearable. His lips and extremities had turned slightly blue. When he sat up, a thin layer of snow fell off him. The ground was hard and frozen.

He had grabbed a nearby tree trunk and pulled himself to his feet. As his hands grasped the trunk, he noticed his knuckles were swollen and bruised. Had he punched one of the trees? Maybe he had gotten in a few blows on Talon and couldn't remember.

Looking around, he saw he had knocked over a sapling as he lost consciousness. The chipped bark matched his damaged hands. One mystery solved.

Dried vomit was caked all over his pants and shoes. Talon's loogie had turned into a frosted grey-white splotch on his hoodie. His phone was dead.

He was dizzy. He smelled his frozen, rotted stench. He dry-heaved for a few minutes. He began to walk out of the woods. It was still snowing. He hoped he wasn't lost.

He heard Raoul and Christine's voices echoing through the trees. He heard his own vile words too. His swollen, bruised hands throbbed at the memory of knocking over shelves. He felt the rage in his heart. He felt the shame soon after.

His beard did a good job of protecting his face, but he could feel the snow landing on his bald head. His father used to tell him that most of the heat in the human body exited through the head, but

Brian had never believed that until this moment. Thankfully, he had woken up not too far from the tree line.

Stepping out of the forest, he saw that his rusted, blood-red Town Car was the only vehicle left in the empty makeshift lot. Struggling to put one foot in front of the other, he tried not to trip over the churned earth. He prayed he would not be spotted by Big John.

Miraculously, Brian made it to his car without falling over or puking. The snow had only accumulated about an inch or so. He didn't even need to scrape off his windshield.

Squinting against the blinding, overcast light, he hopped inside the car. He blasted the heat as soon as the engine started. He shivered, holding himself, desperately trying to warm his hands.

Someone was watching him from the farmhouse porch. He threw the car into gear. He needed to hit the road.

The drive was slow and lonesome. The snowbound cornfields might as well have been the arctic. The desolate journey was made worse by the specters of Christine and Raoul.

When he got home, he stripped out of his filthy clothes. As he took off his shirt, he heard himself screaming at Nikki and Talon again. He looked down at his hands. In his dark, untidy home, they no longer looked so blue.

He felt his hands grab Alexis by the throat.

What had he done to her? What had he tried to do to her? He felt her quavering lips on his. He felt the pulse in her throat against his palms.

He immediately went to the bathroom and puked again. His stomach was so empty, only disgusting yellow bile filled the toilet bowl. He hated himself.

For the next several days, whenever he tried to eat, he puked. Whenever he closed his eyes, he was back in that Target. Whenever he opened them, he was in hell with his creations.

The days bled into each other. Time meant nothing anymore. He was feverish and sweating constantly. His thoughts and memories were so nightmarish any strength to deal with reality fled.

He left his phone next to his computer. He did not touch either device. He spent days shivering naked under his covers.

As the flashbacks faded, he thought of everyone in his life. He wondered how his brother had reacted when he heard he had been kicked out of the party. He wondered if Sabrina or Alexis had even bothered texting him. Alexis had to have written some self-righteous blog about how he had assaulted her. He deserved public humiliation. He had given in to his dark desires.

Had Paul tried to make good on his threats? What was Christine up to? Was she happy with Colin? How would his readership take it when he scrubbed his accounts? Would he ever stop puking? Was this world real? Would the repetitive beasts of anxiety finally kill him? Would that portrait of Bob Dole stop judging him? Would the crucifix stop condemning him? Had Sabrina and the Asian guy hooked up? How much did Sabrina know about *DeathbringerBob*? Was his mom okay? How would he take care of her now?

As his worrying increased, he shivered less. He puked less too. He was able to stomach saltine crackers and water, and then cans of soup. Finally, he was eating again.

Wrapping himself only in his bed sheet, he stared at the crucifix. He tried praying. He gave up. He wasn't worthy enough to talk to God.

He walked through his lifeless home. He stared at pictures on the walls. His family was happy in those pictures. His child prodigy days were better days. Brian sighed. Those days were long gone.

He wrapped his blanket tighter around him. He investigated the bathroom. The roses on the toilet caught his eye. They were black now. They would turn to dust if he touched them. Alexis had turned to dust when he touched her too. Maybe he should refrain from touching things for a while.

His footsteps echoed through the house. He made his way to the back porch. The snow had stopped. The old, dead, white oak towered over the property as it always had. It's petrified; ivory branches vanished into the pale sky.

His bare feet sunk into the deep snow. It was awful. It was nice.

According to family legend, his grandfather had planted the oak tree as a boy. Brian doubted that. The tree was too big. It had been dead for too long. He sighed. He wished his grandfather were still alive so he could just ask him and know the truth for sure.

He couldn't bring himself to kill the tree a second time. He placed a hand on the dry, white bark. It was coarse. Despite being long dead, the tree did not feel hollow. Everything it had witnessed and experienced was still locked away inside somewhere.

Brian felt desperately sad. He wished the tree were alive again. He cried, growing angry with himself.

He cared more about a dead tree than any of his dead fictional women. He cared more about the tree than he cared about Christine. He cared more about the tree than Alexis, Nikki, Sabrina, Zoe, his mother...

Alexis was right. He did have issues with women. He didn't get off on the idea of killing them because he hated them. He got off on killing them because he believed they owed him something. That was worse.

The tree was dead. It wasn't coming back. He was alive, more grotesque than it was. Standing out here freezing to death wouldn't do anything for either of them.

Feet well past numb, he limped back inside. He closed the glass sliding door behind him. He took one last look at the tree. He would have to cut the rot out of himself. Otherwise, someone would cut him down one day.

His filthy footprints made a winding trail from the back door to the living room. He turned on his computer. His background was a photo from the day he had helped Sabrina and Alexis paint the back wall of *Zoe's*. Sabrina was the artist. Alexis had supervised. Zoe had watched in bemusement. He held the ladder. It struck him that he had hurt every single person in that picture.

His phone was having trouble powering on. As it groaned to life, he turned back to the computer. He logged into Patreon. He posted one last good-bye update. He couldn't completely delete the account yet. He still had to wait for the inquiry into Paul.

He began to delete his word documents, but body odor and sickness hit his nose. He gagged. He hadn't bathed or done laundry since before Big John's.

Dropping the blanket on the floor, he hopped into the shower. Warm water washed over him. It felt good.

He scrubbed his dirty body down. His skunky smell was soon sucked down the drain. He hadn't smoked since the rave. That was something.

Once he was dry, Brian applied a little beard oil to his impressive facial hair. He took a breath. He cooked up a plan:

He'd clean this house from top to bottom. It'd be a fresh start. Then, once the house was all clean, he'd ditch his phone. He'd delete all his writing. He'd apologize to Raoul. He'd see if he could apologize to Alexis. Maybe Sabrina could intervene on his behalf.

He stepped out into the hall; towel wrapped around his waist. He heard cars pulling up outside. What were cars doing here? He wasn't expecting company. Maybe Paul had finally showed up. Maybe it was Sam who was coming to murder him. He'd soon know.

A firm knock sounded from the front door. Brian didn't like that knock. It was too formal.

*Oh, shit!* What if something had happened to his mom? The millipede of anxiety unfurled itself in his mind.

He rushed to the door, throwing it wide open. Low, dull sunlight blinded him. He blinked. He made out a group of flashing police cars.

An imposing dark-haired female cop stood on the porch. She was backed by a thin patrolman who looked younger than Alexis and Sabrina. Both officers had intimidating glints in their eyes.

Brian wore nothing but a towel. Sweat hit the floor between his toes. He swallowed nervously.

"Brian Stanhope?" The female cop asked.

"...Speaking?"

"I have a warrant for your arrest. You're being charged with the murder of Sabrina Cunningham. You have the right to remain silent. Anything you say can and will be used against you in a court of law. You have the right to an attorney..."

Brian felt the young cop place him in cold handcuffs. He heard other police officers escort him to a car. After that, he didn't hear anymore.

# XVIII

Alexis Knabusch was living her worst life.

"You're an adult. Just move out." Her father callously suggested.

"I understand your concerns, but he's behind bars now. Besides, with the current market it'd be unwise to sell the house." Her mother coldly rationalized.

Alexis threw her phone at the wall. She screamed that there was nothing for them in Monroe. Her parents were hypocrites for never being *in* Monroe. Clearly, they hated it. Clearly, they were lazy. They didn't want to go through the trouble of selling a house or raising a daughter. They hadn't even attended Sabrina's funeral.

Alexis grabbed her father's three wood from the closet and put holes in the walls. Her parents were hundreds of miles away. They couldn't stop her.

When there was nothing left in the house to destroy, she turned her fury to the internet. Her hatred of Brian flowed from her social media profiles like lava. She did everything in her online power to obliterate his reputation.

Her smear campaign was working. He was now the only thing the local news talked about. The police had discovered hundreds of pages of murder-themed erotica on his computer.

A chill spread over Alexis's body. Just as she had suspected, Brian's whole "fraud analyst" story had been a complete lie. Sabrina had found out the truth. She had been murdered for it.

Why hadn't she seen it sooner? Alexis felt dirty. She felt violated. She had felt the darkness in his gaze that autumn day at Munson Park hill. Why hadn't she done anything about it?

Alexis's eyes were red and puffy from crying. She had developed a nervous habit of running her hands over her throat. Had he planned to kill her too? Had he jerked off after biting Sabrina's throat out? Why couldn't she stop thinking about him?

Alexis feared she would faint again. It was hard to maintain consciousness these days. She couldn't think about fainting or she would lose it. She had to focus.

She sat on her couch, no makeup on her face, days-old pajamas clinging to her clammy skin. Lily snored at her feet, oblivious to her distress. The news droned on and on about Brian's "artistic" day job:

*"So, several of these...commissions...you think they were inspired by actual people and events?"*

*"Oh, yes. Ash Township was mentioned specifically. There was also a piece about two young women on a road trip...*

FOX News Detroit interviewed a forensic psychiatrist. The expert tried to rationalize Brian's fantasies. Alexis thought that the white haired, bespectacled professional was completely unnecessary. Two women? Two *friends*? She could probably guess who they were meant to represent *without* analysis, thank you very much.

*"...throat biting is his motif. Not to mention this hook handed character, who we believe to be-"*

Alexis turned off the TV. She couldn't stand to hear anything about bite wounds, factual or fictional. Her hands shot to her throat again. She forced herself to look at the painting Sabrina had made of Lily. It sat on the floor in front of the TV. She had yet to hang it up.

She started to cry again. She had made such a scene at the funeral. Unbidden memories from that night at Big John's smothered her.

Sabrina had vanished into the crowd. Alexis didn't look too hard for her. She had been too preoccupied by Brian's fumbled kiss. He had not left the faintest bruise, but her insides had still turned to mush. She had been assaulted. He was her buddy, and he had betrayed her. Why? Because she wanted to exploit him for likes?

She had bumped into Sam and Raoul. Sam was pissed that Brian had been kicked out of the party. Brian's ejection was news to Alexis.

"For choking me?" she had asked.

"What? No! He tried to start some shit with Nikki and Talon Keener. He choked you?" Sam was incredulous.

"Your brother's a real piece of work." Raoul shook his head.

Alexis left without Sabrina. She figured Sabrina went home with that nerdy looking Asian skinhead guy with the camo. She would be fine. Sabrina had had weirder hookups.

Alexis went home. She poured herself a glass of cheap wine, showered, and went to bed. In the morning, she would cut Brian out of her life completely.

She had awoken to numerous missed texts and calls from Sabrina's parents. Sabrina had not contacted them. Sabrina had not reached out to her either.

Alexis had done everything you were supposed to do in these situations. She had served refreshments to the search parties every day. She had made the #savesabrina hashtag. She had promoted it to trending with her own money. She had cooperated fully with the police. Sabrina still died.

Alexis hated herself. She was so stupid! She had defended Brian to the detective, like some abused housewife. If she weren't such a victim, she would have gone to the police that night. Maybe then Sabrina would still be alive.

Her hot, angry tears blinded her. She started hyperventilating. She deserved the panic attack. Her own existence had driven her parents away. Now, her existence had led to the savage murder of her best friend. She couldn't shift the blame or control the narrative. She was responsible for Sabrina's death. Panic attacks were the least she deserved.

Her sobs woke Lily. The loyal pooch licked Alexis's red, tearstained face. Alexis grabbed Lily in a big hug and wept, soaking the dog's fur with her tears.

She was disgusted that she had ever harbored tender feelings for Brian. She hoped he would rot in prison. She prayed that the inmates would do unto Brian what he had done unto Sabrina.

By the time she was done crying, it was dark outside. Typical January. Alexis didn't feel any better. She released Lily. The dog was overtaken by the zoomies. Alexis couldn't help but smile.

A deafening rumble rocked Alexis's stomach. The growl was so loud that Lily barked. Alexis clutched her belly. She was starving. She hadn't eaten regularly since Halloween. She had lost a lot of weight.

The angry tears started again. She couldn't let herself starve to death. She had to be her own support network. Two parents gone, one friend dead, one friend in jail…Alexis had no one on earth to talk to at all. Her social media followers only made her lonelier, even when they parroted back her calls of justice for Sabrina.

Alexis strengthened her resolve. She would go out tonight. She would find someone to talk to, and she would get some food in her belly before she keeled over.

Alexis showered for the first time that week. She put on her best makeup. Girl, she was on point! She looked great. A little thin and pale, perhaps, but she would perk up once she got some food. She didn't just need food. She needed burgers. She needed *Larson's*.

*Larson's* was a local dive on Telegraph Road. It had been one of Sabrina's favorite haunts. The place was a little seedy, but Sabrina always swore that the seediness added to the charm.

Alexis would eat at that little burger joint, seedy or not, in Sabrina's name. She would post a nice food pic to Instagram and tag Sabrina in it. Maybe some more digital sympathy would soothe her.

She put on a stylish red coat. She grabbed the keys to her Audi. It was a nice ride, if a bit un-American. She hated the sneers of the proud Ford, Chevy, and GM owners. The more brazen drivers, their vehicles covered with local UAW stickers; would flip her the bird. Some threatened to do worse.

Driving a foreign car in Southeast Michigan was a personal safety hazard. The Audi was a carriage that brought nothing but scorn. From the driver's seat, Alexis observed her house. It was nothing but a lonely castle. At least she had a castle and a carriage. She pulled out of her driveway, leaving Carrington Farms behind her.

After a wistful drive, a windowless brick building with a green terra cotta roof came into view. That was Larson's. The parking lot was full for a Tuesday night. Was it Tuesday? Alexis supposed it must be. That's what the news had said.

Road salt crunched beneath her tires as she pulled into a parking spot.

She made her way into *Larson's*. The place was hopping. Sports fans huddled around the TV, jeering at whatever game was on. A short, slightly plump hostess with a bob cut asked how many would be joining Alexis.

"Just one." Alexis replied.

"Would you like to sit at the bar? There should be some stools open if you want to seat yourself."

Alexis grimaced. Why even have a hostess if you can just hop over to the bar? She forced a smile. Her inner Karen was showing, and she didn't like that. Besides, the bar would be a nice backdrop for Instagram food stories.

"Sure. Thanks."

Alexis weaved her way through the dining room. There was one empty stool at the corner of the bar. The patron sitting next to the empty stool finished a Jaeger-Bomb.

Alexis froze in her red coat. She recognized his full head of hair. She knew those designer glasses. He wasn't wearing camo now, but a bright *Toledo Rockets* hoodie.

The guy doing Jaeger-Bombs was the Asian guy Sabrina talked to at Big John's!

Alexis's heart raced. She was nervous, but full of hope. This was what she had been waiting for: the opportunity to share her grief with someone. If she was feeling *this* horrible, she could not even imagine what was going through this guy's head. He must have been drinking for weeks, *at least.*

"Hey. Excuse me." Alexis took a tentative step towards the stranger.

He turned to face her. No mistaking him now. This was her man all right.

"Hi. Um. Sorry. Were you at Big John's this year?" she asked.

"Uh...who?" The man looked confused.

"You know! Big John's! You were hanging out with my friend all night. You were flirting with her pretty heavily." Alexis sat in the empty stool.

"I'm sorry; I don't know what you're talking about." The man answered hurriedly. He turned away and tried to flag down a bartender.

"No, you were definitely there!" Alexis scooted closer to the stranger.

When the man spoke again, his voice was carefully measured:

"Listen: you're confused. I don't know you."

This made Alexis angry. She had gotten too close to actual human connection to shy away now. Why was he acting like this?

"No, I do know you! I didn't catch your name, but I saw you! My friend...she was..." Alexis faltered, "You know...*Sabrina Cunningham.*"

The man stood.

"Can I get some service around here?" He shouted.

No bartenders came. Cursing, he whipped out a twenty and threw it down on the bar. He bolted.

Alexis was stunned.

"Hey! Wait!

The man didn't look back. He made for the front door. Alexis quickly followed. She almost lost him as she dodged an overworked server. She had already lost Sabrina in one crowd. She would not lose anyone in a crowd again.

The guy ducked outside.

Alexis pushed her way past an overly rambunctious family of five, barely making it out the front door. The night air engulfed her. She looked around wildly. She had to find him!

A rough hand grabbed her by the mouth. Her screams were stifled as the back of her head hit the brick wall of *Larson's*. Her vision spun. Her hands could not pry away the wiry fingers that held her jaw shut. Her legs were paralyzed by terror.

Her ears, however, worked fine:

"You fucking listen to me, you little bitch: You. Do not. Know me. I have never seen you before in my life, and you sure as shit have never seen me. I was never here. I was never at Big John's. Do you understand me, you white cunt?"

Alexis felt herself nod. The man struck her against the brick wall once more. She hit the ground without realizing what was happening. She heard footsteps on the salted blacktop fading further and further away.

She pulled herself to her feet. She heard an engine start. She was scared her jaw was broken. She opened and shut her mouth a few times. Everything still functioned. Her hands ran across her throat.

She saw a green Chevy Impala bearing an Ohio license plate peel out of the parking lot and into the January darkness.

# XIX

Brian Stanhope was living his worst life. Jail sucked. There was no weed. There was no music. There was only anxiety. It was February. Cell 1-13 still didn't feel like home.

1-13 was at the end of the corridor. Brian's only neighbor was the angry, violent inmate in 1-12. 1-12 housed a large black man who was not much for talking, unless it involved taunting the guards into brawls. The correctional officers never took the bait. They simply tazed Mr. 1-12 into submission before wrapping him up in the blue-burrito for another night.

The dreaded blue-burrito was a large, navy-blue gym mat with two red buckled straps. The occupant of Cell 1-12, once subdued, would be placed onto the mat and rolled up like a burrito. The red straps were then tightened shut, securing him inside. Robbed of his mobility, he would moan and curse all night long. In the morning, the jail house faculty would release him for breakfast and bathing. Inevitably, Mr. 1-12 would attempt to assault the staff. They just placed him back in the blue-burrito until dinner, where the barbaric, de-humanizing ritual began again.

*Isn't this a human rights violation? Shouldn't this guy be on meds or something? What's he in for? When's his trial?* The blue-burrito made Brian nauseous.

Brian didn't ask his fellow inmates many questions. The other prisoners only hurled insults at him, calling him a "corpse-fucker," or a "cannibal," or a "fucked-up-perverted-son-of-a-bitch." They usually added that they would rape him until he was dead.

The police explained that Brian was kept in an isolated cell because they were fearful that Monroe County's finest would murder him before his trial and rob justice of its due. So, Brian took his meals in his cell alone. When he showered, he was monitored by two guards.

The loneliness of captivity only set Brian's demons free. The millipede crawled over his entire body. The beast grew tired of thrashing his brain and moved on to his heart and lungs. The ocean of intrusive suicidal thoughts became all-encompassing. Brian didn't realize his self-inflicted emotional labor was nothing more than a mental blue-burrito.

The abhorrent mirror in his cell was a constant judge. He had lost weight. His beard grew untamed. He was not allowed to shave. The police were concerned he might take his own life.

He shook constantly. He didn't sleep. He only stared at the ceiling, replaying the day of his arrest over and over in his head like a worn-out film.

†

When he came to in the car, he remembered feeling calm. He was handcuffed and nearly naked, but not anxious. He was confused.

Sabrina was dead? He had killed Sabrina? No way. He had taken lots of Ketamine, and the substance could mess with your memory, but he would have remembered killing someone! He would have *especially* remembered killing Sabrina. He liked Sabrina, why would he kill her? She was dead?

*No way.*

He tried to remember that night in the woods. He had felt something warm and wet in his mouth. He had heard someone screaming in pain.

*Oh shit.* Maybe he had killed Sabrina. *Oh no.*

Wait, that didn't make sense! He had messed up his knuckles on the tree, but there was no blood on his clothes. There was no blood near him. You couldn't kill someone without shedding their blood.

*Unless you strangled them.*

He was escorted through the backdoor of the Monroe County Courthouse. He wore nothing but that damp towel. Eventually he was given an orange jumpsuit. He was formally booked, photographed, and fingerprinted. Lastly, he was thrown into a mirrored room.

Brian squirmed in his chair. The interrogation room was too tiny. Too quiet. He thought about what he had done to Alexis.

Cold sweat drenched the jumpsuit. Soon he was soaked. How long had he been sitting here?

*This room is bullshit.*

Where was his phone call? Where was his lawyer? He needed a public defender, yes, but he needed legal counsel!

He struggled against his restraints. He was handcuffed to the chair. The chair in turn was bolted to the ground. He wasn't going anywhere. Thank God he had gone to the bathroom at home.

After an eternity, the door to the tiny room opened. The tall, dark police lady entered with a large manila file under her arm. She was accompanied by that younger cop, who set up a microphone and digital recorder on the table. Judging by his hair, Brian supposed he must have been a Stewart. There were a lot of Stewarts in Monroe's public service sector. This was Brian's first *cop* Stewart.

"Mr. Stanhope. I apologize for the delay. I trust you are comfortable?" The female cop sat across the table from him. She set down the thick manila folder with an ominous thud.

"My name is Lieutenant Cassandra Johnson. I'm a detective with the Monroe County Police Department. You can call me Sandra. This is Officer Cal Stewart. I'm just showing him the ropes." She gave a congenial smile.

Officer Cal Stewart placed the microphone evenly between Brian and Detective Johnson. Brian recoiled from the device. He tried to push himself away from the table. As his chair was bolted to the floor, he didn't get far.

"I know my rights. I'm not saying anything unless I have a lawyer."

"I just need your help." Sandra smiled disarmingly. Officer Stewart sat next to her. The sound of his chair sliding against the concrete floor echoed oppressively.

"You need my help? I'm not going to be much help. I didn't even know Sabrina was dead. As far as I know, she's not dead. I need my lawyer." Brian protested.

"Absolutely. You have the right to an attorney when you're speaking with us." Detective Johnson nodded sagely. "I know you've probably seen things like this on TV a thousand times. I just want to clear up some myths before we get started here. We just record these sessions for our own safety, *and* yours. If you have any questions, please feel free to ask them. Don't be embarrassed. We're here to help."

"Sure. Whatever." Brian grunted. "And my lawyer?"

"We're going to set you up with an attorney. The charges against you sound pretty serious. We want you to have a lawyer every step of the way. Right now, though…this is your time." Sandra smiled again. "Before this whole investigation gets underway, we want you to ask us any questions that you have. We're here for *you* right now."

Brian hadn't expected anything like this at all.

"That's very…*accommodating* of you. You guys start doing this because of Sandra Bland or something?" He asked rudely.

"We're aware of the current perspective of police officers by the public. This is just one of the methods we use to combat the stereotype." Detective Johnson explained. "We're not all trigger-happy racists."

"I don't know too much about political stuff." Brian countered lamely. "Do you know how long I've been in here?"

"You've been in this room about twelve hours."

"Twelve hours?!"

"I apologize personally for the length of time. We're a little shorthanded right now, and with the murder investigation, we're running around like lunatics. I'm sorry you've been in here for so long. That's why I wanted to personally offer you this courtesy." Detective Johnson apologized.

"Twelve hours? Come on. Do you have any idea what goes through a guy's head when you keep them alone for that long?" Brian raised his voice sharply.

"No idea." Detective Johnson shrugged coyly.

"Nothing good!" he answered.

"So I've been told." Detective Johnson reached into the heavy manila folder and pulled out a photograph. She slid it across the table to Brian.

"Do you know who this woman is?" she asked.

Brian blinked. His outraged anxiety morphed into befuddlement. A pit formed in his already upset stomach. Staring up at him, red hair in the wind, blue eyes glowing, was a smiling Christine Smith.

"This isn't Sabrina." Brian said. "This is Christine."

"Who?" Detective Johnson asked. She sounded confused. Officer Stewart perked up in his chair.

"That's Christine Smith. She's my ex-girlfriend." Brian explained. The pit in his stomach grew heavy with fear. "Is she…is she…"

"She's still alive, as far as we know." Detective Johnson grabbed another photograph. "Can you tell me who *this* is?"

Brian stared down at the new photo. He knew this man all too well. He was tan. He had dark curly hair and a perfect complexion. His charming smile would have been the focal point of the photo, had it not been for the prosthetic hook giving a friendly wave to the camera.

"That's Colin. He…Christine and I aren't together anymore. He's her new boyfriend." Brian shifted uncomfortably in the hard, wooden chair.

"I'm sorry to hear that." Detective Johnson appeared to be genuinely saddened. She pulled out another photograph and placed it in front of him.

He knew this person too.

"That's Raoul. He's my brother's boyfriend. He…" Brian's brain put the pieces together.

He started laughing. Detective Johnson and Officer Stewart looked at him as if he were a rare molecule discovered under a microscope. Their expressions only made Brian laugh harder.

"Is that what this is about? *Target?*" Brian cackled, "Oh, man. You guys are like, two years late! Isn't there a statute of limitations on this? Hahaha! Is that what this whole song-and-dance about Sabrina being dead is about? She's not dead, by the way. *Man!* Once they made pot legal you all had to make a show about doing real police work? Is that it? Hahahaha!"

"Do you mind if I read you something?" Detective Johnson asked.

She pulled out a stack of papers from the folder. She held them up like a schoolgirl presenting a book report. She cleared her throat.

"Let me guess: the transcript from the security cameras? A pieced together recollection of my tirade penned by Christine, Colin, and Raoul? Go ahead. Read it. It's not like it's been playing in my mind constantly over the last ten days." Brian smirked.

Detective Johnson began to read:

"*The redhead lay twisted and broken. She slumped over the crumpled steering wheel, suspended only by her seatbelt. Life drained out of her wound. Her vision grew dark and blurry. Her extremities twitched uselessly in a feeble attempt to save her life. Her consciousness began to fade. Her final thoughts scattered themselves across her dying mind…*"

Brian froze in fear and disbelief. His heart imploded. His eyes widened as Detective Johnson continued to read:

"*Her train of thought was derailed by a bloodied hook piercing her left shoulder. She screamed. Her broken arms flailed wildly, but to no avail. The charming, sensual smile of the hitchhiker loomed inches from her face. Her blood ran cold at his calm expression. He winked. 'Stranger danger.' He covered her mouth and nose..."*

"Stop." Brian said.

Detective Johnson did so. She looked up, expressionless. Brian tried to catch his breath.

"Where did you find that? Did you guys search my computer?" he sputtered.

*Fuck.* He hadn't deleted his writing!

"I'm going to show you another photograph. Is that okay?" Detective Johnson asked.

"No."

She ignored Brian's protest. She placed another picture in front of him. When Brian saw the image, he gagged as ice formed in his throat.

The battered, broken dead body of Sabrina Cunningham lay in dirty snow. Her one eye stared up at Brian as he sat handcuffed in his chair. Her skull had been caved in. Her face was nearly unrecognizable. A large bite had been taken out of her throat. Brian stared unblinking into the mass of torn, frozen flesh under her jaw. Sabrina's shoes were missing, her fishnet covered feet rested lifelessly in the dirt.

The horrible realization of what he was accused of dawned on him. He opened his mouth, but no words came out. All thought fled from him. Terror gripped him. His legs went numb. His penis shriveled up inside him. He died alongside Sabrina.

Detective Johnson began to read again:

*"He arched his head backwards, still smiling. He bit into her jugular. Echo saw her crimson blood splatter onto the sand. She knew that the pain didn't matter anymore. Her grey eyes closed one last time. The final sensation Echo felt was disappointment. She would never know what it was like to walk all over dry land..."*

"STOP! Just stop! That's enough! No more...no more..."

Brian's tears poured freely down his face. His lips trembled. No further words came out.

Detective Johnson laid the Echo commission on the table. Photographs and papers spiraled over the wood. Sandra merely waved her hands over the clutter, demonstrating what a mess Brian had gotten himself into.

"We need your help, Brian. We just need you to tell us what's going on here."

"It's not...I didn't...I didn't kill Sabrina. These are just art pieces. They're fiction...they don't mean anything."

"So, you are *DeathbringerBob*?"

"...Yes."

"What's up with all the biting in your stories?"

"What?"

"Is it true that your mom was concerned about your teeth?" Detective Johnson asked.

"...I didn't bite anyone. I would never..." Brian stammered.

"Would you get angry at your mom when she brought up your teeth?"

"I mean, yeah, but who likes having an overbearing-?"

"You got pretty violent at Target after Christine ended her liaison with you." Detective Johnson leaned forward in her chair.

"That was...a moment of weakness..." Brian whimpered.

"Was choking Alexis Knabusch a moment of weakness as well?"

Brian did not reply. His tears dried. Panic overwhelmed him.

"What did Alexis do to piss you off?" Detective Johnson asked.

Brian breathed heavily.

"Did Sabrina piss you off when she found your Patreon?" she continued.

Brian's lungs failed.

"The Keeners told us you became *quite* physically threatening."

"I just buy drugs and hacked phones from Talon, that's all." Brian gasped, "You want some real shit, you should look into him, this...this all here...is nothing. What you're saying happened, never happened."

"Why did you bite Sabrina's throat out? What's the significance of Ash Township?"

"I don't-"

Johnson drew forth another page. She read again:

*"That's when the hook pierced her back. She was pulled horribly close to the young man's face. She tried to cry out, but the hook snared her lung, driving the air from her in a bloody spout. His teeth sunk into her neck. Her jugular hit the forest floor. The last thing she felt was her legs giving way..."*

"FOR THE LOVE OF GOD, STOP!" Brian exploded.

"Did Sabrina make you angry? Or was she just an easy target? Another stand in for all the women who hurt you over the years?" Detective Johnson asked.

"It's not like that!" He feared he would pass out like he had with the judge. "This is just...those stories...the snuff...it's just smut...I just write...I just use real life to help me write. Every writer does that! Even erotica writers."

"Real life? Like real murders?"

"No! Well, people like serial killers but I am *not-*"

"If you're just writing, why use an illegally modified phone?"

"My clients like their privacy! This stuff isn't something you just shout from the rooftops!"

"Do you pleasure yourself to your own writing?"

"Oh my God..." Brian's vision began to blur.

"Do you?"

"I'm good at what I do! I find peril fetishism attractive! It's not a crime! No one gets hurt!"

"You use real life for stories? How so?" Detective Johnson's questioning was merciless. Had he not been so emotional, Brian might have realized how screwed he was.

"It's just...I mean...*come on*...I..." his voice broke.

"Did you kill Sabrina because she knew you were *DeathbringerBob*, or were you trying to get some fresh inspiration for your ...*commissions?*"

"I DID NOT KILL SABRINA!" Brian screamed.

"Really? Then can you please tell me where you went after Big John kicked you off his property?" Detective Johnson hit Brian with a withering glare.

"I went into the woods."

"Why?"

"I don't know! I was high on Ketamine! I was just trying to find my car!" Brian felt the icy fear merge with his anxiety. The millipede in his spine would bust out of him and eat his frozen remains.

"Big John saw you the next morning stumbling out of the woods. What were you doing in the forest?"

"I don't know! I heard screaming! I passed out. I hit something. I didn't kill her."

"You say you don't remember?"

"I don't know!"

"Isn't it possible that under the effects of mind-altering substances, you lost control and let your freak flag fly?"

"No. I didn't do it." Brian gritted his teeth. "I'm not saying anything else without a lawyer."

"Excellent. That is your right. I think we've got what we need for now. I look forward to interviewing you again." Detective Johnson smiled.

Her partner reached over and turned off the recorder.

Realizing what was on the tape; Brian lunged at Officer Stewart. His handcuffs, still attached to the chair, which was still bolted to the floor, stopped him. He tore his skin against the hot steel, screaming incoherently until a team of guards dragged him to his cell.

# XX

This was the worst life Brian Stanhope had ever lived. The narrative spun by the police not only seemed plausible, but probable. He had killed Sabrina. The more he dwelled on it, the truer it became. Every memory was a steppingstone towards her death.

The morning after his interrogation, a public defender visited his cell. Mark Navarre was a short, bespectacled young man of sturdy Frenchtown stock. Navarre was not happy that Brian had spoken to the police.

"Let me guess, they told you that they *were here for you*. That this *isn't* like what they do on TV, or some other bull?" Navarre was sweating profusely. He couldn't have been older than Brian, but he dabbed his forehead with a handkerchief like some perturbed old man.

"Yeah..."

"That's the oldest interrogation trick in the book! Why didn't you keep telling them that you wanted a lawyer?" Navarre paced back and forth.

Brian morosely lay on his bed, thoughts devouring his sanity.

"You know...I been thinking. Girls used to come up to me. They willingly flirted with me. I was kind of cute at one point. Isn't that weird?" Brian stared at the ceiling, lost in an epiphany discovered too late.

Mark Navarre slammed Brian's bunk with such force that it threatened to disconnect from the wall. Brian bolted upright, meeting the furious expression on the lawyer's face. He shriveled beneath the attorney's wrath.

"Listen to me! They are painting you as a disturbed individual with a history of problems with women...someone who *fantasizes* about killing them...and when a woman found out about this; you finally acted on your urges under the cover of night." Navarre explained. "Everything you told them yesterday *will* be brought up in court. I come in here and find you raving like a crazy person about girls flirting with you. Are you stupid? Or did you actually kill that girl?"

"Hey man, I thought you were here to help me, why are you yelling?" Brian's head throbbed. He wanted to smoke.

"I *am* trying to help you. I'm going to be real with you: I'm a public defender. I have a duty to serve everyone on my docket. I have a lot of clients. You have a media shitstorm on your ass. I have limited resources to help you, and if you can't help me, you don't stand a chance."

"Well, I'll hire another lawyer."

"With what money?" Navarre laughed in cold frustration. "They seized your bank account. They're trying to see if a real serial killer hired you."

"Well, I'll sell my car."

"They took that too. Civil forfeiture. If they think the car was used to transport evidence away from the scene of the crime, *which they do*, they can take it. You'll never see it again."

"Well, what about my computer?" Brian suggested, "It's worth at least two grand."

"Civil forfeiture. All your murder smut is on it." Navarre shook his head.

"Wow, civil forfeiture is fucked up." Brian replied.

"Be that as it may, it's the reality of the situation. Right now, your options are me, or you can represent yourself." Navarre's face was uncomfortably close to Brian's. "Now: what do you want to do?"

"I'll take you." Brian winced.

"Good." Navarre leaned back. He stared into Brian's eyes. "Now, I need to know, because this will help me finagle what I can do for you: did you kill Sabrina Cunningham?"

"I don't think so."

"You don't *THINK* so???" Navarre exploded. "You're *done* if you say *that* in court."

"No...no I didn't." Brian thought his denial felt like a lie.

"Good. If you didn't kill her, there won't be any DNA evidence, right?"

"Yeah...makes sense." Brian nodded.

"Great. You're not as dumb as you look." Navarre composed himself, "You've got a hearing today. You're going to be formally arraigned. As repulsive as I find your little *novellas*, I'm going to argue that they are artistic creations with no semblance to reality. I will move to have the case against you dismissed. The judge will deny the dismissal. The prosecution will want your blood samples. They will also move to have a mold of your teeth made."

"Why would they do that?" Brian asked.

146

"You saw the bite on Sabrina's throat. They want to see if they can match up your teeth to the wound." Navarre continued. "Now, if you really didn't kill her, the bite won't match up. We will not contest the order to take physical evidence from you. We will comply. Got it?"

"I guess." Brian mumbled.

"Now, let me do all the talking. Don't say anything." Navarre demanded, "Also, they're going to put you in a bulletproof vest."

"Why?" Brian asked.

"If *I* think you're a pervert, and I'm on *your* side mind you, how do you think the people who *believe* you killed Sabrina are going to react?"

"Wouldn't killing me be like, *kink-shaming*, you know?" Brian asked, thinking of Alexis.

"I don't know what the fuck that is, so you better not say that shit in front of the judge." Navarre angrily exited Cell 1-13.

As the public defender foretold, a pair of guards placed Brian in a bulletproof vest. He was surprised at how uncomfortably heavy it was. It complimented the state of his tortured mind.

The courthouse and county jail were connected by an interior walkway, so there was little threat of a sniper's bullet killing Brian. Even so, a retinue of guards walked in tandem beside him. Mark Navarre did his best to repel reporters, who were waiting in ambush inside the hall of justice.

The courtroom was packed with spectators. It was as if the entire population of Monroe had come to judge him. They looked at him as if he were a strange, dangerous animal captured from another land.

"They couldn't get in without going through metal detectors. Don't worry." Navarre quietly reassured Brian.

Brian knew that if given the chance, one of the spectators *would* try their luck, but they would not kill him because they hated him. They would kill him out of a sense of duty. He was a rabid dog that needed to be put to sleep.

When the judge called court to order, Brian only looked down at his shoes. He said nothing. He let Navarre do all the talking.

Navarre argued that Brian was merely a fiction writer, who wrote for a peculiar brand of people, and that nothing he had written had any connection to real-life. Navarre moved for the case to be dropped. The judge denied the motion to dismiss. The prosecution moved to take a mold of Brian's teeth. They wanted his blood too. Navarre acquiesced to their demands.

Brian didn't really pay close attention. He thought about Sabrina. Had he really lost control? Had he done the unthinkable? Hadn't he done it before? In his fiction? He looked at his white jail shoes. He thought of barefoot Echo.

Over the next few days, Dr. Finley the coroner, and a dentist, Dr. Gonzalez, visited Brian in the county jail. They took him to an examination room, where they duplicated his mouth. They worked wordlessly, treating Brian as just another specimen.

At first, Brian wanted to talk to them. He recognized Dr. Gonzalez as one of the many dentists from his childhood. Unfortunately, Brian was unable to communicate. His mouth was pried open so that plasticine models of his teeth could be formed.

The medical professionals spent weeks trying different methods to form Brian's bite. First, they tried making a single mold all at once. Then they tried each tooth individually. Each session caused Brian to spiral deeper into despair.

Detective Johnson and Officer Stewart continued to interview Brian. Having learned his lesson, Brian only spoke when Navarre was present, but it was futile. The damage had been done.

There were more hearings, but the weight of the bulletproof vest never became familiar or comfortable. Brian was positive the vest was another punishment meted out against him. The mute onlookers in the court grew malcontent, doing nothing to pacify his anxiety.

By February, Brian realized his only hobby was staring out his cell window. He had not been outside since November. The full trial was scheduled to begin at the end of March.

Navarre's visits grew less frequent. When he did show up, the public defender always made sure to note how gross and detestable Brian's writings were. He said they would be the key evidence against him.

Sam had not visited once. He had called a few times, but his calls were short and curt. Sam only spoke of the legal and financial issues relating to the care of their mother. He never asked how Brian was doing. Sam knew he was guilty too.

Staring out his cell window, tears rolled down Brian's face. His anxiety, regret, and guilt convinced him he had killed Sabrina. The legal procedure was just political posturing. His sadness deepened with every passing minute. He feared he would kill himself if he got too sad.

"Hey."

Brian wiped his tears away. Yellow sunlight combined with overhead fluorescent bulbs to illuminate his cell. He saw no one.

*Great, I really am crazy.* He thought he might cry again.

"You okay, buddy?"

The voice came from beyond the bars of the neighboring cell. The large, black man in the blue-burrito rolled feebly over to the iron barrier. He seemed concerned.

"Why are you crying?" The man asked.

The guy had messy hair, and a scraggly beard. His eyes, usually wild with insanity, now held a soft gleam. Brian wept. He had not seen concern in nearly half a year.

"Sorry, I just…I think I fucked up." Brian sobbed.

"Man, who hasn't fucked up? What are you in for?" The man in the blue-burrito asked.

"Murder." Brian replied quietly.

"Damn. Did you do it?"

"I don't know."

"Damn…I'm Al." The man answered.

"Brian."

"Do you want to talk about it, Brian?" Al tried to roll closer, but the weight of the blue-burrito kept him where he was.

Brian looked down at Al, seeing only curiosity in the man's face.

"Why not?" Brian rubbed his tears until they were gone. "Well, I didn't want to kill anybody. But I think all these…*things*…ate away at me until I *did* kill someone."

"What do you mean?"

"Like…I write murder themed erotica. It's known as like…a hardcore peril fetish, if you want to be polite." Brian explained.

"Like necrophilia?" Al asked.

"No. That's like…someone who's already dead gets fucked. I used to get requests to write that stuff, but I never did. Not for me. I liked snuff better."

"For sure. Kinda like autassassinophilia?" Al suggested.

"Holy shit, you know what that is?" Brian gasped.

Al nodded.

"You liked writing about killing people?" Al asked.

149

"…yeah. The taboo of it was a thrill. It was like…something just for me, you know?" Brian continued.

"I can get that." Al smiled.

"I never wanted to *hurt* anyone. I got high once, and I choked someone on accident. I didn't want to hurt them, though." Brian shamefully recollected.

"Well, shit." Al chuckled. "It sounds like you're just fantasizing. That shit don't hurt people."

"But it did! I just told you I choked someone." Brian countered.

"You said yourself it was an accident. What happened?" Al asked.

"Well, I was in a K-hole, and I wanted to kiss her, but I grabbed her by the throat when I went for it. I didn't mean it."

"There you go, motherfucker. You didn't mean it! Intention is everything. There's a difference between being a little uncoordinated and wanting to strangle the life out of someone. Isn't that right?" Al offered.

"I guess…" Brian hesitated.

"What's wrong?"

"…intention doesn't equal impact."

"Brian, drugs and emotional hang-ups hurt people. Fantasy don't hurt people." Al argued.

"That's what my readers used to say." Brian sighed. "I never wanted to hurt anybody. Ever. Really. That's the truth."

"Well, your *readers* or whoever they are…they're right! You're just fighting against something that's normal. It's different, sure, but it's no different than if you were gay or something. Don't be afraid to be who you are!" Al exclaimed.

"You don't think it's repulsive, or gross, or dark, or fucked up?" Brian was astonished.

"It's not for me to judge!" Al laughed. "You want to know why I'm in here?"

"Why?"

"I fuck sheep." Al answered plainly.

"No way."

"I'm serious. Best feeling in the world. The world is hard and cold. Sheep are soft and warm. I didn't choose to be this way. You didn't choose to be the way you are either. You just gotta accept your sheep." Al declared.

"That's the problem!" Brian shouted. "Like...I feel like *this*: say I have this fantasy, and I write about this fantasy. I make money off it, so I continue to do it. Aren't I just chipping away at the mental barrier that is preventing me from acting on it and hurting someone?"

"Man, they got you fucked up." Al snorted. "Here's the thing: Life is not a continuum. Say you're feeling sad: you don't get sadder and sadder until you '*break a barrier*' and kill yourself. The key is that you *don't want* to kill yourself. So you never do it! That's the difference between you and me. I *want* to fornicate with sheep. I did so regularly. You don't actually want to hurt anyone, even if you did '*choke someone on accident*' or whatever you've convinced yourself happened. Don't be afraid of these people who say you're a threat. You don't get worse and worse until you go crazy. Your psyche is not a slippery slope. If you were really going to hurt someone, you would've been carving up cats as a kid or some shit. You *don't want* to kill anyone, so you won't."

Hearing this, Brian no longer felt anxious. The millipede shriveled up. The force punching his brain went away. The intrusive thoughts were silent.

His mind grew light. He began to chuckle. His chuckles became full blown laughs. His tears of sorrow turned into tears of joy and relief. He felt alive.

"Thank you...I'm sorry...I just...no one's ever told me that before."

Sabrina entered Brian's mind again. This time, he didn't see her corpse. He saw her playfulness, her goofy grin, her talent, her spacey demeanor. She had once been alive. He had wanted her to stay alive. He couldn't keep Sabrina alive anymore, but he could make sure her memory got the peace it deserved.

"What are you thinking right now?" Al asked from the blue-burrito.

"This girl everyone says I killed...she was a friend. I want to help her. I can't bring her back from the dead, but maybe I know something that the police overlooked...I don't actually know for sure, but I gotta think." The wheels in Brian's mind turned with sober clarity.

"I think that'd be very productive." Al smiled.

"Hey...were you a therapist or something?" Brian asked.

"Nailed it." Al winked.

151

"Damn, you're really good. Or at least I think you are. I've never seen a shrink before. Especially not one who's into bestiality." Brian said.

"I'm not trying to condone it or nothing! I know what I do is fucked up, but I accept that I want to do it." Al laughed. "Sheep fucking is fucked up. I just accept it for what it is. Don't think about it too hard."

"You've been here for a while, right Al?" Brian asked. "What's the punishment for bestiality?"

"It's the lightest felony in the state of Michigan." Al explained. "All these beatings I give these motherfuckers keep extending my stay."

"Why don't you just go with it and let them do whatever they need to do to you so you can get out of here?"

"You gotta be true to yourself despite adversity. Even if you know you're going to fail. That's the *Myth of Sisyphus*, nigga."

"*The Myth of Sisyphus?* The story about the guy rolling a rock up a hill forever?"

"Yup. Find joy in the struggle, my man."

"I don't think you're applying that parable correctly." Brian shook his head with a laugh.

"Brian, I'm fucked up. You're not fucked up. If you accept yourself and remember that your thoughts are not a one-way ticket to murder, you're going to be fine. You just have a little anxiety and some OCD, that's all. Just let it be. Accept your sheep."

Footsteps echoed down the hall. The guards were coming for Al's evening meal and sponge bath. Al growled.

"Speaking of letting it be…" Al began to scream at the guards as they entered Cell 1-12.

"YOU MOTHERFUCKERS! CALLING ME A NIGGER AGAIN! THE ACLU AND NAACP ARE GOING TO RAPE YOUR BITCH ASSES! COME GET ME YOU MOTHERFUCKERS!"

Brian watched the debacle unfold. The guards undid the blue-burrito. Al leapt to his feet, throwing punches. He was wrestled back to the concrete floor.

As Al's swearing faded into powerless moans, Brian couldn't help but admire his unlikely friend's defiance. Al was crazy, no doubt about it. However, the wisdom in the man's tilted words warmed Brian as nothing had ever warmed him before.

He was normal. The path to a murder was not a continuum. He had not killed Sabrina Cunningham.

# XXI

Had Sandra Johnson been more up to date on her millennial lingo, she might have thought she was living her worst life.

"Can we run the tests again? Take another mold?" She asked with injured pride.

"We've run the diagnostics fifteen times." Dr. Finley shook his head. "Sandra, I'm sorry. There is no physically possible way he killed Sabrina."

Finley's desk drowned in meticulously organized evidence. The bright overhead lights reflected garishly off the perfectly copied teeth. Sandra fumed. She couldn't stand to be near those little plasticine teeth anymore. She had spent too many hours examining those denticles for them to be discarded anticlimactically.

Dr. Finley sat in his chair. He removed his glasses and cleaned them slowly. Behind the coroner, leaning against the wall, was Raymond Hoppert.

Hoppert was the District Attorney prosecuting Stanhope's case. Well, he *should* have been prosecuting it. He surely wasn't prosecuting it now. Sandra thought that the tall, balding Monroe native in his overly tight grey suit was worse than useless. He had never been farther from Monroe than Dundee. The man thought that *Cabela's* was the pinnacle of human achievement.

"We should motion to exhume her body. Run the tests again." Sandra demanded.

"Sandra, I know you trust your gut, but look at the evidence. That poor girl's barely been in the ground. There's no way the judge will allow that motion." Hoppert argued.

"Raymond, you read that pervert's backlog. I am telling you: he is our guy." Sandra argued.

"Those snuff stories or whatever they are, disturbing as they may be, are nothing but circumstantial evidence." Hoppert disagreed.

"Damn it, Raymond! You know as well as I-"

"*I* know that without any DNA evidence linking him to the scene of the crime, no jury in the world is going to convict him." Hoppert idly toyed with a vial of blood from the desk.

"For Christ's sake, Alexis Knabusch *heard* Sabrina bring up the Patreon account *to* him-"

"-which Navarre is going to argue is hearsay. Your argument that Sabrina knew he was *DeathbringerBob* is unsubstantiated conjecture. Every judge in the world would-" Hoppert began.

"World, world, world! When's the last time you went out and saw the world?" Sandra shouted.

"Raymond, Sandra, please..." Dr. Finley begged. His colleagues ignored him.

"I know these jurors. They aren't the backwoods yokels you think they are. They *can* discern the truth." Hoppert defended. "Brian Stanhope's teeth do not match the wound in Sabrina Cunningham's neck. Not only are his fingerprints and DNA *not* present at the crime scene; *someone else's* are! What's *worse*, we have no clue *who* that DNA belongs to! It's not in any national registry! The jury *is* going to pick up on all this, and you can be damn sure Mark Navarre will too."

"So what? Navarre is just some public defender. How many open dockets does that man have again?" Sandra interjected.

"He may be young, inexperienced, and overworked, but he's not stupid. This is an open and shut case for him." Hoppert answered.

"What about all the witnesses? The affidavits? The testimony?" Sandra countered.

"I think you mean *character* witnesses. Not one person saw him go off alone with Sabrina Cunningham at that party." Hoppert groaned.

"His own brother was ready to turn him in, for Christ's sake!"

"Just because he has a bad reputation doesn't mean he's guilty." Hoppert folded his arms.

"If people have a bad opinion of the misogynistic bastard, then we should be able to nail him easy!" Lieutenant Johnson pounded the desk.

"Sandra, do you care about the truth? Or do you just want to stroke your ego?" Hoppert retorted. "I swear, you think you're above everyone because you're from the *big city*. Jurors don't ignore cold hard facts. Especially once DNA gets introduced. No amount of gossip, hearsay, or news segments featuring evidence *you* leaked to the press is going to change that."

"Ludington is *NOT* a big city!" Sandra snarled indignantly.

She believed letting those two psychiatrists examine Brian Stanhope's writing on-air had been a master stroke. Apparently, Raymond Hoppert thought otherwise. She scrambled to bring up anything that might convince Hoppert to pick up the case.

"We had that anonymous tip!" Sandra recalled the mysterious email in her personal inbox.

"That tip is unsubstantiated. Sure, it looked strong at the beginning of the case, but no one can contact that individual. They could have been some internet troll. You can be sure Navarre will paint them that way." Hoppert frowned.

"What if we motion for a change of venue?" Sandra asked.

"We could motion to hold a trial in Timbuktu for all I care. It won't alter the fact that there is no earthly way Brian Stanhope laid a finger on Sabrina Cunningham." Hoppert's old blue eyes grew sad. "He's a messed-up sicko, but he's not a killer."

"He choked Alexis Knabusch!" Lieutenant Johnson thrust a finger at the D.A.

"He didn't leave a mark on her. Assault charges need evidence. Evidence we don't have." The prosecutor shrugged.

"I don't believe this." Sandra muttered.

"I'm sorry, Sandra. We gotta let him go before this looks worse for us." Hoppert continued. "This is an election year, remember?"

Sandra was ready to explode. Her entire investigation had been for naught. Her pride bled. She kicked the table angrily. Neither Hoppert nor Dr. Finley reacted to the physical outburst.

"Surely we missed something. There were so many people at that party. Someone else must have been acting strangely that night." Dr. Finley offered cautiously.

"What about those American Guard guys? They're trouble." Hoppert suggested.

"The American Guard doesn't fit the profile." Sandra glared. "They're a white nationalist group. The last person they'd want to murder is an all-American, blonde, blue-eyed white girl near their home turf. If Cunningham had been Muslim, or Black, or Latino, I'd say you might be on to something."

"Maybe they accidentally killed her? Gave her some bad meth or black tar?" Hoppert scratched his head.

"We didn't find any traces of meth or heroin during the autopsy. There was alcohol and marijuana in her blood, and a little Special K, but nothing deadly." Dr. Finley interjected.

"Special K? Like the cereal?" Hoppert asked. "Your tests are getting crazy accurate."

Sandra and Dr. Finley both stared at the District Attorney for a moment.

"Hoppert...no. *Special K* is a slang term for *Ketamine*." Sandra facepalmed.

"Oh." To his credit, Hoppert looked embarrassed.

"A drug deal gone bad, maybe?" Dr. Finley adjusted the molds of Brian's large canine teeth.

"They wouldn't have tried to hide her body. The American Guard like to make examples of people who cross them." Sandra explained.

"So, it could have been anyone." Hoppert's face grew dark.

"I'm not saying it's a stone whodunit. I'm *saying* that Brian Stanhope is still the best lead we've got." Sandra declared.

"That is not going to happen, no matter how much pressure the damn Housing Commission puts on us. It wasn't him." Said Hoppert.

"You think I'm kowtowing to those pencil pushers?! Think more highly of me than *that,* Raymond. Stanhope is guilty as sin." Lieutenant Johnson's pride rallied.

"He's guilty of being a degenerate. He's like a furry or something. We can't link him to anything more sinister than that." Hoppert exasperated.

"Sandra, he's right. I've triple checked every bite mark, fingerprint, and drop of blood. It wasn't Stanhope." Dr. Finley softly said.

"What if he staged the crime scene? To throw us off?" Sandra pleaded.

"You and I both know there's no evidence of that." Dr. Finley set down the canines.

"His mom kept going on about him being a child prodigy or something. He's smart. He's educated." She knew she was grasping at straws now.

Her desperation hurt. It was like the air was being driven from her lungs. Her temples burned.

"I love Monroe, but let's be honest, it doesn't take much to get straight A's at Monroe Public Schools." Hoppert scoffed. "Sandra: You've done a great job. I'm going to meet with the judge and Mark Navarre. They both owe me a favor. We can get them to turn Stanhope loose without too much fanfare."

Hoppert gently placed a hand on Sandra's shoulder. The gesture was surely meant to be comforting, but Sandra felt liked she had been scarred with a cattle brand. She recoiled.

"Raymond, you're making a mistake." she growled.

"I'm not." He lifted his hand from her shoulder, but the burning sensation remained. "Take a few days off. Come back and look at the case with a fresh pair of eyes."

The District Attorney, who was up for re-election, exited the coroner's office, leaving the door open behind him. As soon as he was gone, Dr. Finley sighed. He rose from his seat. He silently walked over to his coat rack and grabbed his belongings. He was defeated.

A wave of impotent anger crashed over Sandra.

"Finley, come on. You've seen what I've seen." Her shame was venomous.

"I'm not sure I did." Dr. Finley replied.

"The Cunninghams are your friends! Don't you owe them justice?"

"That's what I intend to give them. Nailing the wrong guy isn't a viable interpretation of the word. Neither is letting him rot in jail next to that sheepfucker."

"I think the pervert wing is exactly where that animal belongs."

Dr Finley gave a small smile.

"Come on, let's get some coffee. Then you should go home. Spend some time with Ralph. Check on those horses you two are raising. We can come back in a few days. We'll get the right guy." Dr. Finley suggested.

He meekly brushed past her. He too left the door open behind him. His footsteps echoed away. Soon, the faint, monotonous doldrums of the police station were all that could be heard.

Detective Sandra Johnson clenched her hands into vengeful fists. She glared at the molds of the teeth. Those fake, vicious canines were mocking her. She had been so close. Her aching pride tore into her. In her fervor to prosecute Stanhope, she had embarrassed herself in front of her colleagues.

*Unforgivable.*

Doubts slowly entered her mind. Had she really misread the evidence? The irrefutable lack of DNA, and what's more, the presence of *mystery* DNA certainly indicated so.

Despite that, there wasn't anything about Brian Stanhope that she liked. What he wrote was irreparably fucked. His worldview must have been tilted beyond recognition. She would see to it that he suffered for that.

Still, Finley and Hoppert had a point: Stanhope's teeth hadn't ended Sabrina's life. Was there someone out there that was even worse of a monster than he was?

Sandra Johnson closed her eyes and shuddered.

# XXII

"In like a lion, out like a lamb." Al observed.

"Certainly true." Brian agreed.

"Hell of a thunderstorm. Haven't slept all night. Hail hasn't helped." Al maneuvered as close to the bars as the blue burrito would allow.

"Reminds me of my film student days. One of my shorts got rained out for a week straight. March, huh?" Brian sighed.

"You did movies?"

"I wanted to. I did a couple commercials before coming home."

"Who was your favorite director?"

"Brian De Palma."

"Heh."

"What?"

"I get the snuff fascination now."

The storm slowly died down. March's weather was unpredictable, but thunderstorms this early were surely a herald of climate change. Brian wondered if climate change would affect him if he were to remain a prisoner for the rest of his life.

"What's on your mind, Brian?" Al asked.

"My trial's coming up soon." Brian frowned. "My lawyer hasn't visited…my brother hasn't called in a while…and there's no fucking music in here."

"Accept your sheep. Ruminating is not productive. Besides, isn't that him now?"

Brian's cell door clanged open. Mark Navarre and Officer Cal Stewart stood in its entryway. The public defender smiled as he clutched an umbrella and briefcase under one arm. Officer Stewart carefully avoided eye contact with Brian.

"Great news, Brian: You're free to go!" Navarre beamed.

The words did not make sense to Brian's ears.

"Free...to go? Like to trial? Do I not have to wear the bullet-proof vest anymore?" he blinked in confusion.

"No! The case has been dismissed. The physical evidence overwhelmingly proves your innocence." The public defender explained.

"But...you always said I was creepy...or...worse."

"Creepiness notwithstanding, our plan worked out." Navarre motioned for Brian to follow. "Come on! I'll debrief you on our way out. Let's get you out of those blues."

It took Brian a moment to realize Navarre was referring to his bright orange jumpsuit. He looked forward to wearing normal clothes. The jumpsuit was itchy, and a stale smell clung to the fabric no matter how many times he washed it.

Cautiously optimistic, Brian took apprehensive steps towards freedom. He half expected Officer Stewart to taze him the second he set foot outside his cell. He braced for tens of thousands of volts of electricity to wrack his body.

"Let's go!" Navarre impatiently tapped his foot on the concrete floor.

Brian stepped into the corridor unaided. Nothing happened. He smiled. He followed Navarre and Officer Stewart. He was finally free.

"Brian! Don't forget!" Al called out. "Accept your sheep!"

Brian, too bewildered and overjoyed to speak, merely responded with a nod. Satisfied, Al rolled back into the recesses of his cell. Brian would miss the strange man.

Mark Navarre shot Brian a quizzical glance.

"What was that all about?" he asked.

"Being yourself. *The Myth of Sisyphus* too." Brian replied.

"I wouldn't take advice from *that* guy. He's more fucked up than *you*." Navarre rolled his eyes.

The other prisoners stirred. Some taunted Brian. He didn't care. He would never see them again.

The young Officer Stewart led them out of the cell block. He keyed the large double door to the outside world. With an electronic buzz, a pair of guards ushered them all through.

Brian found himself in a large, carpeted room populated with desks. Police officers busily typed away on computers. A few were on formal phone calls. The room smelled like burnt coffee and Ballistol. Brian had been booked in this place.

He felt the gaze of the other public servants in the room. A brief hush fell. Mark Navarre feigned an impatient cough. The clerical hubbub resumed, but Brian still felt eyes on his back.

On the far side of the big room, a large evidence lock-up sat behind a long counter. Officer Stewart shuffled inside through steel-cage doors, leaving Navarre and Brian awkwardly waiting for him. Brian eventually lost sight of the young cop behind columns of meticulously labeled boxes.

After some time, Stewart returned with Brian's towel, wallet, and house keys.

"This is what I've been authorized to release." he set the items on the rough-hewn countertop.

"What the hell is this?" Mark Navarre picked up the towel with disgust.

"That is the…*article of clothing*…the suspect…er…Mr. Stanhope was wearing at the time of his arrest." Officer Stewart explained hesitantly.

"It's storming out there! Don't you have some other *articles of clothing* he can use?" Navarre snidely asked.

"I'll double check."

Officer Stewart re-entered the evidence lock-up. After a tense fifteen minutes, he returned with an assortment of clothes. He laid down a plain grey hoodie, a white undershirt, a pair of blue jeans, some heavily worn socks, and a pair of brown work boots.

"These are unclaimed articles Mr. Stanhope can wear." The cop said.

"Do I have to change here?" Brian asked, keenly aware of the spectacle that was being made.

"Unfortunately, due to protocol, yes." Officer Stewart contemptuously confirmed.

*Fuck it. Let them look. Accept* this *sheep, bitches.* Brian thought with a smirk.

The white undershirt was a little tight. The grey hoodie was a little large. The jeans were far too short in the leg. The socks threatened to come apart at the seams. The shoes cramped Brian's toes. After nearly five months in the can, Brian thought it was the most comfortable outfit he'd ever worn.

He pocketed his house keys. Inside his brown leather wallet, he found only his ID and one credit card. He thrust the empty wallet at Officer Stewart accusingly.

"There was $200.00 cash in here in November."

"Civil forfeiture. You can enter a claim to retrieve your seized personal property. Make sure you fill out the appropriate forms in triplicate and have a property attorney submit the claims with the

D.A.'s office by the specified date on line 3-F." Officer Stewart handed Brian a healthy stack of documents.

"Civil forfeiture! Of course! What a bitch." Brian cursed and looked at Navarre. "I suppose you don't-"

"Public defenders are criminal lawyers, not property lawyers." Navarre shook his head. "I can send you some referrals. Let's get the hell out of here."

Navarre made his way to the enclosure connecting the police station to City Hall. Brian did not follow. He stared at Officer Stewart. The young cop looked incredibly ill-at-ease.

"Brian! Come on!" Navarre cried.

"Just a minute!"

Brian leaned over the countertop, maintaining eye contact with the young cop. For the first time, Brian saw he really was only a kid. He had anxiety, fear, and a little hatred in his youthful eyes.

Brian thought carefully before he spoke:

"Listen, I'm being let go. That means I'm innocent in the eyes of the law, right?" he asked.

"As far as the investigation has determined, yes." Officer Stewart scowled.

"Ok...does that mean Sabrina's killer is still out there?"

"It would appear that way."

"All right...I don't know too much, but I was at that party too. Sabrina was my friend. I don't know who killed her, but there were all these guys there in camo jackets and stuff. I think they're...*American Guard*, maybe? They're wannabe Ku Klux Klan anarchists or some shit. Take a look at them. They might know something." Brian explained in hushed tones.

"We will take that under advisement." Officer Stewart replied, his voice drenched in barely veiled annoyance.

"Please do. I'm serious."

Brian was not convinced that he had been understood. He turned away from the green police officer, leaving the civil forfeiture forms behind. As he stepped out of the precinct, he swore he heard Stewart say "*Stanhope*" into his walkie-talkie.

Navarre was the only other person in the enclosed hallway. The air was tense. Neither man spoke to the other.

"Listen, Mark, thank-" Brian began, trying to break the ice.

"Don't mention it. *Really*. We'll talk in my office. I might have to clear some room for you. The place is drowning in cases."

As Navarre and Brian exited the enclosed walkway, they were met by four reporters. Two held large video cameras, the other two, microphones. Brian recognized the logos of the *Monroe Evening News* and the *Toledo Blade* on the reporters' press passes.

Navarre's cheeks flushed deep red.

"That fucking snake." Navarre swore under his breath. "We agreed there would be no press!"

"What? Who?" Brian asked.

The four reporters descended.

"Mr. Stanhope! What can you tell us about-?"

"Is it true that you wrote a peril fic about-?"

"Do you know who killed-?"

"What do you think your mother would-?"

"No comment at this time, thank you!" Navarre shouted, pushing his way past the journalists.

Brian quickly followed suit. The reporters were right on their heels. Their questions ricocheted like arrows against a castle wall.

Navarre led Brian to the front entrance of the courthouse.

"Aren't we going to your office?" Brian asked as quietly as he could.

"They'd hear us there. No room to sit anyway. Too much paperwork." Navarre responded under his breath.

"Are you really that overworked?"

"Do you know what it's like to be a Public Defender in the United States?"

"A friend told me once…. she's kind of a social-justice-warrior, so I didn't believe her." Brian dimly recalled an Alexis rant.

"Your friend is very smart. Try listening to her more often." Navarre replied sourly.

Brian silently agreed.

The two men broke through the rain-washed front doors. A lone police officer intercepted the reporters, preventing them from following their quarries into the deluge. Brian felt the rain on his skin and grinned. He appreciated going out the front door of the courthouse. When arrested, he had been carted through back alleys and secret police entrances like some sort of tainted refuse. He breathed easier with every marbled step.

Navarre fumbled with his umbrella. When he finally opened the black canopy, he shielded his client from the rain. Brian was certain the umbrella also served to obscure him from prying eyes.

"You need a ride?" The lawyer asked.

"That'd be great." Brian answered.

"Where to?"

"You can just take me to my house."

Navarre's mouth opened in alarm.

"...It's an hour-and-a-half walk otherwise. It's raining." Brian shrugged.

"Are you sure you want to go there?"

"I don't know where else to go." Brian responded simply. There was something the Public Defender wasn't telling him.

"...Stick close or you'll get drenched."

Mark Navarre maintained a brisk pace. The rain soaked into the earth. Brian thanked God it had stopped hailing.

Navigating the storm, they came across the parking lot reserved for court officials. Brian was led to a small brown Chrysler sedan. It was a stereotypical Public Defender's car.

Navarre found the courtesy to escort Brian to the passenger's seat. Brian buckled himself in. Navarre sprinted to the driver's side. He threw the soaking umbrella in the back and tossed his briefcase onto Brian's lap. He fastened his seatbelt and threw the keys into the ignition. The sedan rumbled to life. The radio came on at full volume.

Brian immediately recognized the station as Monroe's own 98.3. The song currently playing was Neil Diamond's *Sweet Caroline*. Tears welled up in Brian's eyes. Finally, music!

"Sorry about that." Navarre attempted to turn the radio down, but Brian stopped him.

"Let it play."

Once, Brian would have derided Neil Diamond as being a little too progressive for Monroe. Now, he was enraptured. A sunbeam warmed his face.

"Hey! It stopped raining!" he glowed.

Though it had been pouring mere seconds ago, the gale had receded. The sun's golden rays pierced through grey clouds. Brian could think of no better song for this occasion than *Sweet Caroline*.

Navarre looked up, swore, and threw the car in reverse.

Downtown whipped past them as they drove. The music softened into a soothing background hum. Moments like this used to call for a joint. Now, they called for answers.

"What was up with all those reporters?" Brian asked.

"Lieutenant Johnson and I agreed we'd keep the coverage of your release to a minimum. She's easy to piss off, but you must have really gotten under her skin." Navarre explained. "Normally, the court would have dismissed the case at the final pretrial hearing. The police were worried about public backlash, though."

*Worried the public might dutifully burn the courthouse down? Like they might dutifully shoot a monster like me?* Brian thought ruefully.

"The good news is the prosecution's entire case was centered on your...*fiction.*" Navarre grimaced. "They were too sure you were guilty. They ended up testing your teeth and blood over a dozen times. They thought they were making mistakes with the DNA."

"So, what does that mean?"

"Your teeth didn't match the bite wound on Cunningham's neck."

"I didn't kill her."

"I know that *now*. Your canines are too big, for one thing." Navarre gave a cold chuckle. "When I saw those things in your mouth, I thought we were fucked."

Brian had never been more thankful for his fangs ever in his life.

"I have a question, if that's okay?" he cautiously asked.

"Shoot."

"They made those models of my teeth pretty early on. They had my fingerprints, my blood; they even took photos of the fading bruises on my knuckles. They must have known I was innocent. Why did they keep me locked up so long?"

"They had an anonymous tip they thought was rock solid. Turns out it was just a bunch of baloney." Navarre said.

"A tip? Like a witness?"

"Yeah. The email is in my briefcase if you want to open it up."

Navarre hit a pothole, which serendipitously popped the briefcase open. Navarre pointed out a printed email. Brian grabbed it. He read it feverishly.

His jaw dropped when he saw the little smiley face emoticons. "That motherfucker!" Brian screamed.

"You know who sent that?" Navarre was genuinely surprised.

"One of my Patreon supporters...didn't you guys subpoena my emails, or Patreon messages, or texts, or whatever?"

"We were in the process of doing that when the forensic evidence came back negative. I think they were kicking around the idea that maybe one of your twisted fans killed Sabrina. If the prosecution could prove that, they were going to go for involuntary manslaughter. Luckily, Sabrina Cunningham's name never showed up in the mountains of pages you wrote."

"Oh no, I never used Sabrina." Brian replied.

"What the hell is that supposed to mean?"

"Well, you know, people say: *write what you know.*" Brian began, "I know a lot of people, and sometimes I would draw from them for inspiration...for my characters." he thought of Alexis and Christine. "I never, ever drew inspiration from Sabrina."

"I'm going to stop you right there." Navarre raised a hand in disgust. "I don't want to hear anything that will make me think my opponents made the wrong decision."

"Sorry, just trying to figure out how to accept my sheep."

"What the hell did I just say?"

They drove in silence for a while after that.

Brian would have to figure out what to do about Paul. That lunatic had delivered on his threats. Just not in the way Brian had expected.

"You know, you're quite the prolific writer. You could be a Stephen King or a Danielle Steele if you weren't so messed up." Navarre interrupted Brian's thoughts.

"Thanks. I appreciate that."

"Maybe you oughta write something different. Happy stories. Or if you need to write smut, make it some good, *clean* smut."

"I'll think about it." Brian paused. Navarre was on to something.

The fields grew larger. Structures became a rare sight. Finally, Brian's house came into view. The car slowed.

"Is this you?" Navarre asked.

Brian nodded. The sight of his small home filled him with emotion. His chest grew tight. Something didn't seem right, but Brian could not place his finger on what that might be.

Before he knew it, the car had halted at the end of his driveway. Something was wrong with the house. He stepped out to take a closer look, but Mark Navarre diverted his attention one last time.

"I better never see you again. You hear?" The Public Defender pointed a finger at his emancipated charge.

"Thanks Mark. For everything. I mean it."

Navarre slammed the car door shut and sped off.

Brian was profoundly grateful for the lawyer's unwilling help. He resolved he would make it easier to separate the art from the artist in the future. He smelled the invigorating petrichor. As his eyes focused on his childhood home, the rejuvenating breath was driven from him as forcefully as if he had been gutted by a not-so stranger's hook.

# XXIII

The house had been completely vandalized. *Corpsefucker,* *pervert,* and *murderer* were spray-painted between penises and swastikas. Each graffitied obscenity bore different handwriting. There had been more than one intruder.

Brian took offense to being called a "corpsefucker" and a "murderer." He wasn't a necrophile. He hadn't killed anyone. He could live with being labeled a "pervert," though. Who wasn't a pervert these days? He thought of Al.

Brian was shocked by the destruction, but a part of him was not surprised. The people of Monroe had been unable to enact vigilante justice. Marking him as a leper would have to do.

Inside, the damage was worse. The computer table had been overturned. His chairs were smashed to splinters. The kitchen was buried in refuse. Cabinet doors hung from broken hinges. His refrigerator was open, and the food inside had decomposed into black slop.

Dirty boot prints covered the floor of his parent's bedroom. A dead rat lay at the foot of their bed. Brian chose to believe that the poor creature had wandered in and died of natural causes.

The bathroom was toilet-papered. The shower curtains were torn. The mirror was shattered. The dead roses in their white porcelain vase were nowhere to be found.

He stared into the broken mirror; his brown eyes reflected back at him many times over. He didn't hate it. He laughed. This wasn't punishment. This was another reminder to accept his sheep.

Sam's room was pristine. Maybe he *helped* trash the place. A gay man with a killer brother in Republican territory? He might have had to, just to save face.

Brian investigated his own bedroom last. Smoke damage on the ceiling combined with a dried pile of human excrement on his fractured bed to create a foul aroma. His half-read books had been shredded; their remains littered the floor. His closet had been gone through; his clothes had been burned.

While the horrible smell of burning shit was strong, it was fading. This must have happened weeks ago. The mob would be unlikely to return now that he was home. If they really wanted him dead, they would have assassinated him at the courthouse, metal detectors be damned. Branding him as an exile was more Monroe's speed, now that Brian thought about it.

The crucifix hung from the wall unharmed. he picked up the little cross. He stared at it. He felt the eyes of God focus on him. To his surprise, they did not pierce him, burn him, or drive him to madness.

*God is not a torturer.* That's what his father would have said.

Brian made his way to the kitchen. The Bob Dole portrait was nowhere to be found. That was just as well. He set the crucifix on the counter. He stepped out the sliding door, and into the backyard, paying no mind to the vile slurs on the glass.

Rage filled his heart when he saw the oak. A large cut had been made at the base of the dead tree. Someone had taken an axe to it. Wooden splinters and shrapnel lay scattered amongst emergent roots. Despite being nearly felled, the tree still stood, defiant in the face of a second death.

Brian quietly approached the devastated trunk. He prodded at the wound. Defiance would be no match against this deep of a cut. A strong gust of wind would knock the poor thing over.

Brian thought of the crucifix. Anxiety closed in. He screamed at the sky. No one answered his cries.

He wept into the wound. The heartwood of the white oak was dry, corpselike. If Brian had an axe, he would have finished the job right then and there. He sighed. He had thrown out his dad's old wood axe during the same anxious episode that had claimed the knives.

He moved behind the tree. He lifted his foot, readying to kick the timber down. He thought of the cross on his counter. He released his leg. He began to laugh again.

Howls of laughter tore from his lungs. He fell on his back. He stared up at the dead branches. Brian laughed until tears poured down his face. Sobs raked his body. He curled up into a ball on top of the hibernating grass. His tear ducts emptied themselves.

He wiped the drying tears and snot from his face. He went back through the sliding glass door. He couldn't bring himself to look back at the tree.

Hunger echoed within his stomach. He was starving. Brian found himself reminiscing about the food they served in the can. The meals at Monroe County Jail were some of the worst he had ever eaten. The powdered eggs they served every morning were one of the most hideous concoctions that had ever entered his body. He would have killed for some of those powdered eggs right now.

The spice cabinet still had a door on it. He opened that cabinet gingerly. The canister of garlic powder greeted him, as did a small jar of minced garlic. There was not a trace of any other substance.

Brian grabbed both garlic containers without hesitation. He snatched a spoon from the silverware drawer, which had been cast onto the floor. He sat cross-legged on the ground. He pried open the lid of the minced garlic. He voraciously consumed the entire eight-ounce jar.

He did not gag. His stomach accepted the meager sustenance with gratitude. When the meal was not flavorful enough for him, he sprinkled more garlic powder on top. Each reeking spoonful tasted better than the last. The scent was intoxicating.

Warm and full, Brian let out a magnificent burp. How he had missed garlic. He could almost cry again.

He stank. His own garlic breath stung his eyes. He grabbed a discarded plastic cup and filled it with water from the sink. No one else needed to deal with his stench.

He gargled, spitting out the water. He filled another glass. He drank this one.

Hunger and thirst satisfied; Brian pulled out trash bags from beneath the sink. He began to clean. He dealt with the rotted food in the fridge first. The feces in his bedroom he disposed of next. When the trash bag was full, he put it in the garbage can outside. He was thankful no one had stolen the big outdoor bins.

Fresh trash bag in hand, he dealt with his burnt clothes. One by one, he discarded charred remnants of jeans, shirts, and hoodies. The blackened husk of his favorite, hideous hoodie caused the anxiety millipede to twitch. He had worn this the day he had argued with Alexis at *Zoe's*. The anxiety turned to sadness.

A perfectly rolled joint fell out of the hooded sweatshirt's front pocket. Miraculously, the little cigarette had not been scorched at all. It landed on the floor ominously.

Brian's heartbeat quickened. Sweat rolled down his bald head and into his beard. With a steadfast hand, he lifted the exquisitely crafted joint to his nostrils. The dank, pungent, musty smell of skunk weed had only been enhanced by the burning of the hoodie. A light, smoky bouquet teased Brian's senses.

Marijuana had given him purpose. It helped him function. This happy little plant elevated him to a greater level of existence. He held up that little joint and stared at it as one might stare into the eyes of a lover.

He then unceremoniously dropped the joint into the trash bag along with the hoodie. He went outside and put the bag into the refuse bin. He could continue his sobriety.

Brian grabbed another bag. And another. And another. After the better part of two hours, He had removed all the trash.

He set his table right side up. He found his router, which still functioned, beneath the splintered chairs. The bed frame he moved beside the now overflowing garbage receptacles. The graffiti he could worry about later.

He buried the dead rat beneath the white oak. He even said a prayer for the rat. It was the first time he had prayed in years. He thanked God that he had found a shovel in the garage.

Brian absentmindedly brought the shovel inside with him. He leaned the earth-covered tool against the wall. He leaned himself over the now upright table. With the house free of clutter, his mind was free to think.

He thought about the hierarchy of needs. The clothes on his back would suffice for now. He had nourished himself on the garlic. The taps in the house functioned; water would not be an issue. He had a roof over his head. A graffiti covered roof, but a shelter all the same.

His needs fulfilled; his mind wandered to his wants. He thought about his car. He thought about his computer. He thought about his phone. He didn't want any of those things.

He only wanted Paul. That bastard had been the reason he spent months in jail. Paul was the reason his house had been ransacked. Paul was the reason why Brian was alone in the world. Yet, if it weren't for Paul, Brian wouldn't have met Al. Al wouldn't have told him to accept the beautiful, dark, twisted fantasy.

*The Lord works in mysterious ways.* Brian clenched a fist.

If he had a computer, he could check Patreon. That was the best chance of uncovering Paul's identity. Where could he find a computer? The nearest library was Blue Bush. Without a car, that was a three-mile walk.

*Is that even an option?* Brian searched his wallet one more time. Snugly tucked behind his ID, serendipitously overlooked by the police, was Brian's library card.

It was still light out. The weather was clear now. Locking the doors to the house behind him, Brian embarked on a long, lonely walk.

# XXIV

Named after the road it was built on, Blue Bush Library doubled as a fire station. In addition to books and public computers, it housed two engines and an ambulance. A smart, white awning delineated the library's entrance from that of the station.

The little brick building with its dark blue roof was a comforting sight to Brian. When he and Sam were boys, their parents frequently turned them loose at this tiny library. Mr. and Mrs. Stanhope claimed it was important to be well read.

In Brian's childhood memories, Blue Bush Library was idyllically surrounded by lush farmer's fields and distant forests. In recent years, a subdivision had grown around it. Brian preferred the memory of a lone bastion in a sprawling countryside.

Stepping through the white front door, Brian stopped at the drinking fountain in the alcove. The humid spring weather had dehydrated him. Between the trek to the library and the cleaning of his house, he'd gotten more exercise today than during his entire stay behind bars.

The interior was roughly the size of a large, one-bedroom Chicago apartment. Three dated desktop computers were clumped together in a corner. The walls were lined with shelves. The shelves overflowed with books. It was within books the imagination resided. The realm of human possibility could never be limited to one single room. Brian wondered if his love of reading and writing, instilled in him at a young age, had paved the road to authoring horrific erotica.

He blinked.

The library's front desk held a stack of newspapers and a clipboard. An elderly female librarian read from a recent issue of *The Monroe Evening News*. The front-page spread was dominated by a photograph of a smiling Sabrina Cunningham. Brian considered fleeing for a moment.

The librarian set down the newspaper before he had a chance to read the headline. The old woman was around his mother's age. Her long grey hair was pulled back into a tight bun. Large, coke bottle glasses amplified her deep blue eyes. She wore a vest patterned with cartoon cats. If she recognized who he was, she didn't show it.

"Uh...hi..." Brian fumbled for his wallet.

The librarian was silent.

"Can I...um...use one of the computers, please?" He thought he sounded like a flustered Christine. "I have my library card."

The librarian pointed a finger at the clipboard. Fresh white paper bore clip art of a smiling computer. The document was entitled:

## "☺ Computer Signup Sheet ☺"

It was empty.

"Oh. Sorry. Thanks."

Brian penned his name and library card number at the top of the list. The librarian nodded. She buried herself back in her newspaper.

The only chairs available were tiny wooden ones salvaged from a Kindergarten classroom. Brian had to tightly draw his legs beneath him just to get comfortable. He squeezed in front of a computer. The monitor was nestled between two large wooden slats, providing some privacy from the other computer users, had there been any.

To log in, all he needed was to re-enter his name and library card number. He grinned. It was a miracle the civil forfeiture had not claimed his library privileges.

*Civil forfeiture? Civil* liberties, *baby.* He thought.

Brian fired up Gmail. He entered the login for his *DeathbringerBob* inbox. He scrolled through months of spam. Eventually, he found what he was looking for. An email flagged as "IMPORTANT":

---

## CONFIDENTIAL NOTICE: THE RESULTS OF YOUR

## PATREON SUBSCRIBER INFORMATION REQUEST

---

The official-sounding email opened with the standard privacy notices. Brian scrolled through paragraphs of cited laws explaining why it would be illegal to use this information for personal gain. The email also advised the reader to delete it once they were finished with it.

None of the legalese was of any use. What mattered was the name on the credit card that had been sending him increasingly large payments every month. Brian sighed in frustration. The name on the card was worthless: *Sarah Lynne Murphy*.

*Of course Paul used a stolen card.* Brian thought. Still, the name was the best lead he had.

The hours flew by. Brian sat in that uncomfortable little chair, browsing page after page of Google search results for "Sarah Lynne Murphy." There were many Sarah Lynne Murphys in the world. They were photographers, mothers, lawyers, business professionals, freelance artists, and Uber drivers. None of them seemed to be into perilous smut.

Just as he was about to give up, Brian found something. He stumbled upon a high school teenager's online blog. She was from Montgomery, Alabama, at least according to www.xxtorturedheartsxx.com, her website's URL. The "About Me" entry made Brian's heart stop:

---

Hi :)

I'm Sarah :)

I kind of hate my life, but maybe you all can get some enjoyment out of it

:)

---

Sarah's blog entries divulged that her father was a defense contractor for the military. Her mother was one of those stay-at-home-moms who sold Herbalife pyramid scheme products from her garage. Sarah lived in a ritzy neighborhood and attended a prestigious private high school. The photographs linked from her Instagram revealed her to be a tall, thin, remarkably plain girl with black hair and green eyes. Judging by the presence of baby fat and acne, there was no way Sarah was older than 17.

Sarah's online persona was popular, but her reality was lonely. Her father was often out of town for work. Her mother was…out of touch. The woman seemed unintentionally belittling. Sarah wrote numerous lengthy posts on her mother's habit of forcing her to participate in activities aimed at young children:

---

Ugh, the old bat took me to see a screening of fucking Snow White of all

things :)

Doesn't she know my favorite part of that movie is when the silly little

bitch bites the apple and croaks? :)

---

In addition to her struggles with her parents, Sarah had a hard
time making friends at school. She often experienced intrusive
thoughts about death and dying. She was jealous of her fellow
teenagers. They had no such mental anguishes:

---

I went to Lucas's party. Maggie was joking around with him, asking what

he would do if his ex Kaneesha showed up :)

"I specifically uninvited her. If she shows up, I'm literally going to kill

myself."

I said it wouldn't even take that much for me to kill myself :)

They all looked at me like I was crazy :(

I hate my generation. :)

Apparently, they don't mean it, despite joking about it a lot :)

I think my thoughts are crazy :(

My thoughts sometimes make me feel blue :(

But sometimes they make me feel red...HOT ;)

Fuck me X(

I sound like a boomer :(

---

After some experimentation, Sarah no longer found her
thoughts alarming. In a rare excursion with her father, he had taken
her to see *Inglorious Basterds*. During the scene where Diane Kruger's
character is strangled by Christoph Waltz's character, Sarah reflected
on how the graphic death scene reminded her of her own intrusive
thoughts:

177

---

In a way, that movie showed me that death is aesthetically pleasing :)

---

This epiphany blossomed into infatuation and arousal:

---

I spend a lot of time watching true crime documentaries :)

Not for the legal procedure or the killer getting brought to justice, if you

know what I mean ;)

---

One night, Sarah experienced every teenager's worst fear: her
parents caught her masturbating. Even Brian cringed with
embarrassment as he read. What made the nightmarish scenario worse
was not the act itself, but what material had stimulated Sarah:

---

Ugh, sorry I was gone for a few days, guys :)

My parents caught me watching The Green Inferno :)

It's not even that good, but man; it really got me going :)

The psychiatrist said my brain's neural pathways are cross-wired :)

She thinks my instinctual fear of death and my instinctual "urge to create

life" (yuck) :P

She thinks they got mixed up somehow :)

They've got me on anti-psychotics :|

I don't think they're working :(

At least my parents didn't check the browsing history ;)

Dad knows better XD

They teach that shit at the NSA :)

I've used the programs Dad brings home. :)

He thinks he's so special. :)

He's not. :)

I could see what he's been up to as well if I wanted to :)

178

Thanks, nerds :)

---

*Well, that explains how she was able to find me.* Brian frowned.

Sarah's access to government tools made Brian easy prey. Her know-how also did a good job of hiding her identity from other fetishists. Sarah spent entire entries bragging about how all her fellow peril fans thought she was a grown man.

Sarah wrote a lot about her beloved hobby of hiking. She wrote about her scriptkiddie codes she programmed for fun. She wrote about her girlfriend, Kayla, and how her parents supported them, despite being from the Deep South.

She posted endless pictures of her and her girlfriend together. Brian thought Kayla looked like a teenage, 100 pounds heavier version of Diane Kruger. Sarah herself noted the similarity. She struggled with it considerably:

---

What if I like her :)

I don't want to act, you know? :(

---

Above all, Sarah adored music. Her favorite band was *Big Thief.* Their lyrics adorned all her blog posts. One entry was simply the lyrics of her all-time favorite song. It was *Big Thief*'s greatest hit: *Paul.*

Brian listened to the song. Its melody was mournful. It was quiet. It was beautiful. Adrianne Lenker's voice was unforgettable. It echoed in his ears long after the final chord dissolved into silence.

Brian leaned back as far as he could in the petite chair. He scratched his head. He inhaled. He exhaled.

Sarah's life was beautiful.

All thoughts of revenge, blackmail, or turning her in to the police evaporated. She didn't need retribution. She needed reassurance.

Without his phone, he couldn't text her. An email wasn't the proper format for what he had to say. Driving to Montgomery in person to talk to a teenage girl about peril fetishism was out of the question.

*Her blog is linked to her Google account...* Brian mused.

Nervously full of resolve, he hit Sarah up on Gchat. He had
no idea if she would even answer. It was still the best shot for what he
wanted to say.

---

Hey Sarah

Maybe I should say:

Hey Paul

Longtime no see

I just got out of jail

Your tip enriched my life

For real

Well, well, well ;)

You know I can trace your IP address :)

Really? A public library? :)

If you're stalking my blog, you must know that coming after me is a big

mistake ;)

You mean your government-guy dad?

Don't worry

I'm not here to threaten you or anything

Then why are you bothering me? :)

Shouldn't you be rotting in prison for murder? :)

That's the thing

I didn't kill Sabrina Cunningham

Press X to doubt :)

I read your work :)

Only someone who's killed could write as vividly as you :)

Yuck, now I feel gross >:(

Why?

It was never a fantasy for you, was it? :)

It was

I just didn't know how to accept it.

A likely story :)

Go on; say whatever you need to say :)

I know you'll just hound me until you do :)

I know how men are :P

That's why I prefer women ;)

Are you scared of killing anyone?

Killing yourself?

Well, I think I may be on to something

You haven't replied in a minute or two because I made you think just now

I didn't kill Sabrina

I never wanted to

She was a friend

I cared about her

So? :)

You're not going to hurt Kayla

How do you know? :)

Because you just have to do one thing:

You've got to accept your sheep

What the fuck? >:(

What does that even mean? >:(

Think of accepting your sheep like this:

Maybe your psychiatrist is right; maybe you're just mixed up in the head

or something

Maybe your friends and parents are right and you're just a lunatic

Maybe Kayla is right and you're pretty cool

The point is, it doesn't matter what other people think of you

At the end of the day, you have to accept yourself for who you are even if
it's hard

It's still hard for me

Wondering what causes your fantasies or intrusive thoughts

Worrying that you're going to act on them

That won't change them or make them go away

Why are you telling me this? :)

I want you to have a leg up

If you can just be comfortable with yourself, maybe you won't make the
same mistakes I did

I used to feel awful anxiety in my head

Constantly

I still kind of do

But it's getting better

You have no idea what's going on inside my head >:(

You don't even know who I am >:(

I know you're worried about acting on the thoughts

You told me they were just fantasy

You're right, even if you don't believe it yourself

Fake it until you make it

The desire isn't your fault, but it is your responsibility

If you accept it for what it is, you'll have a better hang on it

Hmmm :)

What?

If I'm being honest, I just told you whatever I thought would keep you writing :)

I thought if your stories were around, they would keep me from acting on any desires I had :)

You won't act on your desires if you haven't already

You would've fucked sheep by now or something

What? :(

Sorry, still working my thoughts out

I thought writing would stop me from acting on my desires

But I hated myself for it

The hate made everything worse

It made me accidentally choke the one friend I had

:O

It was an accident

I was high

Boy, you really are more fucked up than me :)

I don't want you to have accidents just because you like weird shit

I've been okay since I got out of jail

I see no mention of your release online :)

Do they have computers in prison? ;)

Haha

I got out today

Some secret plea or something to make the elected officials look good

So...you accepted your sheep? :)

I think I'm starting to?

Do I want to know how you came up with that terminology? :)

Probably not

You're really not going to try and hunt me down or anything? For snitching on you? :)

Kink shaming is a big no-no :)

I know, you accused me of it, remember?

Of course I remember lmao :)

I'm not mad

I just want you to be happier than me

Oh, Brian Stanhope, I already am :)

What will make you happy? :)

Accepting this stupid sheep or whatever? :)

Yeah

I'm trying not to be caught up in my own shit

Don't you mean: "caught up in your own SHEEP?" ;)

Hahaha

I wish I could just ask my sheep what to do

I'm completely lost

How so? :)

Maybe I know something, but I can't remember

Something people need to know

Something that could help

Are you seriously going to give a tip to the police who held you in jail for months? :)

I don't know

Why would you do that? Some misguided attempt at redemption? :)

Why do you need redemption if you've accepted your sheep? :)

I don't know. I just feel like God wants me to or something

You're a weirdo :)

I'll think about what you said, Brian :)

Thank you

For what? :)

I don't know

Well...fake it until you make it :)

---

And with that, Sarah Lynne Murphy blocked Brian Stanhope.

The librarian cleared her throat. Brian turned around in his small chair. The little old woman sternly pointed at the analog clock on the wall. Blue Bush Library was open until 8 P.M. on Wednesdays, but that hour was fast approaching.

The diminutive wooden chair squeaked with protest as he stood. His legs were filled with knots. He stretched. He turned off the computer. At the front desk, he signed his name out on the happy little clipboard.

"Thanks again. Don't worry. I wasn't writing smut or anything. Don't trust what you read in the paper." Brian winked.

If the librarian understood what he was referencing in any way, she did not let on in the slightest.

The heavy white door closed behind him. Dark night rolled in. He was still lost. He had an inkling, perhaps, but it felt selfish. He felt like a lost child. He was scared. He needed to go home.

# XXV

"Do you know how far I've walked today?"

"I'm sorry, Mr. Stanhope. Visiting hours are over."

"Look, it's not even midnight-"

"And you know visiting hours end at 9 P.M."

"Check your handbook." Brian angrily slammed the counter.

"I'm not checking anything. If you don't leave, I'm calling the police." The security guard stood threateningly.

"I know your policy says guests are allowed after 9 P.M. on weeknights if there is a medical emergency." Brian doubled down.

"Your mother is fine, Mr. Stanhope."

"Call her then!" Brian demanded. "Call her and ask her if she's having an emergency."

The front desk rent-a-cop paused.

"If you call her and it turns out I'm full of shit, I'll leave." He prayed his mother was either having a really good day, or a really bad day.

The security guard manhandled the phone on the front desk with cold anger. He scowled at Brian and pounded the dial pad. He held the receiver to his ear for a long time.

*Come on, mom, pick up!* Brian was starting to sweat.

Mercifully, she answered.

"*Hola,* Mrs. Stanhope. I'm sorry to bother you...oh...oh...slow down...It's okay...I have your son Brian here...yes, Brian Stanhope...yes...I'm sorry...he'll be right in."

The rent-a-cop went pale as he hung up the phone. Brian froze with worry. If she was actually having an episode...

"*Lo siento,* Mr. Stanhope. You can go in."

Brian sprinted to his mother's unit, anxiety writhing in his belly. The door to her apartment was ajar. He ran inside. He slammed the door shut behind him.

"Mom?" He cried. "Hey...what the...?"

The empty apartment was shrouded in darkness. The off-color couch was gone. The smell of moth balls had been replaced by cinnamon and Lysol.

"Mom? Are you there?"

"...Brian?" Was Mary Stanhope's faint reply.

A thin sliver of light bled onto the carpeted floor from his mother's bedroom. He was at her doorway in an instant. His heartbeat was so fast that the organ threatened to ignite.

Mary sat upright in bed, clutching a telephone in her hand. Her eyes were wild, but clear. She spoke to her eldest son.

"Brian? What's going on? Where am I? Where is your hair?" The phone slid out of her hands and landed on the carpeted floor with a muted thump.

Brian approached his ailing mother cautiously. Was she cognizant of her surroundings? Would she start screaming again?

He pulled the one chair in the room up to the bed. He sat down. The melodious beeps of the machines hooked to Mary Stanhope were deafening.

"I'm here now, mom. I'm here." He said.

"Brian...what happened? Where am I? I was with your father...we were on the road, and...and now I'm in this place. What's going on? Why did you shave your head?" Mary took her son's hand as if it were a life preserver in an ocean squall.

Brian's heart melted. His mother wasn't loopy. She didn't think he was a child. She wasn't screaming. She wasn't trapped in the past. The light in her eyes was more than a reflection. She was here.

A tear rolled down Brian's cheek.

"Well..." He rubbed a hand over his head. "To be honest, it wasn't looking good. I was starting to go bald like dad. I just thought I'd accelerate the process."

"You should use that Rogaine I bought you." His mother chided. "Why am I not at home? What are these *things*?" Mary moved to pull the IVs out of her arms. Brian squeezed her hands tighter.

"I wouldn't mess with those. Doctor's orders."

"What's going on, Brian? Where's your father? Where's Samuel?" She looked quizzically at her son's wild beard. "Goodness, that wasn't what the Rogaine was for!"

"No, mom. I didn't use the Rogaine on my beard." Brian began quietly. "The truth is...this is the first time I've really spoken to you in about two years."

"What are you talking about?" his mother asked in casual disbelief.

"There was an accident. You and dad got hit by a drunk truck driver."

Brian meant to dole out information piece by piece, but the words poured out of him freely. With every word, a weight lifted from him. He threatened to float away.

"You woke up in the hospital. Dad wasn't so lucky. The doctors said you were brain damaged. They said you had early onset dementia and that made it worse. You were in a bad way. I was scared. I didn't want to see you like that. I fainted at court and Sam was declared your guardian and power of attorney. I failed him, Mom. I failed you. That should have been my duty. My responsibility. I was too weak, too crazy. Christine was never dating me, Mom. I made a scene at that Target her and Raoul used to work at. Well, Raoul still works there. Christine left town because of me. I was in bad place, so I hung out with Talon and Nikki a lot and started smoking weed. It's legal now, and I really liked the stuff Talon gave me. I think he keeps it in his toilet? Anyway, I wanted to take care of you financially, because I really felt bad about screwing Sam over, so I got involved with this ring of people who write murder porn. Like, I sexualized the act of killing. My stories made me some good money, so I started paying for all your bills here. You're in River Park Place Apartments, by the way. I know, you said you never wanted to be put in a home, but this isn't a home, the brochures say it's a luxury community-assisted living facility. Luxury for Monroe, I guess. Also, I started hanging out with Alexis Knabusch, and I think I had feelings for her, but I felt really conflicted and confused because I found out I *actually* had a fetish for death, and Alexis and her friend Sabrina invited me to Big John's rave in the woods, and Sam was playing with Raoul and *Parts Unknown*, and I thought things were improving between us, and I thought I was going to apologize to Raoul, but I got too high, I grabbed Alexis by the neck, and Sabrina got killed and everyone thought I did it because I write snuff porn. I got out of jail today. That was fun. All that matters though, is that I am here, and you're here, and I just don't want you to hate me, mom. I fucked up, I've done some questionable shit, and I think I want to help find Sabrina's killer, but I don't remember a lot about that night in the woods, because I got so stupid-fucking-high, but I want to help because I don't want you to hate me, mom. I just don't want you to hate me."

Brian was out of breath. Dreadful lightness consumed him. He felt like a tethered weather balloon struggling for freedom.

His mother's eyes met his. She had sat there, listening intently as he vomited up everything. He was terrified that she would cut his weather balloon soul free and send him rocketing into the void.

She laughed.

He recoiled. Her laughter was beautiful, uproarious. He was sure her guffaws were shaking the foundations. Joyous tears fell down his mother's face. Brian was utterly astonished. Confusion clobbered him.

"Oh, Brian, you don't expect me to believe all *that*, now do you?" Mary chortled warmly.

"What?" Brian murmured.

"You were always a great storyteller. Is this your Dad's idea of a distraction while he gets my anniversary gift ready?" She looked around the room amusedly. "I knew he was going to take me on vacation. Is this place his idea of a hotel? Oh, why did I marry that man?" she teased.

"Mom, I know it sounds crazy, but everything I told you is true." Brian stuttered.

"True? Really? You, hanging out with Talon Keener and Nikole Dalton?"

"It's Nikole *Keener*, now. They got married."

"Well, they certainly are perfect for each other." Mary rolled her eyes. "I can't imagine you getting upset with Raoul. He's a nice boy."

"Mom..."

"In any case, you should apologize to him. Sam really likes him. He'll probably be family soon." Mary placed her hand on her son's face, gazing straight into Brian's soul. "Even if everything in that crackpot story of yours is true, I would love you no matter what. I do love you. You're my son. You're the world to me. You always will be."

Brian wept. His mother didn't judge his tears. If anything, she loved him more because of them.

"Can I spend the night with you, mom?" He sniffled.

"It's your father's dime." She winked.

"Well, actually, it's mine...never mind."

Brian leaned over, half on the chair, half on the bed. He turned his face away from his mother's. The machines whirred in the background. The smell of cinnamon teased his nose. His mother stroked his back. He felt like a little boy again. He was undeserving of such love.

"You and Alexis Knabusch, huh?" She asked him.

"Well...it's really complicated."

"Oh yeah, the murder-sex or whatever. You kids are wild." She chuckled. "Isn't she a little young for you?"

"Totally. Even Sam agrees." Brian swallowed as he thought of Alexis. She deserved better than him.

"Those Knabusch's have weird smiles. Their teeth are way too small." His mother sighed. "If you two do end up together, maybe your genes will cancel out. I want my grandkids to have good teeth."

"Mom!" Brian protested.

"Sorry, sorry. I know the teeth are a sore subject for you." His mother laughed again. "You're my only hope for being a grandma, unless Sam and Raoul adopt."

"Mom?"

"Yes?"

"I love you."

"I love you too. Can you hit the lights for me?"

Brian took one last look at his now sleepy mother. Her eyes were full of joy. He turned the lights off with a calm and steady hand.

In the morning, she was gone.

"Don't miss the bus; I'm not driving you to school again." Mary muttered sleepily.

"Ok, Mom."

He quietly stepped out of her room, gently closing the door behind him. This was who his mother was now. He accepted her sheep as surely as he wanted to accept his own.

Overcast sunlight peered through the windows. Brian wondered if it would rain again. He was hungry. He didn't want to walk in the rain to McDonald's or something. He didn't even have money.

The toaster in the kitchen was still there. Brian scavenged some bread from the pantry. He popped some slices into the appliance.

Once the bread was golden brown, he calmly spread butter on the toast with a knife. He reached up into the cupboards and grabbed a vial of garlic powder. He applied a healthy layer of the seasoning to his meal.

His purpose felt clearer now. His mother loved him. He needed to love himself. Accept his sheep. Bringing Sabrina's killer to justice would allow him to love himself. The thought made his heart glad.

*Big John's...* Brian tried to look back on that evening with fresh eyes. *It had to have been those American Guard guys. Skinheads are violent. Why were there so many of them? I must have seen one of them acting strange...*

His rumination was interrupted by the front door opening.

Sam and Raoul entered, empty cardboard boxes in their hands. Brian stopped chewing his mouthful of garlic toast. No one moved. No one breathed. The space between the kitchen and the front door now felt very small indeed.

"What are you guys doing here?" Brian asked.

"What are you doing out of jail?" Sam seemed more surprised than angry.

"The DNA evidence didn't match me, so they let me go. What's up with the boxes? Where's Mom's furniture?"

"We're moving Mom upstate. There's a community in Petoskey that specializes in brain conditions." Sam spoke robotically, as if he couldn't fathom that his brother was free.

"That's great!" Brian smiled.

Neither Sam nor Raoul smiled back. The air was tense. Brian braced himself. He swallowed his toast. The ass-kicking from Sam was about to commence. He hoped he wouldn't vomit or pass out. He needed to feel the blows. He deserved them.

"I'm not mad you didn't bail me out or anything." Brian began. "I know you didn't have the money. I know you're probably expecting me to blow up on you for not keeping in touch, but I'm not."

There was no response from either of the lovers.

"Sam...remember that day in court when I was all fucked up? That's on me. You and Mom deserve better. I've done messed up things, even outside of what I wrote. I'm a bad brother. You've given me so many chances, and I've blown them all." Brian continued.

"Brian..." Samuel slowly set his empty box on the ground. His hands curled into fists.

"I can't imagine what's going through your head right now. If you want to beat me up, or throw me out, go ahead. I'm sorry, Sam. I'm so sorry. I failed you." Brian was ready for the punches.

Samuel hugged him.

Brian gasped. Sam held him in a warm, desperate hug. Brian slowly returned the embrace. He couldn't recall the last time he had hugged his little brother.

"I thought you did it." Sam's voice was laden with guilt.

"I thought I did too."

"If anything, I'm the bad brother."

"What? No!" Brian broke off the hug.

"I am. I've been resentful towards you ever since that court date. I should have seen you weren't in a good place. Instead, I pushed mom's care back on to you. Look what that did." Sam grabbed him by the shoulders.

"No, I wanted it! It was my duty!" Brian shook his head.

"I still gaslit you into doing it." Sam confessed.

"You had a record deal lined up. I took that away from you." Brian retorted.

"See? Even now he thinks *he* caused that record fuck's homophobia." Sam chuckled to Raoul.

Brian blinked in astonishment.

"Brian, you write some...*questionably horrible* shit." Sam continued. "At the end of the day, though, that's irrelevant. I didn't trust that my own brother was innocent. *That's* fucked."

"I *will* find a way help with the bills again. I swear it." Brian interjected.

"Brian: don't take care of others at the cost of yourself." Sam said.

Brian thought of his half-baked plan to help Sabrina.

"Are you *sure* you don't want my help?" Brian asked.

"Not if it hurts you. Besides, *Parts Unknown* got another record deal." Sam smiled.

"What? No way!"

"A Detroit studio honcho showed up at Big John's. He signed us about a month after you got locked up. I don't think he realized I was your brother, so that helped." Sam's expression went sheepish. "We're going on tour next month. I'm using my share of the advance to move Mom."

"Sam! That's amazing!" Brian hugged his brother again.

Raoul watched the emotional spectacle wordlessly.

"Raoul. Congratulations, man." Brian looked Raoul square in the face. Time to accept a sheep.

"I'm sorry about that day at Target. I'm sorry I called you the f-word. I'm sorry I threatened to kill you and Christine." He would surely get punched now.

"You shouldn't say that word." Raoul answered. "When hateful shit like that slips out, it usually means you're saying things like that on the reg."

"I know you won't believe me, but I don't like that word." Brian explained. "When I said it that day, in that moment...I wanted to mean it. I *meant* it. I was hurt and wanted to say the most horrible things I could think of. I don't know if that makes it better or worse. I'm sorry."

Brian nearly fainted when Raoul shrugged.

"Uh...okay. Apology accepted. I never really cared all that much though."

Brian's brain stopped working. All neurons in his head fired at once and went silent. With three small sentences from Raoul, his entire worldview had been obliterated.

"WHAT? ARE YOU KIDDING?" Brian exploded.

"No. It was never that big of a deal. We all go through shit." Raoul said.

"But...but...but...I made Christine leave town!"

"She left because Colin got a good job down in Texas. You had nothing to do with it." Raoul replied.

"But...but...she comes back! She's scared to show her face!"

"She comes back because her parents still live here. She's pretty comfortable going around in public. You're the one who became some sort of fetish hermit." Raoul snorted.

"I just...I can't believe it. I really cannot believe it." Brian's head was spinning. "I've been scared to apologize to you for years...I thought you were going to let me have it!"

"It's not all about you, Brian." Raoul said.

# XXVI

Lily wouldn't stop barking.

*What is it, you stupid dog?* Alexis bemoaned internally.

She really didn't want to get up. Ever since her assault at *Larson's*, all she could do was sit on the couch, eat Ben and Jerry's ice cream, angrily post on social media, and watch the Weather Channel. None of these distractions dispelled the memories.

Lily needed to shut up. She was drowning out the reports about forming storm fronts. Alexis needed to hear this information. It was quite dark for being nearly noon.

*Is it noon?* She would know if Lily just kept quiet for a minute.

Alexis clutched the three wood tighter. The golf club was close at hand these days. She may have put a few more holes in the walls.

The doorbell rang. Alexis groaned. She looked down at the empty tub of Cherry Garcia in her lap. She hid under her blanket.

The doorbell rang again. Between that god-awful chime and Lily's incessant barking, the empty house seemed full of life. Alexis's mind was fraying.

"Ok! I'm coming."

An uninvited guest might be a good distraction. How did she look? Was she put together enough to receive visitors?

She hesitated. She was only wearing pajamas. She hadn't showered in days. By some act of God, the copious amounts of ice cream had not caused her to gain weight. Depression must have kicked her metabolism into overdrive. That was one small blessing.

She turned off the TV. She tried to evaluate her reflection in the darkened screen. Her grey eyes were bloodshot from a mix of crying and sleep deprivation. She'd have to start wearing sunglasses everywhere like Brian if she-

*Brian...that motherfucker!* She seethed at the thought of him.

The doorbell kept ringing. Lily kept barking. Alexis trembled. What if it was the Asian guy in the green Impala?

She decided she'd go to the kitchen and look out the windows. If she saw angry Asian dude, she'd call the cops. If it were someone else, she'd see what they wanted. Once the door was dealt with, she would go to the freezer, grab another tub of Ben and Jerry's (*Half-*

*Baked would be a nice change of pace from Cherry Garcia*), and check on the status of the impending thunderstorm. Then, maybe she'd write another #bossbabe post.

The doorbell didn't stop.

"I'm coming! *God!*" Alexis exasperated.

Her legs were a little shaky from sitting too long. She grabbed her blanket and empty ice cream tub in one hand and made for the kitchen. She threw the tub away and glanced out the window.

Another ring. Lily went bonkers. Alexis tensed up.

"Who the hell is...?" she cursed. When she saw who was outside, her heart stopped.

"You have got to be fucking joking." Her anger rose like a bloody tidal wave.

Brian Stanhope rang the bell over and over again. His eyes held a frightfully determined gleam. Lily barked louder.

"Lily! Shut up!" Alexis screeched.

Lily dutifully obeyed. The faithful dog went back to her bed. Alexis shook with rage.

She thought about calling the police. She shook her head. This bastard didn't deserve pigs. The perverted, murdering fuck needed to join Sabrina in the grave.

Brian surely heard her yell at Lily, but he did not cease ringing the doorbell. Alexis hefted the golf club. After a few powerful practice swings, she ran to the front door and threw it open.

The bell went silent. Brian's face was overtaken by a look of surprise. The surprise quickly evolved into pain as Alexis beat him with the three wood.

"You! Son! Of! A! Bitch!" Alexis screamed, punctuating each word with a blow from the golf club.

"Hey! Ow! Alexis, stop!" Brian howled.

"You murdering psychopath!" Anger filled every fiber of Alexis's being. "What the hell do you think you're doing here?!"

"I'm trying to accept my sheep!" Was his startled reply. He feebly tried to stop the blows with his arms.

Alexis stopped swinging for a moment.

"What the *fuck* does that even mean?!" She screamed.

"I met a guy in jail!" Brian panicked, "His name was Al, he was doing time for bestiality, he taught me that sheep are soft and warm and you should accept them!"

"WHY THE FUCK WOULD THAT BE HELPFUL?!"
Alexis swung again.

"I'm trying to figure that – oh, shit!" Brian swore in agony.

The club cleanly connected with his right kneecap. He fell to the ground, the cement porch exacerbating his fall. He tried to scramble to his feet, but Alexis knocked him over with a blow to the left shoulder.

"You pervert! You used me and Sabrina as sick fantasy fuel!" Alexis raised the club over her head, preparing to crack open Brian's skull.

"You're right! I did!" Brian groaned weakly.

The confession made Alexis pause. Eyes wild, club still over her head, she glared down at Brian. He clutched his knee. His expression was a mix of desperation and remorse.

"I *liked* you, Alexis. I had feelings for you. My feelings were warped by my fetish. A lot of things were." He explained.

Alexis took a cautious step back. Brian didn't try to attack her. He clutched at his injuries. His voice struggled to hold back the pain.

"Alexis...I did not kill Sabrina." His agonized brown eyes met her infuriated grey ones. "If you need to kill me to believe that...then go ahead. I didn't kill her. I cared about her. I failed her. I failed you."

He broke his gaze and closed his eyes. He lowered his head before the club. He continued speaking:

"If you want to kill me...if you need to kill me...I deserve it."

Alexis kept the club where it was. She stared at her former friend. Her anger felt strangely unfulfilled. She had expected him to beg, or to try and argue, or just flat out murder her. She also expected him to be high, but he was sober. She didn't know what to do.

"You choked me." She finally spat.

"I did. I was tripping balls; I know that doesn't excuse my actions. I'm sorry, Alexis." Brian did not look at her. He stared at the ground, unmoving.

Alexis slowly lowered the golf club.

"How long has this been going on?" she growled.

"My feelings for you? I think the day I met you. The writing...about a month or two after my dad's funeral."

"Why murder...fetishism?" She asked, disgust dripping from her voice.

"Well, the community's term is *peril* fetishism...but...it started off as a way to get back at Christine. It felt good." Brian sounded astonished that Alexis had not brained him yet. "It was fun to write. I found out there were people who wanted to pay me for it. The money was good. It ate away at me though. I hadn't learned to accept my sheep yet."

"You keep saying that." Alexis was annoyed with Brian's strange turn of phrase. The club was now at her side.

"I think, maybe this fetish, or fantasy, or whatever...it had always been lurking there. I was conflicted about it. I still am. I have to accept it for what it is. You know, this guy, Al... he said that if I actually wanted to act on the desires I would have done so by now. I would have actually tried to strangle you. I would have done a lot worse than that before." Brian peeked up from where he was kneeling and lifted an eyebrow at Alexis. "Are you sure you don't want to cave my head in?"

"I'm still thinking about it." Alexis replied.

"Well, if you're going to let me talk...I need your help."

"You...need my *help*...?" Alexis's anger was perforated with confusion.

"I think I need to put Sabrina to rest. I think I need help to solve her murder."

"The police think you did it." Alexis snarled.

"The police let me go. None of the evidence matched me. Please, Alexis, help me remember something about that night. Some clue, *something...anything* I can give to the cops." Brian begged.

"So... let me get this straight: You met a furry in jail who taught you some fucked up interpretation of acceptance. The cops let you go. You come over here to ask me to help you, fully aware of how you used me." Alexis's fury bubbled again. "What's more; is that you know *I* know you used me. Then, you risk me beating you to death, so I can help you give evidence to the police who hate your guts for ruining their murder investigation?"

"Yeah." Brian nodded.

"That is the stupidest fucking thing I have ever heard."

"Raoul and Sam said the same thing." Brian sighed.

"They *let* you come here?" Alexis asked in bewilderment.

"Yeah. They wouldn't give me a ride because they didn't want me getting hurt or something, so I had to walk. They're moving my mom today too."

"You walked all the way here from River Park Place just to have your ass handed to you?"

197

"I guess so. I apologized to Raoul, by the way. Also, I'm not smoking weed anymore."

"Don't virtue signal. It's pathetic."

"Sorry...please, Alexis. Will you help me?"

Alexis studied Brian Stanhope. There was something different about the way he handled himself. He was open. He was honest. Being nearly beaten to death with a golf club hadn't fazed him. This wasn't an act. Maybe he was finally undergoing that change she had once sought for him.

He still had used her. Hadn't she used him, too? Alexis looked at her father's golf club. She thought of her parents. Had they ever been so vulnerable with her?

"Get inside. The neighbors are watching." Alexis said.

"Thank you...Alexis...I-" Brian began. Alexis raised the club's head to his lips, silencing him.

"Let's get one thing straight: I am doing this for Sabrina. Not you." Her icy grey eyes pierced Brian to the core. He did not flinch.

"That's all I can ask for." He nodded shamefully.

Brian struggled to his feet. He limped heavily. He nearly tripped over the doorstep as he entered the house. Alexis almost felt bad. She slammed the front door behind her.

Brian hobbled over to the kitchen table. He winced in pain as he sat down. Lily, upon recognizing him, happily licked his hands. Alexis shot Lily a death glare. The loyal German Shepherd cowered and scampered off.

"I missed Lily." Brian smiled.

"Don't talk about my dog." Alexis kept the golf club ready.

"Sorry." Brian meekly apologized and shivered with pain. "Do you mind if I get an ice pack or something? You really packed a wallop."

Alexis rolled her eyes. She strolled over to the freezer and pulled out a pint of Ben & Jerry's. She threw it at Brian and nearly hit him.

"Use that." She said.

"Thank you." Brian gently placed the ice cream tub on his bruised shoulder.

"So: what exactly do you need from me?" Alexis frowned.

"I just need to run an idea by you. You were at the party...hell, you probably remember it better than I do."

"Of that I have no doubt."

"Yeah, fuck Ketamine." Brian grimaced. "Anyway, if I didn't kill Sabrina, clearly someone at that party did. There was a lot out of place."

"Your behavior for one thing." Alexis leered.

"Yeah. I know." Brian sheepishly agreed. "If you take me, the big red herring out of the question...that leaves only those guys in camo. Do you remember anything about them?"

Alexis was gripped with fear. All anger fled from her. Her eyes widened. She went pale.

"What is it?" Brian asked in alarm.

"A few weeks ago, I ran into one of those American Guard guys at *Larson's*." Alexis spoke quietly, "He was the Asian one. The one who had been hanging around Sabrina all night."

"The Asian skinhead with hair? Holy shit! I thought I hallucinated that!" Brian gasped. "You saw him at *Larson's*?"

"He pretended not to know me. I chased him out of the bar. He...grabbed me. He choked me. He threatened me. He left me in the parking lot. He drove off in a bright green Impala."

There was silence.

"He *choked* you?" Brian looked shocked and a little ashamed. He was clearly thinking of his own accidental strangulation.

Alexis nodded wordlessly.

"That son-of-a-bitch. He killed Sabrina! Motherfucker!" Brian stood, knocking his chair back.

He unintentionally put weight on his banged-up knee. He doubled over; and would have collapsed on the floor had he not caught the table at the last second. He cursed in pain. He shifted the ice cream from his shoulder to his knee.

"Careful, Brian!" Alexis shrieked.

"Damn it...sorry." Brian screwed up his face in agony. "What happened, exactly? Did you ask him about Sabrina?"

"Yeah...that's when he ran out." Alexis answered.

"Holy shit. He killed her...or at the very least, he knows who did." Brian smiled with a mixture of excitement and righteous fury. "Did you get his name?"

"No...fuck! He totally knows." Alexis was annoyed. Brian was legitimately on to something.

"Did you go to the police? After he assaulted you?" Brian inquired.

"No. I didn't get his license plate. No plate. No name…you know how cops are. I tried searching for members of The American Guard online, but I didn't see any Asians in their ranks." Alexis wrung the golf club menacingly. "I'd love to get my hands on that guy, or sick the police on him, or cancel him, or something!"

"I'd like that too." Brian set the ice cream aside. "I think I know someone who might know this dude."

"Who?" Alexis's face brightened hopefully.

"Talon Keener. I saw him making a deal with the American Guard, specifically our hairy Asian friend." Brian explained.

"Great! So, we call the cops, tell them what we know, they arrest Talon, and they take it from there!" Alexis beamed triumphantly. Her glee was immediately waylaid by Brian shaking his head.

"Talon won't cooperate with cops. If we want Asian guy's name, we'll have to ask Talon ourselves. Do you have his number?"

"Oh, so you never remembered Talon's number, but you always remembered mine?" Alexis replied with a rude snort.

"You were more important to me than him." Brian gave a sly smile.

Alexis glowered, wiping the smile from his face. She reached into the pockets of her pajama pants and retrieved her phone. She performed a quick, intense search of her contacts. She grew angry again.

"I don't actually have his number." Alexis set her phone down with dismay.

"Well, if we can't text him, we'll have to go over there in person and ask him." Brian stated matter-of-factly.

"*We?*" Alexis glared again.

"I don't have a car. Also, I don't think I can walk all the way over there now." Brian whimpered painfully.

"I am not driving you to Talon Keener's house." Alexis crossed her arms.

"Don't drive me over there for me. Drive me over there for Sabrina." Brian pleaded.

"*I* can use that argument. Not you."

"Sorry."

"What makes you think he'll want to tell you anything? I heard he knocked you out for talking shit about Nikki."

"Ok, he didn't knock me out, but he did slug me good." Brian pouted.

"Won't he just beat the shit out of you again? I don't think you can take anymore beatings." Alexis eyed Brian as he balanced against the table.

"Honestly, he'll just start shooting. The news said he told the cops I probably murdered Sabrina anyhow. It'll be a bullet for me."

"I'm not driving you over there if he's just going to shoot you." Alexis declared.

"He won't shoot me if I handle the situation right." Brian said.

"Are you sure about that?"

"He was a friend once. I know him." Brian nodded.

"Well...if you can promise me you won't get yourself or *me* shot, I'll drive you. Asian guy's name is worth at least that much." Alexis conceded.

"I promise. We are going to be fine." Brian smiled again. "If it makes you feel better, you can bring your golf club."

"If anything, I'm bringing it for *you*, not Talon." Alexis threatened with the three wood. "I'm going to get ready. I'll be right down."

Golf club in hand, she made her way upstairs. If she was going out in public, even only to question Talon Keener, she was going to look presentable. She reached the first step on the stairs.

"Alexis?" Brian called out.

She turned around. Brian was standing as straight as he could, given his injuries. His expression was one of genuine gratefulness. In a way, he almost looked dashing.

"Thank you." He said.

Alexis nodded. She went into the upstairs bathroom. She propped the mean golf club against the wall. She washed her face. She couldn't believe she was helping Brian at all. Was she doing the right thing?

Unbidden, she remembered Sabrina's closed casket funeral. She began to brush her teeth. Over the sounds of running water and brushing, she thought she heard the front door open. She was reminded of the sound the casket had made when it was briefly opened for her and Sabrina's parents.

She thought of the cruel bite taken out of Sabrina's neck. She thought of Brian's hands around her throat. Strangely, the two thoughts slid apart like oil and water.

She thought of the strange man's hands around her jaw in the parking lot. She snapped her toothbrush in half with anger. Placing the *Larson's* incident next to the funeral in her mind, she found that these two experiences melded together serendipitously.

She ran her hands around her throat.

Darting to her room, she quickly threw on a flannel, jeans, and some tough looking boots. She put on a long tan coat and adjusted her ponytail. If she was going to play detective, she may as well look the part. Once Alexis felt sufficiently intimidating, she took one last look in the mirror. To her surprise, her grey eyes were no longer so bloodshot.

She came downstairs, golf club over her shoulder. She saw Brian sitting on the couch, Lily was at his feet. He tried to play with the dog, but he was moving too stiffly. Alexis felt a pang of remorse over her overzealous beating. She thought about the grey eyes of Echo, and quickly decided that Brian had deserved the beating after all.

"Did Sabrina paint that picture of you?" Brian asked Lily playfully.

He motioned at the painting that sat on the floor in front of the TV. Lily barked. Brian gave her friendly scratches. Alexis looked at Brian expectantly. She still couldn't bring herself to look at Sabrina's artwork. Brian appeared to understand this.

"We gotta go, Lily. We'll be back." Brian groaned in pain. He leaned over and gave the dog a kiss on the head.

"You navigate. I'll drive." Alexis grabbed the Audi's keys off the wall.

Brian stood slowly, with overly straight posture. He was still unsteady. He nearly lost his balance when his injured knee buckled.

Alexis offered an arm, which Brian gladly took. She mused over how unfashionable Brian looked next to her. She gloated internally.

"Do you really think we're going after the right guy?" Alexis asked.

"Oh yeah. A bright green impala? Green's a killer's color." Brian said.

"I thought geniuses picked green. There was a study about that on Buzzfeed a few months ago." Alexis replied.

"Ted Bundy was a genius. Look what he did." Brian countered.

"I remember your mom said you were a child prodigy."

"Don't turn this on me. I'm egotistical enough because of that. Besides, my car was red."

The pre-storm light of the afternoon washed over Alexis and Brian as they were exposed to the prying eyes of Carrington Farms. What an odd pair they made: a smartly dressed young woman toting a golf club, and a recently released murder suspect clad in ill-fitting garb.

Alexis squinted in the overcast light. She hated these days. The clouds seemed to reflect sunlight brighter than blue skies or snow did. The humidity didn't help. It would rain before sundown.

She helped Brian into the passenger's seat. Situating herself behind the wheel, she started the car. The Audi purred to life luxuriously.

She and Brian turned to each other. Their eyes met. They nodded.

"Let's accept some sheep." Brian said.

"Do you want me to drop you off at Custer Statue?" Alexis angrily raised a finger into Brian's face.

"Sorry." He skittishly faced the road. He sat uncomfortably, as if he was holding his body together.

Alexis angrily placed the golf club between the two of them, jamming it upright between the seats and center console. Brian flinched. Alexis smirked.

She backed out of her driveway, driving off into the gloomy day with her friend turned enemy turned uneasy ally. She was unsure about this plan. She thought of Sabrina. She wondered if this is what *she* would have wanted.

*If you're dropping Brian off at Custer Statue, can I come? I need to pass out petitions to get that shit torn down. If that doesn't work, I'll blue-ball the horse again. What do you think?* Sabrina's voice echoed through her ears.

*Oh, Sabrina.* Alexis smiled sadly. *I think I want you to still be here with me.*

She hit the gas.

# XXVII

"I appreciate you not hitting me in the head."

Brian examined himself in the folding mirror above the passenger's seat. Alexis's eyes darted back and forth. She had never been to the East Side before.

"I'm so pale that any bruises would stick out like a sore thumb." Brian stroked his beard as he contemplated his reflection.

Alexis gripped the steering wheel defensively. The blighted houses leered threateningly. In this neighborhood, her Audi might be a fine prize for potential carjackers.

"I'd be in no state to talk to Talon after a golf club to the cranium." Brian chuckled.

"Brian! Can you shut up? We're in a dangerous area! I don't need you preening yourself and providing commentary." Alexis growled.

"Dangerous?" Brian laughed. "Come on, the East Side isn't that bad…okay, it *is*, but if anything, Talon is the scariest guy in the whole neighborhood."

"That doesn't make me feel better." Alexis sighed grimly. "He had better know something."

Alexis double-checked that there were no crackheads, gangbangers, or Juggalos following her. The coast was clear. She relaxed her grip on the steering wheel, but only slightly.

"All we need is a name." Brian squirmed.

Alexis was concerned about his weird posture. He was sitting very uncomfortably. She hoped she hadn't given him any internal injuries.

"Speak of the devil." Brian pointed at a house on the left side of the street.

Alexis's jaw dropped when she saw the flag flying from Talon's porch.

"*Come and take 'em?* Of fucking course." she rolled her eyes. "I just knew he'd be into some stupid Republican bullshit."

"Just wait 'til you see the jack-o-lanterns." Brian winced.

Alexis pulled the Audi up behind the grey Honda on the asphalt driveway. She turned the car off. The AR-15 flag billowing proudly in the gust made her even more uneasy. She slowly reached for the golf club.

Brian shifted painfully in his seat. He clutched at his torso. He leaned over to Alexis.

"Have you ever picked up from Talon before?" he asked.

"No. Sabrina was always the one who…you know." Alexis saddened herself at the mention of her departed friend.

"Ok. So…Talon's a little weird when it comes to picking up." Brian began, "Well, we're not picking up from him, but the process will be the same. All drug dealers are a little superstitious."

"Really?" Alexis raised an eyebrow.

"He knows me. Like I said, he might not be happy to see me, but at least he knows I've picked up from him before. Here's what's going to happen: I am going to get out of the car and walk up to the porch. You stay here for now. Once you see me on the porch, you start honking the horn, and Talon will come out and let us in."

"That's a little convoluted." Alexis answered, her voice dripping with doubt. "If you're a drug dealer, don't you want to remain inconspicuous? I feel like me sitting here honking the horn is just going to draw unwanted attention."

"I know. I know. I've told him that myself, but I don't make the rules." Brian shrugged. "Do you think you can handle honking the horn until he comes outside?"

Alexis nodded.

"Good. Break a leg." Brian winked and got out of the car.

Alexis watched him hobble up the porch steps. His limp had only gotten worse. Why was he clutching his chest? Something about this plan didn't seem right. It would be too easy for Talon to just shoot him on sight; or shoot *her* for that matter. Alexis prayed Brian knew what he was doing.

After what felt like an eternity, Brian reached the top of the porch. He turned to Alexis, smiled, and gave a thumbs up.    Heart racing, Alexis laid down a long blare on the horn.

Brian darted behind a columned corner near the porch's stairs. From that angle, Talon wouldn't be able to see him if he were coming out the front door. He would only see her.

"What are you doing?" Alexis angrily muttered.

She began making short, staccato honks as if to ask Brian that very question. Brian didn't respond. It looked like he was fishing for something inside of his hoodie.

205

Before Alexis could get a good look at what Brian now held in his hands, the front door was nearly kicked off its hinges. Talon stormed outside. He was wearing his signature black hoodie, sweatpants, and beanie.

Just as Alexis feared, all he saw was her. He was oblivious to Brian, who now stood upright behind the column of wood. Fear gripped Alexis. She increased the frequency of the car horn's blasts.

Talon reached into his waistband and produced a black, semiautomatic handgun. He raised his arms as if to ask: "What the fuck are you doing?" He lifted the weapon menacingly in her general direction. She felt the blood drain from her face.

As Talon brought the weapon to bear, Brian lunged out from behind the column and brought down the Audi's tire iron with a metallic ring. Talon yelped in pain, and the handgun went flying. As he clutched his arm, Brian swung the tire iron up into Talon's jaw, knocking him off his feet.

Horrified, Alexis sprang into action. She leapt out of the car and sprinted to the porch, leaving the golf club behind. Brian straddled Talon and wrestled him into submission.

"Brian! What are you doing?!" Alexis shrieked.

"Grab that gun!" Brian grunted.

Talon was cursing egregiously. The drug dealer's lip had been busted open. He wasn't doing a good job of fighting off Brian.

Alexis looked around wildly. She saw the black pistol lying a few feet away from the brawling men. Quite caught up in the moment, she quickly ducked down and scooped it up.

Feeling the weight of the gun in her trembling hands, Alexis thought she was going to be sick. She had spent countless hours railing against firearms on social media. Now she held one of the vile killing machines in her very grasp.

"I will never forgive you for this, Brian." Alexis spat.

"Sorry! I nabbed the tire iron from the trunk while you were-" Brian answered, gripping Talon's throat with one hand.

"No, not the tire iron! The *gun*, you asshole!" Alexis swore. "Do you know how many children get killed by these things every year?"

"What the hell is going on?" A voice called from inside the house.

Alexis, Brian, and Talon all looked up to see Nikki standing in the hallway. She wore matching Minions pajamas. She held a kitchen knife in one hand, and a half-sliced avocado in the other. Nikki stared at her husband and his two assailants for a moment. Her eyes widened when she realized what was going on.

"Get off him! God damn you, Brian Stanhope! Get off him!" Nikki screamed. She hurled the avocado, which splattered against Brian's bald head.

"Nikki! No!" Brian shouted.

Nikki raised the kitchen knife and charged. Seeing the blade held high in the air, Alexis panicked. She squeezed her eyes shut and pulled the trigger.

The pop of the handgun made everyone jump. It wasn't as loud as Alexis thought it would be. She still nearly dropped the pistol from the recoil.

Talon stopped struggling as he tried to get his bearings. Brian, who had a better view, saw the bullet ricochet. It missed Nikki's head by inches. The projectile left a trail of torn up drywall behind it. Nikki screamed and collapsed to the ground, unharmed and in tears. The knife fell from her grasp and embedded itself into the hallway floor.

"Nikki! Nikki! You motherfuckers shot my wife! Nikki!" Talon screamed, blood billowing from his lip.

Brian released his hold on Talon. He got to his feet. The dealer, meanwhile, scurried on hands and knees back into the hallway to comfort his sobbing wife.

"Nice shot." Brian complimented.

Alexis looked down at the gun, and then she aimed it at the sobbing Nikki and bloodied Talon.

"Oh, good idea! Keep the gun on them!" Brian smiled.

"Don't kill us! Don't kill us like you did Sabrina! Please...please..." Nikki sobbed.

"This isn't what I had in mind when you said you just wanted to talk to him!" Alexis snapped. She whipped around in a fury, obliviously pointing the gun at Brian.

"Whoa! Hey! Be careful with that thing! Let's get inside before we attract *more* unwanted attention." Brian grabbed the tire iron.

"Screw this. I'm done. I'm out. I'm leaving you here." Alexis raised her voice so as to be heard over Nikki's wails.

"You're leaving? With a stolen gun that has your fingerprints all over it? A gun you fired at its owners? Yeah, that will go over *really* well with the police." Brian smirked.

"You...you...blackmailing...Brian!" Alexis was enraged. Brian had manipulated the situation masterfully.

"I did say I was egotistical. Get inside. Keep pointing that gun at them. I got the door."

Brian ushered Alexis into the house. He slammed the front door shut. In the poor light of the hallway, Alexis was surprised to see a group of plastic jack-o-lanterns blocking the foot of the stairs.

"See? I told you! Fucking stair pumpkins, man." Brian said.

Nikki's sobs quieted some. Talon held his wife close to him. He glared up at Alexis and Brian with murderous hatred on his bloody face.

"Well, go on then. Kill us like you killed Sabrina. When my boy Nick Bowman finds us, you're gonna be fucked." Talon snarled.

"What? No, he didn't kill Sabrina." Alexis defended Brian before she could stop herself.

"Are you kidding me? Has he brainwashed you too, Alexis? Is this some Stockholm Syndrome shit? Or were you in on it as well? You always were a fake cunt." The hatred on Talon's face darkened with every passing second.

"Oh, they're going to bite out our throats...I just know it...oh, Skylar...Skylar!" Nikki cried harder.

"Hey! Shut up!" Brian roared.

He slammed the tire iron against the wall. Nikki went quiet with a whimper. Talon's eyes narrowed into slits, his red blood making his mousey face appear more ghastly than normal.

"I'm innocent. I didn't kill anyone. We're here to figure some stuff out. That's it!" Brian yelled.

"Figure stuff out?" Talon echoed, confusion creeping into his voice.

"Yeah! But first, Alexis, give me that!" Brian held out a hand.

Alexis eagerly plopped the handgun into his outstretched palm, more than happy to get rid of the repulsive instrument of destruction. Brian aimed the gun at the jack-o-lanterns. Firing wildly, he put a bullet into each of them. Nikki screamed. Talon cursed.

*Why is the gun so much louder inside?* Alexis flinched. She covered her ears. She ducked out of the way of the orange plasticine shrapnel spraying into the air.

Brian tossed the weapon back to Alexis, who caught it with more dexterity than she would have liked. She pointed the pistol back at Talon and Nikki. The couple cowered. Brian angrily kicked over what was left of the plastic jack-o-lanterns. He stormed upstairs.

"Where are you going?" Alexis asked.

"I'm getting to the bottom of this." Brian answered without looking back. He vanished into the darkness at the top of the staircase.

To her surprise, Alexis noticed that Talon didn't seem as angry now. He seemed nonplussed. What's worse, he seemed hurt. Emotionally hurt.

"Alexis...how can you help that burnout? He's a crazy serial killer! He murdered your best friend." Talon pleaded.

"He's not crazy. He's also not a killer." Alexis firmly replied, the gun feeling more comfortable in her hands. She kept it squarely pointed at Talon's chest.

"You saw the news. Can't you see he's lured us all here to kill us? We're going to end up in some murder-porn story. We're the ones who know." Talon argued.

"Oh, you two know. You know more than you're letting on." Alexis countered.

"What do you mean?"

"You know who killed Sabrina."

"Of course I know! It was him!" Talon pointed where Brian had gone up the staircase.

"You are so full of shit. Were you suddenly this articulate before you tried to shoot Damon?" Alexis countered.

"Fuck you, bitch. You don't know what he was like." Nikki spat.

Alexis pointed the gun at Nikki in response. Nikki screamed. She immediately resumed weeping.

Before anyone could say anything further, shattering pottery and loud profanity permeated the air. Everyone looked up at the ceiling, trying to figure out where upstairs the sounds originated. Footsteps and more cursing soon followed.

"What is he doing up there?" Talon asked.

"All part of his plan." Alexis tried to sound confident.

She hoped Brian had a plan. He better have a plan. He certainly had a plan when he hid the tire iron on him.

After a few seconds, Brian returned. He came downstairs holding a pair of soaking wet pill bottles. Alexis recognized the green marijuana contained within them as the skunk weed Brian preferred.

"You fucking son-of-a-bitch! You really did keep it in the toilet tank! You motherfucker!" Brian threw the bottled skunk weed at Talon. The little containers left wet toilet water stains on Talon's hoodie.

"What is this about?" Alexis asked, black anger rising in her stomach.

"Every time I picked up from this guy, he was literally selling me shit!" Brian faced Alexis; arms outstretched with fury.

"Is that why you dragged me here? So you could figure out if he was ripping you off?!" Alexis contemplated shooting Brian.

"I just had to know!" Brian retorted.

"Well...hey!" Alexis reared the gun at Talon in alarm.

Talon had made a grab for the knife in the floor. He wrenched the blade out of the wood. He moved with blinding speed.

Alexis was faster. She squeezed the trigger on the pistol. With another deafening bang, a bullet embedded itself into the floorboards just inches below the location of Talon's family jewels.

Nikki screamed again. Talon looked down at the bullet hole and realized that he had nearly been neutered. He looked at Alexis. Then he looked at the knife in his hands. He let the blade fall back into the floor, where it re-embedded itself. He wrapped his arms around his wife. The Keeners almost looked adorable.

"You're both dead. You're messing in things beyond you. You are both so dead. You don't know who you're fucking with." Talon laughed; his teeth stained with his own blood.

"That's...why we're here, actually." Brian began.

"I ain't snitching." Talon clenched his jaw.

"Maybe we'll call the cops and have them arrest you for all the contraband in here. The black market weed, the gun...are you supposed to have a gun? Aren't you a felon?" Alexis threatened.

"So what? I'll go to jail. I got big friends in there who will look out for me. Friends who are going to deal with the two of you." Talon snickered.

"Oh...your friends...you mean the American Guard, right?" Alexis asked.

Talon gasped despite himself.

"Who's selling to you? The Asian guy? What's his name? And why is an Asian hanging out with some alt-right hate group?" Brian rattled off his questions as if he were a hard-boiled private eye.

"The American Guard split up...it's not like the KKK or anything like that...you know...like one guy didn't like the whole racism thing so he-" Talon started to explain, but Alexis fired a round into the ceiling, cutting him off.

Nikki screamed once more. The hallway smelled as if she had wet herself. Talon's nostrils flared at the aroma. He let go of his wife. He looked like he was going to barf.

"I don't care about the inside drama of some cult! I just want the name of the Asian guy in the green Impala who was hanging out with Sabrina all night at Big John's!" Alexis screamed, pointing the gun at Talon's face.

"Ok! Ok! Shit...you even know what car he drives?" Talon asked.

"He tried to kill her in the *Larson's* parking lot." Brian motioned towards Alexis.

"Look...I don't know the guy that well...he's big trouble in little China, if you know what I mean." Talon replied. "It's like...he's just my distributor, I don't know him super personally..."

"But you know his name, right?" Alexis demanded, inching the gun closer to Talon's skull.

"Yeah! Yeah! Jesus...his name is Tommy Fenton. Tommy Fenton!" Talon retreated from the barrel of the pistol, pushing his wife between himself and Alexis.

Nikki moaned uselessly. A noticeably damp splotch was visible on Nikki's Minions pants. Brian blinked as he too realized what had happened.

"Thanks, Talon. That's all we wanted to know." Brian smiled at Alexis. "Come on, let's get out of here."

Alexis lowered the weapon. Her anger was replaced by disgust. She was violated by Brian's stupid tire iron plan. She was violated by how much she had enjoyed using the gun. She was so revolted she thought she might retch.

Brian noticed the look on Alexis's face. He turned back to Nikki and Talon. He plugged his nose.

"Oh, you might want to clean up, Nikki. That smell is making us gag." He said.

"Fuck you! You two are dead! You hear me? Dead!" Talon roared as Alexis and Brian made their way out the front door. "The first thing I'm doing when you two faggots leave is calling up my friends in the American Guard: Nick Bowman, Tommy Fenton, and the boys! They gonna smoke you raggedy bitches!"

"That's real nice, Talon. Know what else you can do?" Alexis asked.

Before Talon could reply, Alexis calmly and precisely emptied the semiautomatic handgun into the AR-15 flag. The motto *"COME AND TAKE 'EM"* was soon peppered with bullet holes.

When the empty pistol clicked, Alexis seized the bullet-ridden flag with her free hand. She threw the banner over the Keeners. The married couple now looked like they were wearing a misshapen children's ghost costume. They peered out from the bullet holes in the cloth.

"You can take that problematic, ignorant, divisive, self-aggrandizing, offensive, pointless, masturbatory, pro-NRA, anti-intellectual *BULLSHIT* and shove it up your ass!" Alexis screamed.

She slammed the door behind her. This final slam was too much punishment for the poor door. It fell off its hinges.

Alexis hurled the empty handgun with all her might. It landed somewhere in the neighboring house's hydrangea bushes. She furiously stomped off the porch and made her way back to the Audi.

"Wait up!" Brian hobbled after Alexis; his bruises freshly sore from his tussle with Talon. "You were awesome in there."

"I can't believe this." Alexis muttered, anger boiling over.

"Me neither! I mean, maybe it's ignorant of me, and I still have a lot to learn PC wise, but I haven't met too many people of Asian descent with a name like 'Tommy Fenton.'" Brian continued.

"No, Brian! I can't believe *you!*" Alexis shouted in Brian's face. "You used me *again!*"

"I was scared you wouldn't want to be my ride if you knew I was going to beat the truth out of them. It was the only way." Brian explained, shielding himself from Alexis with the tire iron.

"You...you...you include me from now on in these little schemes of yours, or I will leave you on the side of the road as target practice for his hate group buddies!" Alexis shoved a finger into Brian's chest, hard.

"I will! I promise! No more deception. That was unfair of me. I'm sorry." Brian recoiled in pain.

"Good! You're lucky Sabrina was my bestie. Now get in the car." Alexis hoped she had poked one of his many bruises.

Brian sheepishly nodded and followed Alexis into the Audi. She started the car and scanned the neighboring houses. She heard Brian open his mouth:

"With all that gunfire, I'm pretty sure the neighbors know we're here. You can just chill, Lexi."

"Do *NOT* call me that."

"Sorry."

Still, Alexis left the East Side driving much more calmly than before.

# XXVIII

"Like…I think we go back to your place and call the police." Brian began.

"Are we sure we have the right name? How do we know Talon was telling the truth?" Alexis asked.

"What if I check your phone? I'll just do a quick search for *Tommy Fenton* and see if our guy comes up." Brian suggested.

"I am *not* giving you my phone."

"Please?"

Alexis sighed.

"If I give you my phone, do you promise that searching for Tommy Fenton on social media is *all* you are going to do?"

"What do you mean?"

"You're not hatching another retarded scheme where I'm bait again?" Alexis accused.

"No! I promise. I think I'm only smart enough to do that once a day." vowed Brian.

"You were smart enough to recruit me as your manic pixie dream girl." Alexis frowned.

"I took that beating for *you*. Not me." Brian stated.

He went silent. Alexis pondered his words for a moment. She reached into her pocket and withdrew her phone. She threw the device into his lap.

"Here." She said.

"Thank you." Brian smiled, snatching up the phone like a leprechaun would a pot of gold.

"I'm keeping my trunk locked from now on." Alexis huffed.

"That's a pretty good idea." Brian answered absent-mindedly. "Jeez, your phone is almost dead!"

"I was tweeting a lot this morning about how much of a bastard you are."

"Guess that killed the battery. Do you have a car charger?"

"No. We're almost back to my house anyway."

"What kind of zoomer doesn't have a car charger?"

"Do you want me to take my phone away from you?"

"No."

"Then shut up."

"Sorry."

Alexis drove in sullen silence. Brian searched furiously on her mobile device. The rain held off for the moment. The impending weather strangely reminded Alexis of how she had felt while holding the gun.

"Brian?" she turned to face her passenger.

"Yeah?"

"Don't ever put me in a situation where I need a gun ever again."

Brian saw the finality in her eyes.

"Ok." he nodded, knowing that this would be a line he could never cross. "I'm sorry."

Alexis turned her grey eyes back to the road. They did not remain there long. Her focus was broken by an excited exclamation from Brian.

"Alexis! I found him!"

She looked at her cohort's discovery at the next red light. Brian had pulled up the Facebook account of a young Asian man. The name on the profile was indeed "Tommy Fenton."

Alexis's blood ran cold. This was him, all right. He was wearing that same camouflaged jacket he had worn at Big John's. His full, dark hair looked pitch black under whatever Instagram filter he used. His designer glasses glinted sinisterly. His hometown was marked as "Toledo, Ohio."

In one of his highlighted photos, Tommy Fenton was throwing a peace sign in one hand. Alexis felt a deathly shiver slide down her spine. She felt that hand close tight around her jaw. She trembled.

"Ohio! Right? Isn't that American Guard territory?" Brian asked.

"The Southern Poverty Law Center *did* say that." she confirmed as the stoplight turned green.

The Carrington Farms subdivision was up ahead. They were almost home. She couldn't believe Brian had gotten them this far. They had a credible lead! Talon hadn't killed them! They might actually have something the police could use! Alexis could practically see Sabrina sitting with them in the car, smiling and saying *"Hey, thanks for helping track down my killer, guys."*

"Oh, yes! We got him! I can't wait to call the cops on this fucker." Brian cheered.

As Alexis's home came into view, the nervous joy in her heart swelled to a fever pitch. Things were working out! They were golden!

Then she saw her driveway.

Her hands went numb. She almost lost control of the steering wheel. Her heart stopped. Her bottom lip quivered. She was frozen with fright.

"Alexis? What's wrong?" Brian sensed her distress.

In her fear, she was unable to form words. She barely kept the car on the road. All she could do was lift a finger and point out the bright green Chevrolet Impala that was quietly parked in her driveway.

Brian, upon seeing the green automobile, ducked under the dashboard.

"Holy shit. Is that *his* car?" he asked.

Alexis didn't reply.

That was the only answer Brian needed. He poked his head over the dashboard. He tried to take charge of the situation.

"Ok. Just drive casual. Don't stop. Take a side street and get back on Custer." he calmly directed. "He might not notice us."

Alexis barely heard his words. She drove past her driveway. The green Impala was now nothing more than a reflection in her rearview mirror. As the strange car faded away, Alexis had a horrifying realization that shattered her being.

"Lily! Oh my god! Lily!" She panicked, tears welling up.

She went to throw the car into a U-turn, but Brian stopped her. He grabbed her forearm. His grip was firm, but not aggressive.

"Let me go! My dog is in there! Lily!" Alexis cried, tears spilling down her face.

"Alexis. It's okay. Keep driving. We can't let them see us." Brian pleaded.

"Easy for you to say! You never had a dog! She's my only friend left in this world!" Alexis burned with rage and worry.

"They probably have guns! We have what? A golf club and a tire iron? They'll shoot us the second we get out of the car." Brian argued. "If we get shot, Lily is as good as dead."

"What if she's dead already? Oh my Lord." Alexis saw stars. She thought she might faint.

"We should get to *Zoe's*. It's a public place. We can wait for the cops there. We'll be safe in the public eye. I know how these people work."

"You don't know fuck-all!" Alexis gunned the turn onto Custer road at full speed. "Call the cops right now!"

"Get us to *Zoe's*. I'll handle the rest." Brian quickly brought the cell phone to bear.

Alexis gasped for breath. Her tears dried. One foot pushed the pedal into the floor. It was time to see what this Audi could really do.

# XXIX

Brian could barely hear the dial tone over the roar of the engine. The Audi even drowned out the coalescing intrusive thoughts. If this German automobile could go faster, the millipede of anxiety would leave him alone too.

"9-1-1, what is your emergency?" The petite feminine voice of the operator answered.

"Hi. This is Brian Stanhope. The guy you all thought killed Sabrina Cunningham?" Brian began.

He felt Alexis's deathly glare. He put a finger from his free hand into his unoccupied ear. He needed to hear the operator better. He also needed shielding from Alexis's fury.

"Hello Mr. Stanhope. What is your emergency?" The operator repeated.

"I need Lieutenant Cassandra Johnson. She was the detective on my case. I need to speak to her right away, please." Brian demanded.

There was a pause on the other end of the phone.

"Mr. Stanhope, this line is for emergencies only. If you have Lieutenant Johnson's office number, you really should call that to reach her directly." The operator sounded suddenly exasperated.

"This *is* an emergency! I need to speak to Cassandra Johnson!" Brian emphasized. "Tell her I have the name and location of one of the men involved in Sabrina Cunningham's murder. I need to speak to Johnson, and I need to speak to her now!"

The operator sighed so audibly that Brian was sure Alexis could hear it.

"Patching you through now Mr. Stanhope, but in the future-"

"Thank you! Tell her to muster a SWAT team." he hoped that would calm Alexis.

A jaunty tune played on the line as the operator placed Brian on hold. After a few seconds, the little jingle ended. It was replaced by the gruff, world-weary voice of Sandra Johnson.

"Mr. Stanhope. Pleasure to hear from you again." The detective answered. She sounded simultaneously bored and amused. Brian didn't like that combination.

"Lieutenant Johnson! I have an emergency." Brian began again. "I need to report a breaking and entering."

"An emergency, you say? Why didn't you tell the operator you had an emergency? It's almost as if we have a whole system for emergencies so people like you don't have to bother hard working detectives." Cassandra Johnson replied with rude pride.

"I understand, but it's more complicated than that!" Brian continued. "The home of Alexis Knabusch has been broken into by an Asian man we believe to be involved with the murder of Sabrina Cunningham!"

"*We?* Hired some Pinkertons to help you out?" Johnson snidely chuckled.

"Alexis is here with me!"

"I see...how do you know this random *trespasser* is involved with the Cunningham murder?"

"He's the Asian guy who rolls around with the American Guard! He was at Big John's! He was all over Sabrina that night!" Brian desperately explained.

"Really...what makes you think a hate group would '*roll around*' with minorities and foreigners?" Johnson yawned dryly.

"This guy WAS there that night." Brian's heart beat faster and faster. This wasn't going at all how he had imagined.

"Let's say that he was. How do you know he's part of the American Guard?" Johnson countered.

"Talon Keener told me!"

Lieutenant Sandra Johnson laughed.

"What makes you think anything Talon Keener says is trustworthy information?"

Brian could almost see Johnson wiping tears of mirth from her cheeks. He was beginning to panic. Couldn't this woman swallow her pride just once and *help* him? Isn't that what police were supposed to do?

"We went over to his house and beat the truth out of him! We pointed a gun at him, that's how you know he was being honest! The Asian's name is Tommy Fenton. He's from Toledo. He's Talon's supplier. If you go over to Talon's house, you'll find all sorts of drugs and guns over there. I'm telling the truth!" Brian hadn't actually wanted to snitch on Talon out of fear of further retaliation, but given the circumstances, he had no other choice.

"So, let me get this straight: if I send a unit over to the Knabusch residence, I am going to find the man who's going to crack the Cunningham case?" Sandra sounded alarmingly droll.

"Yes! Well...we think so. All Talon really told us is that he's part of the American Guard...not that the guy really knew anything about Sabrina...but Alexis saw this guy, brought up Sabrina, and was nearly murdered at *Larson's* for it!" Brian exclaimed.

There was silence on the other end of the line for a long while.

"You're going to set a record, Brian Stanhope. A record for the shortest stint *OUT* of jail." A horrible edge found its way into Sandra Johnson's voice.

"What?" Brian asked, the blood draining from his face.

"If you ever contact me again, I am going to have you arrested for wasting police resources."

With a grave click, the line went dead. What was worse, the last of the phone's battery gave out. The device died in Brian's hands.

He looked down at the phone in horror. He hoped that Alexis hadn't heard his conversation with Lieutenant Johnson. He turned to face his driver. Judging by the look in her eyes, she had clearly heard every single word.

"You stupid son-of-a-bitch!" She screamed, hitting Brian in the face. "My dog is as good as dead, and my phone is dead too! Now what are we going to do?!"

Brian placed his head in his hands. He could barely feel the pain from Alexis's blows. He scrambled for ideas, a pit forming in his stomach. Even accepting his sheep wouldn't be enough to stop the anxiety millipede this time. It was already puncturing his neck. He was going to have a panic attack. He could feel the pummeling his brain would receive, like the beating a corrupt federal agent would give to a con in a bad movie.

*Federal agent...hey...wait a minute...* Brian looked up at Alexis, a hint of an idea forming.

"Zoe usually has a spare phone charger." He said.

"What?" Alexis asked.

"That's how she runs the jazz music at her place."

"How does that help us?!" Alexis shrieked in disbelief.

"The FBI." Brian stated softly.

"What?!"

"The FBI! The police might not want to help us, but if we can charge your phone at *Zoe's*, we can file an anonymous tip on the FBI's website!" Brian's hands pieced together an invisible puzzle. "The FBI likes murders and weird hate organizations. They will definitely want to help us out."

"You better hope they do." Alexis snarled.

"Ok. We'll wait it out there until they get back to us." Brian motioned out the window. "Look! We're there!"

The large sign outside *Zoe's* was illuminated unusually early. The darkness of the impending weather gave the diner an eerie look. Still, the change in atmosphere had clearly not deterred any patrons from the establishment. The parking lot was full.

The Audi's engine grinded uncharacteristically as Alexis reduced her speed. Brian jolted in his seat from the effort the car was now making. He hoped Alexis's blind anger wouldn't cause her to hit one of the parked cars in the lot. The last thing they needed was to be stuck at a fender-bender. Lily's chances of survival were slim enough as they were.

Alexis circled the diner three times before a handicapped spot opened up. The Audi didn't possess a handicap sticker. Alexis had once posted a blog entry about how abusing handicapped parking was problematic, ableist, and racist. Right now, she didn't seem to care. She sped into the spot so quickly the car hopped up on to the barrier.

# XXX

Zoe was pleased by the size of the early dinner rush. Looming thunderstorms tended to drive up business, but the place had been full all week. At this rate, she'd have to hire more servers. She could kiss her distributor for scoring that deal on prime rib roast. They hadn't had rib roast on the menu since Lou ran the show.

This was the first time the prime rib roast was edible. Lou always insisted on cooking himself, usually when he was black-out drunk. He'd burn everything, and whenever Zoe tried to intervene, he'd smack her and threaten to send her back to her mentally ill parents in Brightmoor. He kept up this behavior until the day Zoe allegedly hospitalized him with her belt.

Zoe took a moment to turn up the Marcus Belgrave and plug her phone into the charger behind the cash register. With a full house and a 20-minute wait for a table, she'd soon have enough money to renovate the place and undo Lou's horrible cover-up job on her lovely mural. She smiled at the thought.

As she checked on the thunderstorm from the bay windows, she noticed the fancy Audi parked in the handicapped spot. The car was half on the curb. It made no effort to correct itself before its engine shut off.

Zoe shook her head. Alexis should know better than to park there. She wasn't impaired. There were no stickers on the vehicle, nor any handicap tags hanging from the mirror.

Zoe excused herself. She intended to politely, but firmly tell Alexis to park somewhere else. She tightened her apron and stepped outside.

The wind hadn't kicked up yet, but the promise of rain hung heavy in the air. Taking a few steps towards the Audi, Zoe saw the frazzled Alexis Knabusch in the driver's seat. In the passenger's seat, struggling to get out; was...

"Brian?" Zoe's jaw dropped. She quickened her pace.

"Hey Zoe!" Brian waved from inside the car. His voice was muffled through the glass.

"You need to leave." Zoe raised her voice to make sure she was heard.

Brian and Alexis both looked at her in horror. Zoe's own panicked frustration caught in her throat. She paused for a second before shaking her head. She had read the papers. She knew who Brian was accused of killing. She knew he wouldn't last five minutes inside.

Brian tried to open the passenger door. Zoe held it shut on him. Brian seemed amazed by her strength.

"Don't get out of the car!" Zoe hissed. "You need to leave right now."

"What? Why?" Brian asked, dumbfounded. He rolled the passenger window down.

"Zoe, please. This is an emergency." Alexis pleaded from the driver's seat.

"I don't care. You know how much of his snuff-peril they've showed in the paper?" Zoe pointed a finger at Brian.

"What? Zoe, c'mon. You know me. I didn't kill Sabrina." Brian protested.

"It's not about what I know or don't know." Zoe snapped. "I've been hearing the gossip all day. Half the town *thinks* you did it, and most of that half is sitting inside eating prime rib. You go in there; you'll start a riot. Are you going to pay me back if my property gets trashed?"

"Zoe, please." Alexis interjected. "We just need to charge our phone. We need to-"

"I don't care!"

Zoe felt Brian struggle against the door. She slammed it on him angrily. She locked eyes with the bearded young man.

"The last thing I need is some redneck seeing you and deciding they're going to be a vigilante." She growled.

"We just need to use your charger! Don't do this." Alexis's voice was filled with hopelessness.

Zoe's resolve faltered for a moment. She made a fist. Whatever was going on here, it wasn't worth her two favorite regulars getting pumped full of lead over.

"Don't you have one of them newfangled car chargers?" Zoe asked Alexis.

"I don't have one. Really! Please Zoe; just let us use the one behind the counter." Alexis begged.

"What kind of Gen-Z kid can't charge their phone in their car?" Zoe exasperated.

"That's what *I* said!" Brian agreed.

"This is not my problem. You've been here too long already. You two need to get going." Zoe stood firm.

"...I've got a lot of followers on social media. I'll plug your place if you just let us use your charger for twenty minutes. I can give you some real business." Alexis offered.

Alexis was playing the trump card now. She had never before offered her online presence as a bargaining chip for anything. Zoe didn't find the proposition enticing at all. In fact, she found it insulting. Couldn't these two see she was trying to help them?

"You need to leave, or I'm calling the cops. Plain and simple." She declared.

"Zoe, we're friends. Don't do this." Brian trembled.

Zoe knew she had to do something drastic. She thought of her marriage. She thought of her ex-husband's impotent excuses.

"Have you two heard the rumors?" Zoe slowly asked.

"Uh...what rumors? About me?" Brian was confused.

"About what I did to Lou Freeman?" Zoe elaborated.

"Who?" Alexis puzzled.

"My ex-husband."

Zoe deftly unbuckled her belt. She whipped it into the air with one hand. The metal of the buckle gleamed menacingly under the light of the large neon sign.

Alexis couldn't start the Audi fast enough.

"Ok! Ok! We're going! We're sorry!" Brian screamed in terror.

"You killed my dog. You killed Lily!" Alexis wept angrily.

Zoe raised the belt as if to strike the hood of the car with it.

"Agh! Okay! We're going! Don't scratch the car." Alexis threw the vehicle into reverse. With a squeal of tires, the Audi zoomed out of the parking lot.

"Dumb kids." Zoe sighed. She put her belt back on. She adjusted the stout metal buckle, making sure it rested snugly around her waist. She then headed back inside.

"Sorry about that." She smiled at the elderly Mr. and Mrs. Vore. The couple had been pretending to wait patiently by the counter to pay their bill. In reality, they had actively observed the exterior altercation with unwavering interest.

Zoe bit her tongue. She tried to push Alexis and Brian out of her mind by focusing on her beloved jazz. It wasn't working.

# XXXI

Brian couldn't stand the silence that now dominated the car. He forced himself to stare at the road. He couldn't look at Alexis. He was terrified of what he would see in those grey eyes of hers.

He needed a distraction. He needed to calm down. He needed weed.

*Damn it...* He wasn't smoking pot anymore.

He needed music. He hit the radio. A Taylor Swift song came on. A little radical for the local stations, but he'd take it. He cranked the volume.

The melody's major key was belied by lyrics that too aptly described the current life-or-death situation. Taylor sang of being outnumbered, raided, and cornered. Sweat formed on Brian's brow. Maybe he was reading too deeply into things.

"Can you turn that off?!" Alexis howled in anger. Clearly, she too had been reading into the lyrics.

"Sorry." Brian killed the radio. "I thought it would lighten the mood."

"Well, IT DIDN'T!" Alexis screamed. "NOW what are we going to do?!"

"Shit. Shit. Shit shit shit." Brian rubbed his temples in frustration.

This whole disaster was his responsibility. If he hadn't forced Alexis to give him a ride, she'd be sitting safely at home. He was reminded of how he had used her as fetish-fuel. All he ever did was use Alexis. Why was he such a piece of shit?

"This is my fault." He said, thoughts racing, anxiety building. "I'm going to fix this, okay?"

"How?! The cops don't believe us, my phone is dead, those psychopathic assholes are in MY house, and we have nowhere to go!" Alexis threatened to cry again.

Brian fought through his deep shame.

"That's not entirely true..." he muttered.

Another idea formed in his brain. Maybe he did have a way out of this. It was time for a little ex-child prodigy mojo.

"Oh, really?" Alexis rolled her eyes, driving erratically.

"Yes! My house!" He snapped his fingers in excitement.

"What." Alexis was nonplussed.

"My house! We can stop at Meijer and buy you a charger. The electricity's still on at my place. We can get a signal there! The civil forfeiture might have gotten my computer, but they left my router! We can get Wi-Fi, and we can contact the FBI."

*Thank you, ex-child prodigy brain.* He thought.

"We can wait out the night. Talon doesn't know my exact address. We might be safe for a while." He continued.

"Wait, how did they know where *my* house was?" Alexis gasped.

"Hmm…when you were ranting about me and organizing search parties for Sabrina online, did you ever tag your address?" Brian suggested.

Alexis blushed in embarrassment.

"You did." He said.

"Just for donations to help find Sabrina." Alexis confessed.

"With your following, you'd be too easy to find." Brian sighed. "Whatever. What's done is done. You'll be safe at my place."

Alexis looked lost in thought.

Brian grew concerned. Whatever she was thinking about clearly weighed heavily on her. He wished she would just accept her sheep and get it off her chest.

Eventually, she took a ragged breath, her fading blue hair shaking with her lungs. She looked pale, even for the circumstances. Brian braced himself.

"Alexis? he asked.

"It's just…the last time we were alone, you choked me." her grey eyes filled with distrust.

That hurt Brian in a way he hadn't expected.

"I know. The Ketamine had me all-" he tried to explain.

"Ketamine is a fucking *downer*, Brian." Alexis interrupted. "It's not the kind of drug that makes people violent."

"Well, okay, that's not entirely true-" he retorted.

"Stop making excuses! You hurt me. When someone tells you that you hurt them, you don't get to decide that you didn't!" Alexis yelled.

Brian suddenly grew terribly angry.

"Are you kidding me right now? You're going to use Louis C.K. against me? That stupid quote is the biggest piece of bullshit that pervert ever cursed humanity with."

"Seems to me that you'd probably get along well with another pervert." Alexis answered.

"That damn meme has been weaponized by every single manipulative leech on the planet Earth." Brian was about to explode.

"Oh! So, *I'm* the leech? You exploit the concept of murder!" she retorted.

"YES!" Brian roared. "*You* feed on negativity and imaginary online numbers! Nothing means anything to you unless it validates you!"

"You're one to fucking talk, Brian." Alexis shouted back. "You didn't get us into this mess because you wanted to help Sabrina. You got us into this mess because you only wanted to help your goddamn self!"

The fight went out of Brian. He knew Alexis was right. He deflated and looked out the window.

"...you know what? Just drop me off on the side of the road." He murmured.

Alexis didn't respond.

Brian thought about Al. He wondered what the man would think about this whole mess. He looked back at his only friend in the world.

"I know you don't believe me, but what happened was an accident. I never, *ever* actually wanted to hurt you." He said.

"Why didn't you just come out and say you liked me? Seems a lot easier than publishing...ew...*murder fan fiction*." Alexis recoiled.

"Because you might have said you hated me."

There was another silence in the car. This was a vulnerable silence. The kind of silence only lovers, desperate comrades, or former enemies shared. Unbeknownst to either Alexis or Brian, it was the perfect silence for where they stood now.

"Why don't we get in touch with your brother? Sam and Raoul might be able to hide us." Alexis's desperation broke the silence like a fracturing glacier.

"No. I'm not dragging anyone else into this." Brian firmly replied. "Besides, who knows what the American Guard might do to some gays?"

"Fuck. You're right." Alexis swore. "Don't ever involve me in any plans you make ever again."

"Sorry."

"What kind of weapons do you have?"

"Well...this golf club...and this tire iron." Brian motioned to the implements in the car. "I also have a shovel."

"That's it?" Alexis growled. "Don't you have guns, or kitchen knives, or *something?*"

"My mom never let us have guns. She thought they'd be a bad influence on a youthful genius like myself." Brian frowned. "As for the kitchen knives, I threw them all out after a really bad panic attack."

"Why would you do that? How did you cook?" Alexis asked in disbelief.

"Well, I didn't cook. As to why I did it...I hadn't learned to accept my sheep yet."

"What did I say about that phrase?"

"Sorry."

There was another silence. This one not in the spirit of deep camaraderie as the last one had been. This one was more frustrated.

"Just tell me how to get to your house." Alexis fumed.

It was going to be a long night.

# XXXII

Contrary to popular belief, the trailer parks of Monroe County were not as bad as the general public made them out to be. Some of the double-wides had nicer interiors than the art-deco homes downtown. The trailer parks also experienced less crime than The East Side, as evidenced by an abundance of Challengers and Vipers parked out in the open.

The trailer dwellers of Monroe dove for cover as the dark sky rolled in. Even a moderate thunderstorm could devastate a trailer park. With no foundations to speak of, strong winds could blow unlucky trailers off into the horizon. Susceptibility to bad weather combined with misunderstood reputation made trailer parks unexpectedly inconspicuous.

Living in a trailer often means one is beneath suspicion. A certain life-long trailer-dweller deeply understood this truth. He *only* lived in mobile homes.

At the end of a cul-de-sac, beneath the only tree in the park, a Jeep Grand Cherokee sat quietly outside a single-wide. The branches of a weeping willow shrouded the lot in a sinister aura. The willow tree was overgrown. The grass was unkempt. The windows of the trailer were covered by curtains, allowing no sunlight inside. The baleful abode was always silent. This was because its owner, Nick Bowman, abhorred music.

Nick would have fit in with aesthetic monks in the middle ages. In those days, back when any music not made by natural sound was considered blasphemous to God's ears, Bowman would have been hailed as a devout man. Too bad he didn't believe in God. Well, that's not entirely true. He was convinced that he himself was God.

He luxuriated in his bathtub, enjoying the scent of lavender bubbles popping on the water's surface. The sound of the wind and rain was a symphony to his ears. A glass of shadowy, grossly ripe red wine sat next to him in a crystal goblet. An American Spirit cigarette dangled from his mouth. The aroma of the tobacco mixed pleasantly with the lavender bubble bath.

Bowman ran a wet hand through his long black hair, examining the only decoration in his bathroom. This oft contemplated artifact was part of his cover: a large flag of the German Reich. A black swastika on a white disk centered against a red field. He hated what the swastika had been transformed to represent, but he adored the dark crimson of the flag itself. In the dim light, it took on the color of freshly spilled arterial blood.

Bowman got hard.

He put out his cigarette in a gold ashtray next to the goblet. He grabbed a wiffle ball bat from the floor and pulled it into the tub with him, caressing it in his arms. He fondly recalled the dark blood that had poured from that vapid girl's throat when he sank his teeth into her.

She had tasted delightful. All white girls did. There was something pure about them, like a fine slice of newborn veal. They were Bowman's favorite. Black women had a smoky, tropical flavor he found disorienting. Asians had a remarkably pungent aftertaste, like a greasy fast-food hamburger. Middle Easterners and Indians were fine, but a little too exotic. Latinos were hit or miss, they were either a five-star meal or reheated leftovers. No, the dependable, clean taste of a white woman was best.

However, Bowman would have taken the most unclean Mexican female over the cleanest man any day. All men, regardless of race, tasted the same. They tasted like body odor and cum.

Holding the wiffle bat against his muscled skin, he thought of his new friends in the American Guard.

*Inbred fucks.* If only they could appreciate the taste of blood.

Southeast Michigan was a slightly better shithole than Ohio. That state had been awful. The women of Cincinnati all tasted like crack cocaine. He had only killed three in that garbage town. Those whores had nearly turned him off blood for good. But Monroe's girl...*Sabrina*...oh, she had been delightful.

He remembered that quaint little rave many months ago. He remembered seeing her with that useless chink Tommy Fenton. She had been dancing to that music the faggots were playing. The tune would have been almost tolerable had it not been for those fruits.

He loved watching her dance. He loved the way her body flowed and contorted in time with the music. When he killed her, her body had contorted and collapsed lifelessly to the cold earth with that same rhythm. The death throes were even better than the blood. Death throes were nothing more than a desperately erotic dance. The spectacle of seeing someone's life leave their body was better than any sex Bowman had ever had.

He released the wiffle bat, letting it float on the surface of the bathwater. He finished his wine, leaving the stained crystal goblet on the vinyl floor. The goblet and ashtray were other trophies. In North Carolina, he had been left in that horrendous boy's home by his useless bitch of a mother. If his father had been there, he never would have let her abandon their eight-year-old son for a life of drugs and parties, but the old man had to go and get himself killed in Desert Storm.

That headmistress at the orphanage was a sour old cunt. Nick had relished bashing her head in with a baseball bat. He had planned that death after she smacked him in the face on his first day at the home. He hadn't yet learned the pleasures of the blood, but he kept her golden ashtray and crystal chalice she displayed on her desk. Now, whenever he used them, he thought of her. How lucky she was.

Reaching out of the tub, he seized a spherical glass pipe filled with crystal meth. The meth pipe wasn't a trophy, but the Zippo he used to ignite it was. He had taken the lighter from a drunk woman in a New York City alley. Life in the Big Apple had been hard. There were too many eyes, and the people there never shut the fuck up. They were so arrogant and full of themselves. The drunk had been no different. She was some aspiring actress. He was convinced that her freckles had given her blood that marbled texture one might find in a wagyu steak. Along with her lighter, he had taken her plaid green flats. He started taking shoes when he realized barefoot bodies threw off the police for some reason.

The New York slut had been kill number seven. Kill number six was the first time he tried blood. She was a yuppie dog walker in Las Vegas. She had fought back. His teeth puncturing her jugular and filling his mouth with her life-force had been a serendipitous accident. Now, *she* had been a savory experience. Blonde too.

*I suppose it's never the same as your first time.* Bowman mused with a smile.

He inhaled the mercury smoke of the methamphetamine. He senses cleared. Energy surged through his veins. He could do anything now.

He pulled the plug on the bathtub and listened to the gentle sound of water draining through the pipes. He watched the wiffle bat float gently down until it came to rest on the basin of the tub. It reminded him of Sabrina clutching her throat and falling to the forest floor. He was getting hard again.

He dried himself with a blow dryer he had taken from a dyke hair stylist in Portland. He stroked his goatee and turned his cold eyes back to the Nazi flag. The American Guard were scatterbrained fools, but it had always puzzled Nick how a group that hated foreigners so much praised Nazi Germany so highly. Surely a system like National Socialism would be too foreign for these keyboard warriors. Shouldn't they decry it as much as they decried the imaginary dark-skinned devils invading their precious American soil?

A sour taste rose in Bowman's mouth. The symbol representing the purity of the Aryan race had been dragged through the mud by dirty inbreeds unfit to kiss the boots of the ideal superhuman. Nick almost spat in disgust. He stopped himself. The Nazis had been wrong too. Eradication was not the way to go. Every race should stick to themselves. That way they could grow into the most ideal forms of their ethnicities by not mixing their blood. Yes, only by clean breeding could the best white people be born. The best black people be born. The best Asians and the best spics and the best ragheads all living in a pure society. Once their flavors had been perfected, then Nick Bowman could truly feast.

Oh, just thinking of the bloody flavors coursing through humanity's veins made his mouth water. He tried spreading this gospel amongst his new criminal associates. To his disappointment, they didn't care about race purity. They only cared about money. Tommy Fenton was the prime example of that. The accepting of a Chinese into a white supremacy group only reinforced Bowman's belief that he was the only human being with thoughts. The only human being with memories. With feelings. With a consciousness. With a brain. With a personality. Nick Bowman was certain that he was the only true human in reality. God, if you will.

Sabrina had come close. She had a personality. Her blood was so pure and fresh, but she had died alone and barefoot just like all the others. A shame, really.

Once he was fully dry, Nick Bowman walked through his dark trailer stark naked. The lack of light did not bother him in the slightest. Meth made his eyes photosensitive, so he kept all lights off unless absolutely necessary.

Wiffle bat in hand, he made his way to the closet. The tiny storage held his few, obsessively cleaned outfits. An unobtrusive trunk took up the floor space.

He popped open the trunk, revealing the many pairs of shoes artfully arranged within. Heels, flats, boots, sneakers, and even a pair of tap shoes all polished to perfection. He placed the wiffle bat next to Sabrina Cunningham's red and black canvassed converses.

He didn't have a better location for the bat than the trunk. Leaving such a recognizable item out in the open would arouse suspicion. None save Tommy Fenton had seen him with Sabrina. He intended to keep it that way.

Hiding out wasn't all that bad. He could smoke as much meth as he wanted. He got to enjoy the media circus surrounding Sabrina Cunningham's death. Oh, the tittering of the vermin as they scrambled for answers was almost as good as the killing itself. This dying town had even framed the wrong man. What great fortune. Monroe was a fit heaven for a god such as Nick Bowman.

He put on a pair of camouflaged pants. He laced up his heavy steel toed boots. He donned a black Kevlar vest and tactical gloves with armored plates covering the knuckles. He wore no shirt of any kind. He liked the feel of the Kevlar against his bare, muscled flesh.

Fully dressed, he closed the lid of the trunk and gave it a tender kiss. He went to the kitchen and made some toast. He pulled a razor-sharp dagger from a drawer. He reached into the fridge and set out a small jar of organic grape jelly.

He smiled as he spread the jelly with the dagger. The blade was a trophy from one of his few male victims, a shut-in college student studying music composition. The unlucky undergrad hadn't succeeded in sticking him, but the experience was enough to convince Bowman to invest in the Kevlar. He never carried weapons himself. All he needed were his fists and his teeth.

He put a piece of toast in his mouth. The meager meal was undeniably scrumptious. It reminded him of that diner in town. *Zoe's,* he believed it was called. That lady ran a surprisingly good joint, for a nigger.

A panicked knocking came from the front door. Bowman frowned through his meth-fueled haze. That damnable sound of fist against plywood was drowning out the natural orchestrations of the falling rain. The sky had not begun its full deluge yet, and Bowman had no intention of missing the first movement of the symphony.

Another panicked knock.

Bowman swore. It was that fool, Tommy Fenton. He was impatient. All Asians were. Perhaps a few centuries of breeding would remove that unfortunate trait.

He set the dagger and toast down, scowling. Tommy would pay dearly for his insolence. A sharp lesson would be in order. Nick lazily opened the front door.

Tommy Fenton burst through at full speed. The young Asian was panting as if he had run a marathon. Nick saw the green Impala parked in the front yard. He rolled his bloodshot eyes and closed the door. The room was plunged back into darkness.

"Nick... my man; we got trouble...what the fuck? Turn some lights on, asshole!" Tommy feebly searched for a light switch.

"Lumination offends my heightened senses." Bowman's rough, animalistic voice belied the pedantic extravagance of his words. He reached into a pocket and pulled out another American Spirit, igniting it with a casual flick of the actress's lighter.

"You are _high_-tened, that's for sure...fucking meth again? Great. Just fucking great." Fenton pouted.

He paced the empty living room. Bowman watched with amusement. It pleased him to see the small-time drug distributor this agitated.

"Remind me, how is it a chink like you got a name like yours? _Fenton_ doesn't sound very...*cultural*." Bowman smirked.

"I'm _half_ Chinese, asshole. It's my father's last name. I thought we were past this whole bigotry thing?" Tommy stopped his pacing and glared. "You guys let me in so I could help bring in the money, remember?"

"Ah, that's right. How goes the quest for the currency?" Bowman chuckled.

"Well, none of us are getting any fucking *currency* if we're all in jail for conspiracy to murder!"

"Murder? Slow down. I don't remember the big man ordering a hit." Bowman gently placed a hand on Tommy's shoulder, trying to calm the young half-Chinaman. "Did someone botch a job?"

"No... It wasn't a hit. Someone thinks we killed..." Tommy lowered his voice. "Someone thinks we killed Sabrina Cunningham."

Nick Bowman examined Tommy's eyes. He smoked his American Spirit. The red glow of the cigarette was the only source of light in the room.

"Fascinating." he finally replied.

"Can I turn on a light? I'm not a fucking bat like you." Tommy grumbled.

Nick pointed to a switch in the kitchen. Tommy fumbled around it for a bit. Eventually, the dull glow of an old Edison bulb provided some illumination. Nick blinked painfully as his eyes adjusted. In this light, Tommy looked like shit. His hair was a mess, his glasses were askew. He looked as if he had been out in the rain too long.

"Now...about this...*killing* that supposedly occurred..." Nick relaxed against the wall.

"Well, my guy Talon Keener just had his shit busted up." Tommy explained, "He said the guy in the news, Brian Stanhope, the guy who actually killed Sabrina Cunningham; he rolled into his house with some bitch named Alexis Knabusch and beat the living fuck out of him. He says they put a gun to his head."

"Brian Stanhope...Alexis Knabusch..." Nick murmured.

The first name had been in the newspapers constantly. Nick didn't own a TV, but he did have a subscription to The Monroe Evening News. He read that gossip-rag ritualistically. Mr. Stanhope was a frequent object of public derision. The second name was not familiar to him, but it sounded feminine, and it sounded white.

*How exciting.*

"He says these two told him they saw me with Sabrina at Big John's. I think they saw you too. Talon spilled his fucking guts man. Those two assholes think it was us. We gotta do something about this. We gotta put an end to this bullshit." Tommy declared.

"Whoa...settle down, Tommy. Let's walk through this." Nick raised a hand. "What do they know?"

"They know everything." Tommy answered.

"Everything? Well, we'll come back to that later. What does Talon know?"

"Nothing. He didn't see me with Sabrina. As far as he's concerned, he thinks Stanhope and Knabusch are insane."

"Where did the perpetrators go after they assaulted your business partner?" Bowman asked.

"I checked out the bitch's house. Only her stupid dog was there."

"And you didn't consume him? My, what remarkable restraint on your part." Bowman laughed.

"Enough with the fucking racist shit! It isn't funny." Tommy folded his arms. "After I left the dog alone, without harming a hair on its head, I hit Talon back up. He thinks they're at Stanhope's house."

"And where might we locate his residence?" Nick asked.

"He doesn't know the exact address. The only thing he knows is that he lives on one of those country roads up near Carleton."

"Well, if he's the same Brian Stanhope who has been published in all the local newspapers, I'm sure we can locate his home address in one of the numerous articles covering his investigation." Bowman took another puff from his cigarette. Smoke now filled the small trailer.

"Or, you know, you could just get a phone and Google it like a normal fucking person. It's a pain in the ass driving out here whenever I want to talk to you. If you had a phone, I could have just called you, instead of driving through the storm of the century." Tommy complained.

"I apologize for being a Luddite. I know it inconveniences you."

"Enough with your fancy-ass words. Let's go! We gotta stop this." Tommy power-walked to the front door and opened it.

Nick Bowman did not move a muscle. He leaned against the wall with his cigarette as if he hadn't a care in the world. He chuckled.

"What are you doing?! Come on!" Tommy yelled.

"Just a moment, my friend. Come." Bowman motioned for Tommy to approach him.

Tommy swore and slammed the door shut.

"What? What are we waiting around for?" he asked.

"I just want to confirm what *you* know, Tommy."

"What I know?"

"Yes. Who sent you here? Do the brothers of The American Guard know about this possibly unfortunate impediment to our business activities?" Bowman asked.

"No. It's just me. Talon called me personally." Tommy puffed up his chest proudly.

"I see." Bowman nodded.

His cigarette was only half finished. He loved American Spirits. They burned forever.

"In that case, do you mind if I ask what you recall regarding the evening at Big John's?" Bowman inquired.

"What I recall?" Tommy asked stupidly.

"What you *remember.*"

"Just say *that* next time…I was trying to hook up with Sabrina. She was fucking hot that night. I love Harley Quinn." Tommy gave a roguish grin. "Anyway, I was chattin' her up; you came up to me and asked to check her out for me. Then you went off into the woods, I ran into you later that night, we were both pretty fucked up, you said she vanished into the crowd, and the rest is in the news."

"Ah! Yes. That's right! I did request a private conversation with Ms. Cunningham." Bowman laughed uproariously. "She accompanied me into the woods for a private chat. She wouldn't shut up. She essentially talked herself to death. Do you know what I said to her when we were alone?"

"No. What?" Tommy nervously laughed along.

"I told her that once we were out of earshot of that faggy music, I was going to bite her throat out." Bowman stopped laughing.

"What?" The half-Asian's eyes slowly widened.

"That's right. She was rather intoxicated, and I believe her answer was to call me a *cunt*. I told her she could keep her cunt. I just wanted her clean blood." Bowman didn't smile. The light from the cigarette reflected in his frozen eyes.

"What…what…" Tommy stuttered in disbelief.

"She was a fighter, too. I like that. It imbues a certain…*spirit of the hunt*, shall we say." Bowman continued.

"…Why are you telling me this shit?" Tommy asked with a quavering voice. "I don't need to know this shit!"

"Oh, Tommy, you already knew this shit." Bowman replied threateningly. "Why else would you come here, by yourself, with no solid evidence from Talon, Brian Stanhope, or this Alexis character that clearly links me to the crime? You only came here because you knew. You knew I killed her. Who else knows?"

"Just Stanhope and Knabusch!" Tommy covered his mouth as soon as the words left it. He slowly withdrew his hands with a coy smile.

"Well, I think they know. Talon didn't know shit. I don't know shit." He elaborated desperately.

"You told no one of your suspicions?"

"No… I mean…I don't have suspicions. You're fucking with me. Are you testing me? I thought we were done hazing me now that I'm a full Guardsman." Tommy attempted to laugh disarmingly.

Nick Bowman gave a sad smile and put out his cigarette on the kitchen counter.

"Tommy...oh, Tommy...I wish I could say that you had such potential. But you really didn't." He lunged with an armored fist.

The left hook shattered Tommy's designer glasses and broke his nose. He fell to the floor, screaming in surprise and agony. Before he could react, Nick Bowman was on top of him. Fenton had no hope of fighting him off. Bowman had an easy 150 pounds on him.

Nick sank his teeth into the thin, sweaty skin covering Tommy's throat. He felt veins give way as he severed the jugular with one clean bite. Blood filled his mouth. He drank heavily. Even the taste of sweat and cum was satisfying while on meth. He spat the jugular out onto the floor. No need to eat something so tainted by years of housing Y chromosomes.

Tommy Fenton gurgled and died on the floor. Bowman watched the body twitch and shudder. He gazed longingly as Tommy uselessly grabbed at the hole in his throat. Another twitch wracked Fenton, and his hands fell lifelessly to his sides.

*Another glorious death.*

The peal of distant thunder broke the disquiet. The increasingly heavy patter of falling rain was deafening now. Bowman gave a wicked, wolfish, bloodstained smile. There would be a hunt tonight.

He would kick in the door and kill Stanhope first. He would drink that interloper's blood. Hopefully, this would frighten the girl enough to make her an easy target. Even better, fear enhanced the flavors in the blood. Oh, he would dine.

When he was finished, he would come back here, collect his trophies, and hit the road. The American Guard were no longer useful to him. He would leave Fenton's corpse here as a warning. The trailer had been rented under an alias. They would never find him.

Thunder rang out. The rain fell harder. Nick Bowman got to his feet, grabbed his keys, and went out the door. His heart raced with excitement.

He thought about his mother. He once asked her why God had taken his father from him. She said that it was God's duty to protect the sheep of his flock. God was the one to guide the lost sheep home to heaven.

*Intolerable bitch.* She had sent him to the boy's home the next day.

Some god she was. Despite the memory, he smiled again. Tonight, god would feast on the unsuspecting sheep.

# XXXIII

Alexis held the three-wood close. It was too dark to see through the graffitied windows of the house. The heavy rain didn't help. Her heightened alertness only added to her panicked imagination. Every flash of lightning became the headlights of a car filled with murdering racists. Every gust of wind became Sabrina's death cries.

A burst of thunder made Alexis jump. Thunderclaps were as good as gunshots to her ears. She wrung the golf club between her hands and wished for a gun instead.

She forced herself to look away from the windows. The interior of the house made her strangely sad. Brian swore he had cleaned the place, but signs of neglect and decay were everywhere.

Brian sat on a table next to the router. He nibbled on a clove of raw garlic he had found in the pantry. Alexis's phone was plugged into a wall socket. Brian hovered over the device, constantly refreshing the FBI's tip page to see if their message about Tommy Fenton had been reviewed.

"What if the power goes out?" Alexis asked nervously.

"Your phone's got power now. That's what matters." Brian replied, garlic breath wafting across the room.

Alexis eyed the heavy shovel leaning against the wall. She wondered if that would be a better weapon than her dad's old three-wood. She took a shaky practice swing with the golf club.

"I'll be honest, I doubt the FBI will get here tonight. Who would want to drive through this mess?" Brian sighed, motioning toward the dark, rain-drenched windows. "With any luck, it'll stop those whackos too."

Alexis didn't answer. Her thoughts were chaotic spirals. She kept thinking about Lily, about Sabrina, about Brian. What would happen tonight? A bad feeling crushed her gut like a hand juicing a ripe fruit. She thought she was going to be sick.

She sat down. Brian perked up. He seemed worried.

"If you want to get some rest, I think Sam's bed is still relatively okay." he suggested.

"I don't think I could sleep." She replied.

"I'll see if there's anything useful in my parent's old room." Brian set the half-eaten garlic clove aside. He journeyed deeper into the house.

Alexis tentatively followed her host down the hallway. She noticed several family pictures still hung from the walls. A young Brian was the main focal point of every photograph.

"You *were* the favorite child." Alexis snarked, trying to take her mind off her impending feelings of doom.

"Yeah...don't remind me." Brian scoffed.

"What? Did they hate Sam for being gay or something?" she asked.

"No, not at all." Brian responded. "Pretty crazy, especially with how religious my dad was."

He paused for a moment.

"My parents always thought I was going to *save the family* or something because I got good grades." Brian's voice sounded very old. "The truth is: the bar at school was so low it seemed like I was excelling. Whenever I tried something that was *actually* hard, I just got bored with it, and I'd think I was worthless. That's why I went to film school. It seemed easier than being a doctor. When I told my parents that, they thought I'd be winning Oscars overnight. They always made me promise to make enough money to never have to put them in a home. Well...look what happened."

"I'm sorry, Brian." Alexis comforted. "That's a lot of pressure to put on a kid."

"Yeah...I don't blame them though. They just had dreams. Don't we all have dreams?" Brian's eyes were crestfallen. "They used to tell me it was up to me to give them grandkids. I almost think I wanted to marry Christine more for my parent's sake than my own."

"Wow...that's...really fucked up."

"Everything was always about me. My grades were *so* good. I was *such* a good writer. My teeth were *too* big. It was suffocating." Brian gave an anxious smile, showcasing his gleaming fangs. "You know what Raoul said to me today?"

"What?"

"He said: *'it's not all about you, Brian.'*"

"He's right, dumbass." Alexis frowned. "Why didn't you leave well enough alone? Why dig up all this shit and try to go after Sabrina's killer? Your selfishness made everything worse."

Brian didn't answer right away.

241

"I guess I just wish someone had told me that sooner. It might have changed my sexual development. It's easy to fantasize about killing when no other human life is as important as your own." He said.

"Brian, I don't think your parents over-coddling gave you a death fetish." Alexis retorted with annoyance. "That type of thinking is some incel shit."

"No, but it certainly didn't help." Brian groaned. "I guess I thought confronting my demons would allow me to accept my sheep."

"You know, you could just call what you're trying to do *'acceptance.'* Every therapist in the world calls this type of mindfulness *'acceptance'*. You don't need to relate it to some madman's ravings about bestiality." Alexis's face flushed red with anger.

"Sorry."

A brief search of the master bedroom revealed only a single cardboard box. Brian wordlessly lifted it. It looked heavy. He struggled to carry it back to the table.

Alexis fearfully looked back outside. A flash of lightning illuminated the sky. The booming roar of thunder followed soon after. The lights in the house flickered; but stayed on. Impossibly, the rain fell even harder. Alexis ran a hand over her throat. She wondered if the rain would wash off the graffiti covering the house.

"What is in this thing?" Brian panted.

He wiped sweat from his bald brow. He popped open the box. Upon seeing its contents, he smiled brightly.

"Oh, sweet!"

A record player and several albums were carefully organized inside the cardboard container. Brian took out the record player and set it on the table. He sorted through the collection of vinyl. Alexis was surprised to see that the albums weren't that old.

"Sam got my dad this stuff for his birthday a year before the accident." Brian explained. "Oh shit, look at this!"

Brian held up an album as if he had discovered a nugget of gold.

"*Charming Disaster! Love, Crime & Other Trouble* is a classic." He grinned.

"Who?" Alexis asked.

"*Charming Disaster?* You never heard of them?" Brian seemed offended. "Jeff Morgan? Ellia Bisker? Ring any bells?"

"No. I'm not a hipster like you and your brother." Alexis scowled playfully.

"Well, well, well. I was an incel a little while ago, and now I'm a hipster?" Brian teased. "I'm moving up in the world."

"The two aren't mutually exclusive." Alexis replied.

"Alexis, *Love, Crime & Other Trouble* was the record that established their whole sound." Brian lectured. "The first song, *Ghost Story*, is a ballad about this couple, and the husband dies…you just gotta listen to it."

"Forgive me for not being excited about your death-related recommendations." Alexis soured.

"Let's play it! You might have to set up the record, though. I was never good with these things." Brian sheepishly scratched his head. "CDs were more my speed."

Alexis fumbled with the cables on the record player. After much effort, she finally dropped the *Charming Disaster* album onto the platter. She lowered the needle.

With some melodic guitar strumming, the song *Ghost Story* began to play. As Ellia Bisker's voice sang out, Alexis found herself enraptured. By the end of the first verse, Alexis realized that she loved the song, much to her chagrin.

She looked over at Brian. She expected him to have a smug "I-told-you-so" look on his face, but he wasn't paying attention. He leaned over the kitchen counter now, staring intently at a wooden crucifix in his hands. She cautiously approached him.

"Are you sure your parents never hated Sam for being gay?" She asked, trying to get a read.

"I'm just trying to think here." Brian glowered.

"About what?"

"About how right you've been." Brian spoke quietly. "I just…you know, I thought that if I helped find out what happened to Sabrina, all my anxiety would go away. Now I'm more anxious than ever before. She's dead. I can't help her. I'm only helping myself. That's fucking selfish. She's just another person I've used. Another human I've fed on."

He turned to Alexis.

"Does it ever get any easier?" he asked.

Alexis stayed quiet.

"…My Dad bought me this crucifix. It's hung in my room for years. I constantly feel like I let him down. Like I let God down."

243

Alexis was sad. She couldn't explain why. She didn't believe in God.

"My dad used to tell us that God is love." Brian continued. "Like, God was the ethereal embodiment of all love. To not love others was to be distant from God. To not be creative in your life was to not honor God...I don't know if God would be particularly happy about what I've been creating. *He who holds murder in his heart might as well be a murderer* or something like that."

His grip on the crucifix tightened. He walked over to the table and sat down beneath it. He dropped the crucifix on the floor in front of him. He stared at it.

Alexis was strangely compelled to join him. Golf club in hand, she sat cross-legged beside Brian. The music continued to play. A few moments passed before he spoke once more.

"This is it. This is the punishment for all my fucked-up behavior. Anxiety is hell. Hell is separation from God. Heaven is peace. Hell is anxiety. I want to change. I want to do the right thing." he said.

Alexis thought she saw tears in his eyes.

"Brian...I don't know much about religion. What you're experiencing, it isn't a punishment. It isn't a judgment against you." she stated. "It isn't something that just goes away because you try and do the right thing. Managing anxiety or depression or what have you...it takes forever."

"Forever?" Brian asked worriedly.

"Forever." Alexis repeated.

The music played on.

"I want forever right now." Brian answered.

Alexis took his hand.

They sat there, holding hands underneath that table until the song above them played out. *Ghost Story* finished somberly, the final harmonies of *Charming Disaster* crescendo-ing above the rain.

The man and woman beneath the table were scared to move. They were scared that one errant, careless motion would erase all the progress they had made together. Despite their best intentions, their tranquil moment ended violently.

The front window shattered. Broken glass and rainfall covered the floor as Nick Bowman hopped over the windowsill and into the house. A vicious smile spread across his face. Alexis Knabusch and Brian Stanhope let go of each other's hands.

Death had arrived. This death was not the words of peril fetishism or the wail of a semi. This death was the tearing, ravaging, primordial specter that hunted the days of mankind. It was more brutal and sudden than any storm, and it would have its due until none were left but the callous winds.

# XXXIV

Alexis screamed.

Brian had no clue who this was. This wasn't Tommy Fenton. This guy had lengthy hair tied back into a ponytail. A goatee surrounded a mouth filled with gore-stained teeth.

The stranger stalked closer, a horrifying gleam in his cold eyes. He was out of his mind on crystal meth. He wore nothing but boots, gloves, camouflaged pants, and a Kevlar vest. He looked like a possessed, white-trash commando.

Alexis and Brian crawled out of their hiding spot at full speed. The man raised both of his fists above his head, bringing them down on the table, smashing it in half. The record player broke against the floor, shattering the *Charming Disaster* album.

Brian's heart threatened to burst from fear. Alexis, still screaming, scrambled to her feet. She swung the golf club at the crazed assailant. The man quickly caught the pole with one hand. He used his grip on the three-wood to pull Alexis close. He kicked her in the stomach. She was launched backwards into Brian's oven, breaking the glass on the stove door as she collided with it.

The golf club was now in the meth head's hands. He towered menacingly over the stunned Alexis. He bent the golf club in half. He smiled.

Brian caught eye of the shovel against the wall. He pulled himself off the ground and grabbed it in both hands. He swung it with devastating force.

Unfortunately, the spade hit the Kevlar vest. The tall man staggered as he lost his balance. Otherwise, he was unharmed.

"Alexis! Get up!" Brian screamed.

He dropped the shovel and leapt onto the violent stranger's back. He nearly gagged. This guy reeked of meth and blood.

Alexis struggled to recover. Glass shards from the oven door dug into her back. Blood soaked into her shirt. She was within arm's reach of the shovel.

Wincing in pain, she grabbed the gardening implement. She aimed a low swing against the tall, pale man. Her blow struck true. The shovel smacked against his kneecaps. The commando hit the floor, Brian on top of him.

The madman laughed.

Brian turned the meth-head over, readying to rain down punches into the druggie's nose. The lunatic forced his face into Brian's, howling with laughter. Armored knuckles slammed into Brian's jaw, sending him sprawling.

Alexis hoisted the shovel over her head, aiming to bring the blade down on the assailant's unprotected skull. With inhuman speed, the commando rolled away, and the sharp shovel blade sank into his shoulder instead. Bright red blood poured down his arm as he yanked the tool out of his flesh.

Now in control of the improvised weapon, the man jabbed the metal end into Brian's face, drawing blood as it cut through the skin beneath his beard. Brian tumbled to the floor. Blood poured out between his fingers as he grabbed at his wound.

Before Alexis could try to grab another weapon, the bloodied lunatic leapt to his feet. With his free hand, he grabbed Alexis's left forearm. He cleanly fractured it with a loud snap.

Alexis screamed in pain. The man took advantage of her agony to drop the shovel and lift her off the ground with both hands. Alexis kicked uselessly against the Kevlar vest. The man smiled with hungry joy. He opened his mouth and brought his gore-washed teeth to bear.

Instead of biting Alexis, he yelped in pain. Brian had sunk his fangs into the back of the man's exposed neck. The pale stranger dropped Alexis and clutched at Brian. He was unable to free himself from Brian's overly large canines. He crumpled to his knees.

Brian released his bite and shoved his attacker headfirst through the graffitied sliding door. However, Brian was too engaged in the grapple. He followed the thug through the broken glass. They were both showered with shards.

Brian winced as his skin was torn to shreds. The stars in his vision grew more spectacular. He landed on the back of the mysterious intruder. The pony-tailed man groaned weakly. He did not move.

Bleeding arms shaking, Brian pushed himself to his knees. He left the meth-head face down in a landscape of rain, glass, and blood. Brian's breathing was shallow. He was scared he was going to pass out.

A radiant flash of lightning brought him back to his senses. Thunder boomed. He had to find Alexis. He desperately cried out her name. Wind whipped through the house.

Alexis was curled up on the blood-soaked kitchen floor, whimpering. She clutched her broken arm. She opened her eyes as Brian stood over her. Judging by the look on her face, he knew he looked worse than he felt.

"Brian...you need to get to a hospital." She groaned, half in shock.

"You okay?"

"My arm...you're bleeding...we need to get you to a hospital."

"You're bleeding too." He countered.

Alexis gasped in pain as Brian pulled her upright. A weird calm fell over him. He held her face, making sure he was heard.

"Alexis...get your phone. Get in your car. Call the police." Each sentence was punctuated by a labored breath. "Get help. Get out of here."

"You gotta come with me." Alexis pleaded. "You need a doctor."

"Someone's gotta keep an eye on this asshole." Brian smiled, gritting his fangs. "I'll get you to your car."

Alexis pushed Brian away.

"Don't play the hero, you dick! Let's get out of here. Come with me!" Alexis's panic escalated with every word.

"Get to your car. I'll be right here. I gotta make sure the cops get this guy." Brian picked up Alexis's phone and handed it to her.

She cursed and stumbled to the front door. She opened it, allowing the vortex of wind and rain to flood the house from two sides. She looked back at Brian.

"I don't want to leave you!" she called out over the typhoon.

"I'll make sure he's unconscious." Brian gestured to the now discarded shovel. He looked at his only friend in the world, a shadow against the light of his house.

Alexis cursed. She bolted for her car. Brian watched her headlights come on. He wasn't satisfied that she was safe until he saw those lights heading towards town.

He gave a contented sigh. The lighting struck again. The thunder followed close behind. The storm was getting worse.

Brian picked up the shovel. He planned to smash it against that bastard's head and make sure he was unconscious all right. He went over to the broken back door, ready to knock that meth head's lights out.

Wind battered against his bloodstained face. He looked onto the back porch, where he had thrust the pony-tailed intruder. There was a pool of blood, but the mysterious attacker was nowhere to be seen.

"Shit." he swore.

He stepped into the backyard, nearly overwhelmed by the tempest. Freezing rain slammed against his wounds. He started shivering.

Another burst of lightning illuminated the tall, white oak. Brian made his way to the tree. Between the rain and his wounds, even walking slowly was challenging. With every step he feared he would lose his footing. At least the frequent lightning strikes kept the dead oak in sight.

"Hey! Jean Claude Van Damme-villain-looking-ass-wannabe! Where are you?" he roared, hefting the shovel defensively.

He felt a rough, eloquently animalistic whisper in his ear.

"Well, I do believe I'm right here."

Brian's right leg exploded in pain as a large, jagged shard of glass mangled his quadriceps. He screamed. His vision went white with agony beyond description. He felt the glass shard break off deep within his flesh.

A vicious kick to the back of his crippled leg broke Brian's knee, sending him careening several feet forward. His vision briefly returned as mud and wet grass soaked his face. The dead tree was practically growing on top of him. He tried to get up. Then he heard the voice again.

"I don't usually ingest males. You, however...you've earned it. I must confess my little sojourn to tie up loose ends has been rather enjoyable."

Brian felt a heavy, steel-toed boot come down on the back of his right shin. Its cleats tore deep into his tender skin. He screamed again. He hit the wet ground with a splash of mud. He tightened his grip on the shovel.

With adrenaline-fueled strength, Brian forced himself up against the weight pressing down on him. What little unbroken bone remaining in his leg cleanly severed as the rest of his body turned in a sharp 180. He flailed the shovel into the air. The weight on his leg disappeared as the stranger ducked out of the way of the arcing spade.

Brian sat on his butt now. The white oak was within reach. He wasn't sure what good the lifeless tree would do, but it was the only thing he had.

He pushed himself backwards, getting closer to his grandfather's tree. Another flash of lightning briefly revealed his wounded limb had remained facing the opposite direction. His right toes sank down into the mud as the flesh of his limb barely held together.

Thunder echoed, closer than ever before. Brian's head began to spin. The white spots in his line of sight grew bigger with every blink. He was so cold he no longer shivered.

Brian realized he was going to die.

"A valiant struggle." The coarse voice rang out over the wind, insane chuckles of a meth addict peppering the man's speech. "You were exquisite prey. You may have even helped bring about my utopia. I hope you remember that."

Brian braced for death.

A blinding bolt of lightning impaled the huge husk that was the white oak. The land was showered in sparks. In the heat of the electrifying light, Brian saw his attacker staring up at the thunderstruck tree in awe.

With a crash that echoed for miles, the white oak splintered in two at the sloppy wound the vandals had made. Its massive trunk toppled over. Even blinded by excruciating pain, bleeding to death, and sporting a useless leg, Brian knew that the weight of the tree would crush him. He used the last of his strength to push himself away from the brunt of the blow.

The tree tore into the drenched earth. Brian missed being pulverized by inches. However, the trunk still landed squarely on his mutilated right leg. The pain amplified for a brief moment and vanished. Now Brian couldn't feel anything below his right thigh.

Nick Bowman wasn't so lucky. He had tried to run away from the falling tree. Whether it was the wind, or the angle of the fall, the tree fell harder and faster than it should have. Nick was tangled and torn, caught by the sharp branches of the dead oak. His limbs shattered as he was taken to the ground. Finally, one long, sharp branch pierced his Kevlar vest. The dead growth staked him through the heart.

Nick choked on his own blood. He looked down in disbelief at his ruptured body. As the last vestiges of life fled from his cold, killer's eyes, he found himself horrified by the revelation that he had not in fact been God.

Rain washed Brian's face as he stared up into the night sky. Every breath was now a monumental effort. In some ways, breathing for the last time was a lot like breathing for the first time.

He felt warm. He couldn't help but smile. Maybe peril fetishism wasn't that far off the mark. Death was kind of pleasant, all things considered.

He thought about how his life had careened out of control, and how he had sabotaged himself. He thought about every choice and revelation that had led him to this moment. He was going to die at night, outside, in a storm. That was okay. He deserved this.

He closed his eyes. He could almost hear a car's engine as the thunder and lightning were swept away by high winds. He heard tires rotating against the earth. Maybe he heard a siren? It must have been the neurons in his brain firing off and replaying memories. He could hear the voice of his father. The voice of Sabrina. The voice of his mother. The voices of Sam and Raoul mingled with the voice of Christine. They were all there. He wasn't alone.

"Brian! Brian! He's over here! Brian...Brian..."

He heard Alexis too. He felt her weight as she lay over top of him. Warm raindrops fell on his chest.

Brian smiled as his being faded. Hearing her sobs and feeling her tears, he knew he was dead. It wasn't so bad, really.

# EPILOGUE: MICHIGAN SUMMER

This year, the sunshine dried out the water-logged farmlands surrounding Monroe. So, the farmers returned to their fields. Local experts predicted a record harvest. Tourists visiting Lake Erie flooded the county. Rumors circulated of a national manufacturer eying the small city for a new branch. The prayers of the town had been answered. Things were finally turning around.

Zoe considered taking advantage of the good fortune to run full service. As it was, she was only doing takeout orders. The renovations weren't complete. Her little diner was long overdue for a makeover.

*Thank you, prime rib.*

The contractors were on their lunch break. The day's meal orders had been filled. The owner, proprietor, and namesake of *Zoe's* took advantage of the respite to lean over the counter, have a cup of coffee, and peruse the local newspaper.

She was engrossed in a two-page spread examining the lives of Talon and Nikole Keener. The Keeners were currently facing a litany of criminal and civil charges. After witnesses reported gunfire at their residence; the local police raided the home and discovered purified crystal meth and black-market marijuana. What was worse, the Keeners also possessed multiple illegal firearms.

Talon, a felon, had an insurmountable case against him. His trial was scheduled to begin the following Monday. His pregnant wife Nikole had turned state's witness. According to the article, she was to testify against her husband in exchange for a reduced sentence.

Zoe clicked her tongue with disapproval. The Keeners reminded her of her own unhappy parents. She would say a prayer for their child.

Beneath the article, a town hall meeting regarding the fate of Custer Statue was advertised. Mr. Cunningham had turned against the official stance of the Housing Commission. He now called for the statue to be placed in a museum, in honor of his late daughter's wishes.

Zoe wondered how Sabrina would have reacted to her father's petition. She had wanted the statue destroyed. Zoe took a sip of coffee.

She turned *The Monroe Evening News* to the back page. She skimmed past the county fair's schedules. She instead perused a tiny, easily overlooked article:

\*\*\*

## POLICE LIEUTENANT REPRIMANDED

*After allegations that 9-1-1 guidelines were not followed properly, Lieutenant Cassandra Johnson of the Monroe County Police Department has been placed on administrative leave, sources say. Lieutenant Johnson, the head detective behind the Sabrina Cunningham murder, is accused of disregarding an emergency call related to the violent break-in that occurred at the Stanhope residence in March.*

*"Our officers are a symbol of trust between the government and the people of this city." Chief McNamee stated during a recent press conference. "If our citizens can't trust our officers to investigate crimes, then we are going to see a lot more incidents like the Stanhope break-in. We need to do better."*

*McNamee provided no comment on rumors of DNA discrepancies present during the Cunningham investigation.*

\* \* \*

Zoe was shocked. Cassandra had always been very cordial. She hoped the detective's leave of absence would not last too long. The woman had obviously fallen under that "detective's curse" the novels wrote so much about. That could happen to anybody.

Another headline caught Zoe's eye:

\*\*\*

## SERIAL KILLER CASE CRACKED BY FBI TIP
\*\*\*

Further reading was interrupted by the sound of a dog barking. Zoe put the newspaper away. She saw Alexis Knabusch tying up Lily outside. She seemed to be having difficulty, as her left arm was still in a cast. Her hair had been cut short. There were no traces of blue dye left. Her grey eyes held no anger. Overall, she looked healthy. Once Lily was tied up, Alexis came inside with a smile.

"I got that coffee ready for you." Zoe handed Alexis a securely packaged Styrofoam cup.

"I'm going to miss you, Zoe." Alexis paid for her coffee. "You're too good for this town."

"Is today the day?"

"Yeah." Alexis answered. "My parents are all set up in Omaha."

"You're always welcome if you decide to come back and visit." Zoe gave a heartfelt grin. "When's the cast coming off?"

"Next week. We're still working out seeing a doctor in Nebraska, but with my parent's insurance, it shouldn't be too bad." Alexis explained.

"Enjoy being on that healthcare while it lasts." Zoe chuckled. "You take care of yourself, Alexis. I can't wait to read your work. Your blog about Sabrina was very touching."

"I appreciate that, Zoe." Alexis's smile turned wistful.

"What is it?" Zoe asked.

"If I'm being honest, I can't wait to get the hell out of here and never look back." Alexis paused. "It's just...if I leave, do you think people will forget Sabrina?"

"I don't think you have anything to worry about." Zoe gestured at the back of the restaurant.

Alexis gasped.

The hideous paint job on the back wall was scraped away. Sabrina's mural was almost restored. The piece was a landscape caricature of *Zoe's* serving food to everyone in Monroe. Sabrina's signature popped out beneath the dried paint. Hanging next to the mural was a photograph of Sabrina, Alexis, and Brian working on its construction.

"Thank you, Zoe." Alexis's eyes filled with tears. She went outside, coffee in hand, and retrieved Lily.

Zoe hoped the girl would find happiness one day. After her favorite regular was gone, she opened a letter from Lou. He was begging for money. Typical.

Zoe unceremoniously crumpled up her ex-husband's correspondence and threw it in the trash. She finished her coffee. She turned on some Miles Davis and lost herself in Sabrina's artwork.

†

"Knee high by July. Isn't that right, Lily?"

Lily whined.

"We're almost there. You can hold it a little longer."

Alexis drove down the lonely road to Brian's house. It was only June, but the cornstalks growing in the once barren fields were well over knee height. Perhaps the rumor mill was right about the harvest this year.

She ruminated on the aftermath of that fateful night at Brian's. She remembered finding what was left of her friend broken and bloody. She shuddered.

When her parents heard that their only daughter was in the hospital, they both took the next flight to Detroit. Half the extended Knabusch family accompanied them. The whole clan was now more than willing to find a new hometown.

The quiet drive out to Frenchtown was pleasant. Every tree burst with green leaves. Fluffy cumulous clouds populated the sky. The golden sun shone radiantly overhead. It was a perfect summer's day.

A lump rose in Alexis's throat as Brian's old home came into view. The graffiti was gone. Fresh paint covered the house. New windows had been installed. A pole topped with a large white block was affixed in the center of the front yard.

Alexis parked and exited her car. She let Lily out. The German Shepherd was immediately possessed by the zoomies. Alexis thought she heard punk music playing.

"Hey! That dog will scare the deer off!"

Brian Stanhope stood on his front porch, cane in hand. The steel of his prosthetic leg glinted in the sunlight. A playful frown peeked through his beard.

"They love that salt lick." He elaborated.

Lily bounded over to Brian, nearly knocking him over. Alexis couldn't help but smile. Brian looked good; all things considered. The cuts on his face had healed well. He looked a little tan too. That was impressive. He had been released from the ICU only a month ago.

"I missed you, Lily." Brian gave the dog a toothy smile.

The surgery required to seal the shovel wound had not interfered with his canines at all. Brian's mother would have been greatly disappointed. Alexis suppressed a knowing chuckle.

"You look great." She said.

"Thanks. The doctors say I won't have any huge scars. Just a few faint lines, things like that." Brian gave a roguish wink. "Or are you perhaps referring to my cybertronic upgrade?"

He posed with his metallic leg and cane. He had gotten some decal work on both the appendage and the walking stick. Colorful flames raced up and down the titanium.

"You like it? I was inspired by *House*. You know, the TV show about the doctor?" Brian explained. "It might have been a little before your time."

"Oh, shut the fuck up, Brian. I know who *House* is."

Alexis finally caught the song playing over the radio on the porch. She immediately recognized the voices of Sam and Raoul. The lyrics of *Parts Unknown*'s latest release took her breath away:

*When the devil comes home*
*In the dark rolling gale*
*You feel all alone*
*As your blood's running pale*
*You thought you were the beast*
*But he's here for the feast*
*Not knowing you've got a trick up your sleeve*
*You're thunderstruck!*
*You're thunderstruck!*
*You wrote every day*
*And you chased them away*
*But you're thunderstruck!*
*But you're thunderstruck!*
*Blood's running wild because its hell where you've been*
*Hell's where he's going to stay*
*If the tree gets its way*
*Cause he's thunderstruck!*

Alexis's jaw dropped. Brian blushed deep red. He clutched his cane and gave an awkward shrug.

"The song mentions you too, but you missed that verse." He said.

Alexis wasn't sure whether to be angry or flattered. Having a song written about you was cool, but the way the words harmonized with the booming drums and the frenetic guitar brought her back to that horrible night. She stopped herself from running a hand over her throat.

"Is it true they have a *record* now?" She asked, pushing aside the memories.

"Yeah. They called it *Murder He Wrote*. Un-fucking-believable." Brian laughed. "He's not helping the ex-child prodigy complex, that's for sure. They're on tour, so now everyone gets to learn about my bullshit."

"Wait, they're on *tour*? No way." Alexis scoffed.

"Yeah way. *Parts Unknown* is the last graduating class of Big John's. He's not hosting anymore raves." Brian sighed.

"Can you blame him?"

"No. Not really."

They locked eyes for a moment.

"I figure you're here to say goodbye?" Brian asked.

"I wanted to see how you were doing. You know." Alexis faltered. Saying goodbye to Brian was harder than anticipated.

"Mind if we sit down? I get tired from standing up." Brian tapped the steel prosthetic with his cane.

Alexis laughed and pet Lily.

"Wow, that's not very ableist of you." Brian teased.

"Oh Brian, it's actually incredibly ableist of me. You still got a lot to learn."

"Sorry."

Alexis offered a hand, which Brian gratefully accepted. They sat down and watched Lily run around the front yard. Neither knew what to say.

"My mom called." Brian started. "She's doing a lot better at that place up north. They got her on some new medication that seems to be helping. She still thinks she's calling from work to make sure I'm doing my homework, though."

"That's something." Alexis consoled.

"Yeah...she would have loved to see you before you left. She might not have remembered you, but she would have appreciated it all the same."

Brian reached into his pocket.

"Remember my public defender, Mark Navarre? He dropped this off after meeting with me in the ICU."

He placed a worn piece of paper into her palm. Alexis opened the small letter. All it contained was a drawing of a cartoon sheep. The doodle was simply signed: *AL.*

"I guess I'm finally accepting my sheep." He smiled.

"Are you though?" Alexis reproached.

"What do you mean?"

"Why would a public defender visit you in the hospital?" Alexis accused.

"I woke up to Detective Johnson screaming about how I was a misombelist." Brian explained. "I just had my leg snapped off, and she was trying to arrest me again. She said I hated women, and murdered women, and that my misombelist writings were proof enough that I had killed Sabrina. She said I lured that Nick Bowman guy here to kill you. I told her I accepted my sheep. I told her sure, I don't have a perfect relationship with women, and I have written some misombelist things, but I'm definitely not a misombelist."

"*Misogynist*, Brian." Alexis snapped, fed up with his ignorance. "The word you're looking for is *misogynist*, and you *are* a misogynist."

"What?" Brian looked shocked.

"You haven't changed at all! All those tears and talk about God…it was just bullshit!" Alexis stood imposingly over Brian. "You made money on erotica about killing women. That's fucked up. You didn't accept your sheep; you *condoned* your sheep. That's the opposite of acceptance! Didn't this Al person tell you that?"

"What are you talking about?" Brian feebly tried to scoot away.

"How'd you pay for your hospital bills? Your little decals?" She asked, turning towards the house. "How'd you pay for all this work on your property? You were broke! You don't have a job! Are you up to your *fraud analysis work* again? Don't lie to me!"

Brian went quiet. He looked Alexis in the face. He took a deep breath.

"I have been writing again. I'm making money off it too." He confessed.

"You manipulative, misogynistic bastard." Alexis spat. "After all the fuckery you've put us through, you're right back to where you started! You think God would be happy about that?"

"No! It's not what you think." Brian interjected. "I've been writing smut again, but there's no murder in it this time. I promise."

"Wait…what?" Alexis was confused.

"When I got out of the hospital, Sam gave me his old laptop." Brian explained. "I was checking my email when I saw a message from a patron of mine. Her name's Sarah Lynne Murphy. I told her about the *accept your sheep* thing too. I told her I didn't want to write peril anymore, but she knew I still had all these conflicting feelings about my fantasies and urges, so she put me in touch with a company called *Wild Ring Cinemas*."

"Never heard of them." Alexis scowled with doubt.

"They're pay per view only, very high end." Brian continued. "They do WWE wrestling styled porn. No one dies! They just get knocked out or humiliated."

"...Really? This exists?" Alexis asked.

"Oh yeah! It's very mild compared to what I used to write." Brian nodded. "I pitched them a storyline about a girl who gets into wrestling to get back at her cheating ex-boyfriend. She's hired as a jobber, but she just dominates everyone she fights. Her momentum as a rising star/baby face builds up, and she finally gets her shot at a championship title. But wait! Plot twist! Who is the current holder of the title? *The girl her ex-boyfriend cheated on her with!* What's worse? *The ex-boyfriend is this homewrecker's manager!* Our hero lets her emotions get the best of her, and she just gets stomped by the new girlfriend. After she gets knocked out, the ex-boyfriend comes into the ring, and he and the new girlfriend run train on her."

Alexis was shook.

"That's...kind of...weird." She stammered.

"Not as weird as killing people!" Brian beamed. "It's a step in the right direction towards accepting my sheep."

Alexis face palmed again.

"Well...if you're happy, that's what counts." she moaned in defeat.

"I'll send you a link if you want to watch it." Brian's metal leg squeaked as he stood.

"I'll pass."

"Why? Taking a break from the internet?" Brian seemed genuinely dumbfounded.

"No. Someone has to educate unwashed misogynists like you." Alexis folded her arms.

Another familiar silence descended upon them.

"Is it that time?" Brian asked solemnly.

"The movers should be wrapping up." She nodded.

"Well...Alexis...I'm sorry." Brian's voice broke. "I got you hurt."

"Brian..." Alexis felt the plaster of her cast.

"Take care of yourself. Keep in touch. Watch out for weirdos."

"Fuck you, Brian."

"Bye, Lily."

"Don't talk to my dog."

Alexis put Lily in the back of the Audi. She felt a pair of eyes on her back. She looked up to see Brian intently watching her from the porch.

"Brian?" she asked.

"Yeah?" he answered.

"Do you still want forever? Right now?"

He was silent for a minute. He looked up into the beautiful summer sky. He looked back at Alexis.

"You know, I'm trying to be more comfortable in my own skin. It's hard. This world is hard. I still want forever...but maybe it can wait for a bit."

Alexis smiled. Her heart was full. He was learning to live with the struggle.

As she drove off into an uncertain future, she glanced back in the rearview mirror. On the night they had almost lost their lives, he had watched her drive to safety. She had felt the embrace of his gaze until she reached the police station. She expected to feel that embrace again. She expected to see him standing on his porch, watching her until her car was no more than a speck on the horizon.

To her surprise, Brian had stepped back into his childhood home and out of sight.

# Acknowledgments

There are a lot of people out there that made *Vampires* possible. I'd like to thank my father, Donald Gerald Burke III. He was my first beta reader, and this book would not exist without his constant encouragement and sage advice. Thank you for giving me my love of reading and my love of John Steinbeck.

I'd like to thank my mom, Leslie, and my sisters, Maddie and Claire. They've always pushed me to explore my artistic side, and make me grow as a person. They're always in my corner, even on my worst days. Thanks for putting up with me being a pig ass.

I'd like to thank Ethan Rath and Trevor Connors. These two guys are some of my closest friends, and their wisdom, knowledge, and love of reading helped make *Vampires* what it is today. You two are more amazing and talented than you know.

I'd like to thank my good friend Marc Schwartz. He was another early beta reader, and our discussion on mothers and anxiety helped me solidify the emotional core of this novel. There isn't a soul like you, and I'm so thankful for your friendship.

I'd like to thank Kyle Ryan, Elliot Bibat, Mark Yacullo, and Grace Heimerl. They have always pushed me to be a better writer and to kill my darlings. This book would not exist without all of you challenging me. Love you guys.

I'd like to thank Amanda Heidorn, who read the working drafts of this novel while she was all the way on the other side of the world. Your friendship means more to me than you know. You're a real one!

I'd like to thank Mickey Novak and Rachel Strolle, who helped me find a home for this book. Their inside knowledge and insight of the publishing world really helped me get the word out about this novel. Thank you.

And finally, I'd like to thank you, the reader, for supporting independent novels like this one.

# About the Author

Erik Burke is an actor, artist, and writer living in Chicago, Illinois. He graduated from North Central College in 2015 with a Bachelor of Arts in Theater. When he's not writing, hiking, biking, watching movies, or acting, he can usually be found playing rousing games of *Dungeons and Dragons* and *Call of Cthulu*. You can find him on Twitter at @erikwburke or on Instagram under the username erikwburke.

Made in the USA
Columbia, SC
09 August 2021